ANOTHER SIDE of PARADISE

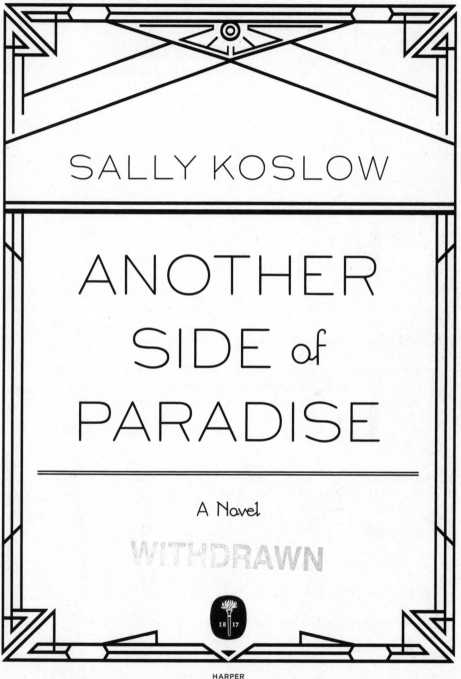

SALLY KOSLOW

ANOTHER SIDE of PARADISE

A Novel

HARPER

An Imprint of HarperCollins*Publishers*

ANOTHER SIDE OF PARADISE. Copyright © 2018 by Sally Koslow. All rights reserved. Printed in the United States of America. No part of this book may be used or reproduced in any manner whatsoever without written permission except in the case of brief quotations embodied in critical articles and reviews. For information, address HarperCollins Publishers, 195 Broadway, New York, NY 10007.

HarperCollins books may be purchased for educational, business, or sales promotional use. For information, please email the Special Markets Department at SPsales@harpercollins.com.

FIRST EDITION

Designed by Leah Carlson-Stanisic

Artwork by CkyBe/Shutterstock, Inc. and supermimicry/Shuttertock, Inc.

Library of Congress Cataloging-in-Publication Data has been applied for.

ISBN 978-0-06-269676-2

18 19 20 21 22   LSC   10 9 8 7 6 5 4 3 2 1

To Emil, Madeline, Yosefina, and William

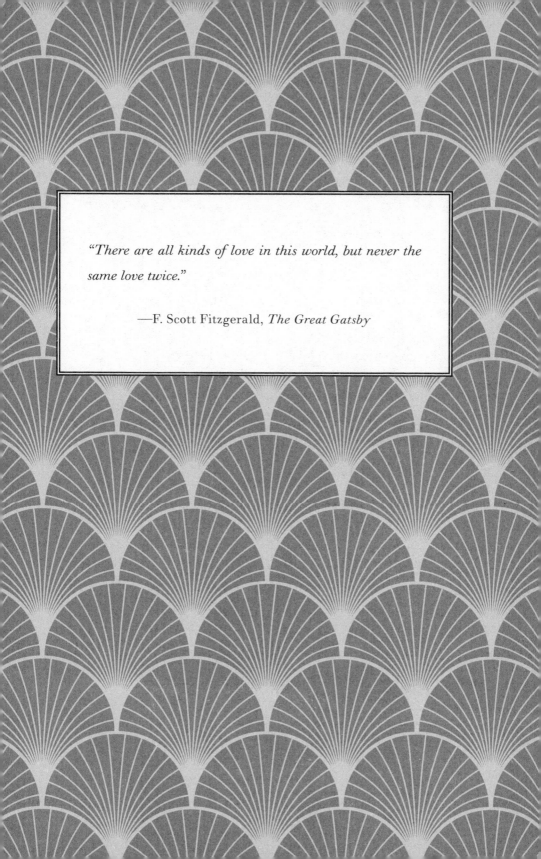

"There are all kinds of love in this world, but never the same love twice."

—F. Scott Fitzgerald, *The Great Gatsby*

ANOTHER SIDE of PARADISE

am not quite a widow, too blunted by shock to weep.

Someone has clicked off the thundering symphony that almost drowned out his last, choking gasp. The glass, too, is gone; I tried to pour brandy down his throat to revive him even as I worried that it might lure him back to drinking. His jaws were clenched. Liquor dribbled along his neck like a crooked amber creek, soiling his sweater. Scott would be embarrassed, I thought, when he recovers from his faint.

Outside it is damp in California's grey parody of the Christmas season. Weak midday light filters through half-drawn blinds, casting his face in shadows. A blur of people swarm as they did when Mama died, seeming to have materialized without being summoned. Their voices crackle with conviction, barking orders. Finally, someone has the decency to whisper, "Shh . . . Sheilah's here."

Why not? This is my flat. Scott is my love. We share a closeness not even death can sever.

I return to kiss his lips, still faintly warm. I stroke his thinning hair, carefully combed over a small bald spot that I have pretended not to notice, and hold the hands that caressed me again and again. His fingers are smudged by the chocolate I offered him thirty minutes and a lifetime ago.

Someone begins to cover him with a snowy sheet. "No," I scream. "He'll suffocate. Take it away." But it is Scott who is taken away.

I am frozen by grief. For almost four years, F. Scott Fitzgerald has belonged more to me than to his Zelda, entombed in her madness, far more than to the public who turned their backs on their literary prince. Like lovers in one of his pages, from the evening we met we began living inside each other's hearts, swallowed by intimacy, cemented by a fierce loyalty. Later, when he knew my secrets, Scott could read me as if I were a story he had written.

With his new book blooming, we had allowed ourselves dreams. If America went to war, we hoped to go to Europe as press correspondents, and after a grand victory and the blaze of that adventure, to trade Hollywood for a cottage in Connecticut. "I'll take care of you, Sheilo," Scott said. "I want to spend the rest of our lives together." His words were fine and true. I believed every one.

Yet decorum dictates that it shall be dear Frances, the noble secretary, who delivers his new charcoal Brooks Brothers suit to the mortuary. What color for his coffin? Dove grey, I tell her. Black is too somber for the Scott I know.

Knew.

Were my love alive he'd say, in a gentle mock as he strokes my face, "You can't come to my funeral, Presh. You understand, don't you?" I do, though I can picture myself in the shadows, eyes downcast under the brim of a black hat, rows behind Max Perkins, Robert Benchley, Dorothy Parker and Alan Campbell, and Gerald and Sara Murphy. Perhaps Arnold Gingrich would have the courage to sit at my side. Scottie, my almost-daughter, would turn and acknowledge me with a look that says *Dear Sheilah, we know how Daddy loved you.* And Zelda? We would eye one another with mistrust, believing our own truths, drowning in questions.

But I will not be with Scott on the day he's put to rest. The unwelcome mourner, I will grieve alone, here on Hayworth Avenue where we breathed the same air and felt as one. With Frances's help, I will pack his things, though I will not part with our pictures, few as there are.

All my life my choices have rendered me an outsider. Why should this be different? I am Scott's Kathleen, *The Last Tycoon*'s seductress, excluded and silent outside the gate of her darling's empire. *The loneliest moment in someone's life is when she watches her whole world fall apart, and all she can do is stare blankly.*

Today, I am mute. But for many yesterdays, I was as happy as anyone has a right to be. Later, should people ask, "What was it like to love and be loved by that great romantic F. Scott Fitzgerald?" I am going to have a helluva story to tell. Does it have a Hollywood ending? No. Should it seem improbable? It does. That is simply the way with the truth.

Chapter 1

1937

Hollywood: I often think my greatest love could have happened nowhere but in the capital of Boy Meets Girl, a city built of dreams imprinted on celluloid lace. Here, the big bands still play. People forget about shanties and flophouses, hunger and hopelessness. As the Depression drags on, Hollywood is designed to pretend.

As Louella Parsons swans by at premieres—her face soft as cream cheese—fans line the red carpet and snicker, there goes the harpy. But when I pass, they look twice. Since I am blond, rather young, and fill out an evening gown well, they wonder, Is she a star? Beverly Hills royalty perhaps, born with a butler proffering chocolate milk, Rudolph Valentino at her fourth birthday party, and a pony stabled next to the tennis court?

In a city of prop department fakes, I am a fourteen-carat sham. Home is neither a mock Tudor mansion nor a gingerbread castle dolled up with seven turrets. I am not even Sheilah Graham of London's Chelsea as I have made others believe. I have, however, grown accustomed to this town, with its sun by day and klieg light by night. I am used to the scent of ambition and desperation mingling with eucalyptus and suntan oil.

I am a scribe who makes her living by watching the wheels go round. At times do I give that mechanism an extra spin? Indeed, I do. Gossip columnist may not be the most honorable of professions, but I wear my occupation with dignity, not merely because it allows me to pay my way in the world. To the motion picture industry, I matter. If Gary Cooper trips in the forest and shatters his leg, will Jimmy Stewart replace him, or will it be Spencer Tracy? Does the studio kill the picture? Readers want to know. I am a cog in the machine that magnifies illusion and trades on private lives.

I am also engaged to royalty and tonight, July 14, Bastille Day, belongs to me. The Marquess of Donegall is a friendly puppy, slender, brown-eyed, adoring; a thoroughly modern aristocrat who likes jazz, flying a plane, and writing a newspaper column of his own. I am to be his marchioness, her Grace, she of the monogrammed lingerie and coronet-engraved notepaper.

I admire my four-carat diamond solitaire, bought at the snazziest shop on Sunset Boulevard, as we kiss, chastely, at our impromptu engagement party. "I love you," I say.

Maybe I do. Maybe I will. Maybe it doesn't matter. I like Don and perhaps it is enough that he loves me and can offer a life awash with privilege.

"Looking forward to our voyage?" he asks.

After our wedding on New Year's Eve, we will be six months at sea. Our unwritten marriage contract requires that I conceive an heir, the Earl of Belfast, as soon as possible, and a doctor has convinced Don that the swaying of a ship is conducive to pregnancy. "Looking forward to everything." That I mean sincerely. Beyond the preposterous frippery and adulation associated with joining Don's ranks, I have always wanted children. My own family.

Our engagement celebration kicked off hours ago at my red-roofed villa tucked into the Hollywood Hills. Don filled the terrace with hothouse roses, dahlias, and nasturtiums illuminated now by torches and fat candles. My home is high above Sunset, set on North Kings Road. As the sky grows inky, the City of Angels glitters like Christmas trimmings. The house is leased and landscaped with palms, which according to my friend Dorothy Parker are the ugliest vegetable God created. But tonight

I refuse to be anything but euphoric. I want to dazzle like the star I am not.

"Hey, shut your traps over there," someone yells, then yells again. My neighbors have a right to complain—this party is loud and liquid, like all the gatherings of the crowd to which I have become attached. Besides Don, who is amused by my circle's boozy warmth, I am the token Brit. With the exception of Humphrey Bogart and his noisy wife and a few directors and actors on the rise, this is a tribe of scriptwriters who drink to forget they are crafting canny movie dialogue when they should be writing their worthy play or novel. But who can blame any one of them for being here? Though you'd never guess it by tonight's shrimp and Champagne, this is the Depression. The average Joe earns in a year what Hollywood's dullest dogs make in a week. Americans flood movie palaces to escape, guaranteeing my own modest but regular paychecks. People eat up the tittle-tattle I dish out.

When another neighbor begs for silence, Robert Benchley, the leader of our pack, clinks a goblet with a spoon and shouts, "Friends, I call this meeting adjourned. Let us alight at the Garden of Allah. To my place. To be continued." Robert is the uncle I never had, the ultimate boulevardier, a walrus waddling in an elegant suit, his mustache as shiny as his slicked hair the color of onyx. He writes and tells stories so clever I often think he speaks in code. I pretend I can make him out, and Robert disregards my ignorance. He plays his game. I play mine. Each of us knows the score.

"Shall we move on, darling?" my fiancé asks.

"You do not say no when Robert Benchley issues an order." I squeeze Don's hand.

We pile into cars, and hurtle faster than we should down the steep, curving road. It takes only minutes to arrive at the Garden of Allah, the headquarters of this artistic armada who blend talent and vice in their own cocktail. It is not an overstatement to call the place a dump. The owner, Allah Nazimova, a sloe-eyed actress whose Russian accent doomed her career when talkies took hold, hasn't made a repair in years, or ever. But it has Schwab's pharmacy down the street, and walls so thin you can hear the inviting tinkle of glasses in the next apartment. This means the revelry rarely stops.

At Robert's, we pick up where we left with liquor poured and bon mots tossed about like sugared almonds. Don wanders away to chat while I listen to John O'Hara detailing a plot I cannot follow.

As I am laughing, which tonight I cannot stop, I feel pinned by a stare behind me, off in the corner. I turn to see a man in an armchair surrounded by a froth of smoke. Behind the scrim, faded gold hair frames a face that could be etched on a Roman coin. The man's suit is one shade brighter than navy. A bow tie tamps down any formality, its polka dots at odds with the sadness of a half smile that transforms his face into a spray of tiny wrinkles, like tissue paper crushed by a fist. Is he young or old? From where I stand I cannot tell, but he smiles at me.

The man looks tragic and alone, as if he were deposed royalty. I am drawn. The air's molecules shift, as they do before lightning strikes, and I mirror his smile, full force. He raises a glass by way of a toast but does not stand and meet me. I am moving toward him when Don taps me on the shoulder.

"The fireworks are starting," he says. He does love his American fireworks.

I join Don, but turn back again. The man is gone and only a plume of disappearing cigarette smoke in the lamplight suggests he was ever there.

Don and I move outside, where someone is butchering *Le Marseillaise*. Bogie strips to his boxers to jump in the pool, which in a nod to the landlord's homeland is shaped like the Black Sea. Two strangers are playing ferocious Ping-Pong.

An hour later I offer Robert my thanks. As we kiss both

cheeks, I nod toward the empty armchair and whisper, "Who was that matinee idol sitting here before, the sad man with the blond hair?"

"Matinee idol?" Robert roars. "That was Mr. Jazz Age himself. The great F. Scott Fitzgerald, a wanton betrayer of his own talent. Poor, sweet schmuck."

The name stirs a memory. Bobbed hair. Dumb Doras shouting "Bees knees!" Flappers dancing the Charleston, splashing in fountains and riding on the roofs of taxis. But isn't F. Scott Fitzgerald as dead as the Roaring Twenties themselves? Extinct?

The way Robert looks at me, I suspect my mouth is agape. "The once-great writer," he adds, filling the void of my amazement, "now, more or less obsolete."

I have never read Fitzgerald's novels, though I know phrases of his that people throw around—*I love her and it is the beginning and end of everything*. In my columns I have brushed aside a certain kind of bone-lazy heiress as a Scott Fitzgerald type.

"He's considered great?"

"Once upon a time, yes," Robert says. "But no one reads him anymore. Too in awe of the rich. Bourgeois reactionary!" Robert throws back his big head and laughs. "Never mind that most people are hypocrites. They scheme to become one of the rich, who destroyed Scott's poor fool, Gatsby. But Fitz would be the last man to defend himself."

None of these are points for me to debate with a Harvard man. "Why did he leave so early?" I ask.

"What fun is it when you're the only one who doesn't drink?"

Except for a proper sherry, I myself rarely drink, lest I miss a scoop that drops in my lap like a juicy California orange. But surely, Mr. Fitzgerald must have a more storied explanation.

Don finds me and we return to my villa for a last night of passable sex. That my feelings for my fiancé fall any number of caresses short of torrid are, I hope, balanced by our ardent friendship. I enjoy Don and I bask in his admiration.

The next day I drive him to the airport. "Farewell, Your Lady-ship," he says.

He is flying to London, where he will beg his mother to al-low us to wed. As worldly as my marquess may be and despite the bauble weighing down my finger, marrying without Mum's approval is out of the question.

Chapter 2

1937

The first person I see tonight is Dorothy Parker. I like Dorothy, and not just because she has never accused me of being a gold digger, at least to my face. A moat of respect protects our friendship. I have never insinuated, in print or otherwise, that her handsome husband is the poof everyone believes him to be.

We're at the Ambassador Hotel, under the billows of the room's tented sky. I'm turned out in my silvery evening gown, sashed with scarlet velvet, here to do my job, as is Dorothy. She has blown her lifeguard whistle and summoned Hollywood's typewriter team to raise money for the embryonic Screen Writers Guild. A palace revolution hopes for better wages, though salaries of thousands per week are not unusual, even now, in the Depression.

"Looking well, Sheilah," she says.

"Let me return the compliment," I lie. "No one can say you don't get into the spirit of the evening." Where most women in the room flutter like butterflies, Dorothy clomps about in a costumer's version of the working class—checkered peasant tunic, babushka, clogs. She looks like an extra in a period drama. Dorothy is barely five feet tall, and while she was once as adorable as one of her interchangeable poodles, she's taking a turn toward matronly, with a thickening waist and bags under her eyes that betray years of overindulging.

I have my insecurities, but I am confident in two things: my plummy accent, newly clipped, which seems to impress Americans, and my sex appeal. Dorothy is as assured of her insufferable cunning as I am not. To mask my deficits I depend on a smile, and to mask hers, Dorothy publishes verses that flash with skepticism: *Love is for unlucky folk, love is but a curse.* Etcetera. She dashes off her corrosive doggerel with aplomb, but I have never been convinced she wouldn't trade half her wit for a scoop or two of my allure.

What Dorothy does have is a passion for political crusades, always liberal. In the past she's mustered the troops to raise money on behalf of the Scottsboro Boys, eight young Negroes accused of raping two white girls in Alabama, and like that vitriol-spitting bully Hemingway, she's also rallied against Franco in Spain. No wonder her scripts are chronically late, as I've been tempted to report.

"I'm counting on you to expose those jackass bosses, Sheilah," Dorothy says.

Tonight's cause is close to home. No love is lost between writers and those who hire them: Louis B. Mayer, miscellaneous Warner brothers, Darryl Zanuck, Samuel Goldwyn, and their colleges of diabolical cardinals who rule the studios and rant about the radical bastards with their Underwoods.

"Then pray that something interesting happens," I say. "You know why I'm here—for a bloody steak garnished with scuttlebutt."

I find it hard to take seriously the labor problems of a proletariat who suffer in sunny splendor and slave, not in a coal mine, but on a studio lot with a commissary that serves banana cream pie. Nonetheless, this is a command performance. A job.

Dorothy recognizes some faces across the room, and with an evangelist's zeal, bounds in their direction. This allows me to find my place at one of the large, round tables. My host is Marc Connelly, a leprechaun notable for his hairless head and the Pulitzer won for a play that retold the Old Testament with an all-Negro cast. I greet everyone at the table—like my mother never said, manners maketh the woman—and discreetly remove a pen and small pad from my brocade bag, hoping for an occasion to take a note.

Dinner proceeds apace, with everyone making harmless conversation—which, for me, is unfortunate. Tonight they're nattering about *The Life of Émile Zola*.

"*Snow White and the Seven Dwarfs* will be the one for posterity," I protest, to which my tablemates laugh. A feature-length cartoon? Let the joke be on them. We sip our vichyssoise and move on to filet mignon. As tuxedoed waiters clear the plates, I look up, trying to find the right adjective to describe the rubies dangling from Ginger Rogers's ears. That's when I see him. At the adjoining table—Dorothy's—is Mr. Fitzgerald. Tonight he wears a dinner jacket with the lapels of another era. His forehead is wide and attractive and he has the most perfect, sharply chiseled nose I have ever seen. Again, I am drawn to his smile, which, when he sees me eyeing him, he flashes. There is a familiarity in the exchange that I find both seductive and disquieting.

This time he leans forward and says, "I like you." His voice, soft and cultivated, drifts in my direction as if we are the only man and woman in this ballroom. His tone suggests warmth and darkness.

"I like you," I respond. In three short words, a ballad. The words hang between us as Scott Fitzgerald picks up a glass swizzle stick and absently stirs his Coca-Cola. His gold band catches the candlelight. Since Robert's party it has taken scant detective work to learn that he is married. His beautiful wife, a madwoman, lives in a sanitarium on the other coast, somewhere down South. People say he still loves her and that she was his muse.

"Shall we dance?" I ask, brazen, unaccustomed to being refused.

He turns his head to the side and says, "Thank you, but I've promised the next number to a friend." With that, Dorothy appears and the two of them walk to the dance floor. Mr. Fitzgerald dances well. As he and Dorothy fox-trot, he seems like a college boy. Her head moves close to his, and I watch them grin and banter as the twenty-piece band in their white jackets plays "It's De-Lovely."

My tablemates are debating whether or not Shirley Temple is actually a brunette with pin-straight hair. There. My next column.

I look Scott Fitzgerald's way again, my flirting emboldened by the diamond on my finger. He has taken his seat and shrugs toward me as the first speaker goes to the podium and the evening's tirades begin. Is Mr. Fitzgerald apologizing for the missed dance or the dullness of the rhetoric? The speeches are each as long as a lease and I soon think, oh do shut up. I feel sympathy for no one in this room except the waiters. Though my column for the North American Newspaper Alliance is syndicated in dozens of papers—not just the *Los Angeles Times* but also the *Lincoln Evening Journal*, the *Times* of Hammond, Indiana, the *Winnipeg Tribune*, and many more—on an extraordinary week, I earn all of two hundred dollars. I will wear this frock until it's tattered or I am nobility.

For a moment, it was the two of us—Mr. Fitzgerald and me, alone together—but I turn to look again and he is no longer at his seat. I am ready to escape this crowd as well and prepare for early studio calls. I didn't cross the bridge to the exceedingly interesting Mr. Fitzgerald. I don't imagine I ever will.

Chapter 3

1937

I am wrong. Saturday, Eddie Mayer—everybody's pudgy, pushy pal—is proposing dinner for that very evening, with Mr. Fitzgerald. Though my friend Jonah and I have plans, I am too curious to decline. Scott Fitzgerald strikes me as a rare osprey caught in a habitat even more unnatural for him than for the rest of us in Hollywood.

When Eddie rings I am in my second-best cocktail dress—a bias cut, emerald, chosen to bring out my eyes. Earlier, I opened a bottle of Elsa Schiaparelli's Shocking, a gift from Don along with the roses reaching full bloom on my cocktail table. I dab perfume in my décolletage. Is it shocking that I am dining out when I am engaged? I tell myself no, because tonight is not a date. I will be surrounded by a veritable Secret Service, not only Eddie but Jonah, a correspondent for London's *Daily Mail*, and a well-known kleptomaniac. When he stops by, I hide the monogrammed tea towels and happily accept the material he feeds me. Fair trade.

You are due for a diversion, I tell myself. Once Don and I wed our life will be as proper as porridge.

"There's been a change of plans," I say when Jonah arrives.

He's troubled himself to get tickets to a concert at the Hollywood Bowl. "Do you have any idea who I had to bribe to wrangle the seats?" He pretends annoyance. Men rarely get angry with me because our relationships swim in a haze of amity and coquetry. Even Johnny, my former husband, remains a close friend.

"When you see who the other two are, I promise you won't be sorry," I say, grabbing my evening clutch.

Jonah snaps to attention. "And that would be?"

"Eddie Mayer and F. Scott Fitzgerald."

"Ah, I heard he'd arrived to work on *A Yank at Oxford*, and you're right." My friend runs his hands through a mop of curls that cover his head like a lap dog. "It could be a real show. Isn't he a world-class drunk?"

"Good God, I hope not." Alcoholics terrify me.

The doorbell chimes and Eddie, a one-eyed mountain with a mustache copied from Clark Gable, fills my foyer. The two of us have silently agreed to overlook last year, when he tore at my clothes in a clumsy pass. His luck is better with scripts and poker, mine with gossip and English nobility.

"Sheilah, may I present Scott Fitzgerald?" he says as though introducing the president.

In defiance of both the climate and the decade, the great author is wearing a nubby salt and pepper suit, a paisley scarf, and a fedora that appears to have barely survived a fight. Los Angeles hasn't seen rain all summer, yet he is carrying a trench coat.

"Miss Graham," he says. "What a pleasure."

I am no stranger to unexpected situations—stalking the vast Surrey estate of Lord Beaverbrook in order to land an interview comes to mind—but tonight seems odder than most. "An honor, Mr. Fitzgerald."

As he takes my hand, Francis Scott Fitzgerald smiles warmly. His teeth are straight and white. "Scott, please."

"Sheilah," I say, "and this is my friend Jonah Ruddy. Eddie, you and Jonah are acquainted, yes?"

I don't hear the answer because Scott, with his hand on my elbow, is escorting me to Eddie's boat of a Buick. He opens its passenger door, settles me in the seat, and slips into the back with Jonah. We are headed a few blocks down the road to our local Sodom, a gangster-owned restaurant packed with luminaries, appreciated as much for its covert roulette tables as its molls and sole Véronique.

The maître d' oozes an oily greeting toward Eddie and me, the regulars—"Miss Graham! Mr. Mayer!"—and seats our party close to the band. Eddie and Jonah order whiskey, and I, a Dubonnet. Scott asks for Coca-Cola. We move on to a first course—I choose the langoustine with lemon—and Jonah attempts to pump Scott about his film project. Scott volunteers little and cedes the floor to Eddie, who rattles off more details than any of us care to know about *The Wizard of Oz*. "The budget is far beyond two million," he says. "Might get to three. Write that down, Sheilah. They'll never make a goddamn profit."

Scott raises an eyebrow. Whether he is reacting to Eddie's coarse language or his declaration he doesn't let on.

The band begins a sassy cha-cha and Jonah escorts me to the dance floor. "He doesn't talk much, does he, Mr. *This Side of Paradise*?" my friend asks.

"This town doesn't need another buffoon. I'd say his reticence is part of his charm."

"Charming is my mum's tea cozy." Jonah swings his arms, not quite on the beat. He is not the dancer he thinks he is.

"You don't read him like a woman does." While we were at the table, I felt Scott's eyes tornado through me in the flare of the candlelight. From time to time, he tilted his head to the side, as if he were memorizing my hair and my cheekbones. Only an equally practiced flirt might notice such a display.

I am glad when the cha-cha ends. "You seemed a tad bored the other night at the Ambassador," I say to Scott, back at the table. "Do you stand with the Screen Writers Guild?"

"I do," he answers, "but I see why the studio bosses aren't rushing to make concessions. Writers may be the farmers excluded from the harvest feast, but a lot of them are lazy oafs who can't keep their mind on their work."

"Would that be you?"

"No. I'm a toiler," he groans, "to a fault. When my mind's on my work that's all I think about. But that's not what I'm thinking about now." He stands, deferential and courtly, and extends his hand. "Care to dance?"

Next to making love, dancing is my preferred physical activity. I adore the sensation of rhythm and music flowing from inside me, and watching Scott dance, I guess he feels that way, too. He is easy to follow, with relaxed but nearly linear posture and a light, firm touch. Straightaway, we synchronize. He is compactly built. In my heels I am nearly his height, which allows us to align in all the best places. Tall men? Overrated.

"I hear you're engaged to a duke," he says, springing to life with an impish grin.

"That's where you're wrong," I tell him. "A marquess."

"Is a marquess higher than a duke?"

"No, no, no." Like the good English schoolgirl I once was, I recite the order of nobility. "First you have the king and queen. Their children are princes and princesses."

"Even we Americans know this much." As he chuckles he looks like the naughty son of the ghostly guest I first noticed at Robert's party.

"Sometimes princes become dukes—but that's beside the point. A marquess comes after a duke. Then it's earls, baronets, honorables, children of lords, then knights."

"So if you and your fiancé have a son, he will be—"

If. Don's heavy solitaire feels grossly conspicuous. I wonder if Scott's interest in me is an egotist's reverse droit de seigneur. But I flatter myself and bring to heel my illusions. I may be conflating civility for something far more personal.

"An earl," I answer, as the band breaks into a rhumba. Scott keeps hold of my hand and we continue to dance.

"How did you become a journalist?" he asks over the song's Spanish lyrics.

"You know, most people say it straight. I'm a scandalmonger, one rung down from a munchkin. You're flattering me." And I love it.

"It can't be easy, picking the grapevine and turning out columns day after day." He, too, has done his homework. "I respect your discipline, because I've been morbidly late on every novel. Ask Max Perkins, my beleaguered editor back in New York. He'll tell you I consider deadlines to be mere suggestions." He pins me with his grey-blue eyes. "Please forgive the way I prattle on, but I do want to know. How did you get your start?"

The band takes five. We stand on the dance floor as I gallop through a practiced résumé: my urbane but Bohemian parents, John Laurence and Veronica Roslyn Graham, deceased, followed by the foolishness of being a London society girl. Bored blind by a French finishing school. The lark of being presented to King George and Queen Mary, a train following me like a spaniel. I tell Scott how I tried acting, for which it was immediately clear I had no aptitude. From there I moved to dancing onstage. Another doomed effort. Then Fleet Street, where the mediocrity of my work was an excellent fit. That's when I became curious about life across the pond. I feed Scott these tidbits as if I were the novelist. As with most fiction, my story has a patina of truth.

"You look too young to have done all this. How old are you?"

"Why Mr. Fitzgerald, aren't you direct? How old are you?"

"Forty," he winces. "Just."

I wish you could have met me fifteen years ago is how I choose to read his tone. Would I have been as drawn to him then as I am this evening? Possibly not. One underdog to another, I prefer a hero who has lost a few brass buttons, as Hollywood tale-tellers say Scott has.

"I'm twenty-seven," I say, erasing five years.

He's too much the gentleman to roll his eyes. "And your father?" he asks. "What did he do?"

"Must we speak of him now? You make me feel as if we're sitting at a story conference. 'Who is this character? She's too opaque.'"

"Fair enough, Sheilah."

I love how my name sounds coming from his mouth, though I am grateful that the music starts up again and the next tune is swing, putting a stop to the turn our conversation has taken. One, two, three, rock step, rock step. As we smile, any nervousness slides away. From here the band switches to a tango and I hesitate. Scott is, as he says, forty. Don's age. Though as he dances, Scott seems younger. The man arches his back comically, eggs me on with the crook of his finger, and begins to improvise steps that cover our corner of the dance floor in widening arcs. I follow his lead, laughing as other couples move aside to let us strut and sway. Perspiration beads on my face and I see the same on Scott's. He deftly wipes his forehead with a white linen handkerchief. My partner looks devilish.

We lock eyes until the band starts a languorous waltz. This allows us to embrace, cheek to cheek, his hand softly on my back. We melt into one another until the other dancers and diners become wallpaper. I close my eyes. I love the way Scott smells, of lime, almond soap, a touch of sweat, and possibility.

"The best revenge is getting the best girl," he whispers, conspiratorially.

"Why Mr. Fitzgerald, are you quoting yourself?" I whisper back.

"Almost, and why not?" He laughs. "Nobody else does."

A mournful trumpet player steps to the center of the stage, slowly performing "Stardust." Scott's breath, cool and clean, is on my neck. I am glad the melody is from a solo horn. Words would only interfere with my thoughts. When Scott Fitzgerald looks at me I feel as if I, Sheilah Graham, am a prize worthy of winning. Men might be stretched out the door, far along the Sunset Strip—all the way to Beverly Hills—for the chance to

cut in, but he will battle every one of them. Let Elsa Schiaparelli try to bottle that feeling.

"With you, I don't breathe quite right, and I don't know what
to say."

"Your beauty speaks for itself." If another man uttered this,
I'd cringe. But isn't the essence of attraction suspending doubt
and allowing yourself to like whom you believe yourself to be,
reflected in another's eyes?

A soloist in peach sequins takes the stage and warbles, "Why
don't we do this more often, just what we're doing tonight?"

"Why don't we?" Scott says. "Dinner Tuesday, no chaperones?"

I restrain the urge to outline his full lips with my finger, but
imagine them on my own lips, soft, urgent.

"I enjoy your company," he adds.

"I enjoy your company. I'd be happy to have dinner with you."

"The correct answer," he says. "Are you always right?"

"That you will have to discover, but I've monopolized you too
long." Off in the corner I see Jonah and Eddie, surely soused and
as bored with one another as Scott and I are not.

We return to the table. I notice that it is Scott who pays the
bill, which, judging from the number of empty glasses and half-
finished baked Alaskas, cannot be insignificant. When the valet delivers the car, Scott takes the wheel, since Eddie is in no
shape to drive. Slowly—the man hugs the steering wheel and
never breaks twenty miles per hour—he delivers me to North
Kings Road.

I thank Scott for a wonderful evening, nuzzle his cheek, and
tell him how much I am looking forward to Tuesday. I walk
inside, alone. Hands trembling, I place Don's ring in its purple
velvet box, and fall into bed.

As I fade into sleep I think, did I pick Scott Fitzgerald or did
Scott Fitzgerald pick me?

Chapter 4

1937

I sit on my terrace and sip an iced tea garnished with mint from one of my pots. I have no green thumb, but California refuses to let a plant die. It is the end of a long day chasing a snip of intelligence about a former beau, King Vidor, which led nowhere. Despite my wasted time, I welcomed the distraction because—I finally admit to myself—I am in a pickle.

I've played along with Don, but the very idea of our marriage is a fairyland of moonlight, mink, and martinis no more real than one of Mr. Disney's animated features. I have never considered that the marchioness might actually acquiesce to my joining her ancient family, but Don wires word to the contrary: MUM IS BENDING SLIGHTLY LIKE A DEEPLY ROOTED BIRCH. Nor have I considered whether I possess the pluck and perseverance required to act the part of a wellborn wife for the rest of my life. I wasn't, after all, the most convincing stage actress. A hundred different Brits could expose me as a woman who knows less about *Hamlet* than Hopalong Cassidy. If that were the case, my own folly—and let me say it, lying—would humiliate, hurt, and anger Don, a man who has been nothing but kind to me. I'd rather not think of how his mother would react.

Yet, I can be tenacious. Perhaps I could bring it off. Don wants me. And to be a marchioness . . .

On the other hand, the other night. With Scott Fitzgerald, something happened. I kick off my shoes, and close my eyes. I need to work out the next step.

The doorbell interrupts my musings. I wonder if it might

be another bouquet from Don. Or if flowers are arriving, could they be from Scott—a Victorian nosegay comes to mind. Too soon for roses.

The delivery is from Scott—but he has not sent flowers. His wire explains that his daughter will arrive earlier than expected and he must cancel our date. There is no effusion in the message or suggestion of rescheduling. Scott is a man of letters who has told me that when he meets a woman he struggles to find the perfect adjective to describe her. Mine, apparently, is *expendable.* I crumple the telegram and toss it across the room.

Twenty minutes later I am still on my chaise longue, shoulders hunched. Darkness falls on the western coast like a hastily tossed cloak and I sit in the twilight and shiver, knotted by disappointment. Scott Fitzgerald is long married, rumored to be in debt, and on the downside of famous. I am engaged to nobility, eager for children, and most likely at the peak of whatever beauty God gave me. I cannot afford to be a fool.

But I am bewitched by this man. I relive us on the dance floor, delighting in our proximity, trying to decide if his eyes are blue or green or grey. I did not merely imagine that for thirty minutes we were bonded, or that with Scott Fitzgerald I experienced an emotion—deeper, more complex—I have yet to feel with Don and don't expect I ever will. My memory is not a mirage. With burning impatience, I pick up the telephone. An operator gives me Scott's number at the Garden of Allah.

"Scott, I'd love to meet Scottie," I say, trying not to tweet like a sparrow. "Why don't the three of us go out together?"

He does not immediately respond, and I feel diminished by his hesitation. This woman is trouble, he might be thinking. Calloused. Unfeminine.

But, finally, he says yes.

Chapter 5

1937

Scottie has her father's face. Whether her high spirits and strawberry blond hair come from her mother's line, I can't say, but she is slender as a green bean, sunny, and fresh. Two of her male friends are in tow from Connecticut, where she attends a genteel boarding school. They are specimens of young manhood in the F. Scott Fitzgerald mold, circa 1922: sun-kissed, blond, dressed in white pants and navy jackets as if they'd leaped from a yacht.

The young men's glossy youthfulness makes my date seem more threadbare than his years. He doesn't stop clucking over his daughter as if she were child, not a young woman. Scott calls her Pie, one of those Muffy-Fluffy nicknames that doting relatives bestow in a show of affection. "Pie, finish your meat." "Pie, sit up straight." "Miss Pie, wrong knife," he chides while he chain-smokes Raleighs and drums his long, elegant fingers on Café Trocadero's least romantic table, ten feet from the hat check.

Where is the jester who tangoed into my heart? Scott is a crank who looks as if he's faded in the wash and yet, it's impossible not to like his daughter. Scottie orders in French far more polished than my own, which isn't dreadful, assuming you are generous about irregular verbs. She asks for her *canard à l'orange* humbly. Nothing arrogant about this girl.

"Miss Graham, can you tell me about your work? It sounds awfully glittery." "Miss Graham, how long have you lived in Hollywood?" It touches me that Scott's daughter, who might

be incensed by seeing her married father with a date, is solicitous. Someone has made it clear that the foundation of civilized
behavior is making sure other people are at ease. I banish the
thought that it was the mysterious Zelda who tutored her in
charm.

"What do you plan to do whilst you visit, Scottie?" I ask.
"You shan't be gone all day and I could show you around."

"*Whilst. Shan't.* Miss Graham, your accent is divine. I'll do
whatever Daddy has lined up." She squeezes Scott's hand in a
gesture both protective and proprietary. Yet she adds, "What a
lovely hat," reaching up to touch the wispy veil that falls over
one eye. "I've been admiring it all night."

Before our date became a family affair and I switched to a
simple black sheath with a bolero, I'd planned to wear a lilac
halter-necked dress that framed my décolletage. My hat, with
its carnelian poppy, is tonight's sole concession to gaiety. I am
tempted to take off the ridiculous adornment and give it to
Scottie here and now, but I merely smile and thank her as the
orchestra strikes up "Afraid to Dream."

"Miss Graham, may I have this dance?" says blond boy number one, ignoring the much younger lady to his left.

"I'm sorry but this dance is promised to someone else," I say,
reaching for Scott. He looks surprised.

"She's enchanting, your daughter," I tell him when we reach
the dance floor.

"She hasn't had it easy." I hear pride, but he clamps down in
a way that doesn't invite probing.

"How long is she staying?"

"A month." *Dear God.* "Tomorrow I've arranged for her to
get a studio tour and meet Mickey Rooney. After that . . ." He
throws up his hands. "I'm so unsettled here I can't take off
much time and that only underscores what an abominable father I am. My daughter deserves better."

"You couldn't be more considerate," I offer, unclear of this man's complicated life, and even less of its details. "Anyone can see how much you care for her, and she, you." He makes a noise short of a grunt. "I could help take Scottie around to see the sights," I say, with hesitation. I don't want him to find me too eager. If there are rules, what are they?

"That's generous, Sheilah. I won't forget the offer." With that, blond boy number two cuts in, and my fretting date fox-trots away with his daughter.

At the end of the evening, Scott drops off Scottie's friends and then drives her to the Beverly Hills Hotel, where she is staying with his friends Helen Hayes and her husband, Charlie MacArthur. It takes only minutes more for him to reach my villa and walk me to the door. Moths buzz around the light and the scent of oleander tantalizes all my senses. I planned to say goodbye with a polite thank-you, but I long to switch on the electricity from the other night.

"Please don't go, Scott," I say, pulling him toward me, speaking in a low voice.

He doesn't move beyond arching an eyebrow.

I take F. Scott Fitzgerald by the hand. Willingly, he follows. In the living room I avert my eyes from Don's roses, whose petals have begun to scatter on my Chinese rug. From my radio, which I've left on to avoid the sadness of returning to a soundless home, a breathy, late-night torch song wafts our way, its lyrics sentimental. *Out of the darkness you suddenly appeared. You smiled and I was taken by surprise . . . but the moon got in my eyes.* Bing Crosby croons what's in my heart as I lead Scott one flight up to my bedroom. I drop his hand to light a candle, ignoring that it is a souvenir from my engagement party. The flame leaps and sizzles in the dewy breeze that blows through an opened window.

"I like you," I say, hoping he remembers our first words. He answers by burying his face in my thick, ash blond hair. His shade, exactly. What else do we share? Little, I guess, beyond the desire to feel each other's warmth and the awareness of a certain complementary loneliness. I am glad for this. I have too little self-love to seek my own reflection.

He slips off my bolero and begins to unzip my dress, which falls to my hips, revealing my black crepe slip.

"Please step out of your shoes," he murmurs hoarsely. I obey. He appraises me down and up and back again, until he reaches my eyes. "I don't deserve you," he says.

I don't deserve you.

He places his serious pinstripe jacket on the velvet slipper chair that crouches in the corner like a handmaiden. I loosen his bow tie—again, a bow tie—and begin to unbutton his shirt so I might wriggle my hands beneath its softened cotton and feel his shoulders. They are muscular and for a man who isn't tall, appealingly wide and strong, like a boxer. He could be thirty. He removes his gold cuff links, one by one, and sets them on my vanity table, next to my tortoiseshell hairbrush. I do not want to think about who gave the links to him, or that a wedding ring remains on his finger. I unpin my hat as he flicks away one strap of my slip, then the other. The garment puddles atop my dress.

"In a minute, I will kiss you, but first I need to drink you in." He doesn't break eye contact as he caresses the contours of my face, the straight slope of my narrow nose, and my full lips, leaving a tattoo of Coronation Red on his fingertip. He dips it in his mouth, then mine. I mirror every gesture. We hold each other, almost dancing.

"Kiss me now," I say.

"First say my name. Please."

"Scott." The sound is both a confession and a puff of hope. "Scott Fitzgerald."

"I want to get to know you, Sheilah. You're like nobody else."

Which I hope means: you are not at all like my wife, like Zelda. Jonah has remarked on our resemblance. I quarantine Zelda Fitzgerald in the same compartment as dear Don, banished from my bedroom. The last thing I want is to be the understudy for a man's absent, celebrated wife.

Scott is down to his boxers now. I sit on the bed, undo my garters, flex my leg, and remove a stocking, then another and slide off my silky panties until all that is between us is my cream satin brassiere. He reaches for its hooks.

"Not yet," I say, shaking my head.

I am built along generous lines with a bosom more ample than I would choose. My assets presented themselves at age thirteen, as if to say, move along now, girlie, your childhood is over, whether you like it or not. Over time I have grown into my body, but I remain shy. My breasts are almost the last thing about myself that I reveal.

I snuff out the candle. The room goes black. Scott and I shimmy beneath my coverlet, a leg and a hand here, a leg and a hand there, mouths and tongues moving slowly, getting to know one another, chokingly vulnerable. A chuckle. A gasp. A moan.

Well. This is how it all began, during a night tender indeed. Only much later did it occur to me that, in those early days, part of our value to each other hinged on how little we knew of the other's past.

Chapter 6
1910

*L*ilye, ayln, mir zenen gegangen tsu zayn shpet," *Lily,* my
mother said, walking two steps ahead of me in her rundown shoes. *Hurry up or we'll be late.* I was old enough to be
mortified by her guttural Yiddish and the *schmatte* tied around
her head, yet not old enough to understand the burdens of her
life. She used to wear a glossy chestnut wig with curls I liked to
stroke, but since Tatte left, it is nowhere to be seen. Perhaps my
father took it with him when he traveled to Germany or she sold
it, along with half of our furniture and the silver candlesticks.

Mama pushed me onto a double-decker bus heading south.
To where, she refused to say. I longed to sit on top and see more
of the city beyond our East End slum, but Mama led me and my
brother Morris to the back of the bus, each grappling with our
own small parcel of belongings, wrapped in brown paper shut
tight with butcher's twine. We were not top-of-the-bus people.
We were not even people who owned satchels.

"Do you think we're going to see Tatte?" I asked Morris.

"Lily, you know Tatte is dead."

I refused to believe that my father, who always found a lico-
rice drop for me in the deep pockets of his overcoat, would leave
me with only Mama, who kvetched far more than she smiled.
I was his *ketzeleh.* His little pussycat. Through our flat's thin
walls, at night I heard Mama wail for him. Louis, Louis, Louis.
From her lips the name sounded like a swear word Heimie and
Meyer, my oldest brothers, used when they told each other to
sod off.

"Are we going past Buckingham Palace?" I asked. "Might we see the queen?"

My mother laughed sourly. "When God was doling out brains, you were asleep," she said, though that was untrue. I could add and subtract better than any other six-year-old in Stepney Green, make the bed I shared with my sisters, and sew a straight seam. I also knew that while everyone else in our family started their life far away in a place called Ukraine, I alone was born in the town of Leeds. That made me British. When my mother would swat my arse, I'd look her in the eye and repeat Tatte's favorite curse. I'd say it in English, which she couldn't understand: *May you run to the toilet every three minutes or every three months.* Mama made me feel as if my being alive had turned her life unbearable.

We changed buses and the scenery shifted from city to country. Except for the cackling of crows, the tumult quieted. Passengers began to get off the bus but few people got on, which allowed Morris and me to peer out the window.

"Lily!" He pointed to a set of stone gates. I hoped this was our destination, but as we passed, I saw it was a cemetery filled with crosses and statues. Even if Tatte had died, this could not be his resting place. The bus bumped ahead over a rutted road. I rested my head on my brother's shoulder, and tried to imagine our father's eyes—toffee brown—along with his dark, bushy beard and *payes,* which he let me pull.

My mother jostled me awake. She urged us off the bus and the three of us walked for blocks, stopping to rest at every corner so she could rub her swollen feet. Finally, we reached a three-story brick building with a slate roof and two short towers sticking up like thumbs. I could read the first two words on the sign over the entrance: *Jews* and *Hospital.* Did my mother need to go to hospital? Did Morris? I had heard "consumption" whispered in our flat. It had killed our neighbor's wife. I tried to sound out the other words over the door, *Orphanage* and *Asylum.* I did not know how to say them or what they meant.

Morris and I followed Mama into a long hall, where a man motioned us to turn right. The smell of floor wax made my nose twitch. My mother straightened her shawl and headscarf and walked forward, her face panicked, as if someone had accused her of stealing potatoes at the market.

"*Ick bin* Rivkah Shiel," Mama said to a woman tall as a horse. She wore an iron-grey dress and sat at a desk at the far end of the hall. The woman's hair was uncovered, pulled tightly into a bun. Silvery spectacles perched on her beak. "*Aun di bist mein kinder, Morris aun Lilya,*" Mama squeaked. Before she pushed me ahead she whispered for me not to say how Tatte died or they'll send me away. How did my father die? No one had ever explained this. And sent away from where? Here?

"*Sei gesund,*" she said, pulled me toward her for a short, unfamiliar hug, and then pressed Morris against her as well, offering the same farewell.

"Come here children," the woman urged, not unkindly. Behind us, Mama let out a shriek and ran toward the door like a hobbled sprint. I started to chase after her, but Morris yanked my hand and pointed to a banner high above us, noble red with gold fringe, as if this were a castle. It showed a woman in a robe sheltering a boy and a girl.

"It will be better here than home," Morris said in English, but I didn't understand where we were, and though I was six and clever, I was a girl who wanted her mother. We continued to walk and reached the woman in grey.

"'Leave thy fatherless children,'" she said, as if delivering a speech to a hundred people. "'I will preserve them alive, and let thy widows trust in me.'" She was reading the words on the banner in an accent I later learned was considered to be better than ours. All that kept me upright was the terror that had unfolded in my bowels like an umbrella. I was afraid I would soil myself.

It was then I admitted that I was more than a fatherless child.

I was motherless as well, a broken broom, cast away. I wanted to run, but I didn't know the way home.

A man patted Morris's yarmulke. "Come along, mind you," he said, disappearing with him down a high-ceilinged hall, while the lady in grey led me to a room filled with girls of varied sizes and ages.

"This is Lily Shiel," she announced, "the last of you we're expecting this month. Lily, this is Sadie, Helen, Freda, Pauline, and Rachel." I hoped I wouldn't be asked to repeat the names, which I instantly forgot. "Say hello, ladies."

Weakly, the group repeated, "Welcome, Lily." *Velcome.*

"For heaven's sake, girls, show some spirit."

They complied, slightly louder this time. The lady pushed up her spectacles, her glance swimming from girl to girl. "I am Matron Weiss. You will follow me and do as I say." I clutched my parcel to my chest.

"Whatcha got there?" said a girl with red hair ribbons, long lashes, apple cheeks, and a ragged calico pinafore.

"A doll, my Shabbos dress, my nightgown, my comb and brush, my toothbrush." All my earthly possessions.

"I'm Freda," she said. "That's Helen, my sister." Standing nearby was a smaller girl missing both front teeth. Snot dripped from her crusty nose.

"Is this a jail?" I asked under my breath. Last week I stole a halfpenny from Mama's bag because I'd wanted a sweet like Tatte gave me. Was this my punishment?

Freda looked at me as if I were a ninny. "It's Norwood, don't ya know?"

I didn't.

"Where you get sent if your parents are dead or can't look after ya," she added. "My older sister lived here. She says the school ain't bad."

It looked nothing like the shabby one-room school that my sisters and brothers went to in Stepney Green.

"My sister says we're lucky to be here," Freda added. "They take only two from a family."

Take. Do they ever let you go? "Where is she now, your sister?"

"She works in a house with six stories and two staircases."

I knew that story. *Cinderella.* For the first time since we'd gotten off the bus, I felt curiosity under my dread.

Matron Weiss hushed us as her oxfords click-clacked on the waxed wood floor. Her cheeks were ruddy and chapped, her eyes as dark as prunes. We entered a steam-choked room that contained two large tin tubs, each half filled. A thick bar of red soap and a brush sat on a table next to a pile of thin white towels.

"Now girls, line up, ribbons out." Freda reached for her plaits. "Freda Rothenfeldt, did you not hear me?" Freda handed over her ribbons as reluctantly as if they were pearls. "Double-quick, no nonsense."

From the shadowy corner a tiny old woman approached with a pair of heavy scissors and in two snips, relieved Freda of her braids and tossed them in a bin. She pushed Freda along to another woman, short and thickset, who held smaller scissors. The second barber cut until Freda's head was a big, fuzzy knob. I held on to my hair as if it were a hat while each girl in front of me was shorn. Someone screamed "no-no-no." Until Matron Weiss grabbed my upper arm I did not realize the shrieking came from me.

"Lily Shiel, stop. We must avoid lice. The rule. Compulsory. Your hair will be trimmed every other week. Now stand still." After each gust of words, I got a good shake, and could smell onions on her breath.

I closed my eyes while the women took to my head. Tendrils, a shade between ivory and straw, fell by my feet like thick worms. I needed no mirror to know I now looked like a plucked chicken ready for the Friday night pot. When I opened my eyes an older girl, tow-headed with widely spaced teeth, had appeared and swept the fallen hair—mine and everyone else's—into a pile. She was not, like us, bald. Hair covered her ears, just. "Don't worry," she said, the corners of her mouth turning up in a half smile. "When you turn twelve, you'll be allowed to grow your hair."

To reach twelve I would need a second lifetime.

From here we were told to strip naked and two by two, bathe in the steaming water. The soap stung and gave off a stink. As we scrubbed with the bristly brush until our skin became as reddened as Matron Weiss's cheeks, we watched her dump out our parcels and suitcases, gather the clothes in her capable arms, and toss them in another tub of suds. After careful inspection, she set aside Kichel, my wooden doll, while my brush, comb, shoes, and socks landed in the bin. "What about my dress?" I whimpered. It was blue, handed down from Mama to Sarah to Esther, worn by one of us on every Shabbos I could remember.

"It will be returned, washed and ironed," Matron Weiss said.

On Pesach I heard the story about slaves. Is that what I was being turned into? I stood, naked, until the older girl, whose name I learned was Mildred, handed me a towel and pile of clothes. Though it was July, I was to wear woolen bloomers and an undervest, dark stockings, and a serge dress with sleeves that buttoned to the wrists. There were stiff brown boots, well worn, that laced to the ankles and a woolen nightdress sturdier than the gown I'd brought along.

We trailed the matron up a wide staircase and into a hall where we were told to take places at the longest table I had ever seen. While a rabbi said a *kiddush* and a *motze,* I searched for Morris on the other side of the eating hall. I failed to find him. The boys looked identical, dozens and dozens of boiled eggs with yarmulkes atop black shirts.

Supper was brown bread, butter, and milk. I had eaten nothing since tea and bread in the East End that morning, and could have gobbled three portions, but there were no extra helpings.

"You missed dinner—it was at half-past twelve," Mildred explained. It was now six. After the meal the rabbi swayed as he led a prayer with many *ya ya yas*. The children—there must have been more than two hundred—shouted "amen" and then there was a clatter as we got up from our benches, pushed them under the table, and lined up two by two. Some were laughing. Mildred held my hand tight as we walked to the other side of the building and entered a shul. From the girls' balcony, I searched for Morris. He was nowhere I could find.

For every night I could remember, I had been the schmaltz between the challah of one sister's plump limbs and the sharp angles of the other's knees and elbows. I had never slept in a cot of my own, or been tucked between sheets stiff as cardboard. I no longer felt like Lily Shiel of Stepney Green. I had become a character in a book that many decades later I learned might have been written by Dickens or Brontë, had their given names been Chaim and Chana. I did not expect my story to have a happy ending.

From somewhere far away in the building, a clock chimed midnight . . . one . . . two . . . but sleep failed to come. The bedroom, which Matron Weiss called a dormitory, was on the top floor of the building, airless and filled with a racket of crying, sniffling, and snoring. Fifty girls, all missing someone. For me it was Tatte, my sisters and brothers—Morris, especially— and even my mother, though she'd tossed me aside like moldy cheese. I felt abandoned, terrified.

God stays closest to those with broken hearts, Tatte used to say. I held back my tears and repeated those eight words.

Chapter 7

1920

At the orphanage, we lived by gongs. Six, rise from your cot, wash with icy water, and slip into a mouse-colored uniform. Six-thirty, gulp cocoa thin as rain. Scarf down bread smeared with dodgy margarine. Seven, scrub floors and pots and pans. Eight, prayers. Nine, go to class, and on and on until evening prayers, supper, and the chime that announced lights out, and the cycle began again. As a bed-wetter, I was exiled to a special dormitory, and swatted whenever Matron sniffed my straw bed in the morning and declared that I'd pissed. Were it not for Shabbos afternoons, when we were left in a park for a few hours, all two hundred of us might as well have been prisoners, separated from the world by a high fence and—until we turned twelve—our baldness. The shearing of heads was not, I discovered, merely a strike against lice. It marked us, should we have the chutzpah to escape.

When I was allowed to grow my hair, it sprouted unevenly, like an old potato. I was scrawny and itched with a rash. My nose never stopped running and my hands were red and rough from chores. After the muckety-mucks emerged from their long black limousines for a yearly visit, some orphans got a pat on the head, but when the trustees saw me, they hurried by. This confirmed what I guessed. I was hideous.

I was also sly. Drawn by the aroma of meat pies—delicacies eaten by the teachers, matrons, and headmaster, but never us—I learned how to steal from the kitchen in order to satisfy my unremitting hunger, though when I liberated a pear from the sukkah I was caught and received a caning on my bare bottom. I found the punishment not altogether unpleasant. On Saturdays, Morris and I stood outside the cinema near the park, looking tragic until a woman gave each of us a penny to see the matinee, a double billing. A cowboy galloped across the Great Plains of America and parents in gleaming houses kvelled at children, even when they disobeyed. I thought I was witnessing heaven, which I knew about only from poetry, since our religion didn't coddle us with the lure of after-life incentives. Our rewards were few, but I aimed to bag them all. I competed in every sport and excelled at my studies. I won top prizes for both Hebrew and writing and was chosen to read my composition, "Why England Defeated the Huns," in front of the entire orphanage.

"It's do or die with you, Lily, isn't it?" Matron Weiss asked after I won a sixpence for reciting "The White Man's Burden" by Kipling, which took me just two days to memorize.

"Thank you, ma'am." I curtsied. But where has doggedness gotten me? I remained an ugly girl in an orphanage.

"You have a good brain," she added. "If you continue to work hard you might become"—she paused—"a typist," hitting on the word as if she were banging the exclamation point key. For an instant I pictured myself wearing a starched blue shirtwaist and patent leather shoes, walking to a spotless office in one of the buildings I'd glimpsed during a trip to the dentist, where we were taken twice a year. I would turn out important letters, stopping midafternoon for tea in a cup without cracks. At day's end I'd retire to a tidy bedsit with its gas heater glowing like a grin. I would never shiver in the clammy cold. But faster than lightning, the image faded.

When I was fourteen I was called to the matron's office. I expected to finally be awarded the opportunity to take a scholarship test. After all, I was the only student who'd been allowed to skip a grade. When Arthur Balfour declared that one day

Palestine would become a homeland for our people, I alone was chosen to write him in thanks. I'd been appointed prefect and sat at a table of honor in the dining room.

The matron, however, said coolly, "Lily, I must convey sad news."

I gasped. "Is something wrong with Morris?" Last week, a boy had died from meningitis.

"Oh no." She fluttered a gnarled hand. "Nothing of that sort."

Perhaps I would have to wait to take the test. I could do that. Only a fool lived in an orphanage for years and failed to develop patience.

"You mother has fallen ill. She requested that you be dismissed to nurse her. I knew you'd hoped for a scholarship . . ." Her voice trailed off.

Disappointment curdled into self-pity, to disgust, to outrage. Despite occasional visits, Mama remained a stooped, jumpy stranger who cleaned public toilets and still couldn't speak or read English. Did she even read Yiddish? The sixth commandment was one from which I had long felt entitled to be exempt, but clearly in this matter, I had no choice.

"You will leave in two weeks."

I stood motionless and unmoored. Matron Weiss rose from her chair, walked to my side, and placed a hand on my arm. "Remember this, Lily Shiel. Destiny is what you make of fate." I wanted to laugh at this platitude, though years later I recognized that it might be the most practical advice I would ever receive.

Orphanage policy required girls to be discharged with a functional wardrobe of their own making. I began a flurry of sewing, at which I excelled almost as much as at cricket, where the team I led trounced the boys. I finished two long-sleeved black dresses with removable white bibs, a high-necked flannel nightgown, thick grey bloomers, and muslin vests. A brassiere, which I could plainly use now, was not on the list. I was also presented with a tweedy coat of indeterminate color and my first hat, a navy straw with a blue ribbon sailing down the back.

The day I left, the other girls, teachers, and Morris lined up to wave me off. In turn, the matrons shook my hand and repeated, "*Gay ga zinta hate.*" This translated to "go in good health." What I heard was, "good riddance."

"I love you, Lily," my brother whispered in my ear as we hugged. As a boy, he was not required to serve his mother.

I left the Asylum and boarded the first of four buses that would return me to Stepney Green. Instead of freedom, I felt fear. Several hours later I reached the tenement of Rivkah Shiel and rang the bell.

"*Kumen in,*" a voice mumbled.

The basement flat where my mother had moved was barely bigger than a closet, with the smallest and oldest coal stove I'd ever seen. I could see that I would be even colder than at the orphanage. The room smelled like unwashed armpits and rotting meat. Huddled on a hard chair in the corner, my mother was ashen from her thin, frizzy hair to the pallor of her skin.

"Mama, how are you?" I choked out the Yiddish.

"*Yeder mentsh hot zikh zayn pekl,*" she muttered. *Everyone has her own burden.* I thought of nothing to say in response. I tried to summon compassion but found a fortress of resentment. I was bright enough for a scholarship that could lead me to respectable employment and a bigger world. Instead, I was sentenced to care for a stranger who had called me back from my abandonment only when she needed an indentured servant.

After I dutifully offered to make her a cup of tea, I pleaded exhaustion, changed into my nightgown, and fell asleep on a lumpy chair. In my dreams I declaimed my victorious essay in front of the whole orphanage, but my sleep was short. I was rousted by someone who hoarsely whispered my name.

"Get up, goddamn it," he said. "Get up, you lazy cunt."

A burly man smothered my mouth with a hairy hand as I shrieked, "Oh, my God," sure my heart would stop.

"Shut up, will ya?" he hissed.

I pushed him off me, shouting, "*Gay avek*," and pummeled the intruder's chest with both fists. "Go away." I screamed again, tasting my terror.

The man's breath was rank with a smell I soon learned was beer. "The duchess doesn't recognize her own family," he snarled.

Thick neck. Scraggly mustache. A long nose with a bump. Heavy spectacles. The man's voice triggered an image of wiry eyebrows and a bristly beard. *Tatte*. Where was my protector now? And my sisters, who I soon learned had each married and moved north?

"Which one are you?" I asked, suspiciously. I barely remembered that I had older brothers.

The man bent close and planted a kiss on my cheek. I twisted away in disgust. "I'm Heimie, and you're in my goddamn bed so move your bloody arse. Go sleep with Ma."

I stumbled to the tiny room where my mother moaned and coughed, half awake. I climbed into the bed, careful not to touch her, less because I worried about waking an invalid than revulsion at the thought of contact. A window, covered with newspaper, leaked frosty air. In the darkness I saw my breath.

The moth-eaten blanket that offered the room's sole warmth was too skimpy to cover both of us. Drowning in self-pity, I put on my coat and moved to the edge of the bed. From the other room, Heimie's snoring matched the throb in my head. Silently, I begin to recite.

Take up the White Man's burden
Send forth the best ye breed
Go bind your sons to exile
To serve your captives' need

When dawn arrived I attempted to muster a self-image of epic sacrifice. I can do this, I told myself, thinking of martyrs in my limited exposure to literature. My goodwill lasted for almost a day. My mother expected me to shop, cook, and clean. I didn't begrudge the first task, since it allowed me to leave the flat, even if the surrounding slums were overrun with vermin, dung, and men who hooted at my bouncing chest or, if they were bold, brushed up against me. But I knew nothing about cooking, having only been in the orphanage kitchen to steal. And though I had plenty of experience cleaning, I was so fueled by ill will that I made intentional blunders. Despite her weakness, my mother berated me continually for my slipshod efforts. Even my dusting offended her.

I tolerated her screeds only because she was too weak to accompany them with beatings, and because her chiding was vastly preferable to the worst of my burdens: nursing. It was stomach cancer, Heimie told me. This required me to cleanse an abdominal hole, the result of a surgery, and that was the more pleasant part of the task. I was also expected to launder her shit-soaked bandages. I would sooner sell myself in the street than perform this loathsome duty. After each washing, I heaved into the loo, again and again.

Such was life at Stepney Green. Not only did my mother shout orders, Heimie did as well, and his were louder. At night when he returned from his factory job, my brother handed over an empty jug to fill with beer from the pub, where stinking boozers made rude remarks about my bum as well as my breasts.

"Bugger off and git it yourself, you pig," I yelled one evening. Already *fershikkit*, Heimie raised a hand to slap me, but when he saw me stand my ground, he backed down.

I sensed a constant looming readiness to lunge, which eventually he did. A jury of my peers might say I deserved his attack. I hated that my mother expected me to scour the cobblestones outside our door, where every neighbor could literally look down

on me with ridicule. As I scrubbed, I pictured myself accumu-
lating accolades at the orphanage. I was no dirty skivvy. But my
memories failed to distract me from my comedown.

One day I refused to clean, and my mother slapped me across
the face. A dybbuk straight from one of the folktales I loved
took charge of my hand and did the same to her, a dying woman
wasted away to eight stone. I could feel the flat of my hand
cracking her cheekbone. At this moment Heimie walked in and
found our mother crouched and crying. As I ran from him in
shame he chased me, yelling, "You fucking twat" for all to hear.

I was startled and horrified by what I had done, and there
was no place to hide in a flat the size of two horse stalls. Heimie
hammered me with his fists as my mother begged him to stop.
Blood dripped on the floor, and I felt a pain in my jaw before I
slumped into darkness.

The next morning I tried to apologize. "Leave me alone,"
Mama moaned. "You're no daughter. I don't want you. *Gal kuk-
ken afen yam.*" *Go shit in the ocean.* I returned to the orphanage.

Two days later I was on a train to Brighton, where a teacher
had found me a job as an under-housemaid—the lowest on
the rung—in a seaside mansion owned by two spinsters. Every day I scrubbed their basement floor and front steps, shined
twenty brass fixtures as well as my employers' shoes, cleaned
nine rooms, served three meals, and washed the dishes. I ate
in the kitchen, was allowed no visitors—though I had none to
invite—and was forced to enter and exit through the back door.

On Thursdays from two to six, my work life suspended when
I was allowed to stroll on the boardwalk. I always stopped to
buy and read *Peg's Paper*. It featured two versions of the same
tale. A peer of the realm hung around places where someone
like me might trip over him and the two would fall in love or,
after a hoity-toity education, a well-born virgin was polished off

in France, presented to the king and queen, and married to a viscount or an earl. The plots might vary by the odd stable boy or lord, but the endings were happily-ever-after identical.

One day a young man saw me reading and asked me my age. "Eighteen," I said, adding a few years. Where did I live? Never before had I brought my daydreams to life, but I said that my home was a mansion down the road. He offered a ride on his motorcycle and dropped me there. While I saw him laugh when the parlor maid scolded me for ringing the front door, I didn't care. Telling lies, I discovered, was no harder than breathing. People believed them, as long as you spoke with conviction.

I idled in this job for months when a letter arrived from Heimie, demanding my return to Stepney Green. Our mother had reached the end. I left with a reference that I tossed in the trash. I vowed to never again clean any toilet except my own.

A few weeks later my nose was buried in a newspaper when I heard a small sigh. Almost incuriously, I checked the bedroom. My mother, pale as milk, had tumbled to the floor and was feebly thrashing her limbs. I was struggling to lift her when she expired in my arms.

I had never seen death, which I learned attracts a crowd. Quickly, the flat burst with neighbors who seemed to care more for sorrowful, doomed Rivkah Shiel than did I, who felt like I was in an audience at a play, seated in the last row. People with names I had never bothered to learn saw to it that the body was removed, and following Jewish custom, arranged for burial the next day. I refused to attend the service, nor did I find out who paid for the casket—Heimie didn't have a pence—or where my mother was laid to rest.

I'd heard that when people die, it's easier to love them, but I hated my mother even then, refusing to consider that this poverty-stricken woman had no choice but to send me away to an orphanage. Had she loved me? I would never know, or ask that question aloud. My sole inheritance was a tiny, dog-eared picture taken when I was about two that I found in her drawer. I was dressed in an apron, wearing little black boots, clutching a wooden spoon.

I thought only of the sullen child in the picture, now a genuine orphan.

Chapter 8
1920

I was ashamed of my absence of grief, but I was *free*. I was also penniless and in desperate need of a job. I wanted to look up and see sun, not raggedy laundry strung tenement to tenement, and longed to forget the percussion that poverty brings. The bawl of starving, sickly children. Never-ending quarrels. The lamentations of hollow-eyed women beaten by husbands reeking from the smoke and beer of their pubs. I was determined to turn my back on the squalor, and was sufficiently naïve to believe that if I willed myself to expunge my past, I could. I did not realize your history is a shadow that follows you everywhere.

I started to look for work in a busy shopping district. With no references, I had no luck. I did, however, have pearly teeth—for that I could thank the orphanage's regular trips to the dentist and complete absence of sweets—and the good fortune of tripping over a newspaper ad: *Wanted, girls with good teeth, no experience necessary, to demonstrate new toothbrush.* I applied for the job and was hired on the spot to start the next morning in a department store close to the West End.

Nearby, on a street whose better days were long past, I found a tiny room. Dark and dank with one small window, it faced a back lane and cost ten and sixpence, twice the rent of Stepney Green and half my salary. While it wasn't Mayfair, it was the West End, the holy of holies. I moved in my paltry belongings and offered goodbye to no one—not neighbors, not Heimie or my other siblings, not even a letter to Morris, who had moved up north and whom I hadn't seen since the Asylum. I cut off my past like a butcher hacks away a hunk of gristle.

On my first day of work I set up my display and practiced my spiel. "Good day, sir or madam." Smile. "Have you tried this new toothbrush that cleans the back of your teeth?" Smile. "You'll see it's as different from old-fashioned brushes as chalk is from cheese." Place in customer's hands and point out feature. "Today we have a special price." Smile.

I heard chuckling and turned to find an older saleswoman. "I can't believe you're going through such a harangue to hawk a toothbrush." She extended a hand and smiled. "Ruth Houghton, cosmetics."

"Lily Shiel," I said.

"Happy to meet you, Shielsy."

That day I sold nine toothbrushes, all to men. The next day, eleven, again exclusively to men. From then I decided I'd try to sell only to men, who clearly cared more about dental hygiene than did women. Let the ladies' teeth rot.

I learned how to josh with customers, who would often say I was beautiful. Was I? My face had turned heart-shaped, with distinct cheekbones. My ash blond hair, uncut since the orphanage and released from its bun, waved to my shoulders. My nose was narrow and pert. My eyes were a mix of pewter grey and the mossy green of an unripe apple. My lips, full with a natural cupid's bow. Skin, classic English, creamy but rosy. I could not claim the pieces added up to beauty, and no one at the orphanage or Stepney Green had made this assessment, but I couldn't dispute that far more men stopped to chat with me than the other salesgirls, and the conversations frequently led to a purchase. Though I could not explain the effect I had on men, I was determined to play this ace. I started to toss my head, bat my eyelashes, and from Ruth bought a red lipstick that I applied carefully each morning. Saying they'd be happy to hire me, several men left calling cards. I tucked them away in a box.

One blustery December, a morning passed with not one sale. It was nearly noon and I was afraid I'd lose my job. A tall, thin gentleman in a bowler hat blew through the door. I nearly assaulted him, saying "Sir, sir, may I have a moment of your time?" Like a bobby, I blocked him with my arm.

"By jove," he said. "Aren't you lovely?" I liked his accent, far more melodic than my Cockney inflections. Thanks to Ruth, I could identify it as posh. He laughed. "Well, if you can sell this"—the gentleman held up the ridiculous toothbrush—"you could sell the Pope a harem." I guessed his age to be late thirties or older, but with the twinkle of Peter Pan, he added, "I'm in sales myself, iron and steel as well as fancy goods. I could always find a place for a girl like you." He handed me a pound along with his card. "You can keep the change if you promise to ring me tomorrow."

I promised, and with that, he bolted into the downpour and disappeared under a black umbrella.

That's how I met Johnny.

Three weeks later the toothbrush company went bust. That evening I searched through my cards until I found one that read *The John Graham Company, Major John Graham Gillam, D.S.O.* The next morning I showed it to Ruth.

"D.S.O.?" she said, impressed. "Distinguished Service Order, Shielsy. It's for military bravery, a decoration from the Palace second only to Victoria Cross."

Now *I* was impressed.

"Call him."

"But what if he wants"—I stuttered—"social favors."

"You take that chance, you daft girl."

I phoned. When I identified myself, a woman immediately put me through.

"What took you so long?" the voice I recognized said, amiably. "My secretary and I have been waiting for your call."

This time, I got to the point. "Could you still find me a job, sir?"

"By jove. Of course."

I didn't ask what the position was, only its salary.

"What are you earning now?"

"One pound, ten," I lied.

"Two pounds and commission then."

I accepted, and the next day I reported to the John Graham Company, comprised of an office and a storeroom chockablock with beaded necklaces, table clocks, lacquered fans, and cartons of reading lamps. My new employer showed off every item, cradling it like a newborn. "I'd like you to sell all of this. You'll be a natural, and before you know it, girls will be reporting to you." He patted me on the arm. "You'll start tomorrow."

Major John Gillam was a hero, my hero, well-dressed, well-mannered, well-spoken—and the handsomest man I'd ever met, with a pencil-slim mustache and statesman's bearing. The suggestion of a shag never came up.

Early that evening, I rapped on my landlady's door. "I need a front room, please," I said. She offered me one for twelve and six with a tall window overlooking the avenue. I moved in my things, settled in a rocking chair and opened a new *Peg's Paper*, trying to see myself on every page. When I read of a young mother's child being trampled by a horse, this was the moment when I began to convulse in weeping for my mother and the ceaseless tragedy that was her life. Then I dried my tears. I was convinced that my future was one happy ending away.

Chapter 9

1920

I hung my black sateen coat on a hook and peered at Sir John Gillam from beneath a hat that tilted over my left eye like a schooner listing in the harbor. Never had I felt more cosmopolitan, or more alive.

"Good morning, my dear Miss Shiel," my new boss said as he rose to meet me. We exchanged a warm but proper handshake. "Won't you be seated?" I settled myself on a straight chair across from his cluttered desk. As he bent his legs beneath him, he lifted a string of beads. "I'd like you to begin your rounds today with these lovely faux pearls. They go for only a few pence a pop. You should be able to sell dozens, and I insist that you wear one yourself. They'll shine against your milkmaid skin."

I'd never met a milkmaid nor had I any idea what *foe* pearls were, but I hung the strand around my neck, filled the valise that Sir John Gillam provided, and set off into the rolling fog. One by one, with an electric volt of enthusiasm, I approached each door on the list of High Street shops he'd provided.

After three days of animated selling—a true Highland fling of effort—I had unloaded not one choker. "You should have visited us at Christmas," any number of proprietors suggested, as if that were obvious. When I reported this failure, my employer dismissed my result with a wave of his hand.

"Fine," he said. "We'll try again before Easter. But meanwhile . . ." He disappeared into the dusty storeroom behind the front office and returned with a small tin. "I daresay that in this dreary weather our Suji-Muji automotive polish is a surer bet." As John Gillam unscrewed the lid I noticed that, like his legs, his fingers were lengthy. "This product contains a secret Oriental ingredient that gives autos a remarkable luster." He beamed and spoke the word "remarkable" in a tone designed to sell *me*, accompanied by the sort of engaging, even-toothed smile I found impossible not to return. "Try the showrooms on Great Portland. You'll find dozens."

I did try, though the closest I'd ever gotten to a car owner was Heimie's mechanic friend, Archie, who always smelled faintly of petrol. At the first six establishments I was turned away. But at the seventh when I walked toward the back of a glassy hall and asked for the manager, a man shaped like a beer keg waddled toward me and listened to me with interest. "If you'd be so kind as to demonstrate your wares, I'll gather the salesmen on the floor," he said. Minutes later, a half-dozen men dressed in identical navy-blue suits assembled for my presentation. I pulled a rag from my carpetbag and reached for the top of the boot.

Politely, the manager stopped me. "My dear, would you dab the product down here? That's the spot that collects the most grime." He gestured toward the back fender.

This required me to kneel. I felt every eye on my arse, raised in the air like a shiny rump roast as a ladder made its way up my best pair of hose. "You see, all you need to do is rub slowly, back and forth, up and down," I cheeped as I applied the viscous polish. I willed my hands not to shake but I could not stop the blood flowing to my face and was grateful for the sweep of my hat's brim. Behind me, I heard a whistle. I struggled to my feet and dusted off my coat.

The manager bought one tin of the paste. One. I dropped his coin into my coat pocket, the delusion dismantled that I could ever become a successful, dignified saleswoman. I hiked back to the office, my valise heavy on my arm, and found Sir John Gillam with his secretary, both stuffing envelopes as they sang a music hall round.

"Miss Shiel," he said, with the greatest cheer. "How did you fare?"

My full bag spoke for itself.

"Never you mind," he said. "You'll go out again after a thrashing rainstorm when every car all but demands a wash. They'll be begging for polish. In the meantime, perhaps you could give us a hand? I don't believe I mentioned our mail-order operation, but every Thursday I send out hundreds of adverts. If you could seal the envelopes and affix the stamps?"

This, I could do. For two hours, the three of us made short work of a mountain of letters, setting aside those intended for foreign destinations. I felt snug in the small, steam-heated office. When I found an envelope destined for Paris, I exclaimed, "Channel! Isn't that a famous perfume?" I'd tried the scent on my wrists when I worked in the department store. It smelled like a life I couldn't imagine.

Sir John Gillam smiled. "Indeed, Miss Shiel. It's a fine French brand, but it's called 'Chanel.' Repeat after me, please. *Cha-nel.*"

"*Sha-nell,*" I echoed. For the second time that day, I felt my face burn. But that was when my true education began.

Over the next few weeks, I had better luck with selling and began to earn modest commissions. More important, I learned from Sir John Gillam that a "debutante" was not a *deb-bunt-ee,* but a young woman—albeit not one born in a hovel and raised in an orphanage—to be presented to society in a ritual as old as Buckingham Palace. I listened hard, and was proud when I put together what it meant to ride to hounds. Unashamed about my ignorance and ravenous for information, I absorbed each drop of intelligence as if it were strawberry compote and I, a slice of angel cake. As my questions grew bolder, my employer became increasingly forthcoming, tactfully recommending that I might exchange my picture hat—not that it wasn't flattering, mind you—in favor of a tidy felt cloche. Never did he make me feel unlettered or unfashionable. If anything, he offered the impression that my gaffes were charming. This, I later realized, was as much the mark of breeding as the filigree of gallant speech and deportment.

Then, a few Thursdays later, he asked me to dine.

I thought of the men who ogled me in Piccadilly, as well as my penny-novel tales of girls who lost their virtue and not incidentally, their jobs, when they accepted such invitations. I admired John—what he'd asked me to call him. But this was a risk I couldn't take. I agreed to join him for tea only when he invited me to see him off for a trip on the boat train setting sail in Dover for Brussels, where he had business. This was an opportunity too star-dusted to decline.

I'd traveled on a train once, to Brighton, third class, squeezed between a family with yapping twins and a wheezing pensioner. But this short trip to Dover was first class. The dining car glowed with resplendent oak paneling and seats upholstered in a shade of velvet John called "claret." I munched on biscuits—six, at least—with cup after cup of milky tea served in translucent china. When I returned to London I floated past a telegraph agency and on impulse, wired John a message of thanks, signing it "Love, Lily." I felt daring. I could do with more of this opulence.

I also frankly adored John, the first grown man who I felt truly wished me well and saw in Lily Shiel what I later identified as potential. The day John returned, he invited me to dinner at a restaurant with an electric candle under an ivory parchment shade. The moment my sole arrived, I inhaled it down to its bones. As time passed, and we continued to dine together at least once a week, I learned to wait patiently for my food and to savor each bite, rather than worry that my plate would be snatched away. I studied how to hold my utensils without mashing my hands into fists, and discovered that a knife existed strictly for fish, as well as how to season my food—at the orphanage, condiments were as nonexistent as handkerchiefs.

The latter contributed to my constant sniffling, causing John to say, more than once, "Do blow your nose, please." Though I couldn't work out why, he taught me to rise when an older woman entered the room but to remain seated when a man approached the table and that—inexplicably—"what?" was the proper response if I needed a phrase repeated, not the shrill of "pardon." He also hinted that my satin coat was more fitting for the opera—the opera!—than sales calls and insisted that I visit his tailor, at his expense, to have him run up a herringbone wool topper.

I became increasingly entranced with this gentleman leading the charge to transform Lily Shiel of Stepney Green into a lady. In the language of the East End, Sir John Graham Gillam knew brass from onions. He was forty-two and I imagined had the maturity and knowledge to navigate any social or business situation with the agility of a mountain goat.

One evening a few months later, when he needed to change into regimental dress for a concert he invited me to attend, I did not decline when asked if I would accompany him to his flat. A uniformed doorman tipped his hat and wished us a good evening as he operated the building's lift. John's flat was small and smelled of leather. Would I like a drink? he offered.

"Fizzy water, if you have it." Liquor was not for me. "And I'd do with a biscuit, please, as long as they got no rise-ins."

John's initial bafflement turned to amusement and he clucked, "The word is raisins, Lily. But your accent, what are we going to do about it?"

In England, your dialect is a straitjacket that locks you forever in the class of your birth. I might have been able to learn to blow my nose and sell a box of ceramic banks shaped like pigs' snouts, but my speech—Yiddish-inflected Cockney only slightly mitigated by my years in the orphanage—was seemingly an impenetrable thicket of wrongs. At the time I did not notice that my *h*'s disappeared or that I'd say *Gimme me keys, will ya?*—spoken in a rush as far from Shakespeare's iambic pentameter as Cambridge is from Cornwall.

John poured me a soda, himself a Scotch, and toasted me. "To dearest Lily. May she learn to speak the King's English." With that, he walked into the other room, shutting the door behind him. He did not beckon me to follow him nor did I feel that was what he expected.

At least ten minutes passed as I nibbled biscuits and sipped my water. When John reappeared, I stared wide-eyed at a toy soldier come to life. He wore full military dress, with a red stripe shooting down the side of his sharply creased pants, his chest spangled by medals and ribbons, shoulders dripping with braid. At the hip, a sword pointed toward boots so spit-shined I was sure they could reflect my face, agog. Absurdly handsome, John walked in my direction, leaned over my chair, and kissed me, deeply, his lips soft and full on my own.

I'd been kissed before, but never with tenderness. I could have happily returned a dozen kisses, but he said, "We need to go now, Lily dear. Chop chop."

I hated to leave John's well-appointed cocoon, and whimpered, "Oh. Could I stay a little longer? Skip the concert?"

John gave me a look I could not read, though he chuckled, "You are an odd duck," and shook his head with good-natured exasperation. "But have it your way." He closed the door behind him and I waited for his footsteps to disappear.

The room echoed with a heavenly calm. I flipped through a magazine, something smart from America called *Vanity Fair*, fingered a row of pipes, and examined John's photographs, taking in a boy in a sailor suit next to a bigger girl with brown ringlets and a silky bow. In the bedroom, from the top of a highboy, I reached for a shoehorn, a tortoiseshell comb, and two brushes, presumably one for hair and another for clothing. I dabbed aftershave lotion on my wrists. It smelled sharply green. No match for Chanel No. 5. A framed landscape painted in muddy shades hung next to a window covered with austere linen curtains. I did not dare recline in the bed, which had only one pillow, rather flat. I opened a door to a closet lined with suits of pinstripes, flannel, and herringbone.

A door led to the bath, where, for the second time that evening, I gasped. Unlike the half tub, cracked and cramped, that I was allowed to use twice a week at my rooming house, here was a rowboat on lion's feet. I could not resist opening a jar of crystal bath salts placed on a small oak table by the tub's curved flank.

I had learned to believe that if I took a risk the world would open up for me. I found my hand letting the tap flow as I allowed a handful of crystal snow to drift into the steaming water. One by one, I stripped off my heavy stockings and my smalls, allowing each item to fall on a plush rug that covered half of the marble floor. Down to nothing, I turned to size myself up in a mirror that backed the bathroom door.

I had never seen a reflection of my entire bare body. I might have been looking at a portrait of a voluptuous stranger, with a nipped waist and rounded hips tapering to slender legs. She had a full bosom, sugary white, with small nipples the color of rosé wine. The womanly hair down below was the color of dark honey.

I blushed and quickly stepped into the tub, where I sank into the billowing froth, laughing for no reason except that I felt grand. As I soaked I allowed myself gauzy dreams, becoming Josephine to John's Napoleon, until the water chilled. I dried myself with a Turkish towel, hurried into my clothes and fine grey coat, stuffed my damp hair under my cloche, and shut the front door behind me.

In the office during the next few weeks, John might say, "Lily, you're so beautiful" or "How did I ever manage without you?" When that happened I remembered our kiss, and fantasized about becoming Mrs. John Graham Gillam, though I quickly flicked away the thought. Our age difference was as vast as our backgrounds. He knew I'd been raised in a slum and orphanage, though he was too polite to probe. That I was Jewish remained a secret. When he asked if "Shiel" was German, I had nodded yes.

Eager, grateful, and attractive as I hoped John might find me, I realized I was no more than his Eliza Doolittle. Nor was I without male companionship. Everywhere, I met men and received invitations.

Chapter 10

1923

One Saturday evening a long black car stopped at my boardinghouse and a liveried chauffeur stood by, as my regular escort, George, rang. He proceeded to sit in the front seat, and his sister Helen and a stout man with puffy cheeks the color of her fuchsia dress shifted to make room for me in the back. He introduced himself as Monte Collins.

Our first stop was to see a play, which George and I watched from the row in front of Helen and Mr. Collins. I tried to concentrate on the plot, but all I could think of was Mr. Collins's rat-like eyes boring into my head. The performance ended at eleven, yet he insisted that we return to his house in Knightsbridge. "Collins is a millionaire!" George whispered. "Hasn't Helen fallen into pudding?"

At Mr. Collins's home, brocade pillows picked up the purple of thick carpets. Vases burst with peacock feathers and pungent lilies. At every turn, silver gleamed. Over sandwiches pinched by his fleshy fingers, our host explained that he had made his fortune through a chain of grocery stores, and despite Helen fluttering around him like a pink bat, he could not stop nattering away to me. Only me.

Did I enjoy the play? Did I notice lilies were his favorite flower? The questions came in such a salvo I doubt he even heard my boneheaded answers. Though he was another woman's escort, Monte Collins, millionaire, was plainly flirting with me. Apparently, he did as he pleased, as I grew to discover could be said of most wealthy men. I became a popinjay, chattering without shame. As the evening wore on, I raised a glass and toasted, "To our friendship," locking eyes with Mr. Collins. George groaned.

Mr. Collins insisted that his driver drop me off last. Soon we were alone in the back seat of his Rolls-Royce. This was when I began to regret that back at the flat I hadn't asked to visit the lavatory. I'd stopped counting how many glasses I'd drunk of Champagne, which tasted like a divine adaptation of my favorite fizzy water. Now, *oy gevalt*, my bladder.

As we approached my rooming house, I exhaled deeply in appreciation of the nearness of a commode. This is when Mother Nature took the upper hand. Beneath me, warmth puddled, soaking my coat and most certainly leaving behind a small lake. As the driver opened the door I hurried toward my stoop; over my shoulder, I thanked Mr. Collins. That's the last I'll ever see of a millionaire—or George, for that matter—I thought, eager to flee my urinary felony. I was right, but only about George.

The next evening, my landlady presented me with my first slim white florist box. In it I found calla lilies and a note on monogrammed vellum.

"Enchanting Lily," it said, "expect me next Sunday promptly at noon. Yours, Monte."

I was too shocked to be insulted by the assumption that I desired this man's company. When I joined Monte the following week in his black car I discovered that we were headed for Maidenhead. Was this a joke? Humor seemed on the far side of the man's range. After he complimented my looks, with a reddened face he pointed out the location of the restaurant's sanitary facilities.

As we sipped our consommé and proceeded to aspic, delicate game birds, and blancmange, topped off by wines, Monte recounted how he had excelled as an "old boy" at Harrow and become a grocery store gladiator. I caught every other word of his monologue, hypnotized as I was by the surroundings.

On Monday when I told John that I'd dined at a restaurant called Skindles, he huffed, "You *must* be careful. That spot is notorious for adulterous assignations." My virtue, however, was safely intact. Monte had ended the afternoon with only a chaste peck.

Monte established a routine that I passively accepted, still pinching myself that a man of wealth fancied me. We dined every Wednesday evening and Sunday afternoon. On other nights I often saw John, who was far superior company. Unlike Monte, who had all the grace of the elephant seal lounging behind glass in the British Museum, John was an effortless dancer eager to teach me the Charleston and the Peabody to records he'd play on his Victrola. Yet while my time with John fell somewhere between friendship and flirtation, there was no question: Monte Collins was courting me. After the fourth Wednesday, we once again wound up at his home.

This time, when he took my wrap, fear uncoiled. I'd held tight to my virginity through the orphanage years, well aware of what had happened to my friend Freda at the park one Shabbos afternoon. I'd defended myself against the swine of Stepney Green and showed reserve even in my physical awakening with John, not that he'd pressed me. But despite the lure of Monte's bank balance, I was unready to surrender to a corpulent man who sat too close and looked too hard, an escort who when he gave me chocolates every Sunday, insisted I eat only one, lest I lose my appetite. When we danced in the snazzy clubs he favored, I wished I could wind up with one of the lordly types who wafted their partners across the floor as if they were made of tulle. Yet who was I to dismiss a mantle of money, especially when I compared him to Sir John Gillam, whom I now knew was far from successful?

Aided by office scuttlebutt, I'd pieced together that the John Graham Company stayed afloat thanks to a noble tradition of which the Shiels were unaware, the financial beneficence of family—in John's case, from an indulgent older sister who'd married above her station. Yet John had attributes finer than business acumen: warmth, humor, an uncanny ability to make me feel that I could soar, and the endearing habit of always wearing a crooked bow tie. I began to suspect that he tilted his necktie intentionally so that each morning I would perform our ritual of my reaching up to straighten it, and saying, "There, John. Got it right."

For my birthday, Monte presented me with a shiny lizard pin, an unfortunate choice, given the comparisons it invited. When John admired the jewel, I admitted that the brooch was from the man we now referred to as Mr. Skindles. I am not necessarily linking cause to effect, but the next week, John made an astonishing gesture. Would I go to Paris to sleuth down French perfume to be had at a rock-bottom price?

Would I ever. I was still beaming from my half-day trip to Dover. That I knew not a word of French and worried that John was Don Quixote, chasing a windmill of eau de toilette, did not deter me. I blurted out the news to Monte when we next met.

"I wish you wouldn't go," he pouted.

"But this is a once-in-a-lifetime chance."

"In that case, while you are away, I will do a great deal of thinking," he said, lifting his beetled brow. To make sure that I did not forget him, he made reservations for me at Elizabeth Arden and Lanvin and gave me a hundred pounds of spending money.

I spent every pence. English-French dictionary and Baedeker in hand, I may as well have been the first Englishwoman to hope that the refinement of Paris would wash over her. On day one of the trip I enrolled at Berlitz, where I was a quick study. On day two I bobbed my hair. On day three, quivering with indecision, I ordered dresses in shades that had previously been too impractical for me to consider—powdery blue and cream— and a sequined silver evening gown, all in the knee-grazing

flapper style with low necks and dropped waists. That this sil-
houette was not in the least flattering to my hourglass shape
didn't matter a whit, since I wanted only the latest fashion. I
also bought matching hats, silk knickers, and T-strap pumps,
though I stopped short of a teasing lynx boa.

When I wasn't in class, I fulfilled my mission for John, ship-
ping crates of perfume to London. Yet I found time to traverse
Paris by foot and by Metro, from Montmartre to Montparnasse,
gaping at the Eiffel Tower, the Louvre, the Arc de Triomphe,
and Notre Dame. I sipped espresso at outdoor cafés while smoking a Gauloise or wandered into brasseries, where, as if it were
marmalade, I slathered foie gras on hunks of freshly baked ba-
guettes.

I returned with a set of leather luggage and a demeanor that
was at least less wide-eyed than that of the girl who'd left London. That evening Monte fetched me for dinner at one of the
city's more exclusive spots. I dressed in my Paris gown. After a
five-course meal, we returned to his flat. With great drama he
extracted from his vest pocket a box of an unmistakable size
and shape, which he opened with precise slowness, and withdrew a diamond ring. Big. Square. Flashy.

"This is an emerald cut," Monte explained, as if he were a
geologist. "You will be my wife." He took my hand.

Monte did not ask on bended knee. He did not ask at all, except to wonder, "Lily, do you love me?" a question I barely heard,
so focused was I on the ring, which exceeded my expectation by
carats. It looked like the paste an actress—or worse—would
wear. I must have appeared stupefied, because he repeated the
question. "Do you love me?"

I loved the security I could batten down by becoming Monte's wife. I also reminded myself that had I lived in my parents'
shtetl I'd most likely have been betrothed to the village idiot,
penniless and slovenly. In Paris I'd had not a scintilla of trouble
spending Monte's stipend, but rarely thought of him. Now that

matrimony was imminent, I pictured him dead weeks after our wedding, leaving me able to turkey trot in John's arms forever. I immediately replaced this thought with the realization that if I married Monte and he did conveniently expire, John would spurn me as the gold digger I was. With these scenarios clogging my mind I stuttered, "I do love you. Thank you."

Monte's face assumed the same satisfied expression I witnessed after he ate a rich dessert. "While I was shopping, my darling, I also bought you this." He watched me take in a bracelet glittering with tiers of tiny diamonds and slipped it over my hand, which was as stiff as if I'd had a stroke. "And to match . . ." He withdrew a diamond brooch from yet another black velvet case.

The ring alone . . . *Dayenu*. It would have been enough, though no one would believe it was real, least of all John. I decided not to show him the ring, which felt heavy as a bolt. "Oh, Monte." I could not get "darling" out of my mouth. I was not that good an actress.

"If you accept these gifts, you will make me truly happy."

The words sounded rehearsed, which embarrassed me on both of our behalves. All I could say in response was, "Golly."

When I returned to my room, I sandwiched the jewels between my sanitary napkins. As I fell asleep I realized I'd never told Monte how thrilled I would be to become Mrs. Monte Collins. At least I hadn't lied.

Chapter 11

1923

led John to believe Mr. Skindles and I had parted ways. In fact, Monte was busy planning our wedding. We spent every weekend looking at mansions on London's outskirts. Did I prefer the Tudor to the Georgian? The brick to the stone? I faulted every one. Too drafty. Too shaded. Too rambling.

"You're very discriminating, Lily," my fiancé pointed out.

"It has to be right. We'll be living there for a long time."

The problem, exactly. A house would be a prison for my life sentence as Mrs. Monte Collins. But as much as I knew I didn't love him, I felt controlled by a despot who spoke in the voice of Matron Weiss, proclaiming that I was in no position to chase castles in the air when a man here on earth was offering me the key to a stately residence, most likely in Surrey. My moony version of living happily ever after with a more appealing sort—John, specifically—wasn't for a slum-bred girl.

For Easter weekend, Monte planned a trip to Brighton, assuring me that we'd have separate rooms in a vast Victorian hotel. On the evening we arrived I slipped into my sequined gown, its luminous ante raised by my ring, brooch, and bracelet. I'd left Brighton as a dim bulb of a housemaid and returned as a floodlight beaming throughout the dining room, turning heads. My fiancé and I were escorted to a prime table. We ordered. We looked at one another. I could not think of one thing to say. If only Monte had come to my room and ravished me. At least we'd have a topic to discuss. I thought of him kicking in my door with his short legs and a chuckle built to a guffaw until I was convulsed with snorts. As my hysteria ramped up, Monte's face grew white.

"Lily," he hissed. "Do stop." But I couldn't. "Everyone is ogling."

Let them. These were people I did not know or care about.

Except one. First I thought I was imagining, but I looked again and there was John Gillam, no more than thirty feet away, staring in disbelief. I covered my face with a napkin as if I were a child who believed it would render her invisible.

A minute later John reached our table and addressed not me, but Monte. "Excuse me, sir," he said in his lovely, low voice, "but may I ask who are you?"

"I am Monte Collins." He sounded as baffled as offended.

"I am Sir John Gillam, the young lady's employer."

Monte twisted toward me. "Is this true?"

I put down the napkin and cocked my head in John's direction. "May I have this dance?" he asked. When Monte nodded his dumbstruck consent, John swept me to the dance floor.

"Lily—that man." He took in my jewels, my gown, and my bosom on display. "Please don't tell me you have gotten yourself into a compromising position."

"I have." John grimaced. As we waltzed, I caught Monte's pin-sharp eyes tracking us like prey. "But I am not a fallen woman. I am engaged."

John winced. "Do you love this man?"

I said nothing as we danced on in harmony.

"Lily, do you want to get married?"

I blurted out, "Yes—to you."

"Good lord." He pushed me away. "Darling, I can't offer you"—he glanced at my jewels—"any of this." But I believed John desired me as much as I did him.

"None of it matters." This was also true.

"Then you must call me in the morning. I am staying at the hotel." John escorted me back to Monte, executed a military bow, and returned to his table.

"Your boss is in love with you." Monte made the accusation as if it were an indisputable criminal offense. "What has been going on behind my back?"

Dancing. Laughing. One kiss. "Nothing of which I'm ashamed." What did shame me was that I had accepted the proposal of a man I loathed. "But I realize I can't marry you." One by one, I removed the jewels and placed them on his empty plate. "I am truly sorry. I never meant to hurt you." I stood up and kissed Monte on the forehead. "And now, if you'll excuse me . . ." In my room, I buried myself under the covers, longing for John's comfort.

John and I met for breakfast. "I never had the foggiest that you were betrothed to Skindles," he said. "Why on earth didn't you let me know?" He seemed more caught up in the aston-ishment of our situation than the decision that we'd made to marry—until we kissed. We held hands, kissed again, and strolled along the boardwalk under a wide umbrella, John's arm wrapped around my waist.

"I really should tell my sister we're to wed," he said in the afternoon.

I knew that was a ghastly idea. "We can tell her later. Let's go to the registry office in the morning." He agreed.

On the following morning, I lied on my marriage certificate. I was claiming to be twenty-one, the legal age of consent. Be-fore a magistrate office in Westminster, with two charwomen as witnesses, I became Mrs. John Graham Gillam, who'd tossed away a millionaire for a wholesaler of dreams. Monte's brooch would have looked smashing on the blue Paris day dress in which I was wed. As I said my vows, that was my only regret.

Chapter 12
1923

After a wedding lunch, we returned to John's flat. My bridegroom swooped me off to bed, professed his adoration, and . . . nothing much. "We shall try again tomorrow—too much to drink," he said, though we'd shared only one split of Champagne.

On the third night, on the third rematch, John deflowered me. I believe he was as relieved by his performance as I was, though it failed to mirror the bonfire of passion novels had led me to expect. Yet John delighted me in so many ways that I laughed off our tepid sexual union, telling myself that with practice, our relations would improve.

At my husband's insistence I stopped working, and my days crawled by. I adored choosing his clothes every morning, taught myself to cook, and filled the hours by reading and, no matter the weather, walks in Hyde Park. This gave me ample time to ruminate on why John hadn't introduced me to his sister, despite vigorous hints. One morning I dressed in a mushroom-brown suit that shouted *married lady*, grabbed my gloves, and decided to rectify the situation. I wanted to meet my new sister, who I hoped would embrace me with the affection I hadn't known since I'd abandoned my brother Morris. By the time I rang at Mrs. William Ashton's home, perspiration soaked the dotted blouse beneath my jacket.

"I work with Sir John Gillam," I stammered to a butler. "I'm Lily Shiel," I chirped when ten minutes later the lady of the house appeared, stiff as a lamppost. My scripted speech evaporated into

"I 'ope this won't come as too gryte a shock but, I may as well say it, your brother and I, we're . . ." Mrs. Ashton appeared to be holding her breath . . . "married . . . a few weeks ago," I added, as if to illustrate the longevity of our relationship.

She backed away as fast as if I'd set fire to the fat dachshund by her side. "No!" she shouted. "My half-wit brother has really done it this time," and then composed herself, patting her silver-streaked bun. Her ring was half the size of my bauble from Monte. "What, may I ask, do you expect from me?" She exuded contempt. "A dowry?"

I summoned my dignity, as well as my brand-new accent. "I merely wanted to meet. We are, after all, kin."

"Ah, that's rich. Did John put you up to this?"

"I'll say not. He has no idea I am here." I regretted that I could not meet her eye to eye: like John, Mrs. Ashton was a tall, thin birch, and I, ground cover.

"Doesn't that tell you everything you need to know, young lady? You do understand he's bankrupt?"

Surely she was exaggerating. Yet I also knew that few people see a person with greater clarity than a sibling. Nonetheless, choosing to ignore grace and good manners, I huffed, "I ask nothing from you."

"Then that is exactly what you will get. Please relay to John that he'll never see another penny from me in this lifetime, and I never wish to see him again."

"But he adores you."

"And I love my brother, but . . . Miss Shiel, is it?"

"Mrs. Gillam." I strived for the self-respect the name warranted.

Mrs. Ashton opened her mouth, but closed it quickly, like a dummy whose ventriloquist has lost his script. Had this been Stepney Green, she'd have flung profanity or at least a shoe. Since Mrs. William Ashton was a fine lady, she merely slammed a door in my face.

Brooding on the insult, I roamed through London. I bought the makings of a fish and chips dinner, and filled the flat with smoke as I prepared it. I was afraid to tell John about my ambush, though more afraid not to. We had enough secrets. After dinner, I acted out my disgrace, expecting John to be enraged. He appeared unruffled, yet another outstanding trait.

"This is not the first time my sister has threatened to cut me off. Once she gets to know you, Lily-love, she will adore you. How could she not?"

As John embraced me, I did a mental tally of all the reasons why. During my wandering I'd also thought about how I'd pushed John's hand when he was in no position to support a wife. The kindest gift I could give my husband would be to leave him. But an annulment would break two hearts. I loved John, and I was sure he loved me. I also admitted to a second truth: I felt as if I was leading another woman's life. I'd known deprivation but never boredom, and idleness was making me blue. In the gentlest way I knew, I told John I wanted to work again.

I was afraid he would suggest waiting for motherhood, which given the rate at which we were having marital relations, was remote. Yet in equally mild but frank tones—a fusion not easy to achieve—he explained that until I thoroughly erased my Cockney curse, I'd never find another job. While I was absorbing his remark, he grabbed me by the shoulders and cried out, "But I know the solution—drama school!" Sir John Gillam had failed to launch a stage career, but based on no evidence—not even in my dreams had I seen myself onstage or in a film—he insisted that I was a natural. He would immediately contact the director of the Royal Academy of Dramatic Art. "The investment's worth it, because soon you'll earn money hand over fist."

John's sister may have sent her brother an ugly message, but she couldn't defeat his optimism—or delusion. His spark of ambition was lit in the cradle, and he hoped to transfer its flame to me. Not for the first time, he seemed to think that confidence could be slipped on like a coat. Because John was showing such zeal, I was willing to give acting a try.

I auditioned a few weeks later on the same day as a young roly-poly from Yorkshire who, while waiting for his turn, sat on his hat. When he discovered this he blushed and mumbled an unnecessary apology. I snickered when he left the room. But once Charles Laughton and I were both accepted—in my case, I have to assume because the Academy had been hard up for blondes— and I heard him perform, I never laughed at him again.

Under the Academy's instruction, my speech improved. My acting, however, never did. Two months into my course, I was asked to play Ophelia to Mr. Laughton's Hamlet. After ten minutes of butchering I was heartily urged to trade Shakespeare for musical comedy. I had, after all, won applause in mime class when I played a cow. John borrowed more money, and I enrolled in lessons for singing and dancing, which I practiced with gusto, using the kitchen sink as a barre.

I was not tone deaf, but my voice was quivery, and I stomped about as if I had stones in my shoes. Stage dancing, I learned, required an entirely different set of skills than social dancing, which I did easily enough. After six weeks, feeling guilty about the cost of lessons, I told John I was ready to apply for a spot in a chorus, hoping that my inevitable rebuff would convince him that our mission was madness.

"You must choose a stage name—you don't want to be dismissed as a housewife," he said. Not that many years ago George V had anglicized the royal family's indigestibly Teutonic name from Saxe-Coburg and Gotha to the properly British, thoroughly benign "Windsor." Why couldn't I do the same? I loved the idea of cutting "Shiel" loose. John suggested "Graham," his mother's maiden name.

"I want to get rid of 'Lily,' too." Monte's lilies had fouled that name.

My husband warmed to this exercise. "Why not 'Sheila'? Our little joke."

"Yes, but ending with an *h*."

"Whatever for?"

"Greater distinction."

I decided who I wanted to be and willed her into existence. John thought it would be advantageous for my career to be seen as unmarried. Sheilah Graham was born and baptized—and she was single.

Chapter 13

1924

To my surprise Sheilah Graham—*I*—was hired for a chorus, most likely because the show, *Punchbowl*, was soon closing. I had three days to practice catapulting into the unfortunate arms of an elfin boy who would hoist me to his shoulders after I did a cartwheel rotation. John and I went through these motions at home seventeen times. The night of my first performance, before my husband—whom I introduced as my uncle—walked me to the back of the theater, he reminded me to smile. Always. I remembered this advice only when I was upside down.

The show folded on schedule, but I got a second big break: winning the silver cup in a competition for London's most beautiful chorus girl. All I had to do was sashay before the judges and dance the Charleston, yet John considered this achievement, for which I was awarded a trophy engraved with *Be Faithful, Brave, and O Be Fortunate*, in the same category as the beatification of a saint. He persuaded a playwright friend to arrange for an audition with C. B. Cochran, the London impresario whose revue was inspired by the Folies Bergère of Paris. After I sang half a stanza of "Rose Marie," Mr. Cochran asked me to do the Black Bottom, and then ordered me to his office.

While his eyes buttered my curves, I, London's second most beautiful chorus girl, bloated with hubris, declared, "I want to be something better than a member of the chorus."

Mr. Cochran hired me on the spot—at four pounds a week—for the new Rodgers and Hart musical, *One Damn Thing After Another*, though I remained in the chorus, third from the right.

One damn thing after another. Story of my life.

The first day of rehearsal I asked Mimi Crawford, the show's lead, "How do you become a star?"

She replied with earnest condescension. "When you're on-stage, Miss, think of nothing but your part."

Every moment I was in the theater, offstage, I memorized her steps and songs, appointing myself as her de facto under-study. This gained some notice. "If you don't get rid of that lu-natic sycophant I will bloody quit," Mimi Crawford wailed to C. B. Cochran after a few days. I retreated—slightly—but in-fluenza intervened. Several weeks into the run Miss Crawford fell ill and I wore down Mr. Cochran with pleas to play her role. Following a hasty costume fitting I heard the audience sigh with disappointment at "Miss Crawford's part will be taken by Miss Sheilah Graham." An overture blared. Curtains parted. I trembled like the earthquake I had brought on by presuming I could be a star, then froze, arms akimbo, chin up, until the stage manager exhorted me to move, pushing me into a circle of apricot light.

I danced. I sang. I seduced the crowd lost in the blackness. When the curtain fell, applause exploded and I swam in glory. I liked it. Oh, I liked it very much.

"Chorus Girl Leaps to Fame," declared my first review, read aloud by John, who might have been even more enthralled than I. "Her fair beauty and dulcet voice enchanted a packed house . . ." I performed for seven evenings, after which the *Daily Express* exclaimed, "Miss Sheilah Graham . . . a great success . . . stepped into her part without even an hour's rehearsal. C. B. Cochran considers her one of the most promising young actresses on the London stage."

My performance seemed to me like a singular act of God, not the result of bona fide talent. But the hyperbole must have con-vinced Mr. Cochran, who signed me for a small speaking role in the next production, *This Year of Grace*. My salary would more than double: ten pounds a week, which would allow me to help John pay off his debts. "There's no limit to what you can do!" he said. I wanted to believe him.

At our first rehearsal, I did not expect to meet the playwright, who stood at the director's side. "As you sing, look at the male lead disdainfully," instructed Noël Coward, a young man with a permanent sneer and jug handle ears.

With no idea what "disdainfully" meant, I grinned and warbled, "I am just an ingénue, and shall be till I'm eighty-two."

He glowered. I sang again, trying a funereal expression. Mr. Coward ground his cigarette into the floor. As bad as my singing was, my dancing was worse. Whatever aptitude I'd shown for movement had vanished. I was out of step, kicked half as high as requested and twirled in the wrong direction. But I smiled so much my face hurt and by default, I became a comedienne. When the show opened, my pictures appeared in tabloids, captioned with the likes of "Sheilah Graham, Winning Her Way."

This led to invitations to midnight suppers that John insisted I accept, "because they will be good for your career—and maybe you'll convince people to invest in my company." Some requests came from Mr. Cochran, who exhibited me as he might a tropical bird, but increasingly, others arrived from the legion of toffs in black tie, tails, and blinding white shirts that filled the theater's boxes.

Among this elegant crowd was Sir Richard North, a man in his fifties who boasted of his stables in Ireland, and how he always wished he'd had a daughter like me. I relayed this to John as a girl might to her mother. What I did not tell John, when I tumbled into bed past two in the morning, was that while I might be fulfilling the *brave* and *fortunate* engraved on my loving cup, I could not say the same for *faithful*. On several occasions, Sir This or Lord That—not Sir Richard, but some of the younger men—had made me their dessert at the end of the evening. I accepted their lascivious summons out of curiosity. I wanted to know how real, completed sex felt. Pleasure was part of the package, I discovered, although I reserved true affection for Johnny.

In short order I became a regular at the Savoy, where some evenings I discovered that every dish had been named for me, from Potage à la Belle Sheilah to Bombe à la Belle Sheilah. The conversation was a mist of hilarity, gossip, and praise punctuated by admiring glances. Within this world my speech began to take on more of John's low, musical quality and I felt increasingly at home. One evening Sir Richard danced me close to the Prince of Wales, whom he referred to as Pragger-Wagger. Later, he told me that the prince had asked who I was. I began to forget who Lily Shiel had ever been, so suffused was I with the myth and marvelousness of Sheilah Graham.

When I came home late soon after that, John was struggling to write an article about Easter eggs, hoping to earn a few shillings. Without fiscal transfusions from John's sister—who failed to come 'round, as he predicted—our bills were past due, despite my contributions.

"Who gives a whoop about Easter eggs?" I asked, immediately regretting my tone.

"What topic would be better?" he snapped.

I was sufficiently self-centered to think people would like to read about a chorus girl, and said as much. My husband skulked off to bed, saying over his shoulder, "Then you write it."

I sat down and scrabbled a breathless reporting of stage door Johnnies in top hats waiting for the chorus girl lovelies after a performance. The next night, John corrected my grammar and mailed my account. A month later he opened one of Fleet Street's tabloids and there was my piece under my name. I called the editor, who told me I would be paid two guineas. Had our rent not been past due I would have framed the check.

I'd like to say that overnight I became a journalist, but I tried to sell seven more articles, and all were rejected. As the months passed I became too exhausted to continue to write.

My days and nights had become a carousel of lessons, rehearsals, pontificating directors, line-dropping performances, late-night suppers, Champagne, flirtations, and occasional trysts before I fell into a fitful sleep in the arms of a husband who never asked indelicate questions. My worry about money was matched only by the fear that our marriage—and my origins—would be exposed. I suffered from unbearable stomach cramps and constant headaches.

Sir Richard, who'd stayed a friend, became concerned about my obvious fatigue. I must see his physician, he insisted, at his expense. The doctor diagnosed me as being on the verge of a collapse, and urged me to rest in a warm climate. Sir Richard wanted to send me abroad and foot the bill. In a spasm of honesty, I told him I could never accept such generosity: I was someone else's wife, Mrs. John Gillam. Full stop.

"Good lord, woman. You must divorce this Gillam at once," he bellowed. "I will be the correspondent."

Only genuine tears convinced him that my husband was not the problem. To his enormous credit, Sir Richard refused to rescind his offer. Not only did he send me to Cap-d'Ail for six weeks of rest, he insisted that John accompany me.

At first John resented that another man was paying our way. But it did not take him long to agree to join me in the south of France, where he quickly bathed in its extravagance as much as I did. "I will reimburse Sir Richard—business will get better," he said, the leitmotif of our marriage.

When we returned, I was twenty-one and close to bilingual, but after weeks of neglect, the John Graham Company went belly-up.

Chapter 14

1926

John took a sales position that required not much more than snake charming, at which he excelled. I also made a change. When we were in France, I admitted to myself that my performances sagged between meager and mediocre. Eventually, I'd be expected to sing and dance at full strength and I did not have the talent or the drive to be a star. I decided to leave the theater. I wanted more.

Then I met my neighbor, whom I'd noticed flying down the stairs, a sapphire blue cape sailing behind her. One day she knocked on our door. Her ice box was broken and could she please store her corsages in mine? Gardenias. Carnations. Tea roses. With her mother, Judith Hurt was renting the flat above us for the season, she explained in a soft Scottish burr.

A lack of friends had been the collateral damage of leading a life bulwarked by fibs. Judith was fresh and lively, and with her I had no need to hide that I was Mrs. Gillam, the young wife upstairs. I liked her immediately and enormously.

"Would you care to join us for skating at Grosvenor Hall?" she asked the next day. I don't skate, I confessed. "My friend Nigel will teach you." He was a classmate of her cousin's. They'd met at Eton in Pop. Whatever that was.

When I considered my plans for the afternoon, shopping for the makings of bubble and squeak, I realized that even if she'd invited me to a sack race, I'd have said yes.

"I hear you were in Pop," I said later to Nigel, practicing my most precise articulation. "Could you tell me about it?" The question lit his face as we circled the rink, my hands in his. He gushed that Pop was the most exclusive eating club at Eton. Its sole reason for being seemed to be to prevent other people from belonging.

Requests to skate continued. I bought a red turtleneck sweater, a black flared skirt that showed off my ankles, and a pom-pom'd tam-o'-shanter. I learned not only how to skate, but also to play tennis and once again took up the squash at which I'd excelled at the Asylum. There was something hypnotic about the thwack of my paddle or racquet hitting the ball. I could practice for hours, and sometimes did. Others at the club, I guessed, considered me acceptably unconventional, the pretty young wife who'd been *onstage* and whose husband was conveniently absent.

One day while I was practicing figure eights, a tall man with silver sideburns glided to my side and introduced himself. Jack Mitford had noticed me at the club. Would I care to waltz? We skated to *It's Time to Say Goodnight* and then chatted over tea.

That evening I described Mr. Mitford to John. "Do you realize he belongs to one of the oldest families in England?" he gushed. "Older than the royal family? His brother is Lord Redesdale, the father to a whole flock of beautiful girls." The next day John presented me with a copy of *Burke's Peerage*, which I studied as if I were preparing for an entrance exam to heaven.

The following week, Jack Mitford invited John and me to dinner; I suspect he wanted to see if my husband existed. John not only appeared, he impressed, and Mr. Mitford asked us to join a group that would be skiing in St. Moritz. John's commissions were rising, and he didn't want to be away, but he insisted that I accept the invitation. I passed two weeks in Switzerland in a flurry of snowflakes and quips traded in English, French—in which I could get by—and German and Italian, in which I knew barely a word. When Jack's nephew, Tom Mitford, another Etonian a few years younger than I, complimented my mellifluous speaking voice, I felt as if I'd earned a diploma. Tom was extraordinarily handsome. I had always wanted children, to be the mother that mine was not. I let myself imagine Tom as the father to my sons, who would look like Saxon kings.

John and I began to be welcomed at country house parties. By day we rambled through venerable gardens bordered by yew hedges, played croquet on emerald lawns, or rode horseback. After we'd heeded the dressing gong, we dined in baronial halls.

At every turn I risked exposure. I had no relations or school chums whose names I could drop, no history to recount. Not that my friend Tom or the Honorable Hortense Hoo-Hah would ever have the cheek to ask, "Sheilah, when did you come out?" Protected by a thin shield of decorum and propriety, I allowed a tragic story to circulate. My parents, rest their souls, were dead. John Laurence and Veronica Roslyn Laurence had lived in Chelsea, a fashionable district known for its Bohemian informality and genteel decay. This would explain my lack of formal education. I'd had governesses before a Parisian finishing school and was seventeen when Papa and Mama died in a car accident. Promptly, the orphaned Sheilah married a family friend, the dashing Major Gillam, D.S.O.

The flaw in the fiction wasn't just that no one could corroborate this tale or my false age, but that I had never been presented at court as a debutante. John solved this problem with characteristic ingenuity. After they married, wives were generally presented a second time. He approached the widow of a colonel with whom he'd fought in Gallipoli. Would she be my sponsor? Mrs. Arthur Saxe, who hadn't been to court in years, agreed. John forwarded my name to Lord Chamberlain and in short order he summoned us to Buckingham Palace.

At this time in England, unemployment was building and the pound was to go off the gold standard, which caused alarm. For the crowd of which we were now marginal members, however, it was considered ill-bred to discuss anything as disturbing as financial restriction. Mr. and Mrs. John Gillam followed through with a not inexpensive proposition. John rented a cutaway, white tie, and knee breeches, and polished the sword I had admired in his bachelor flat. I ordered a sleeveless ivory silk and gauze dress with a modest train from Norman Hartnell, the queen's dressmaker.

The evening of my presentation, my head sprouted three tall ostrich feathers. I felt ridiculous in every way, including ridiculously excited, as Mrs. Saxe, John, and I sat like three bowling pins in a hired Daimler that proceeded from our flat. At a glacial pace, our car joined a queue moving forward until we neared the mall where a crowd of workaday Brits lined the street, sizing me up through the windowpane. Was there a Heimie or a Freda among them, as we were admitted through the gate? I felt a pang of profound shame as I looked out the window, embarrassed to be part of such a spectacle, but I was in too deep to turn back now. Powered by unmitigated chutzpah, I'd left my values far behind.

A footman in scarlet livery escorted us toward a grand curved staircase. The hall was crowded and close, since at least a hundred other women were also being presented this evening. I would have liked to pluck a plume from my headdress and fan my face. Not until past eleven did Lord Chamberlain rumble, "Mrs. Arthur Saxe presenting Mrs. John Gillam." John straightened my train, and in the audition of my life, I followed behind my sponsor, who paraded forward and curtsied. Keeping in mind every lesson through which I'd suffered, I held my chin high and in measured steps, carried on.

In sumptuous robes, on thrones that looked stolen from a storybook, sat King George and Queen Mary and behind them, the Prince of Wales, the Duke of Gloucester, Prince George, Princess Mary, a dowager marchioness whose name I couldn't recall, and all the others, each looking more bored than the next. I curtsied almost to the floor, made a bow, and stood up again while I tried not to trip over my gown. Pragger-Wagger,

I was certain, allowed his gaze to linger on my face for several seconds longer than was necessary.

My magic moment complete, John gracefully tossed my train over my arm and I backed out of the room, as required by protocol. Now a full-fledged member of Society, I joined the horde that had earned the same distinction, forming two human corridors through which the royal entourage passed. The men bowed and the women curtsied before we were ushered downstairs for tiny cakes and sandwiches served on gold-rimmed plates that I assumed were priceless. John lifted a glass of Champagne and toasted our hollow, hallowed achievement. "To my dearest Sheilah, long may you reign."

What was the difference now between the likes of Judith Hurt and me? Everything and nothing. Before, I was an ordinary fake. Now I had taken deception to new heights, from which my fall, should I be unmasked, would be even more humiliating. *Ketzeleh, what have you become?* I could hear my father say, shaking his head in disgust. *My daughter, the fraud.*

With my false honor, I felt more alone and confused than ever. The next day, I pawned my gown and with the money, made an anonymous donation to the Jews' Orphan Asylum, in honor of Louis and Rivkah Shiel.

Chapter 15

1930

became a regular at Tom's lunch circle at Quaglino's, a watering hole for young aristocrats who liked to drink and bloviate in equally indefatigable measures. There I met another vaunted member of the Eton tribe and Tom's cousin, Randolph Churchill. He was regarded as an up-and-coming journalist, but that afternoon I noticed only that he was long and lanky, like John, although decades younger and equally handsome.

His voice roared above the others in Conservative bombast. Rarely did he have a kind word about any politician other than his father, Winston, who was currently out of office. Randolph dismissed most of our country's leaders as cretins, though he saved his highest contempt for Ramsay MacDonald, the leader of Britain's first Labour government, "a bastion of Bolsheviks and Jews" that he considered a threat to the capitalist system. He mocked MacDonald, who was neither a Bolshevik nor a Jew, for being illegitimate: it was public knowledge that the man had been born to an unmarried housemaid.

Though I often felt out of my element during these discussions and simply chuckled or tossed my curls in the background, in MacDonald's case I longed to speak up. I revered this man, who had succeeded through hard work, not connections. But I realized, as I listened to Randy jaw on, that even if you were prime minister—or, let's say, a married lady presented at court in a train and ostrich feathers—what you achieved in life mattered little if you lacked gentle birth. At any point, you could be exposed, reviled, and turned from somebody into nobody.

Randolph's smugness infuriated me, but what bedeviled me more was that while I found him barely likable, he was the first man I desperately wanted to bed. My midnight trysts had ended, but they whet my appetite for more than my marriage offered. Whenever Randy was near me, and even if I was simply thinking about him—which was all the time—I felt a craving. I also sensed, in the way a woman always does, that he felt the same way. Was this attraction magnified by knowing that had Randy been aware of my origins, he'd be appalled? Or had he done me one better, sniffed out my past and in the grand British tradition of upper-class gentlemen soliciting the company of trollops, planned to trap me in his own web? These questions were secondary to the bigger issue: when would we sleep together?

I had not stopped loving Johnny, my anchor and my dearest friend, to whom I owed a high level of loyalty. Johnny was also earning an adequate living for the first time since we'd wed, and encouraged me to spend my mornings trying to write a novel and my afternoons socializing, which, now that I had friends, I was happy to do. But my husband and I had wordlessly abandoned attempts at conjugal relations, and with it, dreams of a child. My flings had meant nothing more than to confirm that I adored sex, its caresses as much as its other physical dividends, though I also realized that I liked being needed by someone who cherished me.

Eventually, one midafternoon Randy pulled out his gold pocket watch as if we'd had scheduled an assignation, extended his arm, and said, "Mrs. Gillam, shall we?" We did, in a discreet hotel where I believe there may now be a plaque that reads *In Suite 901, in 1930, Sheilah Graham reinvented the orgasm.* Compared to my previous lovers, Randolph Churchill was indeed elite.

"Who are you?" he asked after the first of three lush couplings that afternoon and early evening.

"Today, yours," I said, pressing my finger to his lips. "But please, no talk." In bed I found I could silence him far more effectively than at Quag's.

Our affair was short-lived. The last time we were together I was among a group that included Charlie Chaplin. My amazement at meeting a movie star was quashed by the actor's breathtaking subservience to Randolph, who took fawning as his due.

"Mr. Churchill, how I wish I were you, who has had every advantage," Mr. Chaplin said with a flicker of irony that blew by Randy like a feather. "I've had to fight for everything I've earned." He spoke of a father exiled to a workhouse and a mum committed to a lunatic asylum, while as a lad he performed onstage rather than get an education. "How lucky you are to have been born with wealth, position, and your family name. I wish we could trade places."

In response to this raw humility I expected Randy to at least invite Charlie Chaplin to call him by his first name and to defer with, "If only I could trade places with you, Mr. Chaplin. You are all the more a genius because you have overcome such obstacles—and you deserve my greatest respect." Randolph merely said, "I take your point."

Charlie Chaplin went on with what I found to be a discerning analysis of Prime Minister MacDonald's term of office. Randy broke in with, "Charlie, my friend, balderdash. You know nothing. Tell us what you do know. About the American movie colony."

Chaplin spoke of Hollywood, its fresh air and purple bougainvillea, tennis, and marabou, and power-hungry lions that ruled studios like rival jungle kings. But what especially captured my attention was his talk of dashing men and exquisite women who once were waitresses and store clerks and virtually overnight had become stars, beloved from coast to coast. Americans, he claimed, don't give a quid about your birth. If you dare to climb upward, they applaud. If your family name doesn't suit, you change it. Talent and tenacity count more than wealth and position.

The next time Randolph suggested lunch, I decided I was busy. I truly was, trying to write a novel, *Gentleman Crook*. Given that I was no stranger to fiction—I, the living example of fabrication—thought that becoming an author would be duck soup. Wrong. I found plotting to be harder than geometry, never my star subject at the Asylum, and every one of my characters' voices sounded stilted in the same way. After writing two thousand words—many of which were "astonishing," "thrilling," "brilliant," "very," and "awfully"—I decided that I lacked the requisite concentration and imagination to complete a work of fiction. I solved my hero's problems by throwing him off a bridge, put my manuscript aside, and tried my hand again at writing for newspapers.

I began with a short essay, "I Married a Man 25 Years Older, by a Young Wife," and sent it the *Daily Pictorial*, one of dozens of Fleet Street tabloids. They bought it immediately, for the not-unrespectable price of eight guineas. This money came strictly from my brain—no dancing, singing, or high social rank needed—and required no complex storytelling. Journalism, I decided, was my calling after all.

Chapter 16

1932

Would you be willing to accompany me to Germany as a chaperone for my little sister Unity?" Tom Mitford asked one day. "I need a stern Frau Someone to keep our hellcat in line, and I refuse to travel with my aunt."

"Why ever not?" I asked.

"She has ankles like loaves of bread. I couldn't possibly look at them for a whole fortnight."

Our short journey was set. We would be headed to Munich. Sending your daughter to Bavaria had become fashionable among the upper crust, many of whom had German relations. Let their girls have a taste of freedom before marriage. Tom's father scoffed at formal education for women—husbands from within their firmament were all his daughters required. This visit was to be Unity's consolation prize before her debut. She was seventeen.

"I can't promise the trip will be easy, but it shan't be dull," Tom said. His words were prophetic, though not necessarily on Unity's account.

Tom had warned me that every one of his sisters had been cheerfully spoiled in the countryside, six fillies running wild. At the dock where we set sail for the Channel, I spotted Unity immediately, and there was nothing little about her. She was as tall as Tom, the incarnation of the Norse goddess Valkyrie, which was her second name, suggested by their grandfather, a friend of Richard Wagner. Unity was no less lovely than the older Mitford sisters, whose photos I'd seen in the society pages, all fine-featured with long limbs and beguiling smiles. She wore a green tweed traveling suit swathed in a fox fur I could have happily pilfered.

After how-do-you-dos we settled in on deck, where Unity—despite her fierce appearance—complained of seasickness. She retired to her room, and I never saw her again until we debarked and she sprang to life. No sooner had our threesome settled into a first-class train compartment than a German man presented himself in military garb so crisply pressed it looked as if he'd only just unwrapped it.

"May I make your acquaintance, please?" His English was heavily accented. "I could not help but notice all of you at the Gare de l'Est."

I took SS-Rottenfuher Otto von Pfeffel, as he introduced himself with soldierly precision, to be some sort of cadet, older than Unity but younger than Tom. His boots were high and burnished, and his light brown hair barbered to such an extreme that scalp the color of pale pink sherbet peeked through. He proffered cigarettes for each of us from a gold case decorated with an eagle. It's possible that he'd had a professional manicure.

"Where is this captivating group headed, if I may ask?" SS-Rottenfuher von Pfeffel tipped his hat. Tom explained that our destination was Munich. "Ach, but I am also traveling there. I would be most pleased to show you the sights."

I took *you* to mean Unity. Throughout our time together, I would blink and yet another dashing, uniformed devil with preposterously blue eyes would appear, flexing his charm. Every one of these men wore a swastika pin on his lapel.

Unity, Tom, and I spent a pleasant few hours with the cadet, and proceeded to the dining car where we chatted over lunch, for which he insisted on paying. Unity convulsed in laughter at any number of von Pfeffel's remarks, but I couldn't fault her. She reminded me of myself at the same age, a girl in a woman's body, as infatuated as I might have been with von Pfeffel a decade earlier.

"Which military school do you think he attends?" I asked Tom after Unity and her admirer walked ahead of us back to our seats.

Tom chuckled. "He's no student."

"In the army then?"

"Sheilah, he belongs to Adolf Hitler's National Socialist German Workers' Party."

"I see," I answered, although I didn't. I skipped over the serious pages of newspapers. I knew Adolf Hitler was the German politician with a doughy face and an abomination of a mustache who had failed to overthrow the Weimar Republic. This represented my comprehensive knowledge of Herr Hitler. I returned to my seat, and reopened my guidebook to Munich. The semmelknödel was highly recommended.

I had anticipated a trip of merry abandon, with evenings at the opera alternating with pints at the city's ancient rathskellers. During the day, I expected to fill my lungs with bracing alpine air as we hiked the mountains shouldering the city and explored crumbling fairy-tale castles. I did not expect Germany itself to be crumbling.

Our hotel was not the city's most luxurious—the Mitfords' financial resources, like that of many blue bloods, were on a decline—but it was scrupulously clean, a German attribute as highly prized by my visiting countrymen as its bratwurst. We began to walk the nearby area. Munich had a mellow beauty, with a web of cobblestone streets and ancient red-roofed buildings. Tom stopped at a newsstand, stared at a headline, and shook his head in disbelief.

"Could you translate, please?" I asked.

"Unemployment Soars to 40 percent."

"Like at home," I said.

"That's twice that of England. Not to put too fine a point on it, but this country's in the shitter."

As we strolled I looked more closely and saw despair. A one-legged war veteran was reduced to begging. A carton of eggs cost as much as a string of pearls in one of many pawnshops, and I noticed swastikas everywhere, from discreet symbols adorning coats to twisted black crosses on bloody red pennants that flapped high and mighty above our heads. We turned a corner near the Königsplatz, where an especially grand flag roiled in front of a stout yellow stone building. Through its door people came and went, their right arms raised in one-armed salutes to one another. "Nazi Party headquarters," Tom announced, with respect. I wondered if he'd planned our sightseeing so we'd arrive at this destination.

"Isn't it a magnificent spectacle?" Unity asked, breathless.

"Yes, a spectacle," I said and made a show of looking at the glockenspiel on the square. "But we don't want to miss the tea dance." I was eager to escape whatever this garish banner represented.

"*Macht schnell*," Unity said, gaily.

As we walked toward our hotel, I stopped and gasped as I took in a sign with a caricature of a man clearly meant to be a Jew—hooked nose, leering eyes, money grasped in a claw-like hand. Beneath the drawing: *Deutschland Erwache!*

"Whatever does that mean?" I asked.

"Germany, awaken!" Tom roared like a Prussian general.

"Awake to . . . ?" I feared that I knew the answer.

He might have been a schoolmaster speaking to a child who should know that B follows A. "To the Jews," he said.

Willkommen, Lily Shiel. Bile crawled to my throat. "Please don't tell me you believe this," I said in disbelief.

"I'm sorry if I've shocked you, but you don't have to be a don to see it's the Jews who've been ruining Germany since the Great War. They're interested in only their bloated bank accounts, and are eating away at the country like a maggot on a rotting body."

Rarely had I felt more stunned, even more by Tom's assertion than by the vile poster. I adored my friend for his humor and kindness, and though I knew he was, intellectually, no Randolph Churchill, when had he become an outright nutter?

As we made our way back, I walked ahead, alone and ill at ease. At the hotel, a palm court orchestra was playing *Tea for Two* and the room was filled with the burble of German, English, French, and Italian. I spotted dozens of girls near Unity's age accompanied by older women, as well as a spate of young, athletic-looking men, most of whom were in uniform. Tom claimed a table and went to the buffet for biscuits and fruit cups while waiters circulated silver trays of Champagne. I turned to take a glass, and in that time, von Pfeffel arrived, he of the practiced politeness and persistent appeal. He greeted us with an abbreviated bow and handed Unity a nosegay of white roses.

"Would you be so kind as to allow Fraulein Mitford to accept the next dance?" he asked, looking at me.

It was hard not to return his smile. "*Ja*, Officer von Pfeffel," I said, unable to recall the exact wording of his German rank.

Unity walked away on his arm and Tom turned to ask, "May I have this dance?"

I accepted his hand and said, "With pleasure." During this visit, that commodity had been, like eggs, in short supply.

"You seemed upset earlier."

"Everything here is just so . . ." I fumbled. Startling? Horrifying?

"Electrifying? We're witnessing a country in change. They call Munich *Hauptstadt der Bewegung*, the capital of the movement. But I promise to restrain myself from yammering on. As I'm often reminded, I'm a bore." I was glad that for the next hour, *Deutschland, Erwache* meant merely dance your heart out.

During the following few days we hiked the mountains, stopping for cocoa and lebkuchen at tiny cafés. Each evening, we found ourselves sufficiently tired to fall into bed after an early

dinner. I tried to erase the memory of phony Reichsmarks I'd
seen engraved with caricatures of Jews. I wanted to stay in nature, far from Nazi filth. But soon Unity said she'd had enough
stamping about in thick socks and heavy boots. So it was back
to assessing the city's architecture. Twice, on the street, my eyes
stopped at signs that translated to "No Jews Allowed." I hurried
past these barriers as if they were armed and alive.

I was no stranger to anti-Semitism, though I thought I had
put it behind me when I'd moved to the West End and sev-
ered ties to my family. I'd grown up believing Jews were to be
reviled, despite a few exceptions: esteemed physicians up and
down Harley Street, Jewish governesses for highborn families—as
I might have become, had I not been forced out of school—and
the former viceroy of India, Rufus Isaacs himself, Lord Chief
Justice of England, the first Jew to be raised to a marquisate.
Last year I failed to wince when Judith complained that a shop
owner had "Jewed me." When Randolph described a car with
metallic trim as being "Jewish racing gold," I joined the titters.
All my life I'd heard slurs flung as easily as bats at a cricket
match—kikes, Jew-boys, Christ killers, shylocks, sheeny bastards. I was also aware of restrictions—Nigel's beloved Pop, for
instance, surely had no Jewish members. Britain was not exactly a place of enlightened tolerance, but as snide as the insults
were, or as insidious the prohibitions, prejudice was never writ
large on placards.

Only later did I understand that the Tom Mitfords of the
world were hiding in plain sight, more the rule than the exception, and that a mere six kilometers northwest of Munich
the Dachau concentration camp was under construction. But
this was 1932, when Nazi evil was still a mutating cell, not a
full-blown cancer. All I knew was that Germany was no place
for me.

I was thinking of this when Unity asked, "May I have your
permission to go to a concert this evening with Otto?"

Her tone was petulant. I wondered if Tom would upbraid his sister for the insolence embedded in her question, but he said, merely, "If Mrs. Gillam agrees . . ." I did. Let her have her Nazi.

Tom and I had a leisurely dinner, and I returned to my bed to read *The Conqueror.* I was riveted by the story of William, a bastard son who nonetheless made himself the king. At nearly eleven o'clock, I heard Unity, threw on my wrapper, and knocked on her door.

"It's open," she said. "Do come in."

"Did you have a wonderful time?" I asked.

"Dreamy," she said, looking the same. "Otto took me dancing and he gave me a book—in English."

"That was thoughtful," I managed to say. "Now, *Gute Nacht und süße Träume*, and remember, a car is fetching us downstairs at nine." We were spending the day with Baroness von Someone, a distant cousin of Mrs. Mitford.

The next morning, at half past nine, there was still no sign of Unity. As I entered her room a flowery scent wafted through the air. I knocked on her bathroom door. "I'm in the tub," she sang out.

"Could you hurry, please?" I said. "The car is waiting." As I turned to leave I noticed the book von Pfeffel had given her. I glanced at the inscription: *To lovely Unity, with affection, Heil Hitler! Otto.*

I closed its cover. *Mein Kampf.*

I quickly turned the book's pages. First, I laughed. "No politician should ever let himself be photographed in a bathing suit," Herr Hitler observed. But I continued . . .

Was there any form of filth without at least one Jew involved in it? If you cut even cautiously into such an abscess, you found . . . a kike!

The personification of the devil as the symbol of all evil assumes the shape of the Jew.

I closed the book, tiptoed quickly to my room, locked my door, and vomited.

Minutes later, I left a message for Tom to leave without me. Then I wrote a letter explaining that John needed me back in London—I hinted at bronchitis—and I must cut my trip short. I thanked him profusely, and apologized for any inconvenience. Hastily, I packed my bags. An hour later, I was traveling north. The semmelknödel would have to wait.

Chapter 17
1932

The first train I could catch stopped in Frankfurt, where I planned to connect to Brussels and travel home to England. I did not mind the inefficiency of zigzagging around Europe as long as Munich was increasingly farther behind me. In Frankfurt, I waited on a bench and counted Nazi uniforms— *eins, zwei, drei*—while listening carefully to announcements. I was at *fünfzehn* when the stationmaster rang out . . . Berlin. He called it, again and again.

Berlin was in the direction of Poland, not England. But I felt as if my Tatte was commanding me to change my plans. *Ja, Frau Gillam,* an agent said, a seat is available. Hours later, I stepped off the train into an enormous station and bought a map of the city. There it was, marked on Herbert-Baum-Straße.

Weißensee Cemetery had a gate fit for Oxford College. It was eerily calm. I passed a mourning hall and a flower bed as big as a pond. Finally, I found an office and approached a clerk wearing *peyes*. Consulting my dictionary, I asked in halting German, *"Können Sie mir helfen, ein Grab finden Sie, bitte?"*

"Welcher Name, bitte?" he asked.

I had not said my father's name in almost fifteen years. "Louis Shiel." My voice was barely audible.

"Könntest du das bitte wiederholen?"

My confusion must have showed.

"Lauter, bitte."

This time I understood. "Louis Shiel." I let the name ring like a bell.

The gentleman disappeared and returned with a younger man who, to my relief, said, "I speak a little English. May I be of assistance?"

"Can you help me find my father's grave, please? He died in 1910 while visiting Berlin. His name is Louis Shiel. S.H.I.E.L."

"I will check, Madame," the man said, "but with more than one hundred thousand souls here, I cannot promise I will find him." He disappeared but soon returned and instructed me to follow him. The sun was low in the sky, and I felt a drizzle. My guide unfurled a large, black umbrella and offered his arm as we steadied ourselves on a stone path.

I noticed a field of honor for Jewish soldiers who had fallen in the Great War, their sea of graves ringing a monument that resembled an altar. These Germans gave their lives for their country—some had even received the Iron Cross—yet Hitler despises them and their descendants, I thought, maddened by the injustice. Beyond these plots were rows of kingly mausoleums, many of elaborate art nouveau design, where the wealthy would live for eternity. I also saw headstones and obelisks that were simpler, though still elegant. Some were ancient: 1801, 1832, 1877.

Mosse. Plotke, Dorfman, Berger, Teutsch. Jews. Jews. More dead Jews. The cemetery was the size of a village. My companion opened a low gate and we crossed over into a section dense with foliage. He motioned for me to turn, all but bushwhacking until we were forced to travel single file. He stopped in front of a small stone that read 1910.

"I will leave you to your prayers," he said, letting me take the umbrella. "The sixth grave in this row."

I had found my father in the Stepney Green of Weißensee Cemetery. I felt a stab of jubilation soured by grief. Perhaps in *Deutsch* there is a name for this emotion.

"Danke, mein Herr," I said.

Why had I come? To bear witness? To grant my father respect?

I knew only that I felt compelled to be here. As the rain picked up and wind wailed through the trees, I felt as if I heard a descant. My father, I was sure, was telling me not to be afraid. It was the voice that asked me to sit next to his rocking chair every night in our crowded flat. When he returned from the tailor shop, after my mother had become exhausted by her *geshreying*, he listened to Brahms—a discarded Victrola and one record were his prized possessions. As the scratchy music played he would ruffle my hair each time the chair creaked forward. His touch was soft. I could feel it now and a chill ran down my back. "*Meine schöne* Lily," he would say, love nesting in his whisper.

After a father died, a good son would have said Kaddish for a month in shul. Had my brothers? Words I was sure I had forgotten began to fall from my lips. *Yis'gadal v'yits'kadash sh'mei raba* . . . I could picture my father, a simple man but admirable.

"Tatte," I broke into Yiddish. "This is your Lily, a daughter who is bringing you shame. I have disappointed you. I no longer keep the Shabbos. I failed to respect Mama. I married a good man but he isn't Jewish, and I have committed adultery"—I took a wheezing breath—"more than once. And worst of all, I . . ." Tatte would consider what I would say the most unforgivable sin of all, "I pretend to be a shiksa."

My shoulders heaved. "I tell nothing but lies. My life is false and hollow, and I live in constant fear that I will be exposed. I've made mistakes, too many to count, but I'm not sure I can undo them or how else to live." I shrank into myself, disgraced. "I want so much to be loved and accepted. I do not want to be alone in this world like I felt at the orphanage."

I heard footsteps, then the clearing of a throat. The man who'd brought me to this spot had returned. "Madame, the cemetery is soon closing. We must leave."

I found a pebble and placed it on the small marker, as was the custom. "Goodbye, Tatte," I said. "Please know how much I love you."

In the fading light, we walked until we entered the building where he worked. I thanked the man for his kindness, placed some marks in the tzedakah box, and headed toward the grand gate. I was trying to determine in which direction to turn when something hit me in the back. A rock twice the size of the stone I'd left on Tatte's grave fell at my feet. Another hit my leg, and then one more pelted my arm.

Across the street two young boys were pointing at me. "*Jude, Jude*," they hooted. "*Dreckiger, Jude*" came the shouts, ugly and loud. "*Jude, Jude.*"

I started to run, thinking, I have been running all my life.

Chapter 18

1933

Back in England, Tom Mitford invited me to a rally held by Sir Oswald Mosley, the secret lover of Diana, his sister. I found it titillating that in addition to being linked to Diana, Mosley was rumored to have had liaisons with both his wife's younger sister and their stepmother. Nonetheless, I declined; Mosley was the moon to Hitler's Black Sun, the leader of a new party called the British Union of Fascists.

I explained to Tom that at night I was exhausted, since I'd started to play squash with the eagerness of an Olympic hopeful—had squash been an Olympic sport. Every hour I wasn't with Johnny or writing a piece to submit to one of the Fleet Street tabloids, I was banging a small, hard squash ball.

"Why ever do you play so hard," my neighbor Judith asked. Once again she was in London for the winter season. "It's a daft game, not bloody war."

I shrugged off the answer with, "I don't know how else to play." I didn't tell my friend that the squash court was the only place where I had no need for pretense and my mind was free of worry, which, since my trip, would not cease. Never when I played did I feel on the verge of being revealed as a sham. Racquet in hand, I saw myself as confident, even superior, and I forgot that I'd boxed myself into a sexless marriage that would bring neither children nor satisfaction.

I found all this on the squash court and, lately, more: the captain of the men's squash team, whom I noticed whenever I practiced. The Marquess and Earl of Donegall belonged to one of the most revered peerages in the country and had a string of vaulted, inscrutable titles: Earl of Belfast, Viscount Chichester of Ireland, Baron Fisherwick of Fisherwick, Hereditary Lord High Admiral of Lough Neagh among them—and those were merely the noble designations cited by *Burke's*. This esteemed reference failed to add that he wrote the society column I never missed in the *Sunday Dispatch*—or that he was damned attractive, boyish, narrowly built with brown eyes that called to mind comparisons to beloved pets. The tastiest part was that I'd noticed those eyes notice me. This invited a challenge.

One day I contrived to finish a match at precisely the same time I knew the marquess would be completing one as well. I had also won. He approached me with congratulations, and asked, "Why haven't we met before?" *Are you a part of my world?*

I knew I looked my best flushed with victory, when my competitive instincts were as much on high alert as my powers of flirtation. I might have been a spider trapping a fly.

"I've been traveling," I said, beaming, "with my friends Tom and Unity."

"Mitford? He's a cagey one, keeping you all for himself."

The marquess treated me to a celebratory cocktail, and another. This led to country drives, to dinners, to jazz clubs, to boating on the Thames, and to my first visit to Ascot, for which I wore a tasteful saucer hat and carried a matching parasol. After two months he persuaded me to fly in his Gypsy Moth, which resembled an enormous grasshopper. He wore goggles, a white silk scarf, a leather helmet, and a jacket. I wore fear.

Johnny knew about Don, which I started to call him, but thought the friendship was innocent. In the beginning, it was. But it did not take long to become Don's partner in bed, or to feel deep affection. He was better company than Randolph because, not being burdened with surplus brilliance and a haughty temperament, the marquess never made me feel untaught, and I enjoyed him more than Tom, simply because he looked at me with desire.

I never had illusions that our fling would become something more. Don was from a family that protected its bloodlines behind ramparts erected centuries earlier, and I adored him only as deeply as you can care for someone to whom you rarely tell the truth. We kissed and we made love and we chattered about skiing in Switzerland and shooting in Northumberland. Never did we mention Adolf Hitler or Sir Oswald Mosley. Our relationship was a Christmas candy cane, all sweet, shiny surface.

I hadn't bargained on Don falling in love.

"I want to marry you, Sheilah," he said one night at dinner. "I love you with all my heart."

I cast down my eyes and passed the breadbasket.

"Mrs. Gillam," he said. "Did you not hear me? I want to make you my wife."

"And what about Mr. Gillam?" I buttered a roll with slow, sensuous strokes.

"Blast," he said. "He is a hindrance. I guess you'll have to unmarry the chap. Have you heard of divorce? It's quite the rage."

Lily Shiel, daughter of Louis and Rivkah, late of Stepney Green and the Jews' Orphan Asylum, Her Grace, Marchioness of Donegall. I could carry off a romance, but I had my limits. Like squash, Don was sport, and I had assumed he saw me the same way.

"And what of Mother?" I asked.

"The dowager? Not a small impediment. But I believe I could wear her down."

He kissed me ardently. I did not think his offer was in jest.

"Darling," I said, "I am deeply fond of you. But you know marriage will never be in the cards. Please, let's not bring this up again and allow it to spoil our fun."

"Fair enough, but Sheilah, you are everything I want in a woman—beauty, intelligence, grace. You can even hit a squash ball. Please don't forget I asked," he said, kissing my hand. "I surely won't."

Don's words caught me by surprise. Over the next few weeks my jubilance fell away like sequins dropping off an evening gown. I was twenty-nine. My life needed more than diversion. Nor could I continue to return to my husband each night after being with another man, be it Don or a lover who would inevitably follow. Yet the finality of divorce frightened me. I wasn't ready for that step, even though I knew Johnny and I had to stop living together in a distortion of brother and sister.

I longed for substance, meaty and meaningful, and I did not feel I could find it in England, with its rigid castes and my dread of being found as counterfeit. America, I decided, was the country meant for me, its appeal heightened by knowing it was an ocean away from Adolf Hitler. If I was a handful of ostrich feathers short of genuine, people there might applaud my ambition. Or so I hoped.

My metier, I decided, was for short froth like the piece I'd recently published in the *Sunday Pictorial*, "Baby or a Car? By a New Bride." (I picked car.) I went to the library to research American newspapers to see if they included similar whimsy. They did, and to my astonishment, I saw the same articles repeated again and again: in America many newspapers reprinted the identical story in an improbable system known as syndication. A journalist could write one story and be paid for it a hundred times.

God bless the United States of America. I felt as if I'd discovered penicillin. I shared my news with Johnny, who urged me to book passage to New York, where he would eventually join me.

Months later, I was crossing the Atlantic, vibrating with excitement, though no matter what Johnny said, I knew I was leaving my marriage behind me.

Chapter 19
1934

arrived on the other side of the Atlantic with one hundred dollars, a wad of introductory letters, and a rope-hold on skittish hopes. Like London, New York City was crowded and grimy. Gum wrappers and cigarette butts littered the sidewalks, and even before the light turned green on the corner of Forty-Second Street and Broadway, people stampeded across the intersection. With sidewalks hot as griddles, no other woman wore a black velvet suit over a long-sleeved flaming orange satin blouse. The air felt like jelly and reeked of perspiration and pomade. There was nothing fresh or serene about Times Square, which buzzed with neon energy. *Step right up, little lady, here you can be anyone.*

I loved it.

On my second day in Manhattan I walked the seven blocks from my hotel to my first appointment, gaping at legitimate theaters sitting cheek by jowl with peep shows. I found the correct building, took the elevator to the eleventh floor, and entered the hallowed sanctuary of the North American Newspaper Alliance.

"What do you have to show me, Miss Graham?" John Wheeler, the publisher, asked. I had left Mrs. Gillam in London.

Puffed with ersatz confidence, I offered him my stage door Johnnies clipping, which he dismissed with a snort. Next I presented my piece about being married to a much older man, crowing about the attention it received.

"Not for us," he said, waving a hairy hand as if he were swatting a fly. In fact, John Wheeler was swatting a fly. Every window in his office was open in a futile effort to deliver cool air, and the room's sole fan, like Mr. Wheeler himself, moved with grinding calculation. He appeared to have dressed for the role of gritty newspaperman—eyeshade, cigar, and parked on his desk, a snap-brim fedora, suitably battered. It was too early in the day for the glass of whiskey I might expect, but he had the veined nose of a drinking man. "Whadelseyahavefame?" he asked, louder and faster than anyone in England. "Anything that's not goddamn fluff?"

I leaned forward and doled out tear sheets, ending with my masterpiece, a profile of Lord Beaverbrook. I prayed that Mr. Wheeler knew who he was.

"Nah." He looked me straight in the eye and said, not unkindly, "Sorry, Miss—Miss Graham, is it?—but you're not quite ready to be syndicated."

With nine more appointments scheduled that week and into the next, I calibrated my smile to radiant and thanked John Wheeler, asking, "Please, may we stay in touch?"

He took the cigar out of his mouth and appraised me stem to stern. "Doll, I can do you one better. I'm going to ask my buddy at the *New York Mirror* to meet you." He scribbled some numbers on a scrap of paper. "Call this afternoon."

I did and was hired for forty dollars a week.

To celebrate, I bought two flower-sprigged rayon day dresses, one grey and the other brown. I was back to dark colors, and Macy's was a distant cousin to the ateliers where I squandered Monte's francs, but I proudly wore one of the frocks the next night to see *The Gay Divorcee* at the Shubert Theater. When Fred Astaire sang *Night and day, you are the one* I dutifully imagined Johnny. Yet when he got to *hungry yearning burning inside of me* it was my job that came to mind. It might be writing obituaries and police blotter retreads, but I refused to fail.

Meanwhile, I continued to look for more compelling work.

Within days, a competing newspaper, the *Evening Journal,* proposed a freelance assignment, for me to present my first impressions of New York. The next morning I sat on a bench in Central Park with pen and paper and instead, in a jumble of what I considered to be clever prose, fabricated "Who Cheats the Most in Marriage?" Certainly not the Germans, who cared only about sauerkraut and politics. The French? *Non, non, monsieur.* The tradition of men seeing their mistresses from five to seven had become banal to the point that wives were annoyed if their husbands interrupted those hours, during which *les femmes* luxuriated in private ablutions. American wives I compared to heavy carpets banished for the summer, often replaced by lighter, less weathered versions of themselves. The English, I declared—based on no authority whatsoever—took the prize for adultery. Did Americans not realize how common were my country's threesomes? Why did they think shooting weekends in vast estates were invented? No one actually thought we loved drafts, did they? A house party of twenty-four? Consider the possibilities.

The *Evening Journal* published the piece, and I became my own story, the saucy English reporter good for a chuckle. The next day my editor, Mary Dougherty, called me in for photographs. Sheilah Graham on the phone, Sheilah Graham seducing the camera, Sheilah Graham at a typewriter. Never mind that I couldn't so much as peck one sentence on it.

Would I work for the *Evening Journal* full time, she asked? How much money did I want? A hundred dollars a week, I said. I had always liked big, round numbers. She countered at seventy-five. I worked both jobs until my *Mirror* editor informed me that in writing for the competition I was violating a sacred rule of journalism.

"On Fleet Street, journalism has no rules," I snapped.

I was forced to quit the *Mirror* job but kept the other, which evolved into a column called *Sheilah Graham Says*—heavily edited, since I barely knew a colon from a colon. Three times a week I was able to write about anything and anyone I wanted. A press pass opened doors, and not just to Yankee Stadium and the morgue. I covered Lindbergh's return from his world circling flight, crept into Al Capone's home in Florida in order to describe its dining chairs upholstered in alligator hide, and interviewed President Roosevelt's mother, who rambled on the subject of "My son Franklin's bird collection, so fine it's displayed at cousin Teddy's Museum of Natural History." I cornered the Broadway critic George Jean Nathan to ask, "When are you going to marry Lillian Gish?"

"I'll tell you why I'm not going to marry her," he said. I got a better story, and for the first time I let myself dream about where moxie might take me.

Within two years I became what I'd pretended to be, an authentic journalist. I was bold, brazen, and used whatever gifts I had—blond hair, curves, and a bogus Home Counties accent—not strictly in interviews, but to insinuate myself into Manhattan's cosmopolitan life. The Stork Club replaced Quaglino's. Piping Rock in Locust Valley stood in for my London athletic club. And Dorothy Parker helped pave my way.

While interviewing Miss Parker I asked, "Have you been tattooed?—and where?"

"Just here." She rolled up her sleeve to point to a puny star on her elbow. "And you?"

"Where only a gentleman will see." This lie prompted an invitation for cocktails. Despite the fact that I sipped one old-fashioned, heavy on the cherries, to her three sidecars, heavy on the cognac, from then on Dorothy made sure I got invited to the right parties.

My fascination with Dorothy tilted toward envy. Like me, she'd married early and jettisoned a Jewish name, Rothschild—though not *those* Rothschilds. Unlike me, she made no secret of her roots. What she tried to hide was a morose fragility revealed by the most incidental cracks to her brittle exterior. Dorothy simply wanted to be loved.

It takes a woman who feels the same way to recognize this. I didn't, not right away. Back then, what stunned me was how Dorothy Parker differed from every brainy Englishwoman I'd met, all bulky cardigans and dyspeptic disposition. Her sex appeal sizzled along with her zingers. In 1935, Dorothy was a wicked, eyelash-batting pixie willing to catapult into any conversation. Often, she led the conversation, her wordplay surpassing that of the men who danced attendance around her.

Dorothy specialized in games that required brains, not—unfortunately—hand-eye coordination. *If Shakespeare and Plato met today, what would they debate? Suppose FDR, the Pope, and George Bernard Shaw died on the same day. Which death represented the greatest loss?* Such competition rendered me mute, giving me ample time to ruminate on how in America, a smile, a pretty face, and an almost bona fide English accent took you far, but not the distance—although I'd yet to determine the ultimate target of my ambition. It was most definitely not becoming the mistress (his word) of Jock Whitney, no matter how many polo ponies he owned. No, said I.

It was into this stew of self-doubt that Don reappeared—by way of a record that arrived in the mail. I settled down with a cup of tea and heard,

> *My darling Sheilah, I have thought of so many ways to phrase this, and the simplest is the best. I want to marry you when you are free. I am hopeful that I can bring Mother to our side. Please don't send me an answer you don't mean.*

I brewed a second cup of tea, and played the record twice more. I considered Johnny my only family and sent him money religiously, without resentment. But while I thought of him winsomely and indulged in no significant romances in New

York, I recognized that our marriage was long over, with only warm feelings as its echo.

When I had recently visited London to cover the Duke of Kent's marriage to Princess Marina of Greece, I'd broached the subject of divorce. Johnny refused, desolate, but said he wouldn't contest the end of our marriage if after another year that was still what I wanted.

The trip to England had reminded me that there was little I missed about the country, its caste system even less than its climate. I also admitted that while I very much wanted children, I did not ache to marry Don, for whom I felt unswerving love only in my darkest moments of temporary defeat. But becoming a marchioness? What woman could stop toying with that fantasy? Not Dorothy Parker, I would bet. Not I. Nor was Don's title in name only, as were many those days, with peers-of-the-realm able to heat only one room at a time in their stone piles away in the Shires. The Marquess of Donegall was as moneyed as he was socially privileged. As his wife, I would be accorded profound respect. This counted far more than dollars or pounds.

I worked hard, which I enjoyed mostly for the sense of accomplishment it provided. My compensation was secondary, though more than adequate. With my boss's permission I accepted magazine assignments. I earned as much as four hundred dollars a week, enough to double Johnny's stipend—which alleviated an ocean of guilt—while affording me a fine wardrobe and a small leased flat on Central Park South, overlooking the city's greenest oasis. Yet I itched for more . . . for something that eluded me.

I wrote to Don to say I would seriously consider his proposal, but at the same time, threw my hat in the ring to take over a widely syndicated agony aunt column. I did not get the job. Later I discovered that I was considered overly sophisticated for the position. Lily Shiel had pretended too well.

I felt unsettled, the proverbial wandering Jew in pursuit of fulfillment, wondering if I'd trust it to last should I find it. Marriage to Johnny hadn't been the answer. Nor was the stage, hobnobbing with top-drawer London, or the muddle of work and socializing that had become my New York existence. I lacked the intellect for the heady conversation that was the backbone of Manhattan's smart set. In place of retorts and trenchant observations about politics and culture, confusion parked in my brain like a double-decker bus. I was the woman whose sole comment during an evening might be to compliment Claire Booth on her ruby-encrusted compact.

Then a window flipped open. While I sulked over my deficiencies, the contract expired for the North American Newspaper Alliance's Hollywood columnist, who was holding out for three hundred dollars a week. When John Wheeler refused to agree to the reporter's terms, I pleaded to do the job for half her salary. I wheedled and won, willingly selling myself even more cheaply, at one-hundred-twenty-five dollars a week.

On Christmas Eve, 1935, I flew west, leaving behind bone-chilling weather and few friends. I took with me a fresh set of hopes, whittled to a point: I needed yet another chance to start over. This, I decided, was it. Even in London, Hollywood's moviemakers were considered to be ignorant émigrés who just years before peddled gloves or furs. While I'd never been farther west than Philadelphia, I knew Hollywood as the international capital of travesty and sham. Who could be more uniquely qualified to understand both than the former Lily Shiel? And how bloody hard could it be to report on movie stars?

Chapter 20

1936

In Hollywood I became a woman determined to shock. I met Clark Gable and wrote that he "threw back his head and exposed a chin line upon which fat is beginning to collect."

After previewing Jean Harlow in MGM's *Suzie*, I published, "I can't understand why a company with the best producers, the best writers, and the best cameramen should make a picture which has the worst acting, the worst photography, and the worst direction."

At a screening I exchanged pleasantries with a particularly tired, sallow-faced woman. I failed to recognize her as Joan Crawford, and reported just that.

Marion Davies asked me to visit her beach house. "Why does Miss Davies allow her foyer to be cluttered up with horrible caricatures?" I asked in print. Who knew they were paintings of Miss Davies in her screen roles?

After dining at the Trocadero, Hollywood's most fashionable restaurant, I wrote, "Not even the doubtful pleasure of rubbing elbows with Louis B. Mayer can compensate for the high prices charged for rather inferior food." Had I bothered to discover its proprietor also owned the *Hollywood Reporter*, the town's most influential rag? With one sentence I'd alienated a studio titan and invited the *Reporter* to declare open season on Sheilah Graham. Louella Parsons cheerfully announced in every Hearst newspaper:

Publicity heads may take action to ban girl correspondent
for big newspaper feature syndicate. Gal has been sniping
at Hollywood pictures. . . . Several brushes with studios. . . .
Talk of getting Hays to call in hatchet men.

I'd yet to identify the town's sacred cows and what would offend Metro-Goldwyn-Mayer, Paramount, Warner Brothers, 20th
Century Fox, United Artists, and RKO, which *were* Hollywood.
Bombshells that worked in my New York column scandalized the
incestuous corporation that was the country's movie factory. I was
lucky Will Hays, Hollywood's censorship czar, didn't personally
throw me to the sharks on grounds not of moral corruption, but
that I was removing the industry's glamour as handily as if it
were nail lacquer.

It took me three months to understand that privately you
could spread whatever slander you wished, besmirching to the
boundary of libel, but a column had to be written in delicate
code. The point was brought home to me by John Wheeler, who
wired "You are *not* Walter Winchell!" I could sense the invisible expletives.

To put me on a righteous path, John enlisted his friend Robert
Benchley, one of the *New Yorker*'s celebrated wits, who invited
me to lunch at the Brown Derby. It seemed to amuse him that
an English girl of my la-di-da background was scurrying from
studio to studio to rumormonger, and had become despised by
the biggest names in Hollywood. When I made a wry observa-
tion, he was given to explosions of rat-a-tat laughter that made
me believe I was as droll as "Little Sheilah, the Giant-Killer,"
as he christened me.

We discovered that we were neighbors. I'd taken a small flat
on Sunset Boulevard. He lived across the street and invited
me to dinner in the Garden of Allah, a pseudo artist colony of
bastardized Moorish design where my buddy Dorothy Parker
was due to move along with her new husband, the screenwriter

Alan Campbell. I soon started to spend a great deal of time with the three of them as well as the writers John O'Hara and Marc Connelly.

With their help I began to unscramble the paradoxes of Hollywood, where talent and mediocrity existed in tandem. I learned what I couldn't say and what could be put into print, ideally before Louella, my new rival. I also recognized how idyllic the town could be for a girl who was beholden to no man, and whose social and professional life meshed so seamlessly it was hard to distinguish where duty ended and amusement began.

By the second year in Hollywood, my column items, slick with innuendo, came as much from my growing circle of friends as my rounds of studio visits. I had also moved to a small, lovely villa painted peony pink, and met many men happy to squire an attractive reporter to a party at the David O. Selznicks or the Basil Rathbones. When I opened my mail, I found affectionate notes from the diligent Lord Donegall.

In June of 1937 I made a quick trip to London to finalize my divorce. Johnny was solemn—as was I—but we parted as friends. On my last day in town, Don and I had lunch. Only during dessert did I let him know I was single.

He dropped his fork. "Sheilah darling," he sputtered. "How could you have sat through four courses without telling me. Now the coast is clear." His eyes brimmed with emotion as he took my hand and pressed it to his soft lips.

I could learn to love this dear man.

Two weeks later he turned up in Hollywood to cover the funeral of George Gershwin for an English newspaper, took me to a jeweler on Hollywood Boulevard and bought me a ring as big as the diamond from Monte—a temporary stand-in, he said, for a family gem. He got down on one knee, slipped the solitaire on my finger, and asked me to marry him, suggesting a wedding on New Year' Eve—British law required a six-month wait.

My married name would appear in *Burke's* as well as *Debrett's*.

My children would be of gentle birth. I imagined myself at Buckingham Palace, a lady, a marchioness, a viscountess, and a baroness—the four horsewomen of the apocalypse in one patrician package, below only the dukes and princes of the blood royal. Of course the position would come with miles of dusty protocol, and Mama would have to consent. That being as likely as my waking up spouting haiku. I saw no reason not to accept Don's proposal, and enjoy a harmless—if abbreviated—fairy tale. I pretended that I wouldn't see headlines such as "Gossip Columnist and Former Showgirl Marries Marquess," and refused to think that I had the ethics of a grave robber.

I said yes.

Robert Benchley was the first to congratulate us. "We'll celebrate tonight," he said with a cascade of hugs. "It's July fourteenth, Bastille Day. We'll celebrate that, too." Any reason for getting blotto.

And then my real life began, because this was the evening I first saw F. Scott Fitzgerald hiding in a whisper of blue smoke, not quite real, not quite young . . . when I allowed myself to be led blindly by my heart . . . when I threw away my parachute and better judgment.

This was the evening I began to learn to love.

Chapter 21
1937

Best news on earth darling stop mother is on our side stop this makes things so much easier stop wire me sweetheart my love don.

I wait a full twenty-four hours to reply—by letter.

Wonderful, dearest. Thrilled. Sending love to you and your mother. Please give her my sincere thanks. I promise I will write again soon. Busy, busy. Miss you so.

It's not work that fills my time. Louella is beating me on every scoop. I've turned uncharacteristically feckless because I can think only of the next time Scott and I will be together. It's August in Los Angeles and his steady calls have become my day's punctuation, tantalizing ellipses that answer questions far more enticing than "What glitters in the illuminating world of tutting and tattling?" Often, he sends flowers, once—after we'd been discussing gangsters—from F. Scott Fitzdillinger, another time with a card that read "Welcome to the new arrival." He'd drawn a stork carrying a deft caricature of himself as a baby, complete with battered fedora and wrinkled raincoat. The man loves to laugh, especially at himself.

Eager to peel off emotional armor, Scott and I do not tire of talking. On weekdays we speak every few hours. After work his rattletrap Ford chugs up my hill like *The Little Engine That Could.*

I am sure it is motored by a magnetic force pulling my forty-year-old boy to me in his collegiate cardigans.

I'm in a love affair with F. Scott Fitzgerald.

I speak the implausible Dear-Diary words aloud as I hear the wheezy toot-toot of Scott's coupe in my driveway. Typically, our evenings begin at the Garden of Allah with Eddie, John O'Hara, Robert Benchley, or another writer from this rogue's gallery. I sip my sherry and Scott his soda—we never discuss why he avoids anything stronger. Then the two of us leave to enjoy a simple meal—fresh fish, chops, roast chicken—at this or that out of the way restaurant. The point is never the razzmatazz of dining cheek by jowl with stars and power brokers who, as a group, I find as horrid as haddock. With Scott it's intimacy I crave.

Our nights' highlight is what happens when we return to my villa—more conversation, intimate and teasing; barefoot dancing to a crooning radio; lovemaking. More lovemaking. I cannot get enough of this man, with his kind heart and his eagerness to explore my body and my mind, which I reciprocate. I have only to think of him to break into a fever of lust.

For the past month, we have spent every weekend afternoon together. Today we plan to stroll along on a beach in Santa Monica, take a spin on the Ferris wheel, and eat some seafood at a shed with picnic tables. When I walk downstairs in my sundress, sandals, and a straw hat, I see he is wearing old khakis and a white shirt against which his face is as pale as vanilla ice cream. He is examining my photographs in their heavy, antique silver frames.

"Who's this?" he asks, pointing to a small boy on a pony.

As if Heimie, Meyer, or Morris ever wore brocade. "That's my brother David, who died before I was born."

"And this exquisite child—you?" The girl is about seven, with lustrous long curls, holding a kitten. At that age my hair was shaved. I also despise cats, which roamed Stepney Green menacingly.

"My older sister Alicia, who moved to Kenya." I wonder if my fat sister and my thin sister are still that. Has either returned to the East End? "This one's me." I point to a photograph of a girl in a delicate dress with puffed sleeves. Snowy hair, light eyes. She holds a daffodil. Her expression is petulant, as you might expect of a spoiled young blue blood. I remember the day I took the photo buried in my mother's drawer and had it transformed by a photographer whose stock-in-trade was visual hocus-pocus.

Scott peers at the picture closely. "Yes, I do see the resemblance, though you looked snarly. Did someone wash your mouth out with soap?" He moves to a larger picture. "The gentleman sitting atop a thoroughbred? Quite the grand fellow."

"My grandfather." Waxed mustache. No *peyes*. Top hat. No yarmulke. "He had stables in Ireland." Sir Richard.

Scott breaks into four kicks of a step dance and whoops, "Sheilo,"—because this is what he calls me now—"and here I thought you were hoity-toity British through and through. You do know the Fitzgeralds are Irish?"

Please do not ask which county my people are from. Tipperary? Kilkenny? Limerick? They may as well be brands of beer.

"The McQuillans, my mother's folk, were solid potato famine stock, wouldn't have known a spoon from a fork," Scott continues, and I am saved. "May you live to be a hundred years, with one extra year to repent," he adds in a brogue.

This is not the first time Scott has mocked himself, which I consider one of his best traits along with consideration, brilliance, humor, and sex appeal. I have never been this happy. Except . . . there is a significant caveat. It is not, as it should be, that I am engaged, nor that he is married. It's that Scott wants to know everything about me. Where Don requires practiced evasion, with Scott, there is a dangerous pull to tell the truth. I despise lying, yet I am terrified to expose the unpurified facts. This good man merits more than a poseur who was once a ward of charity and spent her girlhood bald, scrubbing, and darning—and that's solely Part I. What of the trickery and facade that followed? At the Norwood shul the Yom Kippur prayers catalogued every kind of sin, including those of omission. Mine could fill the Hoover Dam.

I pretend bravado. "I have a confession."

Anticipation dangles. I am ready to free myself, and then I think of the epidemic of secrets that must ambush my lover day and night. Does he still feel passionate about his wife? Am I a mere stunt double for the headliner of his show? He never speaks of Zelda—we circle around her as if she is a contaminated handkerchief—just as I fail to mention Don. In my case that is because the Marquess of Donegall is out of mind. I have even stopped wearing his ring. But I doubt it's the same for Scott. There are blinks of time when I worry that Zelda walks next to him in private, shared melancholy, casting vengeful looks in my direction. What wife wouldn't?

"A confession?" he says. He walks to me, plants a slow kiss on my lips, and stands back to touch my face. "Are you going to tell me you love me? Because Sheilah Graham, I'm in it big with you, up to my eyebrows."

I cannot lose this. I cannot take the risk. "Darling," I say. "I feel like a blithering idiot. I have never read your books. None of them. There. I've said it."

Technically, I haven't told another lie.

Scott takes a moment to absorb the information. "I figured as much."

"But I want to read them. Every one."

"Do you now?" he says, and beams, making me happy that I made him happy. "I believe this is a problem we can resolve. Follow me, Miss Graham. The Pacific Ocean will wait." He takes my hand and leads me to his Ford.

"Are we going to your flat?"

"No, I packed light," he says. "My books are all back East."

We drive down the road, past Schwab's, a quasi-pharmacy always willing to deliver a bottle of Jack Daniel's to your door, and on to the biggest bookstore in Hollywood. We hurry by the front table, piled high with *To Have and Have Not* by Hemingway, to whom Scott refers as "my former friend," if he mentions him at all. Nearby are displays of novels by John Steinbeck, John Dos Passos, and W. Somerset Maugham, authors I imagine Scott might also know well. I see *Out of Africa* by Karen Blixen, a memoir Eddie Mayer has been urging me to read instead of one of my usual Georgette Heyer romances. Mocking my taste, the other day he declaimed, "The lovely scribe wondered what new seduction she must devise to regain the one man who truly claimed her heart?"

Scott approaches a clerk, asking, "Have you any books by F. Scott Fitzgerald?"

"Let's see," says the salesman, a man about my own age. He scratches his chin. We follow him to a literary fiction section in the back where he scans the F's, and says, "Sorry, sir—none in stock."

"Do you have any call for them?" Scott persists as my breath quickens.

"Not for years," he says. "Might I suggest *Of Time and the River* by Thomas Wolfe?"

"Sorry, I've read it," Scott says, betraying no emotion other than a noticeable tightening around his jaw.

I hurt for him, not just that his books aren't in the stores but because Scott has told me he recommended Tom Wolfe to his editor, Max Perkins, as he did Ernest Hemingway, and both now eclipse him. The other night he went into sweeping detail on the mistake he believes his friend Tom made in breaking with Perkins. "Traitorous bastard. Some spat about editing. Tom could have agreed to disagree." For Scott, loyalty, I have learned, is essential. He gives it. He expects it.

Scott thanks the clerk for his time and we drive to a second bookstore. Again: no Fitzgeralds. The salesman's reaction is a blank, though not the shock I've noticed when I introduce Scott at premieres and dinners. People's eyes widen as they take in that the once-esteemed writer—a name every well-read American apparently knew ten years ago—is alive, albeit consigned to the literary scrap heap. When this happens, I ache. I have always searched for a protector, and in the beginning that's what I saw in Johnny and see again with Don. But in Scott's case, I want to extend the sheltering in return, to be a rampart against indignity. I'd like to wrestle my love away from today's humbling, but he insists on trying a third store, where he approaches a clerk, a man of about fifty.

At last, recognition. "I can certainly get hold of a few titles," the salesman says, amiably enough. "Which would you like?"

"*The Great Gatsby*, *This Side of Paradise*, and *Tender Is the Night*." As the clerk writes them down, Scott clears his throat and adds, almost sheepishly, "I'm the author."

The man's eyes widen. He reaches for Scott's hand, pumps it, and grins. "Mr. Fitzgerald, I have admired your books for years and read every one. I am honored to meet you, sir." I think he may bow.

"Thank you," Scott says. "I'm always pleased to meet a reader such as yourself." I have learned that self-deprecation is for lesser compartments of his life. When it comes to his work, he is never glib.

"Are you working on a new novel?" the man asks.

That is a question I have resisted because I know Scott's mission here is to write scripts, to which he commits long hours in line with his rich compensation. Salaries in this town are no secret to a gossip columnist: he is being paid a thousand dollars a week for six months, five months of which are left. Comparing this to my own salary or, say, a new Chevrolet, which costs six hundred dollars, Scott's salary is a jackpot. But my covert source also informed me that he is in debt for forty thousand dollars. This frightens and astonishes me because after my childhood,

I am terrified by being in arrears or hounded by creditors. I'm a careful spender, without a swell car or a home I own, even with a mortgage. I squirrel away savings and send money every month to dear Johnny. Though we are no longer married, he will have my eternal loyalty.

"I'm always working on something," Scott tells the man. I'm not surprised, because like me, Scott is never without pen and paper. Yet I sense that I shouldn't probe.

The salesman takes Scott's address and promises to deliver the novels within a week. Before we leave, he buys *The Brothers Karamazov*. "Here, Sheilo," he says, "a literary aperitif."

As I accept this dense Russian novel I think of the brothers Shiel: Heimie, Meyer, and Morris. My secrets are always right below the surface, a tangle of roots.

Chapter 22
1937

I can never abandon my poor, lost Zelda," Scott laments a few days later in bed.

This is not the post-coital conversation I had imagined. A moment of bliss, and here's the wife. Nonetheless, my lover blows a smoke ring and strokes my face, saying, "I have no right to monopolize you."

I run my fingers along the golden fur on his chest, with hopes of luring him back to the present and say, "I've never asked you to," though I suspect—with my doorstopper diamond away and half forgotten—that's exactly what he does want. I'm still accepting invitations not only from Scott, but also from, among others, Robert Benchley, Eddie Mayer, John O'Hara, and Arthur Kober, Lillian Hellman's long-winded ex, new in town to write for the Marx brothers. Even collectively, they have the erotic appeal of a gout medication. Yet I count on these escorts to mount a stalwart defense against the escalating emotion I feel toward Scott because he's married, and also has only a six-month commitment from MGM.

John is the gloomiest of the bachelor brigade; his glowers deepen with each cocktail, of which there are many. Last time we were together, he hustled me to my door without shutting down his engine. Did the man think I was going to impugn his virtue? I can't resist dining out on this tidbit when I see Scott a few days later.

"O'Hara's in a perpetual state of just having discovered the world is a lousy place," he cracks. This response makes me want to be with Scott—and only Scott—more than ever, though my impulse runs afoul of any kind of sense, common or otherwise. Unless I am twice as troubled as Zelda, I know I should not let my attraction to Scott run wild. But that's my head talking.

At the end of each workday, late in the afternoon on my patio, I stumble through *The Brothers Karamazov*, tripping over every name and description until my brain quits. Where one word would do, Dostoevsky uses fifty. Several times, I am ready to pitch the book against the wall. More than once I fall asleep, mid-page. Slowly, however, I begin to see why Scott urged this novel on me. Romantic triangles and courtroom dramas take their grip, compelling me to find out whether one of three sons caused their father's death.

Yesterday, well past midnight, I finished. I called Scott this morning to report my triumph. As proud as I feel, I think he is prouder, because my accomplishment affirms that in choosing me, he has picked a winner. This afternoon "Dmitri" sent daisies, the flowers carpeting Russia's hills every spring.

"How's my Grushenka?" he asks in a Russian accent when he arrives that evening.

Dostoevsky's femme fatale juxtaposes two suitors who become bitterly jealous. "Do you see me as a flirt?" I pull a pout. "Please say that's not why you made me read an eight hundred–page book."

"Presh"—short for Precious—"if I wasn't positive you'd enjoy the novel, I wouldn't have given it to you."

Scott and I move on to a bistro, where we dissect *The Brothers Karamazov*'s plot and themes. I've been with other smart men, but all that was demanded of me was to speak casually about the trivial or scornfully about everybody. If I happened to babble something clever, Randy and the other snoots knee-slapped with surprise, as if I'd performed a party trick. They viewed me like a woman who doesn't even know what she doesn't know. Scott is more than the intellectual peer of those uppity English-

men, but he approaches me as an equal, which is how his bracing confidence is beginning to make me see myself. How can I
not love him?

"Sheilo, you are the only woman who can puzzle me out," he
remarks one day. As if he's literally absorbing me, I concentrate
on how Scott appreciates whatever insights I share. This might
be the most appealing thing in the world.

Sometimes we joust about cultural differences between England and America. I will never, for example, get used to how
brazenly Americans discuss money. I'd sooner eat a worm than
tell a friend what a dress cost. Lately, we've sparred over politics. Was it right for the United States to boycott the Berlin
Olympics? Is FDR the greatest president the country's had since
Lincoln? Will America go to war? Scott insists that we will,
which I can't bear to believe.

I find my lover a paradox. He's halfway to a communist in his
instinct to help people, yet enamored by the extravagance of the
wealthy in a way I am not. "We were always on the lower edge
of where the rich lived," he says like an anthropologist, dissect-
ing St. Paul, Minnesota. "I was aware that we were poorer."
This tormented Scott, but his poor was not my poor. Scott's poor
was my dream. I also privately scoff at the moneyed set. If they
can't see through my masquerade, how impressive can they be?

Often, Scott and I simply gossip, the more wickedly, the better. This week I interviewed James Cagney at his Beverly Hills
mansion. Most stars' homes have solariums and movie theaters.
His has a gun room. I can't wait to tell Scott about it.

"How many rifles does this thug own?" he asks, wide eyed.

"At least a dozen and twice as many revolvers. If I were a studio man I'd watch my back. 'Producers are a pain in the neck,'"
I quote, doing a bush league Cagney imitation. "'There ain't
one with more than a baby's idea of the pictures business.'"

"They're all cretins." Scott had recently and unceremoniously
been bumped from *A Yank at Oxford*. Now he's been put on a film

to be made from Erich Maria Remarque's World War I novel *Three Comrades*, about a trio of German soldiers who love the same dying woman. The producer, Joe Mankiewicz, has teamed him with Ted Paramore Jr., a writer from the East whom Scott respected until they tried to collaborate. Now he considers Ted the worst kind of lightweight. But I won't let Scott gripe.

"I asked Jimmy—"

"*Jimmy*?"

"I asked Jimmy if he'll be slugging any women in his next movie." I pace my living room, my hand balled in a fist. " 'I'd sooner sock a woman than a man—they can take it much better.' " Strike one. " 'The best actresses are the easiest to punch.' " Strike two. " 'More than one actor has walked out of my movies 'cause he heard I was going to hit him.' "

At this Scott pops up from his chair and shadowboxes. "I'm gonna wallup ya, Sheilo." His Cagney is far better than mine. And then he kisses me, deeply and lovingly, and marches me to bed.

As summer ends, I stop accepting invitations from other men. I want Scott, and only Scott. I am engulfed by romance.

He calls even more often. "What are you thinking?" "What are you doing?" "What are you wearing?" He details progress on his script and whether he's clashing with his collaborator, which almost always, he is. In the evenings, at the Garden of Allah, he plays madcap Ping-Pong, crossing his eyes, slicing the ball to the left, and pirouetting to make a tricky point. At home, he'll bow, extend a hand—which no longer wears a wedding ring—and ask me to dance, inventing slaphappy steps like he did the evening we first tangoed. Often he acts as if we're both his daughter Scottie's age, just two kids crazy in love. I've stopped trying to square the Scott I adore with the sad sack of his lugubrious reputation.

On days when I interview someone at Metro we eat either in the commissary or wander the medieval villages and Western towns of the back lot until we pick a picnic spot. Often then, I simply listen, because Scott spins a story—about work, his school days, parents, though never his marriage—like a polished raconteur. He starts with a whisper and as the drama peaks, booms like Barrymore.

Charm is Scott's native language. Last night when we were reading—he, cradled in my armchair and I, nestled on the couch—he burst out with, "Where did that gorgeous face come from?" His eyes suggest amazement that he's found me. I tore myself away from *The Great Gatsby*, the most graceful novel I have ever read—*In his blue gardens, men and girls came and went like moths among the whisperings and the champagne and the stars*—and relish that the man who laced those words is beside me, holding my hand. I let myself drift in my own Georgette Heyer plot, both bodice ripper and fairy tale. How can I not be full-throttle in love? A brilliant, handsome man lavishes me with compliments and when I amuse him, chuckles in the most conspiratorial way. A bed laugh, wherever we may be.

He also seems to have a sense that I, like him, have a complicated sweep of sorrows, and that behind my frivolity I am engaged in a struggle I cannot articulate or fully conjugate, even to myself. This is a past that I would never reveal to Don.

How can I marry a man under those conditions? I cannot. As summer ends, with little fanfare and less regret, I write to Don. This is not the first time I have abandoned the chance to be a rich man's wife. But so obsessed am I with Scott Fitzgerald that I fail to miss the diamond I return to Don or what our life together might have become.

Darling Don, I love you dearly but with a heavy heart I must step away from our plans to marry. I will always cherish our time together. We both realize it's for the best . . .

At least I do.

Chapter 23

1937

knew you and the marquess wouldn't go through with it," Scott gloats. "A foolish marriage." He won't grant me the satisfaction of saying he is relieved that I am no longer engaged. My genuinely single status seems, however, to encourage him, he who I learn can be as disarmingly inquisitive as a four-year-old. While most men prefer to talk about themselves, he treats me like research for a thesis. Scott especially wants to know, apart from Don, have I been in love before? How many times? With whom? Perhaps my life will show up in a novel. I'm learning that much of what he lives and learns does.

I've told Scott I'm—God forgive me—twenty-seven, so certainly, I must have a past. Since it's no secret that I'm divorced I offer details about Johnny. I hope this will pacify Scott. It does not. In September, as we are driving to Malibu, he starts in again. "Besides your ex-husband and Don, have there been other men?"

I'd prefer to keep the number to myself, but since the car is proceeding at Scott's standard breakneck speed of twenty miles per hour, he has plenty of time to persist. His questioning becomes a mosquito that I long to squash. At last, I toss off an answer.

"As a matter of fact, there have been a few other men."

I have his undivided attention. "Really? How many?"

By now I've read *Tender Is the Night*. Dick Diver asked Rosemary Hoyt a similar question and she detonated with "I've slept with six hundred and forty men." I might have quoted her. Instead, I say, "Eight." Since I came of age in the Roaring Twenties in London, not Victorian Minnesota, I hope this number places me between laughable and affable, though the true figure is at least double that. I launch right in with a tale from my worldly past.

"One of my first serious suitors—his name was Monte—took me to an exclusive restaurant. I ordered turbot, and couldn't wait to take a bite. Then I glanced up. Monte was looking at my face in the same lip-smacking way I'd eyed my fish." I continue to rattle away. "The bugger danced like a wounded kangaroo, hopping from one foot to the other, and he assumed I'd marry him without a formal proposal. 'You will be my wife,'" I say, mocking Monte Collins's not-quite Oxbridge accent.

I leave out the parts where he gave me a diamond brooch and bracelet, took me to see a country estate where he hoped we'd live, and that at this time, my name was Lily Shiel. Still, I jabber on, attempting to tell a story as well as Scott.

It takes me minutes to realize that the man beside me, who scandalized postwar America with tales of flappers who had the temerity to cast off their corsets and pet in the back seats of roadsters, is dripping with disgust. Lurking beneath Scott Fitzgerald's impeccable wardrobe—gracefully aged but still supremely well-cut heather tweed jackets with patched elbows, grey flannel slacks, and white shoes with an oxblood saddle that makes him look if he were just years out of Princeton—is an old-world gentleman who has yet to allow me to see him naked. In his own sweet way, Scott is a prig. He is also not a casual philanderer but a monogamous adulterer who prefers a tasty entrée to an assortment of appetizers, making one lover at a time the centerpiece of his passions.

I am a woman who has made a profound tactical error in our romantic poker. The scorn I see announces that Scott is pickled with retroactive envy at the thought of me luring man after man. Madly, I backpedal.

"I'm kidding. I lied about the number," I say. That part is true. "I'm teasing you." But his frown fails to conceal that I've stepped deeper into a bog.

For twenty minutes he won't speak, and I short-circuit with exasperation. Did he take me for a virgin?

"A man can have a past and a woman can't?" I taste the acid of having unintentionally caused our first squabble.

"When a man falls in love, it's entirely new every time." Scott is not so handsome when he sneers. "For a woman, it's an additional experience to those she's already had."

Is he suggesting that women compare one lover to another and men don't? Has he wiped away every memory of Zelda, who he's visiting in North Carolina next week?

We drive in silence until he says, "It's all right. These other men don't matter."

But apparently, they must. As lonely as I feel with my secrets, and as different as he is from other men—no one else I've met since Johnny is half as gentle or truly interested in me, and in bed, I've not met Scott's rival—I am now convinced that I can never tell him the whole truth, which in lovesick moments, I had allowed myself to imagine.

I hoped Scott's anger would burn off, but on the ride home from Malibu, the badgering starts again. "What's your father's full name?"

"John Laurence Graham." John and Graham for my former husband's first and second names. Laurence for Olivier, who I regard as the finest living actor.

"Your mother?"

"Veronica Roslyn Graham." Chosen from a pulp novel.

"What was she like?"

"Do you resemble her?"

"Where did you live in London?"

"What kind of child were you?"

"Where did your people come from?"

"Is Graham Scotch? English?"

"Was your father in business?"

On and on, the queries hammer away the feeble scaffolding of fables that lash me together. As soon as I answer one question, another flies toward me like enemy fire. Scott won't stop, and I can't duck. My head begins to pound. I start to cry. To my shame, I am minutes past any semblance of composure when he pulls over to the side of the road.

"Sheilo, what is it, darling? What have I done?" he asks, wrapping his arms around me. "You must miss your family terribly. Since I never do"—he rarely has a good word about either parent, though he saves his most bracing disdain for his mother, whom he described as the homeliest woman he ever met—"I often forget others may."

As tears stream, I furiously shake my head to disagree.

"I've upset you. I've hurt you. I'm sorry. What is it?" He holds me so close my mascara streaks his white shirt.

I thought, *he has chosen me.* I am in love with Scott Fitzgerald, who must never feel that I was once a grubby waif who has gotten to him by a series of deceptions. I am shamed by my ancestry, which I have entombed so deeply in my mind I have a hard time recalling it. I want him to be proud of me at all costs. I will not reveal the truth about myself. *Je refuse.*

Chapter 24

1937

stand before a microphone, clammy and panic-stricken. I tell myself I can read a five-minute script, but a spook lunges at my throat, choking away sound. I am here but not here. As I rehearse, Scott's smooth words become marbles in my mouth.

I've been asked by one James Wharton to contribute to a weekly radio show originating in Chicago, though my portion will be broadcast from Hollywood. The offer came last spring for a not-ungenerous hundred dollars a week. When Scott heard about it, he insisted that I demand double. The sponsor agreed to the higher fee, but now I knit my brows and worry that my performance will be held to a loftier standard.

I worked on my script for days. "Mind if I read it?" Scott asked.

If he sees my columns, which appear in the *Los Angeles Times* and dozens of newspapers in other cities, he fails to comment. We both know my reporting is purely functional, seasoned with laugh lines and innuendo. In the kingdom of tattletale, polished prose places a distant second to divulging a grapevine gem. Yet I handed over my script. Scott read it quickly and asked to make a change or two, though he had to be bleary from a long day of wrangling over *Three Comrades* with his cowriter, Ted Panatere.

He pulled out a pencil stub and a pack of cigarettes, loosened his tie, and scratched away. Three cigarette butts and a half hour of fidgeting later, an insubordinate crest of hair stood on end like a tuft of grass while he concentrated on the rewrite.

When he finished, I could scarcely read the words given the crosshatching of cuts and corrections.

"What do you think?" he asked, displaying the same gravity I'd expect were he presenting Chapter One of a novel to Max at Scribner's. I am beginning to understand that Scott sees his talent as a trust from the literary gods for which he's taken a holy oath to cherish and respect. When he abuses his genius he's angry with himself and anyone who collaborated in the mistreatment—a producer, for example. He also has only one speed: intense.

"Where are my exclamation points?" I asked when he reworked the script.

"Gone."

"But no one would ever see them."

"An exclamation point is like laughing at your own joke. Shoot for droll, not slapstick."

"Scott, I'm not Dorothy."

"Be yourself. Just remember, what's interesting to you is interesting to your audience. You have to try to make listeners see the people you're talking about. Small details add up to big pictures. That's what brings news to life." He counted off each point on his fingers. "Here, I underlined the passages you need to emphasize."

Where my words were choppy, his are liquid. Where I'd larded my speech with superlatives, he'd pared it to perfection. "Won't this be over the head of my audience?"

"Nonsense." He circled my waist and swung me in a jitterbug. "You're going to be wonderful, darling. A star."

Now, days later, I'm in the local CBS radio studio. After an excruciating delay, an announcer booms, "A special treat awaits, Hollywood's voice-in-the-know, Miss Sheilah Graham." A highway of forty seconds stretches before me while invisible technicians pull levers and push buttons. Finally, a director slices the air with his hand, signaling me to begin. Only after he mouths "Start, start"—followed by what I am sure is a queue of exclamation points—do I squeak out, "Hello . . . this . . . is . . . Sheilah Graham in Hollywood." A pant follows every other word as my voice climbs to a yip, and my English accent, which has shriveled in the western sun, returns. Cary *Grant* rhymes with "flaunt." James *Cagney* becomes "cog-knee." My whinny sounds as if I'm parodying a British underling's wife trying to impress the Viceroy of India as she serves him tea and crumpets. When five minutes ends, the silence in the studio echoes with my failure.

Scott calls immediately. "You weren't bad, sweetheart. A little breathless perhaps . . ."

If ever there was a time when I wished he'd lay off the accolades, this was it. "I flopped and don't try to tell me otherwise."

The advertiser, I learn the next day, agrees, though he liked my—Scott's—script. I have a six-month, unbreakable contract, but going forward, an actress will read my words. I report this to Scott.

"Insane. There's nothing wrong with your voice. You simply need practice."

"And no forty-second delay. I thought I'd die waiting."

I see his mind cranking away before he breaks into the grin of a politician. He pounds his fist. "You'll go to Chicago and do it in person."

"Are you mad?"

"Maybe, but not about this. Sheilo, your employers solicited you. They owe you this job. Ask for what you want. Be tough."

"I'm not tough," I say, though a lifetime of evidence would suggest otherwise.

"I'll go with you," he adds. "The tickets are on me. I insist."

I'm incredulous. Not only can Scott not afford the extravagance, this is an inauspicious moment for him to leave. Ted will surely claw through their script, rearrange Scott's lines to claim as his own, and turn a war novel into overripe slop and chop. But my knight-errant persists.

I follow his advice and receive a second chance—all expenses paid by the company in Chicago, and Scott Fitzgerald will accompany me to lead the charge toward Sheilah Graham's soaring professional advancement.

Chapter 25

1937

On a cool October evening a few days later, Scott walks toward me in the Burbank airport. I wave from a distance, though my smile is purely ornamental. While I'm pleased that we'll be together at a swank Chicago hotel, pressure trumps gauzy expectation.

It turns out, I have every reason to worry, but not about my presentation.

As soon as Scott saunters—I can think of no other word to describe his walk—toward me, I realize something is wrong. His pale cheeks are as red as if rouged and his grin like Mickey Mouse. His jacket hangs off-kilter and he is unshaven. As we embrace, he reeks of booze.

Of course I'd heard about F. Scott Fitzgerald the world-class lush, but in the months we've been together, I'd seen him drink nothing stronger than a Coca-Cola. I thought he'd outgrown any need for alcohol. But in the lingua franca of my brother Heimie, my lover is shit-faced and I, in turn, am fucked.

"Presh, ready for the big flight?" he says, and ogles the young female press agent standing next to me. She's arranged for an interview with a starlet waiting in the lounge. Both women hope I'll drop the actress's name into a column.

I don't want to embarrass Scott or cause a scene. When I say, "Darling, please meet Mary Crowell," he genuflects, sweeping an imaginary plume to the floor as if he were Cyrano de Bergerac in a doublet.

The woman blushes. I cringe. "Scott, I'll need to step away for half an hour," I say. "I'm sorry." And relieved.

"Mr. Fitzgerald, why don't Miss Graham and I meet you at seven in the bar?" the press agent jumps in to suggest.

"Stupendous. Simply marvelous." *Stoo-PEN-dus. MAHve-lus.* Adjectives Scott dismisses as the vocabulary equivalent of antimacassars. Nor does he usually mimic Tallulah Bankhead loudly enough to turn heads.

We leave Scott and I sprint through the interview. As soon as it's over, Miss Crowell and I dash to the three tables and six chairs that constitute the airport's bar. Several glasses sit in front of Scott, empty. His eyes are half closed.

"What will you have, Miss Graham?" the press agent asks.

"A brandy, please," to steady my nerves.

"And Mr. Fitzgerald?"

"Make mine another double." The words roll out in a smear. The bartender places a glass in front of Scott, who says, "Mud in your eye," gulps it down, belches, and asks for another, which quickly arrives.

I push the drink away, saying, "Scott, you've had enough." With surprising force, he grabs my wrist. Half of the gin spills on the floor, but he all but gargles the rest and wipes his mouth with the back of his hand. Miss Crowell gets up from her chair and takes a few steps back. She is blushing. A loudspeaker announces our plane. "Time to leave, sweetheart," I say, struggling to modulate my voice.

"Aye-aye, Captain Ahab." He salutes Miss Crowell, then me, and grabs his trench coat, which he struggles to put on and fails to button. I hastily say goodbye to Miss Crowell and we walk to the tarmac, where Scott's coat balloons with a gust of air. He resembles a fedora-crested crane attempting to take flight. When we find our seats on the plane, a bottle of gin clunks to the floor.

"Please tell me you won't drink any more," I plead. I feel

a filmy heat in my face and perspiration under my arms as a stampede of anger and shock floods my body.

Scott takes a swig directly from the bottle and raises it higher than his head. "To the intrepid Miss Sheilah Graham, who will conquer Chicago, hog butcher for the world, toolmaker, stacker of wheat, player with railroads and the nation's freight handler; stormy, husky, brawling, city of the big shoulders. They tell me you are wicked and I believe them—"

"Enough," I hiss. Passengers are gawking. "Cut it out."

To my relief, when the airplane rumbles to life, Scott begins to doze. Los Angeles vanishes as we lift into the meringue clouds. Is the bliss I've known for months a fool's paradise that will also disappear because the real Scott has been revealed as a common drunkard? I'm clenching my hands so tightly my fingernails leave half-moon indentions in both palms.

He continues to sleep, softly snoring, but when a stewardess walks down the aisle proffering cigarettes and magazines, he wakes up, touches her arm, and coos, "Do you know who I am?" I can smell the gin on his breath and am sure she can, too.

"I'm sorry, sir. I don't know who you are," she says. "Do you have a special request?"

"I'd like it to be 1925."

"Excuse me?"

"1920 will also do."

The year he married Zelda. He barks a laugh. "I demand that you tell me who I am."

The girl looks away, perhaps in hopes of being rescued.

"Never mind. I'm F. Scott Fitzgerald, the writer. The famous writer."

I could easily rip out every page of each magazine in the woman's cart and stuff them down Scott's throat.

"Would you like something, Mr. Fitzgerald?" Her voice trembles.

He empties his glass. "A Gin Rickey, easy on the fizzy water."

The stewardess honors the request and moves on to the next passenger as I sink into my seat. "Do you know who I am?" Scott demands of a man sitting across the aisle.

"No, pal, I don't," he replies.

"I'm Francis Scott Key Fitzgerald." His tone is not entirely unpleasant. He hums a few bars of *The Star-Spangled Banner*. "You probably know me as F. Scott Fitzgerald, the inventor of the now extinct Jazz Age."

"Well, I'll be damned."

"And who are you?"

He responds with "Holy cow, I've heard of you," and adds what sounds like "Humbert Hinklefeather."

It's unclear to me if the man is being comic or respectful, but Scott says, "See, Sheilo, I'm not dead yet. Hum here knows me. I'malivegoddamitandI'mfamous. Hum, do you know Hem? First-class bum, Hem."

"Ernest *Hemingway*?"

"Señor Machismo. Also known as the Prick."

"You know him?"

"Know him? I made him. Always ready to lend a helping hand, my friend Ernest—especially to the guy on the rung above him."

Scott commits the mortal sin of laughing at his own joke while I watch with shock and curiosity. How is it possible for my stallion to change into such an ass? I remember a line that struck me in *Tender Is the Night*: "There is something awe-inspiring in one who has lost all inhibitions." But there is nothing awe-inspiring now in seeing Scott. "When we stop to refuel, I want you to go back to Los Angeles," I blurt out. "Going to Chicago together is a mistake."

His expression turns sweetly sincere. "But you need my help, Presh."

"Perhaps, but you're in no position to offer it and"—I choose words as anodyne as possible—"I don't like you . . . this way."

"In that case, fuck off," says the banner carrier for verbal rectitude, a man who's been known to flinch at "menstruate." I am as shocked by Scott's language as its intent. "Go fight your own battle," he says, then assumes the tone of a revival-meeting preacher. "But I'm warning you. You'll always be alone, Sheilah Graham. Which is why we belong together. Two lone wolves."

I close my eyes to staunch the tears I won't allow. For all of my adult life I have felt isolated, marooned by my lies. Perhaps Scott's talent, which people have ceased to honor, sequesters him, too—or he is set apart by the chip he carries on his shoulder about being one down from the rich. It's also possible that he's simply an exceedingly nasty wino others abhor and learn to ignore.

The only step that strikes me as viable is to send my he-wolf packing. "When we get to Albuquerque, please get out," I say. "In fact, I insist."

"You're casting me off?"

"Not at all. We'll see one another back home."

"You'll regret this," he growls as the plane taxies to a halt.

Perhaps, but I don't stop him. When the door opens, he grabs his hat and coat.

"Goodbye, darling," I say, feeling protective as Scott wobbles down the aisle. Does he have any money? Can he even find his wallet? If he flashes it about, won't he be vulnerable to thieves? Part of me wants to rescue him as if he were a child and insist that he stay, but my wiser half takes control, adding, "I'll miss you. I'll call you from Chicago and I'll be back in Hollywood in a few days."

Scott stomps out the door into feral New Mexico.

About fifteen minutes later, the stewardess unfolds my seat into a berth and pulls the curtains around me. I let the revving engine muffle my sobs and try to pinpoint how my sweet, dignified love could degenerate into a creature suitable for James Whale's next production. As the propellers begin to whirl I turn this over repeatedly. Liquored up and tongue-loosened, Scott is an ugly contradiction I do not know. For the past few months he's been such an attentive listener and cross-examiner that I realize most of our time has focused on my history and my problems—to the extent that I am willing to reveal myself. I feel unequal to understanding what has brought on his binge, just as I am ill-equipped to restore this corruption of Scott to the man I know and love.

The draperies in front of me part. I expect the stewardess, checking to see if my seat belt is buckled. It is Scott who sticks in his head.

"Honey, I thought you'd got off the plane."

"I did. I needed more gin." Beaming, he holds up his trophy. "I wasn't quite pickled."

I open my arms to welcome him into my sleeping compartment, and as the plane rises into the night sky, rock him like a baby.

Chapter 26

1937

In the morning Scott staggers into my bedroom at the Drake, drains the few drops that remain in a bottle he is holding, and rings room service for another.

"Gin is the last thing you need," I say.

"The sergeant has spoken."

A bellboy almost as small as a munchkin delivers the liquor and lingers for a tip. Scott starts to chase him, whooping with glee, until the terrified man flees in a streak of red. Scott runs into his bedroom and slams the door. Where I—to a fault—am aware of the social costs that come with defying the world's social order, for Scott, propriety has disappeared down a bottle.

James Wharton, the show's producer, arrives. We begin to chat in the sitting room of my suite when Scott barges in, wrinkled and groggy.

"Mr. Fitzgerald, what an unexpected delight to meet you," he says, masking any surprise.

Scott accepts the greeting as if it's a package he expected. "Mr. Wharton," he says, pumping his hand, then drops clumsily into a wing chair. I try to judge the level of drunkenness by the ruddiness of his face. Medium-rare.

"I've brought my scripts with me, Mr. Wharton," I say. "Under different conditions I'm positive I can deliver exactly what you want. It's the delay that throws me off." Forty seconds of hell.

"Yes, you've made that clear, Miss Graham. Now, if you'll

allow me." He takes all six scripts, sits down at the room's table, and begins to read.

After ten minutes, I flash my toothiest smile and break in with, "You are going to let me go on tonight, aren't you?"

He doesn't respond for another few minutes, when he tidies the scripts into a pile and looks up. "What you've written is fine, but I have to think this over and discuss the situation with my betters back at the office."

"But I've come all this way—and I know I can vastly improve if I'm not alone in a Hollywood studio where I may as well be on the moon. I'm happy to do this live from Chicago."

"Like I said, it's not strictly my decision."

I feel Scott's eyes following our conversation. As if a puppeteer yanks his strings, he comes to life. "You rat-faced twit," he shouts as he stands. "Does she go on or not?"

"Excuse me, Mr. Fitzgerald." Mr. Wharton backs away.

"Put up your dukes, ya little creep." Scott takes the stance of a boxer, shouting, "Show me what ya got." He raises his fists, lunges, flails, and collides with his opponent in the third punch. The poor fellow's lip spurts blood.

"My God, stop it, Scott," I scream as he stands over James Wharton like a victor. I shout, "Cut it out. Stop," afraid he will pounce again.

I run to the bathroom for a towel. "She's going on and that's that," Scott says when I return. "No two-bit chump is stopping Sheilah Graham. Let's see you try."

I bend over the producer, dabbing away blood. "Mr. Wharton, please. I am so sorry," I say, repeatedly, and to Scott, "Calm down. Compose yourself. Please—"

I'm interrupted. "Of course you can do the show tonight, live, Miss Graham—as long as you come alone," Mr. Wharton croaks, his voice nearly lost in the bedlam. He clambers to a stand, holding the towel tight to his wound. "Be ready at six."

"Thank you, thank you, thank you," I say as he escapes, the

door slamming behind him. I take a deep breath and face Scott, who stands across from me smirking, his arms crossed. The silence between us is a taut wire.

"I believe some gratitude is in order," he says, drumming his fingers on his arm.

"Is it now? Gratitude?" I yell as loud as I am able. "I'd like to kill you. How dare you behave like such a horse's ass? You've almost ruined me. I hate you. I despise you." If he were closer I'd be pounding his chest.

Scott stands stock-still and stony. I can't tell if my rant penetrates his blanket of intoxication. Mortified by outrage and self-pity, I run into my own room and throw myself on the bed.

Minutes pass. I gather my wits and return to the sitting room. Scott isn't there. I check his bedroom. Empty.

That evening in the studio, after a round of read-throughs, I do justice to my script and collect a chorus of praise. Heroically vindicated, I race back to the Drake, praying that Scott will be sober and stoop-shouldered with apologies, his bag packed for our midnight flight.

I find the door to our suite ajar. He is sitting in a chair and a stranger is kneeling, feeding him as if he were a toothless invalid. A large linen napkin is tied around Scott's neck like a bib, yet despite this coverage, he is spattered with dark spots, as is the other man's shirt, its sleeves rolled to his elbows.

The stranger howls, "Fitzgerald, you fucking bit my finger" as Scott leans forward, grinning maliciously, ready for another chomp. "Be a good boy. Have more coffee, and then you'll get your steak."

"Excuse me?" Hearing my voice, the man swivels in my direction. He's about my age with even features, dark hair, and a spiffy mustache.

"Oh, hello," he says, as amiably as if we were meeting at church. "You must be Miss Graham. Scott's been telling me all about you."

"I'll bet." I wince. "What, may I ask, are you doing?"

"Getting Scott sober."

"And you are?"

"Arnold Gingrich, Scott's editor," he says and chuckles. "I'd shake your hand if mine weren't otherwise occupied and most likely injured. Sorry you had to walk in on this Mack Sennett comedy." He turns to Scott. "You don't have rabies, do you?"

"Show my doll the 'Crack-Up' stories, will ya?" Scott calls.

"Pipe down there, cowboy," Mr. Gingrich says to Scott. "I gather you haven't seen any of his articles in my esteemed *Esquire?*"

This new magazine had been earning kudos among the Garden of Allah battalion, but I didn't know Scott was a contributor. Robert Benchley recently went on and on about a piece Ernest Hemingway published citing seventeen books he considers so exceptional he claimed he'd rather reread any of them than have a yearly income of a million dollars. I laughed at Ernest's pretension, though I bought the issue. I'm embarrassed to admit that the only book I've gotten to is *The Brothers Karamazov*—because Scott urged it on me. *Anna Karenina, Wuthering Heights, Madame Bovary, War and Peace, Huckleberry Finn*, all the others—I've read none of them.

"Arnold here will do anything to pry a goddamn story out of me," Scott bellows, juice from the steak dripping from his mouth. "He'll rip out my liver if necessary."

"Keep up the drinking and you'll have no liver for me to rip out."

"Is trying to sober up authors part of your job, Mr. Gingrich?" I ask. He laughs as he continues his mercy mission. "And are you having any luck?"

"Not yet, but I'm a patient guy." He turns back to Scott. "First things first, right, my friend?"

"Another drink. Another drink." Scott might be cheering on the Princeton Tigers.

"How did you know Scott was in town?"

"He called—my offices are around the corner. He wanted me to bring over some articles of his I'd published so you could read them." He nods toward a large folder on the table.

"Have you ever seen him like this before?"

"I can hear you, Sheilo," Scott yells, his eyes glittering. "I'm right here."'

"Many times, but never quite this bad." Arnold Gingrich pinches Scott's nose and pours coffee down his throat. Scott spits it back in a geyser of black.

"I'm grateful for what you're trying to do, Mr. Gingrich, but if you don't mind me saying so, this is demented."

"Arnold loves me," Scott says. "Don't you?"

"You know what, Scott? I do," Arnold says. "I've admired your work since I was in high school. You've always been my idol."

The sincerity of the admission quiets Scott.

"Shall I gather, Miss Graham, that you've never read 'The Crack-Up' or any other of Scott's pieces I published over the last few years?"

"Never." Nor have I heard of them.

"They may explain a lot. I visited Scott in Baltimore two years ago to see why he'd stopped sending us stories we'd already paid for. It had gotten to where the damn auditors were circling my desk with spears."

"Pimps like Arnold expected me to write about young love, tra la," Scott sniggers. "The last fucking thing on my mind."

Arnold continues to ply Scott with steak and coffee as he explains that he'd told Scott even if all he turned in was a pile of pages printed with "I can't write, I can't write," he needed something—anything—to satisfy his publisher for advance checks that had been cashed. Scott promised to try. The result was "The Crack-Up" and a list of other titles that helped him torpedo through a writer's block that had, apparently, stretched for years.

"You do know that Scott Fitzgerald plus liquor is as different from Scott without liquor as night is from day, don't you?" I hear Arnold Gingrich's compassion.

"I do now, but my more pressing concern is how I'm going to fly him back to Hollywood. He has a meeting tomorrow with Joe Mankiewicz—"

"The fearsome Monkeybitch," Scott shouts.

I ignore him. "Scott's contract is up for renewal. We've got to get home, and our plane leaves in a few hours."

"Jesus," Mr. Gingrich says, "we better stop the small talk."

He continues his routine until Scott nods out. At eleven, the airport limousine arrives, and Arnold and I manage to bundle Scott into his coat. He and I fall into the car, where another couple is waiting.

"If you need me, here's my number." Scott's editor hands me a card along with the folder filled with Scott's past work. I thank him again and Scott, now fully awake, bids goodbye to Arnold so lavishly you'd think one of them is being deployed to battle.

Halfway to the airport, he says, "Doesn't she have the most delightful curls?" pointing to the young brunette in the seat in front of us. The girl smiles at her escort. "Isn't she pretty?" He continues to ladle on the flattery, sotto voce—"utterly ravishing . . . exquisite"—until the woman turns and flashes us a smile.

"Who are you looking at, you silly bitch?" Scott hoots.

"Apologize!" I say as the woman's escort raises a fist. Fortunately, this is the moment when we arrive at Midway Airport. The limo stops. The other couple flees as Scott stumbles out, tripping on the pavement, ripping his trousers. With the driver's help, we hoist him upright and slowly escort him to the check-in counter.

"We're sorry, sir, but we can't permit you to board in this condition," a clerk says.

"In that case, I'll buy a plane," Scott replies, bloated with indignity.

"If only you could. The next flight doesn't leave until five in the morning." In desperation, I phone my messiah.

"Get Scott in a cab and just keep circling till it's time to go back to the airport," Arnold Gingrich advises. "I'll call every bar in the area and tell them if a man in a dirty raincoat and fedora shows up, to serve him only beer. By two, most of the taverns will close."

Scott passes out on my shoulder while we take a trip to nowhere. Every few minutes he wakes to say to the man, "You motherfucker—I asked you to stop at a saloon" or, to me, "Hello, baby," after which he promptly shuts his eyes and begins to sleep. Throughout the ride, I ruminate on how impaired my judgment must be to have allowed myself to fall in love— twice—with a weak man. My coat of arms may as well say *Make a mistake, then make it again.*

At four-thirty a.m., an hour when nothing good ever happens, we return to the airport. Scott is allowed on the plane. He dozes through the entire flight.

On my way home in Los Angeles, I drop him at the Garden of Allah. In a moment of complete sobriety, as if the real Scott has been restored, he says, "Sheilo, my love, I'm deeply sorry for my behavior. You deserve a thousand apologies."

"Oh?" My voice is ice water.

"Can you forgive me?"

I offer my most lacerating stare.

"I want you to know this was the first time I've had a drink in almost a year. Worrying about my script and whether my contract would be renewed and Scottie and well, other things— it's been too much. I'm sorry. I fell off the wagon."

"Fell off the wagon? There's a vast difference between a drink and this sideshow." My tone continues to be artic.

"Please, I beg you not to worry, Presh, I can stop this whenever I want. I'll report in sick to the studio for a few days, and see a doctor, and get a nurse." He kisses me softly on the cheek. "I can dry out. I'm sure of it. I've done it before."

"We'll see." I hustle him out of the taxi. "Get some rest."

When he wakes, will he remember a word he just said, or any of the last two days? Is drunk Scott the real Scott, or vice versa? Does he love me? Do I still love him?

I know the answer to only the last one. I have caught Scott as if he were a virus. I am no longer naïve enough to believe that we get to pick whom we love. The only thing I'm sure of is that I can no longer look at this man, nor can I listen to him.

I am sick of F. Scott Fitzgerald.

Chapter 27

1937

Arnold Gingrich's package sits like a sulfurous dragon whose breath sours my flat. I am tempted to toss the manuscript in the fireplace. Bloody hell. Let my romance incinerate along with it.

Swimming through the motions, I dash off the last item for Tuesday's column.

> Harry Warner walks over to a child at the Coconut Grove to say, "You're the prettiest little girl I've ever seen. Would you like to be in pictures?"
>
> "Well how do you do, Mr. Warner?" she answers. "I'm Shirley Temple." His studio's top box-office draw for the last few years.

Thank you, Harry Warner, for never recognizing a soul.

I go to a concert with my friend Jonah, clean my closets, make a pot of vegetable soup, and devour *Gone with the Wind* while munching on peanut brittle. None of these distractions keeps me from thinking of whether I owe Scott the courtesy of reading his essays. Three days pass and then I break. As much out of curiosity as loyalty I begin reading, and then must force myself to stop several times and mop up my tears. "The Crack-Up," "Pasting It Together," and "Handle with Care" are the testimony of a man flying his fear like a flag. All pretense is gone, revealing a raw human stalk riddled with emotional shrapnel.

I suddenly realized I had prematurely cracked. Scott writes of

sleeping twenty hours a day and in his few wakeful hours, making lists, hundreds of lists—of popular tunes, suits he owned
since he left the army, women he idolized, people who snubbed
him, happier times. *I slept on the heart side now, because I knew
that the sooner I could tire out, even a little, the sooner would come
that blessed hour of nightmare which, like a catharsis, would en-
able me to better meet the new day.* He likens his condition to
being overdrawn at the bank, mortgaged physically and spir-
itually. Scott compares himself to a cracked plate you consider
tossing, and—few writers see to the truth at the bottom of a
murky pond better than he—notes that at three in the morning, a forgotten package has the same tragic importance as a
death sentence.

I need to stop when Scott writes about the novel, no longer
the *supplest medium for conveying thought and emotion.* Scruple-
free Hollywood merchants, capable of reflecting only the most
superficial thought and emotion, will make fiction extinct, he
rages in his own wily way. Yet here, I think, is Scott, throwing
himself at the mercy of producers, another greedy author struggling to write scripts. It was he who suggested that the mark
of a first-rate intelligence is to be able to balance two conflict-
ing ideas in your mind at once and still maintain the ability
to function, but it was my Tatte who said, *Keyner zet nit zany
eygenem hoyker.* No one sees the hump on his own back.

Every genius scribe in America wants a bite of Hollywood's
apple pie because elsewhere, Americans are starving. Here,
even if film industry folk aren't floating gardenias in their pools
and importing Napoleon's parquet, no one lines his shoes with
cardboard. Even lesser acolytes—I, for example—live flush
with snug comfort. I am willing to own up to this. I may be a
liar, but I'm not a hypocrite.

Scott is right about movies trumping books. I can't help but
think that's not merely because books cost a few bucks and
films, two bits. In Scott's case, the subjects he's written about

became his undoing. He gave voice to a decade that roared as it rode on the roofs of taxis, and he rhapsodized about that hedonism better than anyone. Now, most people can't afford taxis, shut up and get on with it.

I never expected life to be all cherry cheesecake and Cole Porter lyrics. I figured out how to put one foot in front of the other, with no allowance for suicidal gloom. Perhaps this has left me a tragically sensible Brit who can't accept that the man she loves has a lesser will. The half of me honed by a slum and an orphanage is shocked by Scott's naked self-pity. But maybe Scott's falling off the wagon is more. I pray it's not the beginning of a second severe breakdown.

It's a sad business to prospect for feelings alone. I call Dorothy. "He's a fine writer and a beautiful person, our Scott, but when life frustrates him and his sweets are taken away, he kicks and screams like a spoiled brat," she says. "That's when the drinking begins."

This is not helpful.

Next, I speak to Robert, to whom I give the condensed version of my trip to Chicago.

Ten minutes after I sound my alarm, he arrives. I point to the *Esquire* essays piled on the table. "What did Scott's friends make of these?"

Robert sits back, lights a pipe, and the woodsy scent of tobacco turns my living room into a men's club. His bulk threatens to capsize my armchair. "Public opinion was divided," he says. "Most of us admired Scott's honesty and writing—it's sublime, and I wrote to him saying as much. *True Confessions* in poetry. But there were those who saw him as a whining, melancholy baby. Ernest, in particular."

"Did he read Scott the riot act?"

Robert takes away his pipe so he won't choke on laughter. "Oh that he were that subtle. He wrote to Scott to say he jumped 'straight from youth to senility without going through manhood.'

Ernest thinks everyone's spineless until he goes mano a mano with a grizzly."

My face must show that I like Hemingway even less now than an hour ago.

"It gets worse, pet. Ernest published his own story, right after Scott's three, and slandered our boy. I brought the evidence."

He pulls a clipping from his jacket.

He remembered poor Scott Fitzgerald and how he had started a story that once began, *The rich are different from you and me*. And how someone had said to Scott, Yes, they have more money. But that was not humorous to Scott. He thought they were a special race and when he found they weren't, it wrecked him as much as any other thing that wrecked him.

Most people are taken in by the rich. I certainly was, once. But after Monte and Randolph and Tom and Unity and Johnny's carnivorous sister, the silk stocking crowd underwhelms me.

"Ernest is more than cruel," I say. "He's disingenuous, always with his hand out for some noble cause or other."

Robert pats my leg as if I'm an overexcited dog. "There, there. We all know the man is a big, talented brute. With Scott, the animosity goes back to Zelda. It was hate at first sight with those two. To Ernest, she's the bitch that dragged down her talented husband, competing with him and draining away his gift. Zelda called Hemingway a pansy with hair on his chest and accused him of having a homo's interest in Scott. She's suspicious of any man so fixated on physical bravery."

For the first time, Zelda comes alive. I suddenly like this woman I manage to forget for days on end, the wife for whom I do not exist. I imagine her as someone I might want as a friend.

"Ernest has been an extra limb in the Fitzgerald marriage,"

Robert explains. "His first mistake is to be convinced he under-stands it better than Scott does."

"Didn't Scott help Ernest get his start?"

"Sadly true, despite everything. Yet Scott has never tried to get even. He and Ernest will never be thick as thieves as they were in Paris, but according to Dorothy, he even wrote to Ernest and complimented him on his *Esquire* piece, though Scott told him to lay off." Robert switches to a spot-on mimic. "When you incorporate the story into a collection would you mind cutting my name? The 'poor Scott Fitzgerald' rather ruined it for me. Approximately."

Hearing how gallant Scott was toward Ernest is a bold-faced reminder of who Scott is when he's not inebriated: generous, eloquent, lovable. "I could sink a knife into that man's heart."

"Whoa, little giant-killer. Forget Ernest and give Scott some rope. He'll stop drinking. He always does. Hell, whatever his failings, I love the bastard."

My problem, exactly. Scott has his addictions and I have mine. Him. After Johnny, he's virile. After Randolph, he's kind. After Don, he's appealingly complicated, and compared to all of them, he's the best listener I've ever known as well as the best lover. I could go on.

The next day a box of long-stemmed tulips, shamelessly red, arrives with a note,

Darling,
These are the color of my face. I have no words except I miss
you. Will you take me back?

Your forever fool,
Scott

This is the man who has said, "Loving you is a luxury like everything else about knowing you, dear face, dear heart, dear

Sheilah." My anger about his drinking looms less when I re-member the tenderness. I think not exclusively of the sex—though I do miss it—but of Scott's small gestures, and the pleasure we take in one another's company . . . of how the eve-ning before we went to Chicago, when I was soaking in a bubble bath, he brought me a small pillow for my head, yet averted his eyes from my naked body. I remember our last UCLA Bru-ins game. While he patiently explained football, he stroked my neck and held my hand, dropping it only to jump up and cheer giddily when our team scored a touchdown.

It boils down to this: when I consider the past, I try to im-prove on it. Scott reaches for the gin or writes a requiem. But he is also generous and forgiving. If he can pardon Ernest Hem-ingway, shouldn't I at least hear him out?

I agree to meet him that evening to walk on the pier. When I get out of my car and see him waiting, my heart pounds in excitement. I had almost forgotten how handsome Scott is. He embraces me and for just a moment my head rests lightly on his shoulder. We fit together as if designed to complement.

"Alcohol is a gift in the sense that I can't remember much about Chicago, but it must have been wretched, whatever I did. I am very sorry, Sheilah," he says, a bit formally, as he pulls me toward him with both hands on my shoulders, looking straight into my eyes. "I embarrassed you, I know, and I no doubt did the same to myself. I beg your apology."

My heart is pounding like the surf. Who am I to not forgive?

"I accept, Scott, on the condition that this never happens again." If he was on the wagon for all the months before Chi-cago, surely he has the willpower to climb up there again. Rob-ert Benchley has said as much.

"It won't, I promise. I love and respect you far too much."

I blink back tears. "Thank you for saying that." Respect is something I need as much as love, since whenever I think of my lies I have only the lowest regard for myself.

"Do the essays explain me at all, Presh? I'm just now, here in Hollywood, finding pieces of myself and trying to reassemble them. I'm a jigsaw puzzle hit by a tornado."

"Oh, Scott. What you've gone through . . . I hate even to think about it, and wish you'd told me everything sooner."

"I was trying to forget it. Fresh starts and all that."

"You're entirely right, by the way. The rich *are* different."

"Oh?" he says.

"This is a subject on which I feel qualified to speak." He smiles for the first time, his teeth even and white, betraying no sign of his ubiquitous Raleighs. "But not now." I want only to love and comfort Scott, and get the same in return. We walk to our cars and meet at my home, where we start with dancing and laughing, move on to a striptease, and end in bed, for hours, athletic yet vulnerable. I feel as if Scott has been put on earth to give me pleasure and I am happy to return the favor. We graft a new beginning onto our own crack-up.

Scott wants to celebrate Christmas together. Scottie will stay East, where Robert and most of his troop are heading. He doesn't suggest visiting Zelda, whom he quietly saw this fall. Johnny and I never made much of the holiday beyond a hotel lunch with the requisite silly hats; all Christmas has ever meant to me is another December day. But I am determined to create a Noel of wifely domesticity, though I suspect Zelda has never gone beyond toasting bread. I should invite Dorothy and Alan, but I am selfish. The last few weeks have been sweet, and I want Scott to myself.

I buy *The Settlement Cook Book* and create a menu of oysters from Santa Monica, roast turkey with cornbread dressing, potatoes—sweet and mashed—and Brussels sprouts with chestnuts. For dessert, mince pie from Sunset Bakery. No plum pudding, because every recipe calls for whiskey, brandy or rum, and I do not want to find Scott under the Christmas tree.

On Christmas Eve, Scott finds the last and stringiest tree in Los Angeles, sold off the back of a truck on Pico. I spend a full day in the kitchen and at five o'clock, we stuff ourselves with fat, briny oysters, dry turkey, perfect potatoes, limp sprouts, and plenty of pie. He reminisces about Christmas in St. Paul. A twelve-foot Norwegian pine he and his father cut down at a farm for the foyer of the big house on Summit Avenue. The cook's goose, slick with grease. His grandfather's declamation of "Twas the Night Before Christmas," which Scott repeats in finest thespian fashion.

"No stockings hung by the chimney with care, I'm afraid."

"Next year," he says.

I thrill to words that suggest a shared future. As the fire crackles, Scott plays a recording of carols that he has brought and sings along in a fine tenor. "We Three Kings of Orient Are." "O Little Town of Bethlehem." Songs I do not know.

"Sheilo, join in," he says in the middle of "Deck the Halls." "Don't leave me standing alone on the stage at Carnegie Hall."

"You know I can't sing."

"But you were on the stage, and I've heard you in the shower. You're a natural soprano."

"Got me. Darling. In England we sang different songs."

He breaks into "Hark! The Herald Angels Sing." "You must know this one. The melody is by Mendelssohn."

Why has Scott mentioned a Jew? "Meet me by the mistletoe," I say, trying to hide my alarm. "My visions are not of sugarplums."

His mouth is a holiday of its own, tasting of longing and sweet whipped cream. I cling to Scott, and almost pray. If an entire religion can grow from the idea of a virgin birth, perhaps he and I might be able to find our own peace on earth, an armistice without drunken tirades, perhaps even including a child.

Mistletoe leads to a trip upstairs, joy to the world and all that. When we finish, I ask him if he wants his present now or tomorrow.

"But we said no gifts—though I believe I just got mine?"

"This isn't from Bullock's or Saks Fifth Avenue," I say. "It isn't even from me."

When curiosity lights Scott, the corners of his mouth turn up and he is ten. I want to emboss this face on my memory. "Carry on, Cleopatra of gossip."

"MGM is picking up your option." Hedda Hopper, my officious new rival—now I have two—leaked the news to my friend Jonah. Scott wasn't banking on it, and neither was I. His Chicago trip was unauthorized—grounds to cancel. I smother Scott in a hug. "And you're getting a raise, and I'm going to trumpet the good news in print."

Scott will be making $1,250 a week, a fine sum, though there are those like his St. Paul friend, Donald Ogden Stewart, who rake in $5,000. Still, Scott's wage will be almost as much as what the average Joe makes in a year, a cause for celebration in every way.

I fall asleep knowing I've lived my best Christmas and let myself believe that New Year's, and the future it will bring, will be even better.

Chapter 28

1938

A few weeks later, as we share our morning coffee and read the *Los Angeles Times*, Scott discovers that the Pasadena Playhouse will perform a play based on his satire from 1922, *A Diamond as Big as the Ritz*. He hops up from the table, jingling with excitement. Could the next step be Broadway? An F. Scott Fitzgerald renaissance? I sense that Scott allows himself to imagine the literary equivalent of a ticker-tape parade. Life feels plumped by potential.

He calls the theater and requests two tickets in the back. The evening of the premiere, Scott gives me a corsage of camellias and lilies of the valley to pin on my grey silk. He wears his tuxedo, touchingly dated, that he had on the night we first danced, and hires a car. We start with lobster at the Troc, where I am grateful to be *someone*, not another leggy hatcheck girl waiting to be discovered.

I discreetly comb the room for Bugsy Siegel or Mickey Cohen, who are buying the place, and offer air kisses—which I'm struggling to master without feeling like a British stiff—to William Powell and Merle Oberon. I keep my pen and pad in my evening bag. This is Scott's night, and the first I hear of a novel he wants to start.

"No one's written a serious book yet about Hollywood, Sheilo," he says. "The idea's been simmering since I was here in 1927. I see the main characters as stand-ins for Irving Thalberg and Louis B. Mayer. Art meets commerce." His fists crash together like silent cymbals.

Scott always did like a fable. Ten years ago, both he and Irving Thalberg had been boy wonders and Scott has spoken of how impressed he was with the man's honesty and brains, a golden mogul with a celebrity aura. He was married to a movie star, Norma Shearer, and did it all—picked and rewrote scripts, cast, directed, edited, and produced. If someone told me he made the crews' baloney sandwiches, I'd believe it. For Scott he is a kindred spirit with the soul of a poet, all Louis B. Mayer is not.

"Old Louie is a lout who represents everything money-grubbing and coarse about the movie business," he says, "starting with the word *business.*"

Here is where Scott and I differ. A more judicious sort—I, for example—would flatter, not offend, LBM, who has the ultimate say over his employment at the studio he owns. Not Scott. "Thalberg's a hero?"

"Power at its best."

"Even after he died." Last year, when he was only thirty-seven.

Everyone has a favorite Thalberg story, and I share mine. "By mistake, an invitation to be a pallbearer was sent to Harry Carey, a cowboy actor from before talkies, instead of Carey Nelson, the producer. Afterward, everyone thought Thalberg had reanointed the cowboy, and now he's a star all over again."

Scott takes out his notebook, jots down the story, and I feel proud. I like the idea of his book, assuming he can disguise Louis B. Mayer so the man doesn't roast him on a spit. I love that Scott is hoping to write any novel, and has gotten past Stutz Bearcats and pink Champagne.

"Baby, I used to have a beautiful talent once," he says, stroking my hand. "It was a comfort to know it was there. I've been only a mediocre caretaker but I think I have enough left to stretch out over another novel or two. Maybe what I write won't be as good as the best things I've done, but nothing I write can be completely bad." Now he looks into my eyes and with pure joy says, "I may be the last of the novelists for a long time."

Arrogant as the statement sounds, I believe it to be true. Like his shoe size, Scott's gift is nothing for which he can claim responsibility. It's his to use or abuse.

We leave the restaurant in a bubble of bliss, but when we arrive at the Pasadena Playhouse no other limos are discharging fancy theatergoers. I wait in the empty lobby while Scott checks to see if we've made a mistake about the time and place.

"It's the students," he says when he returns. From the tightness in his throat, I see he's reaching for nonchalance. "They're doing the play upstairs."

In our finery, we climb the stairs and sit on a bench in the back of a hall. There is a small, bare stage. About a dozen young people in casual clothes and a few adults who might be their parents or teachers eye us curiously before the show goes on. Scott roars louder than anyone at every joke. When it ends, he claps longest.

"I'm going to go backstage and compliment the cast," he says, after the one and only curtain call, though there is no curtain. "They may find it encouraging."

Years of practiced pretending keep me from displaying any sign of pity toward this proud man. Along with criticizing his drinking, sympathy, I now know, is *verboten*.

He returns minutes later. "Nice kids," he says. "Though they seemed a little awkward."

Of course. They assumed you're dead.

Scott applies himself to the task of mastering screenwriting as if he were solving an algebraic equation. If X is characterization and Y is dialogue, what is the square root of plot? Almost every night, we find ourselves at a film. He prefers obscure theaters to splashy premieres, because—I suspect—he finds it humiliating to go unrecognized as I forage for the rare mushrooms a gossip columnist craves. In fairness, however, his interest is in analyzing what makes the hoi polloi laugh, cry, or offer their harshest critique, the thunder of silence, and a premiere's audience wouldn't dare be mute with studio fat cats in the next row.

Scott is never silent. On our rides home, he loves to talk shop and so do I, because the film industry may be the one area where I know more than he.

Bringing Up Baby, or at least Katharine Hepburn's bone structure, earns praise from both of us. The razzle-dazzle of *Comet Over Broadway* also rates a gold star. I mention that John Farrow directed after Busby Berkeley fell ill, but only Busby received a credit. "Half the heroes in this town are unsung," Scott grumbles.

Scott allows that Louis B. Mayer got it right in hiring Josef von Sternberg, one of many refugees fleeing Germany, for *The Great Waltz*, though he calls the script for *Test Pilot* "dreck." I bite my tongue at his Yiddish. We chew over other films MGM should not, in his opinion, have produced—*A Christmas Carol* ("Dickens is already dead, fortunately"), *The Girl of the Golden West* ("Get me out before Nelson Eddy yodels"), and the complete Andy Hardy oeuvre ("Not at all how boys think"). Scott, at forty-two, is the authority on what boys think. We even endure *A Yank at Oxford*, finished after he was dismissed as a writer. "Drivel." Scott also appraises actors: Ronald Reagan ("plank of wood") and Olivia de Havilland ("born without oomph").

Scott is spending long days working on *Three Comrades*, but his greater ambition is to move forward on his novel. Constantly now, I see him scribble phrases and whole conversations he overhears, because "a writer wastes nothing." I am flattered when one of my remarks—"if only I could walk into your eyes"— merits the notebook.

Since there is not a movie to see every evening, plenty of nights we stay home, insulated by love's narcotic pleasures, which make me feel that his other goal—not necessarily in third or even second place—is to please me. I own barely enough vases for the flowers that arrive, and the phone rings every hour. "What are you wearing?" "When will I see you?" "What are you thinking of?" During the evenings at my apartment we jitterbug or fox-trot to the radio, gorge on homemade fudge, or I listen as Scott declaims poetry from memory in the melodramatic tenor he reserves for T. S. Eliot or Swinburne. He is not always reverent, and may shuffle off to Buffalo as he recites. But sometimes he wants to see his friends, and then it becomes New York all over again.

Often I am conscripted for charades, a game taken so seriously by Scott's tribe that when Marc Connelly's team was up against Ira Gershwin's, they held rehearsals. I am at the same marked disadvantage on the West Coast as I was on the East. I rarely catch on to the clues and am eaten by humiliation. The Thirty Years' War? Never heard of it. I try to compensate by spewing studio gossip and lavishly apologizing.

Scott gently reproaches. My desperation makes me look pitiable, he informs me. "Don't try so hard," he says. "Pretend everyone bores you."

Oscar Levant bores me. Ogden Nash bores me. George S. Kaufman bores me. The truth is, none of them are half as interesting as they think they are. Even Dorothy bores me when she yammers on about her dogs. At parties, I prefer to huddle in a corner with Scott where, as if drawn to wet paint, I struggle to keep my hands off him. This leads Dorothy's husband to say, "You two always look as though you have a secret you're going to talk about later."

We are the secret. Our romance holds us captive as we see in each other what others miss. This is the first time that my feelings burn at a blue flame. I look at Scott dressed and imagine the silk of his skin next to mine and the look on his face as our lovemaking reaches a climax.

A few days after Scott turns in his final draft of *Three Comrades*, the interoffice mail unceremoniously delivers his copy of the script. Approved. More-stars-than-there-are-in-heaven MGM has blessed and ratified his labor. Nonetheless, that night he seethes. "Ted Paramore rewrote my best scene."

"Pollyanna would like to point out you'll get a credit on a major film," I risk saying. I despise a sore winner.

Next week's news is even better. Eddie Mayer pops into Scott's office to announce that Hunt Stromberg, one of the greats, wants Scott—single-handedly—to write a script for Joan Crawford. "You'll like this guy," Eddie promises. "Rare as an albino elephant, a producer who actually respects writers."

"Stromberg's a Gatsby fan," Scott reports after he and the director meet. Hunt is calling the film *Infidelity*, to be based on a splinter of a story around which Scott is expected to build an entire script. Joan will play a wife who discovers her wealthy husband with a strumpet—Stromberg's term—played by Myrna Loy, a star clipping at Joan's heels.

"It's a universal subject," Scott says. "Everyone's life has locked doors. Married couples know the chance opening of one of these doors may lead to trouble." He must realize I am thinking of the distress I may be causing when he opened the door that led to me, and quickly shuts down that train of thought. "The problem is they want Joan to be all kitten fur. She was, once. I remember her gowned in the apex of fashion, droll expression, laughing eyes. But that was years ago. Only the leer is left." He shakes his head in disbelief. "Have you seen her lately?"

I have. This town has baked the softness out of her. I hope it won't do the same for me.

The following weekend, we are invited to the home of the sociable Warner brother, Jack. We drive Scott's rattletrap under a canopy of sycamores that leads us past a gurgling fountain to a wide cobblestone courtyard. Scott's hand is on my thigh. I have one of my pinch-myself moments as a valet drives away the car to an unseen parking lot.

Scott goes directly to the pool and tennis party outside, but I sneak into the mansion, designed in a style you might call Spanish clunker. Every furnishing is oppressive, most likely selected by the studio art department. The entrance hall wallpaper, claims Louella, was imported from the imperial palace of China, and has plenty of foo dogs to go around. In the library, the paneling might have been ripped from the Mitford family estate, with leather-bound books bought by the yard, arranged by color. Everywhere, drapery is dense with layers of turquoise shantung, blocking out the dappled California sunlight. Off the main hallway, goldfish swim in a porcelain powder room fixture that may be a bidet.

The rich *are* different. Their taste is worse.

Outside, a Hawaiian buffet starring a roast pig stands untouched; the unwritten law is that guests don't partake before Jack Warner digs in, and he is nowhere to be seen. Starlets in orchid and tuberose leis strum ukuleles and undulate their hips as they sing aloha this and aloha that. I spot Scott across a rolling lawn. Joan Crawford is by his side, drinking from a coconut shell.

"I believe you know Sheilah Graham," he says. "Joan is sharing her ideas for the script." I read his tone. Joan Crawford is a pinhead. "She thought the wife should be an equestrienne. She sees herself in jodhpurs, perhaps with a whip."

Miss Crawford gives me a cursory nod, and though we have met many times, doesn't call me by name. Immune to my smile, she picks up mid-speech. "Remember, Mr. Fitzgerald, in my movies I never lose my man and I never, ever die."

"Duly noted," he says, doing an excellent impression of a sycophant.

"Write hard, Mr. Fitzgerald," Joan Crawford says with queenly disdain as a waitress in a grass skirt refreshes the rum in her coconut shell. Scott isn't drinking. Fortunately. "Write very hard."

"Indeed," Scott says as Joan swans off, her perfume competing with Jack Warner's rose garden.

"Get hard, Mr. Fitzgerald," I whisper in Scott's ear. "Get very hard." First, Scott looks shocked by my vulgarity, but a moment later he lifts me off the ground, spins me around, and says, "Why Presh, aren't you the tart? But yes, I will try my best."

Five minutes later, we are on our way home.

Scott is on a tight deadline, with weeks ticking away, and as excited as I've seen him. He has his own project, with no incompetent sidekick, and is reporting to an esteemed producer. But on Wednesday he learns that Louis B. Mayer is changing the movie's title to Fidelity. "Infidelity" has landed in the linguistic ash can along with "fanny," "gawd," "hell," and "madame" as Hollywood genuflects to the Hays Code.

"I have moved to the principality of prudes, where an animated cow can't have an udder for fear of offending America's milk drinkers," Scott squawks after an early dinner. "The brains come in and sit around a table. They don't know what they want or where they're going. The only infidelity you can have in a movie now is asking another man's wife to pass the salt. Wardrobe must be working overtime sewing bloomers for Joan fit for my Grandmother McQuillan."

That evening he returns to the Garden of Allah to work. In the morning he phones to say he wrote all night.

It is a blessing and a curse to be the first person to hear gossip. A few days later I discover that LBM is killing the movie. I keep the news to myself, though in a blink, Scott knows he is out of a job.

The next morning he announces that he will visit Zelda. That afternoon deep purple irises arrive with a note in Scott's loopy, straight-up handwriting.

Missing you will be my privilege, exquisite Sheilah.

Your admiring slave,

Scott

He does not say how long he will be away.

For months Scott and I have been one, our love as close as tropical air. I know he adores me, in bed, out of bed, and he's strung my life with fairy lights in such a way I thought it meant he couldn't live without me. I was wrong, as hoodwinked as any innocent who ever lusted for a man owning a wedding ring, even if I've stopped seeing it on his hand. I feel stupid, as well as betrayed, underestimating the bond that must link husband to wife. It must go far beyond the sense of gallantry toward a sick woman that he has intimated. Scott has heard the mating call of marriage and escaped to his madwoman for comfort.

I dump the flowers in the garbage. What rot. Fidelity. Infidelity. I am a victim of both.

Chapter 29

1938

With Scott on the run, I refuse to weep. Resolute as a soldier, I marshal my resilience and call on agents, attend back-to-back screenings, and write a chatty letter to Johnny. For the first time I wish I had a close woman friend, a whole-souled female confidant who doesn't have Dorothy's misanthropy, but I have never dared to let anyone become overly familiar, lest they divine my true identity. Within a town where I know everyone, I've become an island.

Lily Shiel had sisters, lost to her even before she willed Sheilah Graham into existence. Where are my fat sister and my thin sister now, though what could a sister or friend possibly tell me that I cannot tell myself? It requires no keen insight to conclude that in getting involved with a married man, I have risked trading happiness for pain. In that bargain, I am certain to lose.

The days and early evenings go by, and not bitterly. But after midnight, when I am facing sleep, a faceless woman lurches from the shadows to attack me. Zelda. I remain wide-eyed at two, at four, at dawn, my mind running a B-movie loop of despair. I am tempted by the Nembutals Scott swallows as if they were after-dinner mints, but they terrify me as much as heavy drinking does. Instead, I heat a mug of milk and reread Margaret Mitchell. On my bookshelf, I reverse Scott's novels so the spines face inward. If I saw even a title, his voice would fill my head.

It is after the third sleepless night, with visions of Zelda

careening like pinballs, that I decide, if Scott is in North Carolina, I will fly to London, report on hits from the West End
theaters, and enjoy the gentle company of my ex-husband and
constant champion, to whom I continue to send a check every month. He deserves it. Were it not for Major John Gillam,
I might still be Lily Shiel, crippled by a Cockney accent and
graceless manners, her snuffling nose pressed to the glass of
the shiny life I enjoy.

With John Wheeler's blessing and pounds I check myself
into the Dorchester, an upper-crust port of call where on my
first afternoon Johnny and I meet for tea. What a custom, tea.
I didn't realize I missed its civility until I enter the room, done
up in soothing shades of apricot and salmon. Walking to the far
corner, I pass tables set with bone china, serious cutlery, and
three-tiered stands proffering finger sandwiches—succulent
roast chicken, cucumber with minty cream cheese, egg salad
flecked by cress—piled below raisin scones waiting for clotted
cream and strawberry jam, all beneath a crowning display of
pastries, each like a brooch in a jeweler's window.

Around the large room, muted light glows like Lyle's Golden
Syrup from lamps topped by tasseled silk shades. My skirt rustling, I catch the muffled twinkle of chin-wagging. I hear "bol-
locks," "peckish," and twice, "rubbish," but never once "damn,"
"dame," "cute as a bug's ear," "shake a leg," "what's your story,
morning glory?" or "you and me both." With the exception of
a few sylphlike debutante-types squired by handsome beaus, by
Hollywood standards the clientele is proper to the edge of fus-
tiness. Dotty, perhaps, but not flouncing in a cloud of Jungle
Gardenia.

Scott might love it, or at least want to write about it. I also
wonder where, at four o'clock in the afternoon, I would be in
California. Just ending the first shift of my workday, perhaps,
beginning the drive from Burbank. I'd be rolling down the
window in the hope of catching a breeze while longing for an

icy drink, a cool shower, and the release from my girdle and hose, tethered by pinching garters.

Depending on his degree of sobriety, I might be dreaming of Scott.

Here in London, am I home? Not exactly. This London was never truly mine, but Johnny was, and there he is in the corner, his smile a floodlight.

So, my former husband, the man who saved me from being forever Lily Shiel. He stands, bends slightly—not quite a bow— and in his sonorous voice, with enunciation as crisp as a hospital corner, says "Sheilah, dear Sheilah, I can't believe you're here." He extends both hands as I hear the soloist on the grand piano croon, *I'm no millionaire, but I'm not the type to care, 'cause I've got a pocketful of dreams.* Did Johnny tip the musician to play what could be his theme song? I don't recall him having quite that heightened a sense of self-deprecation, but it's another reason to smile as he kisses my hand. In California such a greeting would be riddled by insincerity, but coming from Major Gillam, the gesture is natural. We embrace for seconds beyond perfunctory.

In my pumps, I stand almost eye-to-eye with Scott. I stretch to look up to John; I had forgotten how tall and reedy he is, the sort of Brit who grows older but no less elegant. In the handful of years since I've seen him, his precisely combed hair and flick of a mustache have become as silver as the teapots on each damask-dressed table. His posture remains lance straight, and grin broad but not foolish. I can barely believe this living testimony to England's propriety was once my husband. For a moment, I think, what if we had stayed together in our cordial but sexless marriage cobbled together by kindness and trips to the theater? Then I'd never have met capricious, stormy Scott, thoroughly sauced, equally lovable, and studded with surprises.

"You must tell me everything you leave out of letters," John insists when we get past my flight, accommodations, and plans. "Who is your favorite film star?"

"Spencer Tracy, without a doubt." Knowing he is a Kipling fan and would have seen the movie, I fill Johnny in on the making of *Captains Courageous*.

"Ah, one of my favorites. *Right now, I sorry I speak English,*" my thwarted thespian says, in a fair imitation of Spencer. "That cast sparkled with luminaries."

I give him a rundown not just on Spencer Tracy, but on Mickey Rooney, Lionel Barrymore, and Melvyn Douglas before we cover John's sister, with whom he's had a rapprochement now that he and I are divorced and I'm slumming it thousands of miles away. He does not say, "she told me so," though I'm sure Mrs. William Ashton did. Then we get to his latest job, selling antiquarian maps and ephemera, as well as news of the Nazis marching into the Rhineland and the Rome-Berlin Axis formed by Hitler and Mussolini.

I did not come here to speak of battles. As I finish the last of a lemon tartlet and my second cup of Darjeeling, Johnny reads my mind and signals for the check with a discreet arch of his eyebrow. "What do you say to some fresh air and a bit of a ramble?"

"Hyde Park? Alfred Hitchcock told me this hotel would be ideal for a murder, given the possibilities for burying bodies across the street there." I am name-dropping, but John chuckles, seemingly in appreciation.

"Shall we?" He offers his arm and we walk through the lobby and out the grand front door.

"Are you happy in Hollywood?" he asks as we stroll.

It's a question no one raises, not even one I ask myself, because the answer has become bound up with Scott.

"My work is a challenge, the sleuthing more than the writing, and not nearly as featherbrained as it might appear. I do like it, especially when I one-up my rivals."

"Are there many?"

"First there was only one cunning old cow, but I now have a second even more obstreperous archenemy, and we've formed the unholy trinity from hell."

"Good lord, is there enough gossip to go around?"

"If there isn't, we stir the pot and practice the fine art of innuendo."

"Clever girl," Johnny says, swooping down to place a kiss on my cheek. "Do you imagine you might tire of this Americana and practice your dark art here? Plenty of scandal to monger on the West End alone."

The midday rain has stopped, but fog hovers like a secret over the city, rendered in shades of charcoal as reserved as the populace. I'm surprised to realize I miss the jagged Technicolor glare of Los Angeles, its buildings so new and low they look half-finished, as well as the breezy ocean scent. In London car exhaust makes my nose twitch, and history freights every building, as if to say, wait a few years and you, too, will pass. Even though Scott is as mismatched to Hollywood as a goat is to a petticoat, it's also the only place where I've known him, another point in the city's favor.

"I try not to plan too far ahead, John."

"If you'll forgive my curiosity, whatever became of the Marquess of Donegall?"

I turn to him and shake a finger while I laugh. "Shame on you. You know better than anyone that our match was doomed." Though I have been debating whether I will let Don know I am in town.

"No dashing actor or well-heeled director proposing marriage? I'd hoped that if we weren't together, you'd find a man worthy of you who would give you children, love."

Silence is my answer. John knows my true age—thirty-four— and that if childbearing was my goal, I'd best get a move on.

"As I said, I try not to plan too far ahead," I answer. "Let's talk about tonight—and the next few days." We have lined up several plays. John will be my escort.

I have missed live theater. Johnny suggested *Operette*, Noël Coward's latest, which to my ear falls flat. Noël has done better. *The Fleet's Lit Up* is more to my liking, with a fast pace, brassy music, lavish costumes, eye-popping sets, and broad comedy, topped by a ballet in a newspaper office that I might have to perform for John Wheeler. *Under Your Hat* turns out to be the show I write about, because I know my readers will admire a drama about film stars called upon to track down spies who've stolen some sort of thingamabob of great consequence to the British Air Force. The female lead waltzes across the stage while suffering the hiccups, and, in the guise of a waitress, serves a drink garnished with a goldfish. Pure idiocy, but the antics keep me laughing—and for several hours, my mind off Scott. The point of this trip.

For two afternoons I play tourist at the usual haunts—Big Ben and Parliament, Westminster Abbey, the Tower of London, and the changing of the guard at Buckingham Palace, which I admit to Johnny I'd never seen. But on my third day, rather than tackle the V & A Museum, I set off early for Stepney Green, where the singsong patter of Yinglisch—*oy gevalt, zhat is vun fershtinkene fish*—surrounds me along with the German of somber, well-tailored people I take for refugees.

I wind through crooked lanes: Mile End Road. Frying Pan Alley. Princelet Street, with fine old houses chopped into tiny, airless flats. The streets are as crowded, malodorous, and littered as I recall. Behind every door, I imagine my father. But he will not be found in the Great Zionist Synagogue on the incongruously named Jubilee Street. Tatte davened in one of the humble *shtiebels*—I have no idea which one—that hide behind mezuzahs on every other block. Nor is a doppelganger of little Lily in any of the kosher restaurants on what passes for a high street. The Shiels did not dine out.

I must look lost—I am, in the smoke of memory—when a kindly woman about five or ten years older than I am taps me on the arm as I stand at an intersection, trying to decide whether to turn right or left.

"Help you, Miss?"

I blink and search the face, with its apple cheeks and dark eyes fringed with long lashes. Names swim from the past. What became of my friend Freda and the other bald girls from the Asylum? Could they be walking these streets, pushing prams while older children tug at their long, modest skirts or trail like ducklings? "Freda Rothenfeldt? Is that you?"

I move a few inches closer and the woman tenses so fast you'd think I was Charles Lindbergh Jr.'s kidnapper. She holds tight to her young son, his curly sidelocks bouncing in the wind.

"Ah, pardon me," I say. "I thought you might be a friend of *meine schvester.* I am mistaken." The woman stares. "I lived here as a child," I offer by way of explanation.

"Nu?" she says, still suspicious of a gibbering blonde with an alligator handbag and burgundy-red suit tailored to show off her waist and legs.

There's no way to explain why I am here or what I am looking for, because I do not know myself. A connection? A ghost? An acquittal? I thank the woman and walk on until I find a small café wedged between a wig store and a photographer— Boris Someone—whose window display features wedding couples fancied up for the camera. The faces look happy, or at least not unhappy, as do most of those who stride with purpose up and down the streets.

I sip hot tea in a tall glass and nibble a biscuit, wondering how my life would have turned out had I never broken loose from Stepney Green. Perhaps I would have married someone decent and upstanding from the neighborhood—a taxi driver, let's say, or a butcher with his own shop. By now I'd be as round as a tea cozy, surrounded by an armada of children. Every Friday

I'd braid a challah and light candles for a Sabbath table. I never would have heard of Louella or Hedda, signed my name to a column, driven a car, flown in an airplane, or traveled to Paris, Munich, or Berlin. I'd never have concocted Sheilah Graham or had reason to lie. I'd never have known Sir John Gillam, Randolph Churchill, or Tom Mitford, fallen in love with Scott, or become engaged to the Marquess of Donegall, nor would I have broken off with this good man via a curt letter.

It's the last thought that prompts me to pay my bill, leave a bountiful tip, and return to the Dorchester to wire Don. I don't expect a response. But he phones, immediately, asking if we can meet for a cocktail in two hours' time.

Now I've done it. I get to the lounge early, the least I can do, and consider how, without saying anything overly dramatic, I will be able to channel a woman able to put Don at ease. I do not care to be hated.

Because Scott has become the standard by which I measure males, the first thing I notice when Don walks to my table is how young he looks. The second is his deep suntan.

"Sheilah," he says, kissing me on both cheeks. "Lovely as ever."

"Don, you're the color of a bronze statue." I expect him to say he's been on a seaside vacation. Fiji, perhaps.

"I've been covering the war in Spain."

I know Don to report on wherever his mind meanders—to Dixieland jazz, the maiden voyage of the Queen Mary, vintage cars, Sherlock Holmes, aviation, and the alpine world ski competition in Switzerland. Never politics. "Good Lord, whatever made you put yourself in harm's way?"

Do I see a grimace?

"When the woman you love gives you the old heave-ho, you figure nothing will take your mind off heartbreak faster than a little war. A clash between democracy and fascism is a fine distraction, especially in a warm climate. And, of course, I've long outlived my usefulness as a marquess."

I try to hide that I'm utterly flummoxed. "Where were you?"

"Spain's northern coast, for about five months, filing stories for British newspapers while I hoped I didn't get my legs blown off."

"What you must have seen . . ."

He shakes his head. "I'd rather not talk about it, actually. Or think about it."

"I'm glad you're safely back," I say, though I resist placing my hand on his. I do not feel I have the right.

"I plan to return."

"I wish you wouldn't."

"Why not, Sheilah?" His tone is strident. Not the Don I remember.

"Because I care about you."

"That's rich." Don laughs. "Shall we order?" He catches the eye of a waiter. "For the lady?"

"A martini, please. Dry." Today I need it.

"And for me, my good man, a Thunderstorm."

"Whatever might that be?" I ask when the server steps away, grateful for a benign topic.

"Whiskey, Benedictine, and bitters. My new poison."

I have the feeling this will be the first of several cocktails. He takes a sip, sits back, smiles, and says, "I'm being glib and harsh. That's not fair. You were kind enough to get in touch." He takes another sip. "May I ask why?"

I regain my equanimity, force a smile, and try to find words that aren't threadbare aphorisms. Are there any?

"I wanted to apologize for my abrupt behavior. I am the one who, for no reason, was glib and harsh. I should have treated you differently. I couldn't marry you, but . . ."

He signals for a second drink, while my martini remains untouched. "Couldn't or didn't want to?"

"I simply couldn't see us married." I cross my ankles and will myself not to squirm in discomfort.

"Because you'd met your Mr. Fitzgerald, a man, I might point out, who was and is already married."

Is it Don's wartime experience that has hardened him? I down the rest of my drink in three gulps. "Scott had nothing to do with my decision," I lie.

He takes my hand and softly strokes my empty ring finger. "In that case, could you see reversing it? Because I'm hoping you'll come to your senses and return to me. I miss you, Sheilah. Why let an engagement ring gather dust in a vault?"

"Don, it's been years."

"My feelings haven't changed."

Nor have mine. I regret that I am an intractable romantic rather than a pragmatist. "I can't see it working, Don."

"Even if I fly you to Paris tomorrow in my plane?"

I am happy to see Don smiling. "Tempting as both offers are, tomorrow is when I return to the States. But I thank you."

"And so our story ends," he announces, as if he were narrating an Agatha Christie novel.

"Oh, you never know," I say, and we kiss. I feel . . . nothing but a profound ache for Scott and home.

Chapter 30
1938

The day after I return, Scott calls while traveling West. He will be home tomorrow. I respond coolly. "No, I can't have dinner. Terribly busy." Then there is more.

"Sheilo, we can marry."

"Excuse me?" I shudder.

"You're going to be a beautiful bride, and you will make me happier than I deserve to be. I love you. I want you to be my wife. We belong together . . ." and more, as if there weren't enough ordinary words to capture his joy. "We'll make a baby together, Presh. I want a son, a better version of me. No, I want another daughter, one who looks just like you. Tomorrow I'll take you in my arms and we'll begin the next Fitzgerald."

"Oh, Scott." My heart is a hummingbird, beating its wings. I never imagined a proposal or a baby together—or let myself hope for either. It's unexpected, terrifying, and thrilling. I may melt into the rug.

"Truly?" I ask Scott.

"Yes, my Presh. You are the heart and hope of freshness. I will see you soon and show you how I feel."

I hang up and with ticklish glee, push aside the typewriter on my desk, pick up a fountain pen, and like a schoolgirl, begin writing over and over, *Mrs. F. Scott Fitzgerald. Sheilah Fitzgerald. Sheilah Graham Fitzgerald. Sheilah Graham Gillam Fitzgerald.*

And a baby? A child offers the promise of unconditional love and being loved in return. I admit to myself that the prospect of motherhood was the best part of marrying Don, better even than his title. I thought he would be a devoted papa. Judging from the concern Scott shows for Scottie through his constant letters, he, too, will be a fine father. I feel a silvery skyscraper of warmth and desire for Scott, whom I sometimes believe reads me better than I read myself. He has asked me to marry him because he realizes I want to create the family I never had.

After a night when I sail on crests of joy, confiding in my pillow, and surely do not sleep at all, I fill my flat with tulips and daisies, and buy juicy sirloins and the greengrocer's freshest artichokes, each like a rose in full bloom. It is when I remind myself that I cannot serve Champagne that I slam into the truth. Scott may be my *beshert*. My destiny. But do I dare marry him? Whatever am I thinking? I have never cared for anyone this deeply, but he is not a man I can wholly trust.

Rubbish, I tell myself. It's your nerves talking. But like mold on fruit, the worry spreads.

At seven o'clock, he calls from the airport, elated. "Be there in a half hour, Sheilo." Thirty minutes pass. I have set the table in the spot on my terrace that catches a refreshing twilight breeze. Fifteen more minutes tick by. An hour. Could Scott have been in an accident? I picture him hurt or worse. Finally, with profound relief, I hear his car grind up my hill. I run to the door.

He spills onto the sidewalk, unkempt. When he gets closer I see his eyes are bloodshot.

"Sheilo, how I've missed you." He literally falls into my arms, all stubble and alcoholic kisses.

My expectations calcify to a veneer of disillusionment.

"Do you know what the bitch did? Tried to get me committed. She's the devil, that one. Untethered and dangerous." Inside, Scott sucks on a cigarette as if it's oxygen he needs for life support, and while it's still lit, lights another, as he paces in circles.

The sense of romance that for the last twenty-four hours

wrapped me in a wedding veil has blown out the window, through which I would like to hurl Scott. "Our conversation?" I ask. "Are you getting a divorce or not?"

"Damn right, I am. I've had it this time. I'm done. My marriage is dead. R.I.P. to the saddest family in America." He makes the sign of the cross.

"What did Zelda say when you told her?"

With dead eyes he stares over my head.

"Does Zelda know you're divorcing?"

Plans to leave Zelda may have crossed his mind—I will give him that—but there is no separation in the works. I am a child whose birthday cake has been snatched and trampled and yet he doesn't notice.

"Back in a minute," he says, and runs to his car.

I could pick up the paperweight on my table and throw it at the back of his head, but my internal brake is still on.

"Baby, I'm glad to see you," Scott says when he returns with a bottle in his hand and gives me a sloppy kiss. "You have no idea."

I squirm out of his embrace. "Oh, but I do." I know the crush of disappointment and the swell of anger. "I have the idea that you'll never get another job in this town if people know you're drinking again."

"Don't tell a soul," he says dramatically.

"Get out of here." I dismiss Scott in the voice of Matron Weiss. "Go home and sleep it off."

"But Sheilo," he says. "It's you I love."

What does that matter? "Go home. Go home. Go home."

He does.

At two o'clock in the morning, the doorbell rings. Of course it is Scott. His car has announced him. He bangs on the door and yells my name as I get out of bed and throw on a wrapper.

"What now?" I ask peeking over the chain lock.

"My shoulder—I think I broke it."

There is a story I can't follow about a brawl in a parking lot. "Get in my car, now," I say and drive to the nearest hospital, run by an order of nuns who could make a general cower. Scott's shoulder is only sprained, and he is discharged.

"Take me to your bed," he begs.

"Not on your life. I don't want to see you till you've stopped drinking. You're a brilliant man. How can you do this to yourself again? It's degrading, and it's not only to you, it demeans me as well. Do you think at all of how your behavior makes me feel?" I cross my arms over my bosom and won't avert my eyes until he answers.

"I can quit, you know." His voice is barely a murmur.

"So you say."

"It's hell, but I'll dry out. I'll get a doctor. Nurses."

"You should copyright that speech."

We drive to the Garden of Allah, the twenty-four-hour cock-tail party that is the last place Scott should live. I'm not fully listening as he describes the cure, though the words "vomit" and "intravenous feeding" escape.

A week later, the inevitable flowers arrive with a note of apology. Scott begs me to visit. I refuse. More flowers. More apologies. Days pass. I have two choices, love him—which truly isn't a choice—or leave him. But I think of a third option and agree to visit.

Scott is wobbly and pale, though he has made an effort. Sober Scott always makes an effort. When I arrive he's in a bow tie and a pink shirt. Like a sentencing judge, I spell out my terms.

"If you want to see me, not only must you stay sober, I want you to move to a cottage I found at the beach, in the movie colony." I exalt Malibu's advantages as if I were a real estate agent. "It's cheaper than your flat, three times as big, only a forty-five-minute drive to the studio, and the housekeeper—Flora—is willing to stay for fifty dollars a week."

With its green shutters and clapboard, the shack could have

been transplanted from Long Island, albeit not anywhere near West Egg. If Scott has a late evening, I tell him he can stay with me on King's Road. Instead of smoky rooms with clinking ice cubes, he'll be surrounded by fresh sea air while he, ever the observer of human nature, can take notes on movie stars enjoying illicit assignations. I'll visit often and we'll walk on the beach, swim, soak up the warmth, and go to sleep to the lull of waves crashing against the rocks. Nothing, to me, is as vitalizing as the ocean. I refuse to believe its soothing powers can't restore Scott Fitzgerald.

Malibu is my fantasy, not Scott's, but the man is too weak to object. The next Saturday, I help him move his meager possessions to 114 Malibu Beach.

We fall into a gentle rhythm. I spend every weekend there along with one or two weeknights. From what I can tell, he takes to the tranquility of the sun and surf, praising Flora's fried chicken and reporting that he is positive he saw Errol Flynn skinny-dipping with a girl who couldn't be older than sixteen.

Chapter 31

1938

Scott is switched to Clare Boothe Luce's Broadway hit *The Women*, yet another exploration of adultery, which lately—perhaps I'm hyperaware of this, being the poster girl for the topic—seems to be Hollywood's pet subject. It's a comedy of manners that reflects the viewpoint of females, on which Scott considers himself an authority, though I'd say he idolizes women far too much to truly understand us. Were Scott on the project alone, it could be a good fit. But boo-hoo. Donald Ogden Stewart and Anita Loos are collaborating as well, and Scott has proven he doesn't play well with others, especially if they're friends with top-flight screenwriting track records. "Nothing is as obnoxious as other people's luck," he complains. My role of consoling him is wearing me down. To distract both of us, I suggest luring our friends to Malibu for a beach party.

He has orchestrated the afternoon as if he were planning a military campaign: volleyball, relays, boxing matches, a tug-of-war, and a Ping-Pong tournament, for which Scott compiled teams, handicaps and all. There's plenty of beer and lemonade, though Scott promises to drink only ice water.

It's a fine day with a light breeze scattering clouds that rise like small soufflés. Flora and I have set out her deviled eggs, fried chicken, and macaroni salad along with watermelon and chocolate chip cookies. Our friends start arriving at noon—Dorothy and Alan, John O'Hara, Jonah, Eddie, Nunnally Johnson and his wife, Marion Byrnes, and about a dozen others.

Scott greets each arrival like the lord of the manor, oozing charm as if he were Dick Diver at the start of *Tender Is the Night.*

"Hey, old man."

"Looking fetching."

"No party without you, my friend."

"Watch out, O'Hara, you rank amateur."

He wraps one arm around my waist and I think how there are times when a hug means far more than a kiss. I am standing next to my beloved, the sun bouncing off the sea as if it is reflecting my happiness. Though it's common knowledge that Scott and I are together, this is our first party. I feel like a bride. I wear a white eyelet sundress trimmed with ruffles, a broad straw hat, and a proud smile. I want everyone to have a good time, Scott especially.

About an hour after the guests arrive I point out two children peeking over the fence that separates our property from the next. The girl has long blond plaits; the boy is a towhead with curls and freckles. They must be about eight and ten.

"Come along," Scott says to them in a friendly voice. "Join the party."

I have never seen him with young children. He pulls a deck of cards from his pocket and begins to do tricks. "Here's one I learned from a murderer at San Quentin," he stage-whispers. "Now watch carefully." He shuffles the deck, closes his eyes, and pirouettes three times. "Abracadabra." Four kings appear.

When Scott wills it, magic surrounds him. I close my eyes and wish the children were ours.

The afternoon flits by and my ringmaster showers the same attention on our friends that he shows the children. More card tricks. Jokes. Songs. Also an odd prank played on a writer named Charlie, who is recovering from back surgery. Scott asks to speak to the man's date in private. "I hate to be the messenger of bad news, but your Charlie is suffering from syphilis. Hence the brace. Without it he'd fall apart."

The girl shrieks and demands that someone give her a ride home, abandoning Charlie. "You haven't said anything to offend her, pal, have you?" Scott asks him, all innocence and nectar.

I take Scott aside. "The joke's gone too far. You owe the poor guy an apology and tomorrow, you better send that woman a flower arrangement bigger than her head."

"Mind your own fucking business," he snaps, and as the verbal blow lands, I know. That isn't water in his glass. Whatever brio has carried Scott along since noon has turned to reeling intoxication. It is also too late to hope that no guest heard his disrespect. As if on cue, people gather their partners and possessions, heading for cars.

Nunnally and his wife are walking out of the house with their bag when Scott yanks him by the arm and shoves him back inside and into the front bedroom, which—strangely—locks from the outside, making me wonder if our landlord routinely kept prisoners.

"Open that door at once," I shout to Scott.

"Listen boy, get out of Hollywood before you're ruined," he yells to his hostage. "I can't see you sell your soul."

"What the hell?" Nunnally barks, pummeling the door. "Let me out."

"Let him out!" I echo.

"In a pig's eye. Not till you promise to do as I say, Nunn. Hollywood sucks the blood from every decent writer. If you have talent, it will kill it." Scott begins to list all the writers who he believes have been destroyed by writing perfunctory plots for movies. Anita Loos, Donald Ogden Stewart, and Ted Panatere make the list, though, curiously, he himself does not.

"I'd be a chump to give it up," Nunnally bellows from his jail cell. "I earn more here than anywhere. Good God, why would I run away?"

"To preserve your gift, my friend."

"You're a literary lion—" I hear a facetious tone, but Scott nods, taking the praise as his due. "I don't have a special gift. I'm a penny-a-line guy who needs the work. A drudge."

"Sweetheart, no. You're much better than that," wails Marion, his wife.

"Darling, I'll handle this," Nunnally says, his voice muffled yet irate. "Now let me out, Fitzgerald, for Chrissake."

"He's right. Let him out," I say for the umpteenth time. I cannot fathom why Scott fails to grasp that Hollywood writers are mere hired hands, expected to bootlick. They stick together not because they like one another—though occasionally they do—but to share grievances. None of them actually roots for the next guy.

"Sheilo, stay out of this."

"You'll not speak to me that way, Scott."

"Listen to Sheilah," Nunnally says.

"Please, Mr. Fitzgerald," Marion moans.

Perhaps it's the "Mister" that makes Scott say, "I'll open the door, you sorry sonofabitch, so long as you give me your word you'll make plans to return to New York and protect your talent."

"I promise, I promise." Nunnally's voice is hoarse and frantic.

Scott unlocks the door. Nunnally and Marion make for his car like greyhounds, with Scott—slower, drunker—in pursuit. He bangs on the car door. "You'll never come back here. Never."

"Nunnally, we hope you and Marion will visit again soon," I say and feel the eyes of the other guests, though I'm long past embarrassment.

"No, he'll never come back because it makes him sick that I live here with my paramour," Scott hisses, and turns to the few people who remain, "and all the rest of you feel the same way. You're disgusted that I'm living in sin with Sheilah"—he looks me up and down—"in her ridiculous virginal dress."

"Sheilah, ignore the bum." Dorothy turns to Scott and adds, "For fuck's sake, shut up, you jackass."

But Scott repeats "paramour," a word from an era of less forgiving morals. I slap him, hard, across his face, for this unforgivable coda to my storybook afternoon. He stands still, mumbling,
"What the hell?" while the guests who remain pile into cars.
I send them off with hasty goodbyes, summoning a residue of
dignity. Then I turn to Scott. "Why can't you behave like a
gentleman?" But I don't wait for the answer. I run to the ocean.

Scott is a beast. Scott has an illness he cannot control. Scott is
a childish mess on whom God made a grave error when He bestowed on him talent of staggering proportions. Scott is infected
by Zelda's craziness. Scott made Zelda batty. Scott hurts those
he loves and drags them down with him.

I hate Scott. I love Scott. From the distance, I see him peel
away in his car. I believe he is exceeding his twenty-mile-an-
hour speed limit.

I muster my equanimity and help Flora clean the cottage
before I send her home. The air is turning cold, but I return to
the beach and let the waves drown out a new wave of sobs. I'm
standing at the water's edge when Scott returns with a fresh
bottle of gin, and walks toward me. I expect an overweening
apology, but he continues on as if I don't exist, into the ocean,
fully clothed.

Scott has chosen tonight for his inaugural swim in Malibu.

As if it were a spear, I throw the first item I can find, a rotted
oar. My tennis arm refuses to fail me, and the oar smacks Scott's
shoulder as he bobs in the surf. "Are you trying to kill me?" he
shouts.

I head for my car and drive back to Hollywood, hoping he
drowns.

The next afternoon, the roses arrive. A note dripping with con-
trition follows, and then calls that would plead for forgiveness
did I not hang up, again and again. I have made sure I do not

have an empty evening looming by planning a dinner with Robert Taylor. It's a work-related engagement that I initiated, but I dress in a raspberry pink, form-fitting cocktail suit. Robert escorts me to his Cadillac, where his driver waits. Halfway down the block, Scott is parked, stalking me.

All Robert seems to have in common with Scott, who is fifteen years older, is chain smoking. Though it's nothing like the bond I feel with Scott, I sense a frisson of electricity with Robert, whose version of indigenous midwestern American appeal is entirely his own; the man does not allow his emotions to hang out like shirttails. "In Nebraska," he says, "should a feeling come up, we shoo it into the barn and lock it up." It's a night sealed by a more than pleasant kiss shortly past midnight. By that time, Scott's car is gone, but at ten in the morning he calls.

"Looking for your paramour?" I ask.

"That slur was unforgivable, Sheilo," he says. "You know it was the gin talking. I'm so very sorry."

"But why were you drinking?" My voice rises. "Your promises are hollow. Tell me, what was the point of suffering through your cure?"

"I realize even my friends think I'm a dissipated carcass. I was trying to be an impresario, a natural-born host, like Gerald Murphy back in the day. I couldn't, not without liquid to blur the lines."

"You're stronger than that."

"I'm not, evidently. I'm fallible, a flawed fellow who loves his Sheilah. Do you love me?"

I remain angry. "That's never been in question. The point is, you hurt me."

"I'm so sorry—I will say it a thousand times. Hurting you hurts me. Please, Presh. Another chance."

"Why?" My voice rises. "You'll only hurt me again. I need you to promise you'll never do that."

"I won't. I adore you."

Do I dare believe him? I want to, but I'm afraid. "I also need to know, do you drink to find yourself or to lose yourself?"

He pauses before he answers. "I honestly can't say. Probably both, and it's always a mistake."

I am familiar with mistakes. I have made a tradition of them.

My mind ticks off an inventory of Scott's best qualities: gentleness, kindness, humor, self-deprecation, generosity, myopic devotion—is there anything I have ever said to him that the man doesn't recall?—and his willingness not to blame anyone but himself for his shortcomings. Apart from the drunk lives the real Scott, an entirely different man. There are two Scotts, and I apparently can't have one without the other.

I can now chart the cycle of our reconciliations. Biblical indignation. Disappearance. Flowers and apology. Then it gets to the dangerous part, where I fall in love all over again, never failing to expect that the high will be higher than the last low.

Inevitably, with Scott, this brew leads to reconciliation, his Puritan temporarily locked away in the closet. We reunite, insatiable.

Scott is addicted to alcohol, and I am addicted to the only man who has ever truly *seen* me. "Sheilo, only you can figure me out," he has claimed. That works both ways. Others have admired my appearance, even temperament and charm, but he alone penetrates beyond these attributes to love me for my intellect, my heart, and my character. We are each the answer that completes the other's crossword puzzle.

Scott responds to me as no one has before. He listens and takes me seriously, and it has been this way since the moment we met. The minute he breaks into a smile, tilts his head, looks at me a certain way, and calls me "Presh" or "Sheilo," I'm there, adoring him, ready to spontaneously combust.

Speaking to Scott now reminds me of how much I miss kissing him and being kissed. My resolve begins to wash away like a sandcastle crumbling at the beach. I want to strip off his shirt, bury my head in his chest, and savor the salty smell of his sweat mixed with his citrusy aftershave. I'm willing to overlook a wide swath of ghastly behavior to have that again with the closeness it brings. No other man will do. I want the real Scott. I cannot give him up. Why am I torturing myself?

"We'll give it a try," I say.

I take him back once more and try to forgive not only him, but also myself. Later that night we begin with dinner at our favorite Italian joint, where we can't keep our hands off one another, and make each other dessert at my place. As I offer Scott amnesty, our lovemaking weaves the real and the imaginary while my feelings flood back. I am exactly where I want and need to be, in his arms, hearing him murmur, "I love you. Please don't leave me. I depend on your love to get me through the day and night." This brings on a contentment that echoes in my dreams, even after Scott has fallen asleep. I curl myself next to him, our arms around one another. I could stay here forever.

Chapter 32

1938

It's a given that in each of his novels a lovesick hero, one of the characters Scott refers to as "his brothers," is his own dead ringer, besotted with someone like Zelda—or at least like Zelda once was—cultured and wealthy. I pretend to be a working girl version of Daisy Buchanan, but if I resemble any of Scott's characters, it's his twenty-four-carat fake: Jay Gatsby. Both of us changed our names, concealed our pasts, and with a blast of bravado have created an alias that we pray society will admire. Our similarities extend even to the photographs we display to disprove our deception. We are successful, Jay and I, albeit in undignified fields, bootlegging and gossipmongering, and to the world, we are all confidence. Inwardly, we feel perpetually second-rate.

I am sorry I have read to the end of *Gatsby*.

After lunch at the MGM commissary, as Eddie and I walk to our respective appointments, I admit that sometimes I'm baffled by Scott's love for me. He throws back his head and roars, "You're gorgeous and bright. How many women would be happy with him?"

I turn my voice icily British. "Because he often drinks to excess?"

"You do have a gift for understatement. The party in Malibu?"

"He was trying too hard to show everyone a good time," I say in Scott's defense. "He apologized for days afterwards."

"Let's not forget he's also married, and I don't predict a divorce."

"Harsh, Eddie." But true. I concede to myself that most women past thirty who aspire to becoming a wife and mother would have moved on. They also wouldn't stick with a man who complains about his health, which Scott has started to do, though he continues to smoke nonstop, live off canned turtle soup and Hershey bars, and pop pills to sleep each night and more to rise and shine every morning.

"You could have anyone in this town," Eddie says. "Me, for example. Why him?"

I flash a grin. "You don't know the Scott I know," although I am not sure how well I, or anyone, understands the man I love.

After my afternoon appointments I drive to Martindale's Book Shop in Beverly Hills. Perhaps I'll find the answer to why I want Scott so in Marcel Proust's novel, which Eddie and the others were discussing today at lunch. It intrigued me when Eddie said, "Swann was insanely in love with Odette, but when it ended, he said, 'She wasn't even my type.'"

That night when Scott sees the books I've bought, his mouth drops open. "A little light reading, baby? Whatever possessed you?"

I slink off to the kitchen. He follows me, and puts both hands on my shoulders. "Did I insult you? I'm so very sorry. You have the brains for Proust but to tackle him, you need to bite off only a morsel at a time." At the kitchen table, he grabs the pad I use for grocery lists and hands it back a minute later. "This is what Professor Fitzgerald suggests." He assigns me ten pages a day of *Swann's Way* until I'm a third through, then thirty pages a day. For the last third, I'm to read forty pages a day. Only then can I start the second book, and so on, until I've read all seven. He hands me the first volume. "I'll keep the others for later," he says.

Over the course of many months—when Scott is back on the wagon and our life is smooth as cream—I read *Remembrance of Things Past* so slowly I might have been scaling the Alps with a twenty-pound pack. But I smell the madeleine. I drink the tisane and I begin to relive not just the author's childhood, but my own. I see my white-blond hair fall to my feet as it's snipped close to my skull. I gag on orphanage potatoes, eyes still sprouting in them. I smell my own urine each morning on the straw mattress where for two years I'm forced to sleep.

Proust's characters come alive, in particular a Madame Verdurin, who buries her face in her hands at a crisis. Much to Scott's amusement, I begin to do the same if Flora burns the soup or I forget to return a phone call. As I turn the pages I stop looking for why Scott loves me and I love Scott, and revel in the fact that I can decode the arcane language and enjoy exercising my mind in this new way.

"I've never met anyone who's as quick a study as Sheilah," Scott boasts to Dorothy.

Months pass—happy months—and when I finish the seventh volume of Proust, he treats me to lobster at the pier, and gives me the novel *Vanity Fair*, liberated from the studio library. "You need this book more than MGM does," he says. "You'll like Thackeray."

I see myself in Becky Sharp, who fights for what she wants, which, in her case, is position. I fight for acceptance and decide they're not unrelated. I want to be seen, not as a dumb blonde, but as the intelligent heroine of my own life. Scott sees me that way, the very foundation of our bond. I feel closer to him than anyone else in my entire life.

He follows *Vanity Fair* with *Alice's Adventures in Wonderland* and *Through the Looking Glass*, books I read long ago with only a token understanding. He explains their satire. I realize that around him, I might actually be developing a public sense of humor. Since I've always obsessed about how I'm judged, I have rarely permitted myself unrestrained laugher. But his gaiety is infectious. He guffaws so hard he almost chokes, taking special pleasure in puncturing pomposity. In front of our friends, I hear myself laughing, too.

One Friday night we attend a screening for *Jezebel*. At the opener, the voice-over proclaims, "From the Old South, a gorgeous spitfire who was loved when she should have been whipped," and we both snicker. Our tittering stops, however, as the story unfolds. Jezebel is an impetuous Southern belle cut from the same satin as Zelda. As the plot unfolds, he sinks lower in his seat, and when *Jezebel* ends, says only, "Terrible casting. Bette Davis was too hard-boiled for the role."

I disagree. Bette's strength did not diminish her appeal. I plan to publish exuberant praise.

For most of the drive to Malibu, Scott is quiet. Shortly before we arrive he comes to life and begins to recite:

Fair youth, beneath the trees, thou canst not leave
Thy song, nor ever can those trees be bare;
Bold Lover, never, never canst thou kiss,
Though winning near the goal yet, do not grieve;
She cannot fade, though thou hast not thy bliss,
For ever wilt thou love, and she be fair!

His voice is a caress. Eddie, I think, this is the authentic Scott, not the party drunkard. I feel his love in each phrase and surprise myself by crying. I repeat the lines, *"Beauty is truth, truth beauty."*

"Isn't it unbearably brilliant?" he says. "Each word is as perfect as a note in Beethoven's Ninth. After Keats, most other poetry is like humming."

When we get to the house, Scott reads me all of "Ode on a Grecian Urn," followed by "Ode to a Nightingale," from which he borrowed "tender is the night" to title his novel. Although I suspect that I am not the first woman to have been the recipient of one of his private poetry recitals, it becomes its own seduction, to which I willingly succumb. With each line, he removes a piece of my clothing as I do the same for him. After we make love, he declaims "To His Coy Mistress" as, under the covers, he lazily traces the contours of my body.

"I'm amazed that men and women who lived hundreds of years ago feel the same way about love I do."

If my remark is naïve, Scott shows no disdain. "Exquisite writing captures those passions. You discover your longings are universal and you're not lonely and isolated. That's part of the beauty of all literature."

Writing like his. "You hope to be immortal, don't you, darling?" I ask in a rush I regret; one thing Scott never kids about is his writing.

"For a few years I thought as much," he says, after a considerable pause. "Now the second printing of *Gatsby* is gathering dust in a warehouse and the joke's on me. But I'm like the athlete who's let himself go to fat and has decided to make a comeback. That's why I want to write another novel, Sheilo. I still hope."

As do I. I squeeze his hand and know better than to speak. He lights a cigarette and turns on the radio. I expect him to find music that matches our mood, perhaps even get up and ask me to dance, but instead, Adolf Hitler's invective explodes in our bedroom like a volley of grenades, overpowering even the crash of waves we hear through open windows. No translation required.

"I'd like to fly over there and assassinate Herr Hitler before he starts another war," Scott says, not for the first time. During the Great War he never saw combat, which he regrets, especially when Ernest chides him about this as if it illustrates a character flaw that Second Lieutenant Francis Scott Key Fitzgerald, in his custom-tailored Brooks Brothers uniforms, should have corrected.

"I've been to Munich, you know, six years ago," I say, "with my friend Tom Mitford and his sister."

"Oh? You've never mentioned it."

"I expected Mozart and marzipan, but I wound up terrified."

Scott bombards me with questions. I summon answers I've shared with no one. I relive the Nazi banners and inescapable swastikas. The boisterous Party headquarters where soldiers Heil Hitlered each other as they goose-walked in glossy, knee-high boots. I paint a picture of SS-Rottenfuhrer Otto von Pfeffel and his gift to Unity and speak of the no-Jews-and-dogs signs and the placard that read *Juda verrecke*, which I learned meant not just that Jews should die, but that they should come to an agonizing end. I drag it all into the light.

Scott appears spellbound. "You did understand that Hitler is a monster who wants to kill democracy?"

"Not completely. All I wanted was to leave."

"Did you sense how much he reviles the Jews?"

What I sense is a whiff of rebuke, as if I, Sheilah the giant-killer, missed the chance to single-handedly wage war against the German chancellor. I reel with culpability as well as the cowardice that I spoke of at Tatte's grave. But I am also getting angry.

"Most people see Jews as noisy, evil, pushy, too smart for their good." *Our* own good. "Everyone despises the Jews." I stop short of adding, *even you.* My declaration stuns Scott to silence—unfortunate, because I plough ahead. "Your Meyer in *Gatsby* had not one redeeming trait. He's a moneylender, obese and disloyal, with hairy nostrils and cuff links made of human molars, and his Yiddish accent is a parody right out of vaudeville."

I can't read Scott's expression. Horrified? Contrite?

"In *The Beautiful and Damned* isn't there a Jewish storekeeper with 'suspicious' eyes?" I ask, my voice toughening. "Once you portrayed a Jewish movie studio head as slimy and power-grubbing and somewhere"—the tirade gathers speed until I can barely breathe—"I'm positive you wrote of a 'little kike'?"

Scott's face flushes. "These are low blows," he snaps in a voice as loud as my own. "I modeled Wolfsheim on Arnold Rothstein, a gangster who happened to be a Jew. Good Lord, he fixed the 1919 World Series, which to me makes him fascinating, not unlike many of our Jewish friends, and we have plenty. And Jewish bosses." He knits his eyebrows. "Thalberg was Jewish and a king."

"Yes, I know, you've practically canonized him."

"Call me provincial—I deserve it—but I'm not malicious. Where is this coming from?"

I'd like to think Scott's characters simply mirror prejudices of the day, not what's in his heart. But how can I be sure? "I'm sorry I brought it up. May we change the subject?"

"No, because you're attacking me," he says in a slow drip. "I'll admit my mother, who was as small-minded as she was hideous, probably believed Christian boys were killed at Easter so Jews could drink their blood. But my father wasn't a bigot and neither am I." He grasps my wrist and pulls me toward him. "I deserve a clarification."

I try to wriggle free. "Stop badgering. Please."

He releases me but asks, "Whatever caused this harangue? You're being irrational and that, darling, is my department. Tell me, please, what set this off." His voice is still curdled, though no longer loud. "You're acting like a child."

I feel like six-year-old Lily who lost her doll, Kichel. "Scott, I'm sorry. I . . . I . . . ." I explode with tears, race downstairs, and slam the door behind me, barricading myself in the small, front bedroom. Scott stands outside and calls my name. After twenty minutes I hear him walk away.

I sob until I have no tears left. I'm crying about my lies to Scott, my lies to myself, my lies to the world, my lies to God. I've tried to wear them lightly, but they feel like a hand pushing me under water. In time I am crying simply because I am crying. I wail until I fall into a vacant sleep.

Early the next morning, I walk to the bathroom for aspirin.

My head is pounding, and my face is puffy with eyes swollen to slits. I brew a cup of tea and sit on the patio, waiting for sunrise. Hours pass before I hear Scott.

He comes to my side, takes my hand to his heart, and kisses my cheek. "Good morning," is all he says.

"Scott, I'm sorry," I say after minutes of silence. "I don't know what came over me." But of course, I know. I have been a dormant Mount Vesuvius for half my life. *Bei mir bist du schoen.* "Please let me explain. But one condition, please," I place two fingers on his lips. "Do not cross-examine me." I am ready to crack the seal on my secret, and blurt out the story I never told anyone in entirety.

Chapter 33

1938

I've never wanted to reveal the truth about myself to Scott, thinking he has chosen me and I want him to be proud. He shouldn't feel that the woman he loves is a grubby little waif with a history of deceptions. But I count to ten and begin.

"My parents are dead—that part is true—but they weren't John and Veronica Roslyn Laurence from Chelsea who perished in a car crash. As I'm sure you've guessed by my lack of education, I wasn't taught by tutors, nor did I attend a French finishing school. I was forced to quit school at fourteen. I did marry Sir John Gillam, but he was my employer, not a family friend. Often we couldn't pay our bills unless I made some money and"—it feels disrespectful to Johnny, but I feel compelled to tell the truth—"he was impotent. He encouraged me to be with other men."

Scott hops up from his chair, his eyes widening. "What kind of husband would act this way? He was a pimp?"

"Don't say that. Johnny is a wonderful man." I refuse to think otherwise. "Sit down and listen, please. My childhood, I assure you, was the real humiliation." I'm in the thick of it now and cannot stop, my voice mechanical as I try to tell the story straight. "I come from one of London's filthiest slums. My father's name was Louis Shiel. He was a tailor from a shtetl in Russia. My mother spoke only Yiddish and cleaned toilets for a living. After Tatte died, she couldn't afford to take care of me, so she left my brother and me at a charity institution. That's where I grew up and went to school, with a shaved head, clothes that barely kept me warm, and inedible food—at the Jews' Orphan Asylum."

"The Jews?" Scott gawks as if he is watching a movie. "An asylum?" I expect him to say, "Stop right there, Sheilo—I need to grab a pad and pen."

I start with the first day at the orphanage, and try to confess every indignity. "I was raised among poor, shabby people. I'm a phony. A sham. My name's not Sheilah Graham. Those family photos you saw are fakes, and I used to speak like this." I exhume my Cockney. "Did ya clock the bloody size of that rat?" I describe the squalor of Stepney Green, not just the vermin, but the lice, the squalid basement flat, the stink of the brewery, and the vomiting drunkards, who terrified me and tried to touch my breasts and bum as I passed them in unlit lanes.

"As bad as Stepney Green was, I am worse. Scott, I slapped my mother as she was dying. I've abandoned the faith of my mama and Tatte, who was a pious man. I adored my brother Morris, but cut him out of my life as if he never existed. I have no idea where he lives, or even if he is alive."

I could have been in a synagogue on Yom Kippur ticking off my sins as I retch up details that reflect my shameful burden. "Before the Marquess of Donegall I was engaged to a rich businessman I loathed. When I broke it off, he"—here is something I have kept to myself all these years—"hung himself because of my rebuff. If Jews believed in hell, I'd burn for eternity."

The shock on Scott's face is matched by my own. I'm surprised that I am able to release my sewer of facts, but my lies have been choking me. I've talked for an hour, and am left thoroughly drained.

"You can never tell anyone what you know," I say. "Never."

As I gave vent, Scott's face contorted along with mine, but now he turns solemn. "I'm baffled. You say 'Jewish' as if it's your worst humiliation, but almost every tycoon in this town probably grew up in a village one mule ride away from your father's. The Warners, Louis B. Mayer, even Thalberg with his yellow Rolls."

I drop my shoulders and sigh. "But you don't see them making movies *about* Jews, do you? These men practically invented the American dream, which their films perpetuate."

It's Scott's turn to be breathless. "Granted, but this is also what confuses me. To the refugees who wash up here, Hollywood is a rubbish heap. They'd give anything to have their old life back, *mit schlag*. They'd return to Berlin or Vienna or Warsaw or even Minsk in a heartbeat for serious philosophizing and some decent pastry. When Max Factor opened his salon, he invited what, a thousand Jews who were also here from Europe?"

Why can't I get through? "You're speaking of refugees raised with culture, refinement, and education. No one was an underfed, bald-headed girl held hostage in hand-me-down boots at an asylum—and plenty of refugees who arrive here don't admit they're Jews."

He pulls me to him. "Sheilo, if only I'd been there to save you from all this—those other men especially . . . their hands on you." What seems to trouble him most is the junction where my past encroaches on his territory. He embraces me tightly. "I think I may be ill."

I break away. "I can't face you. I don't even want to face myself. Could you please drive me home?" In the car we do not speak, though my confession echoes in a silent squall. When we reach my villa, Scott walks me to my door, takes three Nembutal from his pocket, presses them into my hand, and kisses me on the forehead before he returns to his car. I swallow the drugs, crawl into bed, and close my eyes. Were I a gambling woman, I'd bet I'd never see Scott Fitzgerald again.

Chapter 34

1938

sleep until the next afternoon and wake, my linens tangled and moist with perspiration, to a persistent ringing of the doorbell. If it's Scott, I do not want to face him, but the sound will not stop.

Even though it's Sunday, a delivery boy who must have earned a hefty tip drops off a bouquet of jasmine. *For your grace and intelligence, Scott.* The note is gallant but distant. No *Sheilo*, no *Presh*, no *love*. Nor does Scott call, though we had planned to meet friends at the Santa Anita racetrack. I had been looking forward to cheering on the thoroughbreds and their jockeys in flamboyant silks.

I spend the day wondering what part of my fraud sickens Scott most? That I have the temerity to become enraged by his drinking, a common shortcoming, when my defects are far more egregious? The irony that despite my deceit, I have the chutzpah to make my living by spilling secrets more innocent than my own?

Marlene Dietrich is contemplating *a divorce* in order to marry Douglas Fairbanks, Jr.

After playing the signature role in *Dracula's Daughter*, Gloria Holden is seen as a ghoul and can't get work. She's had her nose shortened and her hairline plucked higher in hopes of capturing the delicacy of Myrna Loy.

Dear readers, Ernst Lubitsch suffers from the immortal sin of being short.

Is Clark Gable the father of Loretta Young's baby? Just asking.

Well, not entirely innocent.

There is still no word from Scott, who I hoped might stop by on the way to the studio. But I cannot enjoy the luxury of sulking. I drive to one of Burbank's most distant back lots to interview Gary Cooper. Even in eyeliner Mr. Glamour-in-a-Saddle is six feet and one hundred eighty pounds of prime American beefcake, the ultimate *shaygetz*, who both Warner brothers, Louis B. Mayer, and Samuel Goldwyn would pay a cool million to be.

I may be the only woman in Hollywood with whom Gary hasn't slept. I've never been drawn to his brand of perfection, though I wouldn't mind if he'd remove his pants to verify what Lupe Vélez reports about the size of his manly parts.

Gary and I banter, but I could get a better interview with Rin Tin Tin. After twenty minutes of fruitless chitchat, I tell him I must return to Hollywood. To fill my column, I'll ask Jonah to supply some fodder and pay him for his trouble.

At home, I find two-dozen long-stemmed roses, sunny yellow, resting inside a florist's box with a note: *With love from your Scott.* I am as relieved as Little Orphan Annie on the day Daddy Warbucks adopted her, thankful for the *love.* I search *your* as if I am a British spy decoding a telegram from Hitler to Goering.

There is also an envelope addressed in Scott's handwriting. *FOR SHIELAH: A BELOVED INFIDEL*, it says. This is not the first time he has misspelled my name—or other words. Scott has a vast vocabulary. I am the better speller.

I immediately open my dictionary. *Infidel: a person who does not believe in religion or who adheres to a religion other than one's own.* I break the envelope's seal and slide out a poem written on two sheets of paper.

That sudden smile across a room,
Was certainly not learned from me
That first faint quiver of a bloom
The eyes initial extacy,

Scott and his spelling.

Whoever taught you how to page
Your loves so sweetly—now as then
I thank him for my heritage
The eyes made bright by other men.

My "heritage"? That's one way to put it.

No slumberous pearl I valued less
For years spent in a rajah's crown
And I should rather rise and bless
Your earliest love than cry him down.
Whoever wound your heart up knew
His job. How can I hate him when
He did his share to fashion you?
A heart made warm by other men.
Some kisses nature doesn't plan.
She works in such a sketchy way.
The child, tho father to the man
Must be instructed how to play.
What traffic your lips had with mine
Don't lie in any virgin's ken.
I found the oldest, richest wine
On lips made soft by other men.
The lies you tell are epic things
No amateur would ever try
Soft little parables with wings,
I know not even God would try.

He got to my *lies*. I knew he would. He seems to be impressed by my audacity, and there is more, ending with:

> *But when I join the other ghosts*
> *Who lay beside your flashing fire*
> *I must believe I'll drink their toast*
> *To one who was a sweet desire.*
> *A sweet fulfillment—all they found*
> *Was worth remembering. And then*
> *He'll hear us as the wine goes around*
> *A greeting from us other men.*
> *—S*

No one has ever written me a poem, least of all about my epic deceit and sexual history. Stepney Green and the Jews' Orphan Asylum don't merit a line, though perhaps the only rhyme Scott can think of for Jewess is St. Louis. I can only laugh at this bizarre tribute, which I find schmaltzy, seductive, and an immense relief. My sentimental romantic is offering me a pardon, though of all the things about myself I wish I could change, my sexual resume isn't on the list. Yet this, apparently, is what riles him most.

I dial MGM. There is no answer at Scott's desk, nor does he pick up at the Garden of Allah. I decide to drive there and wait for him to appear. I begin to speed down my curvy road when I spot Scott chugging in the other direction. We both stop. He walks to my car and reaches through the open window to cup my chin in his hand. "Were you running away?" he asks, his thumb gently stroking my cheek.

"I was looking to thank you for the flowers, darling, and the poem. Especially that. I'm overwhelmed with gratitude."

"I'm no Keats, but I wrote what's in my heart."

We drive up the hill to my flat. Scott takes my hand as we enter, sits by my side on the patio, and he turns to me. "Presh, if you think I would ever end things over your name or your background, you know nothing about me," he says. "Whoever you are I want you, the real you. And for God's sake, Lily Shiel, half of Hollywood has taken a nom de guerre."

He stands, sniffs like a society matron with his perfect nose in the air, and in a falsetto asks, "Madam, may I present Lucille LeSueur?"

That would be Joan Crawford. "Of the green pea LeSueurs?" I ask. "Charmed."

"And Sir Frederick Austerlitz?"

"Fred Astaire of the Omaha Austerlitzes?"

I could add Spangler Arlington Brugh of Filley, Nebraska, more commonly known as Robert Taylor, but after our dinner, Scott forbids me to mention him.

"Indeed," he says, "but I'm sure you don't know Archibald Alexander Leach."

"Oh, but I do. We have met. Across the pond." Cary.

"And Josef *von* Sternberg?"

He acquired the "von" while sailing the Atlantic. The director owns no German schloss. A yarmulke, perhaps.

Amusing as this is, I say, "Scott, it would be one thing if an agent or studio had christened me, but I renamed myself. Your poem didn't get at that."

His voice turns as serious as a doctor's delivering a fatal diagnosis. "It's you I love, not a footnote like where you're from. Sheilah Graham, don't you know that by now? Why do you doubt me?" He pulls me close and we kiss. "If I tried to craft a heroine, I couldn't create one as interesting, complicated, and giving as you," he insists. "We're also not so very different. Most Protestants despise and look down on Catholics, which I am, technically, though I haven't been in church for years. Social climbing is the Catholic boy's favorite sport. What do you think John O'Hara and I reminisce about half the time? For centuries wars have been fought between our kind and Protestants and we're still at it. They don't want us in their clubs or for their daughters' husbands, and I doubt there'll ever be a Catholic president."

Scott seems unstoppable.

"Also—hear me out—I admire people who've pulled themselves up," he insists, gathering steam. "Every Midwesterner does. You've made yourself somebody from nobody. You have grit. Courage. Qualities I envy, which I lack." He takes me by the shoulders. "You're the American dream incarnate, and my kind of dame."

I've been called worse, usually by Hedda Hopper.

"You may think you have a sketchy past," he continues, "but mostly, it's tragic. Sheilo, with me you'll always be safe, I promise. Remember, I don't just love you. I *like* you. Isn't that the first thing I ever told you?" He lets go of my shoulders and clears his throat. "There's something I do need to know, though." I stiffen. "Did you call things off with Donegall because he discovered your story?"

"Certainly not. You're the only one I've ever told."

"But were you worried that he'd find out?"

I was. My divorce from Johnny was considered odious all on its own, and if Don knew all my lies, our marriage—if it got to that—would have crashed in a hail of headlines. But I believe Don never learned the truth, nor did I love him one percent as much as I do Scott.

"I ended things with Don because I wanted—want—to be with you. The sole reason." And why not admit it? "I still want to be with you, more now than before." Two broken people who together make a whole.

He turns his face toward the darkening twilight. "Sweetheart, I feel the same way."

I am wilted from the last few days, but when we adjourn to my bedroom to seal our contract, for the first time, in a gift to one another, both of us strip to our skin, in all its vulnerability.

I place my hand on Scott's beating heart, and then feather the whorls of soft blond hair on his chest, working my way down his pale, slender torso. He does the same, fondling and praising my curves. "You, my love, are a goddess," he says.

The candle burns low as our sweat mingles and dries. I feel as if my past is simply my past. I am understood. I want to own this man, my knight, my stable boy, my novelist. I want him to own me, and I want this for eternity.

Chapter 35

1938

F all is coming on, with dampness in the air. Scott wraps himself in his ancient flannel bathrobe, ripped at the elbows, showing his grey sweater underneath. A pencil sticks up over each ear, and the stubs of a half dozen others peep from the breast pocket of his robe like so many cigars. A pocket bulges with two packs of Raleighs. My handsome lover, trying to write.

I worry what winter will do to the nineteenth-century lungs that Scott is convinced are ridden with latent tuberculosis. Time to find a place for him to live that isn't the beach. I have two jobs now, author of "Hollywood Today: A Gadabout's Notebook," and the wifely chore of organizing Scott's life. I love both. With Scott, I have the family I've always coveted, and it includes Scottie, who has recently visited. We are relaxing into a cordial friendship. Since "mother" is taken, I've cast myself in the role of older sister, eager to spring to her defense.

Yesterday Scott read a letter he planned to send to his daughter, who is now at Vassar. "I am intensely busy, working like hell, though I wouldn't expect you to understand," he says.

"Don't you think you're being a little snide? For all you know Scottie's working as hard as you are."

"I worry she's falling in love with Cro-Magnons, natural-born stevedores, and future members of the Shriners while she's taking only the easy courses."

If I had a daughter, I'd lay off the scolding and be the kind and understanding mother I never had myself. I say as much to Scott. He softens his letter. Slightly.

Today we are driving north on Laurel Canyon Boulevard, over the summit and down into the San Fernando Valley to Encino. A squadron of hills grandly called the Santa Monica Mountains crouches in the distance and protects this lowland from ocean fog, ensuring that the weather is always warmer and dryer than in Hollywood and certainly Malibu. We pass citrus groves and ranches and finally arrive at a large white cottage surrounded by rolling lawns and old-fashioned gardens in full bloom. Bees and butterflies circle honeysuckle and zinnias.

"I hate it," Scott says immediately. "Looks like a dusty crypt." Perhaps it resembles the drowsy institution in North Carolina where Zelda lives, which is why Scott also says, "I'm not a dead man, at least not yet, and how can I tell anyone I live in a place called Belly Acres?" Which the owner, the prissy-voiced actor Edward Everett Horton, has named his estate. Ed realizes that film careers aren't eternal. Land is.

The rent, however, is reasonable for a pine-paneled living room, gracious dining room, four bedrooms, a maid's room, and a long balcony off the master bedroom where Scott can pace, as he's done virtually every day on the widow's walk in Malibu. Beyond a white picket fence, there are deck chairs under a magnolia tree, a tennis court, and a pool—currently unfilled. I declare it ideal.

Despite Scott's gripes, he agrees to the rental. Once again we move his meager belongings. Like his parents, he has never owned a home. All his life, Scott Fitzgerald has been a vagabond.

His sarcasm persists until our young friend Buff Cobb visits and declares the house charming, especially its fence, which she compares to tombstones on a Confederate graveyard. The image reverses Scott's opinion.

"Come live with me, Sheilah," he says the evening of Buff's visit. "I'm lost in this big place. You can give up your villa, rent something small in Hollywood for appearance's sake and when we want to stay overnight in town. Your Catholic boy is ready to live in sin, not see his girl only on weekends."

I find a small flat on Hayworth off Sunset. As if we are newlyweds, we buy furniture for Encino at Barker's Bargain Basement. I pick a green chintz sofa and after settling into several armchairs, bouncing in each, Scott chooses one in green velvet with an ottoman. To our purchases, I add four fluffy goosedown pillows and a yellow chenille coverlet. I chase away the inner choir that tells me I am investing in a doomed future, but for almost a year, Scott has been attentive and abstinent to the point of saintliness. I have buried the memory of our Malibu party.

When I'm not running down gossip or attending screenings, I now spend most of my time at the house, where we each have our own study. At night we sit on the balcony—I with my tea and Scott his Coca-Cola—and occasionally hear voices carried by the wind from the RKO Western lot a few miles away. "All quiet, everyone! Camera! Shoot!" The air fills with gunshots and the stampede of horses' hooves. It is a long way from Stepney Green.

Autumn ticks past as Scott tries to turn *The Women* into a screed on females who don't work. "I reserve special contempt for girls given every advantage with no price to pay for these privileges," he rants one night, to my delight, since it's the last rebuke anyone could sling at me. "They accept mink coats and fabulous jewelry as if they own the earth." I feel his approval—at Zelda's expense.

Days later Scott is yanked off *The Women* on the grounds that his approach is off the point. I believe the true reason is that Hunt Stromberg, the producer, can never settle on what he wants. Scott reports that the man is a drug addict. This is not, regrettably, column material.

Next up for Scott is a movie about Marie Curie, and he becomes even more evangelistic about this project, sure it's the one that will ennoble his reputation as screenwriter. Again, he approaches his script as a moral treatise, presenting Dr. Curie as the prototype of a modern woman. This time he gets caught between Mummy and Daddy: one producer agrees with his approach, the other wants a formulaic love story.

"I'm once again at liberty, taken off another picture," he says no more than a week after the assignment began, more astonished than hurt. "No one here wants to be corrupted by raw talent." He writes to Scottie that, "I'm convinced they're not going to make me czar of the industry right away like I thought. It's all right, baby—life has humbled me. I am willing to compromise for assistant czar."

Surely this will lead him straight to gin, I worry, and try to brainstorm a mounting defense. But there's no need, because the future assistant czar gets lucky.

When *Gone with the Wind* won a Pulitzer last year, Scott sputtered, "If that's literature, I'm Eleanor Roosevelt. The novel's got no new characters, no new technique, no new observations, and no new examination of human emotion. I lament the soul who considers that woman's book the supreme achievement of the human mind."

The American public should clearly be reading *Gatsby*.

Now that I know what a Hail Mary pass is—thanks to umpteen Saturdays cheering on the UCLA Bruins with Scott—I realize he just got one from David O. Selznick, who asked for him to be traded to Warner Brothers to work on the film adaptation of *Gone with the Wind*. Scott may be the seventeenth screenwriter tapped. My lover, however, is eager for the project despite his outright condemnation of the novel when it won the Pulitzer the year prior. He argues, "The book is surprisingly honest and interesting—if workmanlike."

David O. Selznick turns out to belong to the lamentable herd that considers Margaret Mitchell's oeuvre to be the supreme achievement of the human mind. "I'm forbidden to use one word or phrase that isn't in the book," he reports at dinner after the first day at Warner's. "To Selznick, it's the Torah."

My hand freezes as I deliver a piece of sirloin to my mouth.

"Excuse me, Presh. But you won't believe the reverence. I was asked to portray Aunt Pitty 'bustling quaintly across the room.' Can you please explain how anyone 'bustles quaintly'?"

"Happily." I stand up, and swivel my hips as I circle the table. "Oh dear, oh dear, Captain Butler," I say in a spidery drawl, the back of my hand to my forehead. "Where oh where are my smelling salts? I do believe I shall faint."

"God's nightgown, Aunt Pittypat." Scott slips on his own Deep South accent. "There's nothing quaint about you. I swear you're into the brandy. Not again?"

He eats two bites of peach pie, excuses himself, and disappears to write well into the night, living up to his personal description as a toiler. In the morning, Scott is gone before I wake.

The next evening I learn he's been asked to draft the big staircase scene. "Every woman's favorite part," I inform him. "Rhett and Scarlett are like dogs in heat."

"Subtle, that Margaret," Scott grunts. Again, for the next two evenings he works beyond midnight. Tonight we are sitting in the parlor after dinner, each with a coffee, when I beg him to read me his script. From his battered briefcase in the hall, he retrieves a fistful of heavily marked up pages.

Every time Scarlett opens her pouty little mouth the dialogue turns stilted and flat. I choose to be direct. "I don't think you're there yet."

"I knew it." He rips the pages to shreds. "Rhett Butler's drinking and passion and pride are familiar, but I can't get a bead on Scarlett. She's mad for her husband yet torments the poor heel. I could wring her skinny little neck."

It shows. "You've got to find a way to like Scarlett. Think of her as a wild panther only Rhett can tame, and while she adores him, the girl is too pigheaded to admit or recognize it. It's a classic power struggle."

Is this the underpinning of his relationship with Zelda? Was their sex like our sex? When they're together, do they still make love? Is she as besotted with him as I am? I can't imagine anyone more attracted to Scott than I am.

He interrupts my preoccupations to ask, "A clash between top bananas?"

I have a different image in my mind and am grateful to shake it away. "Maybe we should try acting out the scene and see if the dialogue comes to you."

"Why Mrs. Butler," Scott says, as if I've offered to drop my drawers. "Bless my cotton-picking heart, you are the very reason to rejoice."

We walk to our own curving staircase. I stand at the bottom by Scott's side, pretend to lift a long skirt to show a pert ankle, and bat my eyelashes.

He leers. "I've always admired your backbone, my dear."

"You sound like an orthopedist. How about 'moxie'?"

"'Moxie' is for floozies. Too brittle. Pluck? Fortitude? Resolve? Sass?"

"Try 'sass.'"

"Scarlett, I've always admired your sass." He twirls an imaginary mustache as I snap my imaginary fan.

"Captain Butler, did you say *arse*?"

"Scarlett, I admire your *resolve*, but it will never work with your Ashley Wilkes, that . . . twit. That twerp." He shakes his head. "Sheilo, I cannot figure out why Scarlett cares for such a nincompoop. Hemingway would call him a fairy."

I won't point out how Scott is far more like Ashley than Rhett. "Stay in character. You're just jealous, Rhett, a snake in the grass unfit to wipe Ashley's boot. You're coarse and conceited, and you're no . . . gentleman." I work myself up to the point where I shed a tear. If only I'd performed this well in London.

"Sugar, don't get your knickers in a twist, and hold on." He races back to the dining room, returns, and pulls a white dinner napkin from his pocket. "Never in your entire life have I known you to have a handkerchief when you needed one, Scarlett dear." He glowers. "You're no lady, and this is one night when I won't let you act like one. You're not going to turn me out." He delivers this line with ringing conviction.

"Oh lawd, yes I will." Oh lord, no I won't.

"I know you down to your bones in a way that buffoon Wilkes never will. If he truly understood you, he'd despise you. All you care for is money and what it can buy."

"You scoundrel. Not only are you wrong in every way, you're skunk drunk."

"I intend to get a lot drunker before the night is out."

Please let life not imitate art.

"But not before——" He sweeps me into his arms and begins to carry me up the stairs. Maybe Scott is Rhett after all.

"Take me to the promised land," I moan. "Ravish me."

If I remember the book correctly, Scarlett gets pregnant and tells Rhett later that she wishes the baby were anyone's but his. This is where Scarlett and I part company. I would love to carry Scott's baby. He would look like both of us, light-eyed and fair-haired, with his talent, humor, and brains, and my stamina, self-control, and hand-eye coordination. Scott would be the same extraordinary father he is to Scottie, whom he writes once or twice a week—heavy on the advice—and misses dearly.

This is what I am thinking when he deposits me on the third step, draws me into an embrace that stops at friendly, and bows from the waist. "Very, very helpful, Sheilo. Thank you. Why did you abandon the theater?"

Before I answer he vanishes into his study, closes the door, and works into the night.

⊷⊶   ⊷⊶

A week later I hear steps behind me. A woman with a hat like a floral tribute for a murdered mobster taps me on the back as I cantor off to an interview at MGM. "Why Sheilah Graham," says the newest member of our holy order of gossipmongers, "wherever you're going I'm sure I've already been there."

"Why Hedda Hopper."

Weak chin, pointy nose, dull brown hair—as ZaSu Pitts has pointed out, she does resemble a ferret. I try to keep my distance because Hedda can lacerate. Unlike Miss Hopper, I am not indifferent to societal rules. My bottomless need for people to like me is too powerful for me to become flat-out malevolent. I abide by the catch-more-flies-with-honey-than-vinegar theory, while Hedda's approach stops just short of extortion.

"How fortuitous to see you," Hedda says with a flounce of arrogance, her standard imperious expression intact. Has she tailed me? "I believe my news will be of interest."

I have news, too—my best scoop in months. Tomorrow I intend to publish that Katharine Hepburn has acquired the film rights for *The Philadelphia Story*, the Broadway hit in which she played the lead. She will produce the movie on the sole condition that she stars, a highly unorthodox step and to my knowledge, a first for a woman. This, she hopes, will turn around her career. A good thing, since, after last year's *Bringing Up Baby*, the Independent Theatre Owners of America put her on their box office poison list.

"Care for a sneak preview?" Hedda asks.

"Go on."

She approximates a smile that fails to include her beady eyes. "Mr. Selznick was just window-shopping when he brought your lover on board. Not only will he be dropped from the picture, his MGM contract will be canceled and . . ."

I cannot feel my legs. "That's not news," I interrupt, though it is, of the most painful sort. "Scott quit." Scott will be devastated. Scott will be blackballed. This was the last stop for him.

"He has another project lined up." Will Scott abandon both Hollywood and me, fall off the wagon, and flee to Zelda as he did before? "We knew yesterday." Which is when, buoyant, he turned in new pages to David Selznick.

"I think it *is* news, Sheilah, though that your Mr. Fitzgerald is a washed-up drunk is not." She sidles away, her hatted head held high, flowers wobbling. I picture Hedda making the hat herself, gluing on plastic cherries from Woolworth's.

I walk as fast as I can to my car and drive to the pier, *washed-up drunk* ringing in my ears. The pounding of the water always helps me concentrate, and in January, seeing anyone I know is unlikely. I pace the boardwalk, shivering, my thin sweater buttoned to my chin, arms crossed and clutched to my chest. The wind kicks up, and salt water stings my eyes, but this is not how I will let my love story end.

After an hour, I return to the lot and nose around for Hedda, whom I intercept on the arm of George Cukor, the director who yesterday was also ingloriously relieved of his obligation to *Gone with the Wind.*

"Ah, Sheilah. Your boy was doing fine work," George says when he spots me.

"That's terribly kind of you to say. I realize great minds don't always think alike, but I'm sorry you and David have parted ways."

George rolls his eyes. "Buy you a cup of coffee?"

It's Hedda I need. "Rain check?"

With that he busses both of us on the cheek, excuses himself, and I'm left with the ferret.

She waits for me to speak. "Spit it out. Why are you crawling back?"

"What would you say to a horse trade?" Our conversation is abbreviated, but the deed is done. We are businesswomen first, writers second, each looking out for our own interests.

From there I drive to Paramount to call on B. P. Schulberg, head of production.

"You're home late," Scott says. Since this morning, wrinkles seem to be etched more deeply across his cheeks and forehead. "You've heard?"

I will my own face to go blank. "What is it?"

"I may have set the screenwriting record, Presh. Dumped again. *Finito.*" I hear an echo of the strain I recall from the Pasadena Playhouse as he slides two fingers across his throat execution-style. "I couldn't make the grade as a hack. Like everything else, it takes a certain amount of practiced excellence. Whoosh. My contract's gone with the wind."

I shake my head and gasp. What I do not say is that perhaps he'll be offered a contract from another studio. Hollywood is not that forgiving, nor is Scott that gullible.

"I see you're worried, Sheilo."

Nor am I the actress I think I am.

"It's going to be all right," he says. "I want time to start my novel and maybe some stories. You know the *Saturday Evening Post* used to pay me four thousand a pop?"

Ten years ago.

"And maybe there's freelance work in town."

I think of Scottie's tuition at Vassar. Zelda's fees at her very expensive sanitarium. Scott's bills for Dr. Nelson, who visits often. Scott's made a dent in his debts, but his expenses loom large, and even if I earned enough money to help him, he'd be too proud to accept it. But I say, "Of course you'll find work, darling, and I want nothing more than to see you writing again."

Late that afternoon I take Scott by the hand, lead him to his bedroom, and try to show him how the contract between the two of us is eternal. As his words fill every empty spot, I believe he is telling me the same thing. I touch each faint seam engraved on his face. My fingertips graze him everywhere as I bask in our tenderness. I want our lovemaking to last forever.

Over breakfast, I dive into "Hedda Hopper's Hollywood" in the *Los Angeles Times.* "Good God," I shriek. "Katharine Hepburn's snagged the rights for *The Philadelphia Story.* She's going to try to line up a producer and director who'll let her star."

"Smart," Scott says, "because she can forget landing the part of Scarlett. Selznick would never believe her as a woman Rhett Butler chases for twelve years."

I grimace. "I wish I knew how Hedda got that item."

"She probably threatened to castrate someone." Scott shrugs. "Could you hand me the sports section?"

Ten minutes later, on schedule, the phone rings in the hallway. "Would you get it?" I ask, feigning interest in a review of *Gunga Din.*

Scott returns fifteen minutes later, doing the McQuillan jig. "What did I tell you, Sheilo? I'm not the last-place hack after all. Maybe penultimate. Looks like I'll have to dredge up the old youthful razzle-dazzle one more time. I landed a job, fifteen hundred a week, and not only that, I'm going back East, to college."

Chapter 36

1939

B. P.'s son Budd could be taken for a Bar Mitzvah boy, tall and gangly, with a halo of dark curls and an unfortunate stutter. In fact, he is twenty-five and writing a movie about the winter carnival at his alma mater, Dartmouth. I prevailed upon B. P. to convince Budd to hire Scott to coauthor the script and pray that Scott never learns of my conniving.

The job requires a trip to Hanover, New Hampshire. I am accompanying them as far as New York, where I've scheduled an overdue meeting with John Wheeler. I also plan to indulge in Broadway shows, shop at Bonwits, and shriek with the Roseland Ballroom crowd when Frank Sinatra performs. After Scott joins me, we'll go to El Morocco and up to Harlem for jazz—when I'm not arranged like a bouquet of flowers, awaiting him in peach silk lingerie at our hotel suite.

I would be elated were I not alarmed. "My TB's flared up," Scott informed me—night sweats, coughing, fever—and New Hampshire in February will be far from hospitable. But canceling is not an option, and as I look at Scott now from across the aisle on the plane, he seems to have willed himself to become healthy and not much more than twenty-five himself. Since we boarded, he and Budd haven't stopped yammering about their hallowed Ivy League, Scott's Roaring Twenties, and primarily the Fitzgerald oeuvre, which Budd studied at Dartmouth. Could there be a more flattering reprieve from literary extinction?

After a few hours, I put away my book, say good night, and climb into my berth as the old pro regales his disciple with tales of E.E. Cummings, Edmund (aka Bunny) Wilson, and Ernest Hemingway, and draws Budd out on what it was like to grow up as a Hollywood prince. Novel fodder.

Seven hours later I wake to Scott looming over me. His skin has lost its rosiness. On the floor by his seat he points to "a gift from Dad" and flashes a lupine grin. "To toast our success."

The empty magnum of vintage Mumm may as well be a destroyer headed toward his career. Scott is blotto. "You've got to stop this now," I whisper, "or you're going to regret it."

"She's back, the high priestess from hell," he says, and stumbles to his seat.

We land at Idlewild, and hail a taxi. Scott is invigorated—too invigorated—but Budd most likely sees only his partner's high spirits. Before they meet with the movie's director, they drop me at the Weylin. My suite is complimentary, management's appreciation for putting their hotel on the map when I reported that Lupe Vélez was charged a hundred twenty dollars extra for carpet damage. ("An overenthusiastic tango with Gary Cooper.") I wish Budd good luck and Scott a tearful goodbye.

"Better not call me," he says, his voice sweet as jam and miraculously sober. Perhaps he didn't drink as much as I'd feared. "I'll phone you from Hanover."

As the days pass I find myself too worried to parse the attributes of gabardine over chiffon, nor am I in the mood to applaud the Rockettes, cheer Frank, or watch movies at either the Roxy or the Paramount. I muster enthusiasm for *Pins and Needles* and *DuBarry Was a Lady*, the best plays of the season, because keeping up on the theater is, after all, my job. Mostly, I brood about Scott. When he finally calls on Wednesday, his remarks about Dartmouth—"Princeton's earnest kid brother"—are so thoroughly carbonated with happiness, I sense his overindulgence from two hundred and sixty miles away.

"Please don't drink," I beg. He terminates the conversation, reminding me that he will be home by Friday.

Friday comes and goes. The phone is silent. Frantic, I wire Scott and receive no reply. After ten minutes of the play *Stars in Your Eyes* I leave and stay awake all night. In the morning I wire again: PLEASE TELL ME YOU ARE SAFE AND WHEN YOU WILL RETURN MISS YOU MORE THAN I CAN SAY.

Early Saturday, with still no word, I call the Hanover Inn and receive a frosty reply. "Mr. Fitzgerald and Mr. Schulberg are no longer guests." Only on Sunday do I hear from Budd. "B-b-bad news, Miss Graham."

I imagine my love staggering 'round the campus, under the influence, burning with fever. "Scott's dead!" I scream.

"N-n-no. Mr. Fitzgerald's alive, but s-sick, very sick. We went on a real b-b-bender. I shouldn't have g-given him Champagne. But I've never enjoyed listening m-more."

Liquored up, Scott can schmooze with the grandiosity of an Oxford don, whether he's discussing the downfall of the House of Medici or the hairdo of Alice B. Toklas. Budd reports a garbled tale of a missed train, a lost overcoat, a slip on an icy ski jump, a fraternity house brawl, and a reception hosted by the English department that, he admits, was "inauspicious."

No wonder. Professors prefer their authors dead, leather-bound and shelved, not arrogant, sly, and pissed.

"I'm also sorry to say we were both fired."

The least of it. "When will you and Scott be back here?" I manage to ask.

"That's the thing. Mr. Fitzgerald—"

"I think at this point you can call him Scott."

"We're in town—"

"For Chrissake, where?"

"The Weylin wouldn't check us in given . . . let's just say we're both a bit . . . mangy. I tried six more hotels. Then S-Scott came up with D-Doctor's Hospital. He has a fever of almost 104 degrees—and"—I swear Budd is crying—"Miss G-Graham, if you c-come down here and t-take over, I'd b-be eternally g-grateful."

Twenty minutes later a taxi drops me at the hospital. I thank a teary Budd, who, when I turn around, is gone. A physician on Scott's case explains that the patient is being shot through with penicillin for a bronchial infection and appears to be responding. Thank God.

I find Scott alone in a large room, tucked under a sheet that matches his pallor. Stripped of drunkenness's veneer, he looks fragile as he gazes at me with glassy eyes. I kiss his high forehead and stroke his hair. Nothing will scrub away my love. Were anything to happen to Scott, I would be a husk, stripped to nothing. I think of how cruel I was to my own sick mother and I am flooded with profound remorse and a need, this time, to do better.

Scott's latest drinking saga has unleashed no demons toward me. Yet despite my worry and desire to comfort him, I'm finding it hard to completely forgive. He should have known better. Still, had it not been for me, he'd never have met Budd and for that I have myself to blame. I accept my guilt and say, "A fine mess," as I offer him a sip of water.

"I shouldn't have left Hollywood, Sheilo," he replies. "But I'm running rather low on what is tediously known as financial resources. Years ago, dollars rained down on me every month, but I'll never know where they went. Zelda didn't even own a string of pearls. I need to start a new chapter, and I—"

I place my finger on his lips. "What you need is help, darling," and not solely for the body. "Close your eyes, and I'll be back soon."

John Wheeler gives me the name of a psychiatrist, Dr. Richard Hoffman, who says he remembers meeting the Fitzgeralds in Paris more than ten years ago.

"You know about his drinking?" I ask when I call.

"Yes, but I admire his work very much." The doctor arrives two hours later and I present him to Scott.

"You know Dr. Hoffman, don't you, sweetheart? He's a psychiatrist," who has probably dined out for years on meeting you and Zelda.

"Herr Doctor," Scott says, reaching for the man with such exaggerated politeness that I realize he is faking. "Where's your straitjacket?"

"Now Scott," I say. "Be nice." I offer my own impish look. "I'll leave the two of you."

"Fine, as long as you and the doc don't talk about me behind my back later."

But we do. Scott, depleted by worry and exhaustion, believes his career and creativity have skidded to a halt. "I don't have it anymore," he confesses to Dr. Hoffman. "My skills are gone." I'm surprised and pleased that he is this forthright.

I prevail upon Jonah to file my column during the two weeks of Scott's convalescence, when the doctor visits every afternoon, trying to convince my mulish lover that his talent still shines under boyish illusions. I become hopeful, but on the Friday when Scott is to be discharged, I walk into his room and find him blithely analyzing Dr. Hoffman's marital problems. No doubt the doctor will pop up in a novel. I may as well have hired a plumber.

Finally, we pack up for California. I request Dr. Hoffman's bill. He waives it. "Use the money to buy a wreath for the grave of Mr. Fitzgerald's adolescence," he says, "and go on from there."

Chapter 37

1939

Perhaps Dr. Hoffman did some good. Back in Encino, Scott begins to crank out stories for *Esquire* about a character he christens Pat Hobby, a script stooge and drunk, age forty-nine, scrambling for screen credits. Pat is older than Scott, less talented and devoid of scruples, but endowed with the same humor. One night, about three weeks after we return, he hands me a story to read.

At the studio Pat had eaten property food—half a cold lobster during a scene from the latest movie; he had often slept on the sets and last winter made use of a Chesterfield from the costume department. Benzedrine and great drafts of coffee woke him in the morning, whiskey anesthetized him at night . . . and . . . he developed a hatred against his collaborator, which served him as a sort of ersatz fuel. . . . Working frantically . . . he substituted the word "Scram" for "Get out of my sight!" put "Behind the eight-ball" instead of "in trouble," and replaced "You'll be sorry" with the apt coinage "Or else!"

Pat may be lazy. Scott is not. He not only generates story after story about Mr. Hobby but also completes a minor bone of a script his agent tosses him. With money coming in—not much, but something—*the gift of hope remains through his misfortunes*, like it does for Mr. Hobby. This makes Scott determined to spend more time writing his novel, which he's decided to call

The Love of the Last Tycoon. His main character, the Irving Thalberg stand-in, will be Monroe Stahr.

"Why Monroe?" I ask.

"Jewish parents often give their sons names of presidents," he explains. Not in my experience, says Heimie's sister, though I keep that to myself.

Scott decides to hire a Girl Friday to type narration he writes in longhand and to take dictation for dialogue, which he prefers to talk through. I expect that this assistant will also poach the occasional egg. Today Rusty's Employment Agency has sent the first candidate, one Frances Kroll, age twenty. In a preliminary interview I find her cheerfully direct, and able to type and take dictation as fast as I speak. She is slim with short hair, but not distractingly gorgeous.

I escort Miss Kroll to Scott's bedroom. At eleven o'clock, he remains in his frayed dressing gown, unshaven.

"Please excuse my appearance," he says, as if it's standard practice to interview employees from bed. "I have TB that flares up." Or, as others call it, a hangover. Despite Scott's sustained production, I know he drinks. Only a week after we returned I opened a closet and found a stash of empty gin bottles taunting me like a float of snapping crocodiles. Bickering about it served only to put me in the position of a priss, and so I have stopped trying to intervene.

"Don't worry—I'm not contagious," he says to Frances Kroll and doffs an invisible hat. "My friend Miss Graham applauds your qualifications. But Miss Kroll, how do I know I can trust you?" He turns his voice low. "I'm writing about Hollywood, and I can't have a secretary who'll snitch."

Miss Kroll answers with a New York cadence. "Your secrets are safe with me, Mr. Fitzgerald. My father is a furrier, my mother is a housewife, and my brother composes music at UCLA. We've only just moved here and don't know a soul in the motion picture industry."

"You're correct." Scott lights a cigarette. "It's an industry, not art."

"But an intriguing business, from what I can tell."

This is the right response.

"Could you go to that bureau, please, and fetch my note-book?"

I cringe as I watch Frances Kroll open a drawer and find six full bottles of Gordon's gin, neatly aligned. Sent to the bath-room, she'd discover a pint or two hidden in the toilet tank.

"What do you say?" Scott asks.

"I'd say you're throwing a party."

I honestly can't tell if this young woman is exceedingly droll or has just fallen off the turnip truck.

"I have a favor to ask," Scott says. "I have a daughter about your age, Scottie—actually, her Christian name is Frances, too. She's at college back East. Vassar."

I'm afraid Scott may humiliate Frances for her lack of formal education beyond business school, until he says, "My daughter's not the most judicious. She often gets into financial scrapes. Would you be able to wire some money to her on your way back to town?"

"Certainly," she says. He asks her to count out thirty-five dollars from his wallet while he writes down Scottie's address as well as our phone number. "Please call after you take care of this at Western Union." He thanks her and she is on her way.

"What did you think?" I ask. "The agency has more candidates."

"I like her," Scott says. "She has an intelligent manner."

An hour later he answers the phone. Mission accomplished. "The job is yours if you want it," Scott says. "I can pay you thirty-five dollars a week"—a rather rich wage—"and you can start tomorrow."

I realize that the wiring of money had been Scott's honesty test. Frances Kroll did not abscond with his cash.

I know amateur psychologists in the Garden of Allah crowd amuse themselves by drawing parallels between Zelda and me. They can get back to work, because Miss Kroll is not much older than Scottie, the other Frances. Frances Kroll completes the reconstituted Fitzgerald triangle, of which I now stand in for Zelda, almost giving me the happy little family I craved.

F. Scott Fitzgerald, creator of the loathsome Wolfsheim, will now have two women spinning around him like dreidels. It is obvious that Frances is Jewish.

She is also efficient and congenial, and folds into our Encino life like sugar into egg whites. With his writing Scott himself is a disciplined baker, not a haphazard cook. He churns out plot outlines and notes that Frances—soon upgraded by Scott to Franny or Françoise—turns into a thickening manuscript. Her other top job takes place every Friday. Before Frances leaves for her Shabbos dinner, she puts Scott's bottles into a burlap sack and flings the evidence of his imbibing into a ravine near Sepulveda Canyon.

I appeal to Robert and Dorothy about Scott's drinking. One by one, both suggest that I relegate him to the pantheon of permanent drunks. They understand neither how, when he is sober, we nurture one another, nor the depth of our attachment. Thus I'm pleased when Arnold Gingrich, my most reliable ally, sends me a jar of pills he's discovered that purportedly help alcoholics reverse their habit by making them nauseated. Their only drawback: the pills turn drinks blue.

I drop a tablet in Scott's bottles. "How odd," he says that afternoon as he sips a gin and tonic. "Sheilo, would you call this shade cerulean or cobalt?" He gulps, suffers no ill effects, and refills his glass.

Twice he has hired a nurse to help him dry out, but soon the drinking resumes. It's painful to witness Scott's declining state—grubby clothes, airstrikes of anger, fibs, and foul language. There is also his diet. He'll starve all day, then make dinner of crab soup and fudge. I begin to spend more time in Hollywood, joining him only for weekends.

One Friday, around noon, Scott phones, asking if I'll come to Encino early. Frances couldn't be there that day. Dr. Nelson had given him a shot that is making him sleepy. Until a nurse arrives he wants company. Scott sounds coherent, sweet, and solicitous.

"Of course," I say.

A few hours later as I get out of the car, sage perfumes the valley air, but Scott's bedroom exudes alcohol. He is propped up in bed, writing on the board he uses as a makeshift desk and in his classic, hardworking pose, his hair is twirled to the spike that grows from his concentration. One pencil is in his right hand, another behind his left ear. We kiss and he yawns.

"Thanks for coming, Sheilo," he says. "I've missed you, my love."

"You too, darling," I say, which is true. "You sleep. I'll wait downstairs for the nurse." He slides under fresh sheets our housekeeper, Earleen, put on the bed before she left, and closes his eyes.

Across the room, I notice my most recent press portrait displayed on the bureau in a silvery frame placed next to a picture of Scottie. I'm pleased. I stop to look at it and gasp. Behind the photo is a black revolver. I have no idea what Scott is doing with a weapon—protection from a wild-eyed lemon farmer, perhaps? I have never held a pistol, but instinctively, I slide it into the pocket of my coat.

I turn and Scott, tubercular and dopey as he may be, runs across the room and tries to grab the gun. I hold it tight. As if we're in a schlock Western, we tussle, standing, and then fall to the floor, rolling like animals, panting. I had no idea that Scott was as powerful as he is, but now I feel my own unexpected strength and slip my fingers into the trigger guard.

"Why do you have a gun?" I shout. "Planning to bloody kill yourself?"

"None of your bloody business," he says and yanks my hand so violently I bleed.

"You're a fool," I shriek and throw the pistol clear across the room. We struggle to our feet. "Go get it and shoot yourself, you sonofabitch," I yell. "Kill yourself for all I care. I didn't pull myself out of the gutter to waste my life on a drunk like you."

Rough language, but as heartfelt as anything I've said to anyone.

Scott stares at me, his hand frozen as if to hit me back, but I strike first. I reach his face with a satisfying slap, but I'm not going to stay for the Punch and Judy show that may follow. I run out of the room, down the stairs, and into my car. Pebbles fly as I speed down the gravel driveway.

Not until now have I hated Scott for his self-destruction and his cruelty, though during the drive back to Hollywood I force myself to think rationally. Would he have actually hurt himself or me? Probably not. Can he rekindle his talent? Yes, if he works hard enough. Does caring for me—which I don't doubt—magnify his guilt about Zelda? Most likely, it does. Will he conquer his addiction or will it conquer him? That I can't answer.

All night long I tell myself that because of my duplicity I am in no way above Scott. His ugly drinking is balanced by my rejection of family, my denial of Judaism, and my string of lies. Call it even.

In the early morning causeway between sleep and waking, my rationalizations scatter like a flock of crows after a thunderclap. I think only of how when Scott's drinking is in check, our romance is everything for which I could hope. I remember how it feels to be reading next to him on the sofa, my feet in his lap, when he looks up and says, "How did I get lucky enough to find you, Presh?" How he closes his book, and leads me to the bedroom, which seems to be our natural home. How when I don't see him for a day, every time the phone rings I hope it is Scott, simply so I can hear his voice. I have never felt this way about another man. I can almost see and smell and feel his body next to me in bed, and trace its familiar contours.

But I also need peace. There are limits to how much I can take of Scott Fitzgerald craving infinite succor and I can no longer let myself be tortured. "Every man has his own burden," my father used to say, although the tongue was Yiddish. Scott has many burdens and I have Scott. I don't feel I can stop loving him—that's not even a choice—but I can force myself to stop seeing him.

Sheilah Graham is not a victim. In order to be a woman of courage, with sincerity and flaming self-respect, she's going to have to call it quits.

Chapter 38

1939

What I need now is distance. My column, also, will not write itself. If I'm not careful, I'll be swallowed by the slapstick of Scott's life and let all I've worked for slip away, especially since I've developed the unfortunate habit of rejecting millionaires and titled gentlemen who'd like nothing more than to make me their pet. And so, I accept a coveted invitation from Cecil B. DeMille to join a select group in his private train car that will travel to where *Union Pacific*, his latest film, premieres. I'd let the request languish for weeks, worried that I needed to be available for Scott's well-being.

What the hell.

A taxi drops me at the new train station, an unapologetic jumble of Spanish Colonial, Mission Revival, and Art Deco. Like much of Los Angeles, the building feels unfinished, at least to a Londoner used to the grandeur and grime of Paddington.

I plant myself in the shade of a potted lemon tree to discreetly adjust the tilt of my new blue felt hat, and see him, half moviemaker, half mythmaker, wearing a cream-colored suit although it's not yet summer. I enjoy this maestro who strives to create epics, not mere motion pictures. Part of the package is Cecil himself.

"Sheilah, my angel." He bends to kiss my hand with his thick, rubbery lips.

"I can't begin to tell you how honored I am to be included in this group." With directors, when isn't fawning in order? "How is your health?"

I had reported, to the indomitable Mr. DeMille's delight, that following surgery he directed much of *Union Pacific* from a stretcher.

"Fit as a twenty-year-old," he says. "Put *that* in the papers. Now, if you'll excuse me . . ." He heads toward Barbara Stanwyck, who is approaching Joel McCrea, her on-screen love interest.

Cecil DeMille's rolling mansion turns out to be a parlor with lavishly upholstered easy chairs, soft lighting, and mahogany tables; a dining car set with Baccarat crystal and Bavarian china on which we're served meals prepared by a French chef; and two Pullman cars, their crisp sheets monogramed with CBdM. Jonah and I find seats blessedly distant from Hedda and Louella, and as we chug east, the steady clacking of the train becomes an opiate that puts me into a welcome trance. *You will not think of Scott. You will not think of Scott.* As the landscape turns rural, I unspool, tension dropping by the mile.

My first interview is with Cecil, who points out how superior his movie is to a low-budget Western before I am passed like a baton to a nervous young actor, Robert Preston. "You look familiar," I say, attempting to put him at ease. "Won't you tell me a bit about your background?"

He mentions a few forgettable movie roles and adds, "I was the lead in a student production in Pasadena of *A Diamond as Big as the Ritz.*" This tidbit will not make my column. That evening, after the requisite posturing with men who flirt back— which reminds me that my skills in that department have not atrophied—I let the chuffs of the train lull me into the sweetest sleep I've had in weeks.

Not until the third day do I get to sit down with the top-shelf stars. "What was it like to swim with a nude Dolores del Río in *Bird of Paradise*?" I ask Joel McCrea, a stunt double who ripened, virtually overnight, into a leading man. "Were you nude, too?"

I get only a tolerant half smile. Joel is a husband excessively content in his marriage, a gossip columnist's washout.

Finally, I meet with Barbara Stanwyck. I am last in line, but what should I expect? To my knowledge, neither Louella nor Hedda has let herself become distracted by gun-toting drunks.

I've always felt Barbara's best talent is convincing people she is stunning. When I ask if she has roots in the West, where the movie is shot, I learn that no, she is from Brooklyn. We're roughly the same age, both exiled to orphanages because our parents were dead or absent. Our schooling ended at the same age, fourteen, when Ruby—Barbara, too, invented a glossier name—went to work in a department store. Barbara Stanwyck, my secret alter ego.

"I knew that after fourteen I'd have to earn my own living, and I was willing to do that," she says. That, too, we have in common. At sixteen, she auditioned for musical theater, much the same as I did. From there, she became a Ziegfeld girl and soon, a Hollywood triumph. I wish I could make a friend of Barbara and privately celebrate how we've both risen above our stations, but while the actress boasts of her history, I hide mine in shame and remind myself that she didn't need to contend with the whalebone of English class distinctions or its history of spurning Jews.

"I've always been a little sorry for pampered people, and of course, they're 'very' sorry for me," she adds. I admire that Barbara can admit this, which she does with a wink. Would people say the same of me, if they knew my truth?

We move to a subject dearer to readers and of not insignificant personal interest. "Are you and Robert Taylor keeping house?"

They're dating. They're not dating, which is what I heard from Robert the last time we had dinner. They're sharing a house, flaunting movieland's unspoken decree. Then not. Is it true love or all for show?

"If you're asking me if I want to get married"—which I wasn't—"I'm not ready to take the plunge again."

I press on. "I know you lovebirds see a lot of each other."

"Robert will always be a close friend." I detect steel in her chirpiness. "I'm someone he can trust to show him the ropes—he's a real Nebraska boy, you know?"

I do.

"We both love riding, hiking, fly fishing, that sort of thing."

"So you're sort of an older sister?" Barbara is five years Robert's senior.

She coughs, clears her throat, and a lackey materializes from the seat behind us to say, "Sheilah, your time is up."

I believe Barbara is clever enough to land Robert if she truly wants him. Which is more than I can say about my own romance, if I can even speak of it in the present tense.

A few hours later, we pull into Omaha for a conga line of parades, banquets, radio broadcasts, and, almost incidentally, a screening of the movie. The next day I fly to California. The five-day spectacle almost made me forget Scott. But not quite.

At home I find a pile of bills, a post from Johnny alive with details of his latest get-rich scheme, and *Esquire*, to which I now subscribe. As I put aside the mail, an envelope flutters to the bare wood floor. It's postmarked from Encino. I rip it open, expecting an apology or even a love letter—possibly a poem. Am I not Scott's "beloved infidel"?

I find a two-thousand-dollar check. "For your time," sniffs a smudged note, as if this settles our account for sexual favors bestowed.

My pendulum swings back to outrage and sticks there. I recognize that Scott must expect me to boil with indignation and rip up the check. But two can play the game. I will deposit the check. That it may bounce is not the point.

Over the next few days I swell with vengeance while I bang out columns, clean my closets, and pull errant weeds—and the lemon verbena, dammit. Exactly a week later I'm surprised by a call from the wife of Frank Case, who owns Manhattan's Algonquin Hotel as well as the Malibu cottage Scott rented. Could I please help poor Mr. Fitzgerald? After some sort of hullabaloo, he wound up in a hospital—again—where he stayed until he was well enough to travel back to Los Angeles. Evidently, he returned yesterday, "in frightful condition."

I had not realized that even before I'd left town, Scott had, too.

"He needs some support," the woman begs.

"Why was he hospitalized?" I ask.

"Zelda says . . ."

Zelda. I catch only Scott's standard whitewash: "tuberculosis."

". . . but you can't trust a word from that girl," Mrs. Case clucks. "Quite the lost soul, and in no condition to have traveled. Her sister took her straight back to Asheville."

Until this moment, I've felt nothing but compassion for this broken woman, but now, sick or well, I wince with disgust. Did Zelda provoke Scott's latest emergency? May she and her husband roast in hell.

"Who gave you my number?" Was it Scott?

"Dorothy."

I thank Mrs. Case and hang up. I owe Scott nothing. But again, I am reminded of how I failed my mother. What if he is seriously ill? Tatte lectured all of us on the importance of *rachmones.* Mercy. Where is mine? I may pretend I'm no longer Jewish, but I've never stopping believing in my faith's basic tenets, and one is the milk of human kindness. I call Scott in Encino and consider it a mitzvah.

"Mr. Fitzgerald is sleeping," Earleen says. "He can't talk."

I call again the next day. "Mr. Fitzgerald, he working." *Do not bother the great man.*

Now I'm aggravated, especially when the following day Earleen informs me that Scott is away.

"Did he leave town again?" Without a goodbye. "Is Mr. Fitzgerald avoiding me?"

"I'm sorry ma'am, but he don't want to speak to you."

"Thank you. I won't bother you again," I say when a muffled voice asks her to hand over the phone.

"I know how put out you get when people fail to call you back." Scott, somber as a saint. "I have no wish to cause you that discomfort."

Only now do I realize the extent to which I feared I'd never again hear the cultivated speech of the real Scott—not the seedy alcoholic—and how I hope this olive branch will grow into a truce. "I'm sorry I slapped you, and said those ugly things." That I hope aren't true. "You know I don't believe them." Or want to believe them.

I could rattle off the Pledge of Allegiance waiting for him to reply. "Perhaps there is blame on both sides," he concedes, his voice shaky.

Scott was the pistol-packing crackpot, the reprobate whose drinking has made him all but unemployable and most likely unwell, and the one whose moods exhaust me. I'm the girl whose father taught compassion, as well as the optimist convinced that bona fide Scott can vanquish his boorish imposter. I believe in happy endings. I see us together. Forever. Swans. Zelda or no Zelda. I tell myself that being kind is not the same as being a victim.

"I hope you will visit," concedes the swan prince.

Late the next day, I join him on the patio at Belly Acres. He is pale as an old ivory carving, badly shaved and thinner. His hair needs cutting. I brush it off his forehead, rest my hand on the back of his neck, and stare into my favorite eyes. In the dusk they are the blue of the delphinium climbing a nearby trellis.

He sits in a rocking chair and sucks Coca-Cola through a red-striped straw. "I'm sorry, Sheilo. For everything."

As am I. "I never should have made those slurs and—"

He reaches for my hand and presses it to his lips. "We won't speak of it." A rogue's grin creeps across his fine face. "That gun, you know, was loaded."

"Why in God's name?"

"Oh, you know. Lions and tigers and bears."

"Tell the truth or I'm leaving."

I don't expect him to meet my eye, but he does. "After Dartmouth and New York, I had a bad day. A string of bad days, actually. I thought it was crack-up time again. I wanted to have it on hand, just in case."

I'm too shocked to respond.

"Then I thought of Dorothy's ditty 'Razors pain you, rivers are damp, acids stain you and drugs cause cramps.'"

"'Guns aren't lawful . . .'" I continue. "'So you may as well live.'"

"I kept your portrait—and Scottie's—in front of the gun to remind me of those six words, though Sheilo, I'd be the last man on earth to take his own life. I'm way too big a coward."

"Jesus H. Christ, you are a madman."

"Nor am I proud of it."

For the next half hour, Scott narrates a saga that starts in North Carolina, where he whisks Zelda, now a Bible-toting fanatic, to Havana, "because Ernest loves it." Scott did not. The filth. The sway-backed donkeys. The rumor of a ship in the harbor carrying German-Jewish refugees whom the government barred from entering the country, dooming them to God-knows-what. Zelda was terrified and hid in their room, praying, in order to escape people who stared at her shopworn 1920s dresses. Scott rambled, pie-eyed from rum. He is warming to his yarn while I remind myself that my lover is an inventor of fiction and hope this is at least fifty percent tall tale. The part about the Jews, especially.

"One night I stumbled into a cockfight. When I tried to separate two mangled roosters I was attacked by both the birds and the Cubans, short men with no necks, foul-smelling cigars, and reeking armpits. They chased me down the street and beat me bloody. I got a black eye, bruises everywhere, and couldn't find my hotel."

The story is as preposterous as it is unpleasant. "Oh, Scott," I say, because I must say something.

"The next day we flew to New York City and checked into the Algonquin, where we'd stayed as newlyweds . . ."

We. Newlyweds.

". . . but Zelda began to wail"—Scott mimics a banshee. I feel as if I am sitting around a campfire while logs burn low, not that I have sat around a campfire, ever. At the Algonquin he took to the halls and shouted—though it isn't clear at whom—and the "cacophony"—*great word*—drew complaints.

I offer Zelda a private apology for the injustice I did her days ago by thinking she caused Scott's problem; she may be the saner half of this pair.

"I tried to throw a waiter down the stairs," he deadpans, as if he is proud of the feat. The manager carted Scott off to the alcoholic ward at Bellevue. From there, he transferred himself to Doctors Hospital.

"Presh, no one knows how to have fun anymore," frets my middle-aged juvenile delinquent.

This story would be shocking had it not become tiresome. Nonetheless, seeing Scott next to me, sober and contrite, my love renews. I do not want to be separated from this man. I start to hope that he detours into announcing that he is leaving Zelda. It's a marriage in name only, he says. Their time together was too—he doesn't complete the sentence. Painful? Sexless? He couldn't stop thinking of me, with my good health and goodwill. But at the end of his soliloquy, Scott brushes his hands together as if he is sweeping away crumbs. "And this is how I spent the last few weeks." That's that.

We turn silent as the gilded light fades into dusk and the setting sun casts purple shadows over the San Fernando Valley. Birds warble a hushed descant as fireflies flicker in the darkness. The temperature has cooled, and a breeze tosses my hair. Our eyes are on each other.

"This nonsense in Cuba and New York is all history," Scott says. "In the ledger you must be keeping of my ill deeds, record them, but please use invisible ink, because I can change."

"I want you to. I need the real Scott. Show me."

He stands and draws me to him, takes my hand once more, and leads me through the French doors, up Rhett and Scarlett's staircase. Embracing, we back into the bedroom and tumble onto linen sheets that carry the scent of citrus and sage. Opened windows let in the wind as our clothing falls away and we erase the past.

"Baby, I missed you," he whispers, holding me tight, his touch silky. "I need you. I'm sorry." These are lyrics to the song I long for him to sing. I sing it back.

Chapter 39

1939

In the morning, I find a letter to Zelda typed by Frances. "You were a peach throughout the whole trip," it reads, "and there isn't a minute when I don't think of you with all the old tenderness. You are the finest, loveliest, tenderest, most beautiful person I have ever known . . ." I relive last night's lovemaking and Scott's promise, and choose to lock away any corrosive jealousy, though I do make a note of Zelda's address in North Carolina. Then I get on with life, which quickly assumes the brightness of an operetta. When I'm not tracking movie stars or fending off shameless agents, I pour myself into the F. Scott Fitzgerald College of One, which is what we have decided to call my ongoing education. College is now fully in session.

"You shall be my Galatea," Scott declares. I learn that's the name the sculptor Pygmalion of the Greek myths gave to a statue he fashioned and brought to life.

For as long as I can remember I have been on a relentless quest to improve myself, with a major assist from Johnny. The College of One, however, is different from what I experienced with my husband, whose ambitions for me were his, not mine. I want to expand my mind as much as Scott wants to see it happen, with the presumption that my intellect knows no limits. He boasts to our friends that he's never met a faster learner, which makes me angry all over again that my formal education ended at fourteen.

Because lists are the spine of his life, Scott has outlined a curriculum of a liberal arts college. Since he does not claim to have a well-rounded education—reasonably informed about literature, history, and religion but not math or science—the latter aren't part of the plan. This is fine. My arithmetic is better than Scott's, and I do not aspire to succeed Marie Curie. I spend at least three hours a day reading and studying before evening cross-examinations. If we stay on course, I may graduate by 1941. Currently, I am devouring *Great Expectations.*

Scott sends Frances to scour secondhand bookstores in downtown Los Angeles to nab his favorite editions of Chaucer, Melville, Cervantes, and other literary knights. She returns with signed copies and first editions for as little as fifty cents.

Sometimes I get a surprise. "When I was naughty, my mother called me a bad brownie and when I was good, I was her good brownie and got a lollypop. Here's yours, for doing Darwin so well," Scott says today, presenting me with Dickens's *Bleak House.* Each time I master a challenging book—Plato's *Republic* almost broke me—the pearl in my oyster is an easier book.

Scott includes Hemingway, whose talent he admires despite the man's affronts. I find Ernest engrossing but gruff; Scott may be able to overlook his disloyalty, I cannot. *Look Homeward, Angel* by Tom Wolfe, another of Scott's cronies, may as well be a Nembutal. When I admit this to Scott, he confesses that he agrees. "I'm a taker-outer and a changer," he says, "but Tom's a leaver-inner."

Scott hires a carpenter to build a set of golden oak bookshelves for my flat in Hollywood, a generous and thoughtful gift. Soon I have two shelves filled with books inscribed *Encino Edition,* covered by jackets of heavy brown wrapping paper he fashions with scissors and glue. My collection reflects Scott's panoramic mind and the glimmers of my own waking brainpower. I love to learn and he loves to teach, which means taking the time to expand my vocabulary.

Today he is quizzing me. "Miss Graham, please define 'nihilism.'"

"A rejection of religious principles. Not like I've done with Judaism, because I believe in the commandments and the morals. It's more extreme skepticism."

"That will do," he says. "Next up, 'umbrage.'"

"Taking offense. I take umbrage at the suggestion that you don't think *Dark Victory* is a superb movie."

"Well, I don't. It was a bore. Now, 'torpor'?"

"A state of mental or physical exhaustion. How I feel in this soupy heat."

"Too easy. 'Escutcheon'?"

"An emblem with a coat of arms. Johnny had one."

"Way too easy. This leads me to 'Anglomaniac.'"

"Randolph Churchill."

My answer earns me a smile. "Correct, Miss Graham. Now, 'desultory.'"

"Lacking a plan or purpose. How I was before the College of One."

Scott devises ditties to help me remember facts. When we study the history of France, *Saint Louis was a pious blade/Who vainly led the last crusade* falls off my tongue as I drive into town to make my rounds. I am up to seven columns a week, syndicated in sixty-five newspapers. This means stopping by the studios daily and all but harassing movie stars, publicists, producers, and agents—in person, by phone, at banquets, at galas—as I pursue leads. I also must travel for press junkets and entertain visiting editors who seem always attached to six-year-old children requiring amusement. When I return to Encino every weekday late in the afternoon, I am breathless.

I know Scott's drinking quietly continues—I see empty bottles—yet not to excess, and he is similarly productive, subdividing his day into compartments marked by almost military precision. Along with maintaining an unflagging correspondence with Zelda and Scottie—letters go East every week—he writes to friends and to magazine editors from whom he wants assignments. He is also plotting and writing sections of his novel. *Colliers* is willing to publish installments at twenty-five hundred dollars apiece, providing that he first submits fifteen hundred words of which they approve. Sitting in bed, invigorated by doctor-administered vitamin shots, he works on his lap desk and the yellow pages of his manuscript pile up for Frances to type along with Pat Hobby stories ("Pat was employed to discover how a live artillery shell got into Claudette Colbert's trunk . . ."). There is also the odd screenwriting job, plans for my college courses, and newspapers he devours for coverage of sports and the war in Europe, which he follows on the radio more actively than ever.

Well done, us.

"Read when your mind is freshest," he advises me. Since I wilt as the day ends, my breakfast is toast, coffee, and a book. Before, during, and following Earleen's sumptuous dinners— roast chicken, barbecued ribs, salads garnished with zucchini blossoms and garlic scapes, frothy desserts—we chew through the current lesson.

Talk, eat, study, laugh, play tennis or Ping-Pong, make love, and listen to Scott read the latest addition to his novel—Stahr is falling deeper in love with the Irish girl he calls Kathleen, which I take as an affirmation of our relationship. This is our life, cloistered, close, and complete.

With no prompting, Scott has also started to read from Zelda's letters. He presents them with a certain detachment, as if his wife were a case study that fascinates both of us. Her writing is enchanting. "The moated mornings remind me of twenty-five years ago when life was so full of promise, and is now of memory." Scott has described how the young girls in Montgomery would put on their makeup before they went out and then take cool baths before their beaux arrived. Though now Zelda must be about forty, I see that young girl in her words.

I suspect Scott wants me to hear her letters to let me better understand his ordeal. To me, Zelda sounds more wistful and otherworldly than mentally ill. I begin to picture her as a character in the sort of novel I used to read, a diaphanous romantic trapped in a summer afternoon fifteen years ago. I never get tired of taking note that she signs her letters with "devotedly"—not "love" or "I love you," as if she and Scott were brother and sister, not man and wife. I am reminded of Johnny and me.

Zelda's letters make me both twitchy and curious. Were we to meet, would we be friends? I decide to introduce myself. Whether my wish comes from pride or insecurity, I cannot say, but I feel a desperate need to make my love for Scott—and his for me—known and acknowledged.

Dear Zelda, I write one day.

I am a close friend of your husband and I want you to know that Scott worries about you constantly, as you must worry about him. Rest assured that I am taking good care of him. I watch over his health. I have become very attached, as I believe he is to me, but that he loves you dearly will never be in question. You are his center, because without you, there is no legend. I admire and accept this, but it does not diminish our love. We share a bond built on mutual respect.

With affection,
Sheilah Graham

I reread the letter several times a day during the next week. Ultimately, I tear it up, wary of hurting this woman and fearful of how she—and Scott—might respond.

Just when I think our days could not be more idyllic, Scott adds music to my education. Morton Kroll, Frances's brother, advises him on composers to choose. Melodies of Beethoven, Schubert, Bach, and Brahms become "our" songs, and with music comes art. We begin to visit the Los Angeles Art Museum to learn about painting and sculpture.

This is where we are on a spring day, strolling. I stop in front of a Frans Hals. "Every one of these men is smirking exactly like Robert Benchley," I announce.

A few galleries later I decide that Bogie is a Hogarth, always larking about in a crowd. Jonah is an able-bodied Toulouse-Lautrec, and a Madame Renoir with a poodle reminds me of Dorothy.

"You're generous, Presh. His platter of onions, maybe," he says. "And who am I?"

I consider Van Gogh with his explosive energy, but the painter is not sufficiently handsome—no self-portraits of any artist are—and he also came to a bad end. I adore Degas, because like Scott he is a romantic, but worry that his fascination with ballet, which Zelda threw herself into before her breakdown, will be a regrettable association.

"You might be a Durer. The intricacy of his woodcuts reminds me of your writing." Then I change my mind. "No, you're *The Thinker* by Rodin."

"But he's naked, and I'm a shy guy."

"A girl can dream. And who am I?" I ask, kittenish.

He replies immediately. "Botticelli's Venus on the half shell. Obviously."

I approve.

We leave the museum around noon. "I'd like to take my Botticelli shiksa out to lunch," Scott says. "I know just the place."

He drives not to an Italian restaurant, as I expect, but to Greenblatt's Deli, a *heimische* hub of lox and paranoia where studio regulars kvetch as they eat the food of their fathers.

"Is this your way of apologizing for the way you've besmirched Jews?" I ask, only half-joking.

"Yes, Venus. Will you accept my apology?"

I appreciate Scott's peace offering. I've tried hard to believe that his work has reflected prejudices of the day that he himself does not hold.

Scott skims the menu and smiles. "Kneidloch. Now what is a kneidloch?" he asks the waiter who appears, a plump fellow who combs his diminished strands of grey hair over a broad brow and speaks with an echo of Slutsk.

"It's a matzoh ball, sir, like a dumpling. Very tasty, light as air, served with Greenblatt's famous chicken soup."

"Say it again, please?"

"Kneidlach."

"Ka-NADE-lock." Scott is chuckling. He repeats the word three times, tilting his head right and left.

"Gargle the end, my friend," the waiter suggests.

"We shall take the soup and ka-NADE-lach-ch-ch under advisement. What else is good today?"

The waiter warms to Scott's interrogation. "Our customers kvell over the kreplach."

"Dough filled with mashed potatoes," I say. "You'd like them."

"But we're also noted for our knishes."

Scott turns to me. "I defer to Miss Knish."

I blush, look around, see no one I know, and add, "I'm partial to blintzes, like crepes, but I also love tzimmes."

When there was money, Mama cooked it on Shabbos. I can smell the succulence of carrots, yams, and prunes mingled with cinnamon, piled next to juicy flanken awash in gravy, fat floating in golden dots. I am back in Stepney Green, missing my Tatte and my mother—not the sour hag who exiled Morris and me to an asylum, but a woman wearing an ironed blue kerchief and a smile. I could easily cry, if Scott didn't, at that moment, declare himself a schmendrick, a term he informs me that he learned at the studio from one of the other boychicks.

Our feast arrives: chicken soup with parsley and kneidlach

along with potato kugel and a sandwich to split—four inches of tongue piled on seeded rye, soft and freshly baked. Scott polishes off his kneidlach in three bites. "Twice as tasty as Zelda's," he says. He devours the kugel and half of the sandwich, as do I, and orders rugelach and tea with lemon and honey.

"Did I tell you that Frances's father got Mrs. Kroll a live carp before Passover?" he asks while shoveling it in.

"Personally, I'd prefer sable."

My feeble pun is lost on him. "The fox jacket I gave you doesn't cut it?"

"I love my jacket and you know it." My first birthday gift from Scott, undeniably the most appreciated present I've ever received. If it were alive I couldn't care for my fox more lovingly.

Scott bites into a rugelach. "The Krolls kept the carp swimming for days in the bathtub until Mr. Kroll bludgeoned the poor sucker with a mallet and Franny's mother gefilte'd it." Now he gobbles the rugelach. "I don't know why they didn't just fill their tub with gin and let the fish simply drink itself into oblivion, or why I didn't get invited to the Seder. I'd make short work of those four glasses of wine."

He laughs almost as much as I do, but stops abruptly. "Did you read about how the British Parliament is allowing what they're calling the Kindertransport? German-Jewish children are being sent to England on the eve of war."

Not for the first time, I feel shamed by my ignorance about current events. Given my professional commitments, I'm having a hard enough time preparing for our College of One. Except for Louella's and Hedda's columns, I read nothing much in a daily newspaper.

"I didn't know. They're being saved. That's wonderful, darling."

Could we take a child? Scott's baby is, of course, my first choice, but my heart breaks at the thought of a tiny German

Lily or Morris, clutching her Kichel or his teddy bear along with a small valise. I would happily be that child's mum.

My fantasy rams into reality when Scott says, "It's not exactly wonderful, Sheilo. The English care only for the children. None of the parents are being given visas. It's as if the little ones are already orphans."

Chapter 40

1939

*S*heilah Graham *is scared to do her lectures, and scared if she* *doesn't.*

I hate when Hedda is right.

Louella, gossip's yenta emeritus, is embarking on a national lecture tour and John Wheeler has booked me on one, too, to give readers the inside line on Hollywood and meet the real me. I am terrified. When I appeared on the stage, third from the right, I could pass off my flops as comedy. Not so for these speeches. I've become a woman with a professional reputation to uphold.

I worry, as well, about abandoning Scott. If I'm away, will his sobriety, such as it is, end in a waterfall of gin? Canceling is not an option, so I draft a speech spangled by Hollywood glitz, spiced with familiar scandals—Fatty Arbuckle's 1921 rape charge and Charlie Chaplin's proclivity for underage girls. I will omit my juiciest material, the sort that makes it into a column only as blind items—rumors about swishers, drag queens, and Marlene Dietrich's lady-loving sewing circles, bed-hopping on the Hearst yacht, various crabs and pornos, and Louis B. Mayer's attempt to strong-arm Jeanette MacDonald into aborting Nelson Eddy's child. Real Hollywood and the town's gutter press run on parallel tracks: personal earthquakes rock the ground below the studios with regularity, but the industry protects its own.

When I show my speech to Scott, he scowls. "You're feeding people the pabulum they expect. I can't let you deliver this, Presh." Scott means well, but he can unintentionally reduce me to a speck of lint. "Tell people how movies actually get made. What's interesting is the mechanics and pecking order. Who's the most important cog in the machine?"

"The writer?" I venture.

"I wish. We're bottom-feeders. Our best work can be destroyed by any second-rate actor." He pauses only for a second. "I give you John Wayne. But the actor is just a puppet that can be destroyed by the industry's swaggering cartoon general, the director. That's what you should dig into." Scott is getting warmed up. "And I'd love to see you point out how movies affect the way we talk and look, why we say 'ix-nay' or 'yeah'—well, I don't, but others do."

"Okay, I'll rework the script."

But he refuses to relinquish it. "May I?"

Scott owes *Colliers* tens of thousands of words in order to earn an advance. Nonetheless, he takes my speech and doesn't return it until the next afternoon, rewritten and neatly typed by Frances. It's brilliant.

"Now don't memorize," he warns. "Review the address often enough so you practically know it by heart and can maintain eye contact with your audience."

For days I repeatedly read the speech aloud, hoping it will sink in. I also visit the studios' libraries to borrow books about cinema history and technique. As once I rattled off the names of the royal family, starting with Egbert of Wessex, I memorize lists of Oscar winners and learn more than I ever wanted to know about film equipment, to be ready for anything lobbed during the lecture's question-and-answer period.

A few nights before I'm to depart, when I arrive in Encino I discover that Scott has built a makeshift podium and borrowed a music stand from Frances's brother. It's placed at the far end of the living room, past the dining room and onto the porch where he sits with Earleen and Frances. "We're waiting to hear your speech, Miss Graham," Svengali announces. "The ladies in the cheap seats have to be able to hear."

"Won't I have a microphone?"

"What if it breaks?" asks California's most worried driver.

"Good evening," I begin. "Tonight, my friends, I'm going to share the secrets of how motion pictures are truly made." I dissolve into giggles.

"Cut it out, sweetheart," Scott calls out. "You're an industry authority. Don't hesitate. Now start again and remember, you're Sheilah Graham."

Sheilah Graham, movie maven. "Good evening . . ."

"Look up!" he shouts. "People want to see your pretty face. You're not some gorgon like Hedda or Louella."

Head high but terrified, I complete a speech that takes forty minutes. My audience of three claps politely.

"Any questions?" I ask.

"Miss Graham," Frances pipes up, "who was the first movie star?"

"I'd have to say Mary Pickford. Twenty years ago she made ten thousand dollars a week and cofounded United Artists with Charlie Chaplin, D. W. Griffith, and Douglas Fairbanks. By the way, he became her second husband."

"What was the first movie made in Technicolor?" This from Scott.

"*Becky Sharp.* One of my favorites. That would be 1934."

"Is there a movie that won all the major Oscars?" Frances asks.

Bingo. "Yes. In 1934 *It Happened One Night* won Best Picture, Best Actor, Best Actress, Best Director, and Best Screenplay."

"I also wondered, what was the first picture that talked?"

"*The Jazz Singer.* 1927."

Now Scott waves. "The handsome gentleman in the back, please."

"Is it true that a munchkin fell into a toilet during the making of *The Wizard of Oz*?"

Scott has cautioned me that no matter how preposterous, I'm to answer every question with sincerity. I gather my dignity and reply, "Sadly, that is true—one of his legs got stuck—but the MGM crew came to the rescue and the small fellow suffered no harm."

Earleen flaps her hand. "I hear little Miss Temple is actually a midget? Is that true?"

I work to keep a straight face. "I have heard those rumors, Madame, but I assure you, I know Shirley Temple and she's a young girl, unusually bright for her age."

In this way, we continue until Scott walks forward. "Miss Graham, you were riveting." He presents me a bouquet of snapdragons snipped from the garden as well as a lingering kiss. "I believe you are ready for your tour."

When I leave the next morning, I do not tell him that I have seen a lawyer and written a will. I bequeath to F. Scott Fitzgerald all my earthly possessions as well as my life savings, four thousand dollars. Two thousand rightfully belong to him, because, to my astonishment, last year's indignant check didn't bounce.

Scott insists that I borrow his battered brown leather briefcase. The engraving reads: *Scott Fitzgerald, 597 5th Avenue, New York*. It is the address for Charles Scribner's Sons, because Scott has no permanent address, not now, not ever.

Chapter 41
1939

In New York City the North American Newspaper Alliance puts me up at the Roosevelt Hotel. I unpack a photo of Scott and my powder blue hat—not a parade float with canaries and grapes, lest I be confused with Hedda. My suit's shape shows off my waist and my hair is a shade blonder, thanks to Carole Lombard's hairdresser.

John Wheeler wraps me in a hug when we meet for tea at the Palm Court. "The minute you walked into my office six years ago I predicted your success." Revisionist history—another term Scott has taught me.

A few hours later I walk onto the stage of the Town Hall. It's filled to only one-third capacity, five hundred curious listeners, give or take. I grip the podium and feel stage fright so severe all I can do is drone through my speech without looking out once at the audience, who are too bored to ask even one question. "That Louella Parsons was much better," I overhear a woman sniff as she leaves.

When I return to my hotel, a telegram waits. KENNY WASHINGTON RUNNING WELL THINKING OF YOU SCOTT.

Kenny is the star quarterback for the UCLA Bruins. I crawl into bed, exhausted, but can't sleep. I haven't failed this publicly since Noël Coward's play.

I tell myself I'm like Kenny, an athlete who needs to limber up. Philadelphia and Washington are slightly better, and by Cleveland I'm able to flash a few smiles at the audience. Each evening a wire waits from Scott. Cleveland's is signed YOUR

HOLLYWOOD ADMIRER SCOTT. I kiss his portrait good night and thank him for the kindness.

By Louisville I'm both confident and famished. After a sold-out performance I gorge on fried catfish, hush puppies, and banana pudding. Scott's telegram: ROOTING FOR YOU LOUELLA AND HEDDA. I STILL MISS YOU TERRIBLY.

This, to me, is as good as "You are the finest, loveliest, tenderest, most beautiful person I have ever known."

In St. Louis I'm in fine form. ANXIOUS FOR YOUR RETURN LOVE SCOTT.

By Kansas City, I end to rousing applause. In the question period, a woman asks, "Miss Graham, what is Loretta Young like?"

"Charming. Loretta always presents a happy appearance to the world." She's an actress, for Christ's sake. "But it's hard for one woman to judge another woman. If you really want to know what Loretta is like underneath, ask a man."

The audience roars. "Oh, my God!" I yelp. "What I should have said is, ask Clark Gable." They like that even more.

Tonight, I splurge on a call to Scott. "I had them in the aisles, darling."

"Baby, I knew you would."

The following morning I fly home on a billow of relief. Scott meets me at the airport, carrying princess-worthy roses. He is frisky enough for me to suspect drinking, but I am too elated to give him the third degree.

Two days later Frances makes an unexpected, early morning appearance at my apartment. The lack of her customary smile signals distress.

"Has something happened to Scott?" I shriek. His TB, his drinking, his sleepless nights and days of getting by on only chocolate and cigarettes, his mood swings, his anxiety over debts. Until that moment I hadn't recognized to what degree worry freights my love.

"Nothing like that, thank God, but here." She hands me *The Hollywood Reporter,* which features a Page One editorial.

"Two junkets, headed by motion picture columnists, Louella Parsons and Sheilah Graham, had a good and bad effect on the business," writes the editor. Billy Wilkerson has been carrying a vendetta toward me since one of my earliest columns, when I sounded off about the inedible food at the Trocadero, which he owns. "Miss Parsons is to be thanked. But Sheilah Graham is another thing altogether."

A "thing"?

He quotes a Kansas City reporter, who I know skipped my lecture. "Sheilah Graham got two hundred dollars for a one-night stand at the Woman's Club. The studios should have paid her to stay home. The lecture was a dirt-dishing that left none of the movie mighty unsmeared."

It is *I* who's being smeared.

"The nocturnal pastimes of an adult star were hinted at. Hollywood, its players, producers, writers, and directors, won't countenance Miss Graham's further dishing. Dishing is NOT CRICKET. On the other hand, Lolly . . ."

Lolly! Who pays spies to lurk behind palms at the Brown Derby and prints whatever Randolph Hearst orders?

". . . spreads news from her rostrum that helps the picture business."

"Franny, this is—"

"Reprehensible?"

I can feel the redness of my face. "Does Scott know?"

"I'm off to Encino next."

She drives away and I call, waking him. As I snivel, I read the editorial.

"This is insane and unfair," he says, his voice stiffening. "That man is trying to get you fired. Sheilo, love."

"He's had it in for me for years."

"I can't stand by. I'm going to challenge that chump to a duel, with John O'Hara as my second. I demand satisfaction on a field of honor."

Is an affaire d'honneur an Ivy League tradition, perhaps? Aaron Burr, he once bragged, was a Princeton man. I found the duel scene in *Tender Is the Night* bizarre and think so all the more now.

"Don't be ridiculous," I say, shocked into clear thinking. "I just need your commiseration. This isn't an opera. I'm not looking for you to defend my honor. I'll call the editor of the *Kansas City Star* and request he write a protest to Wilkerson and ask John Wheeler to demand an apology and retraction."

I doubt Scott even hears me.

Late in the day I find out that Scott arrived in Wilkerson's office, gin bottle in hand. He paced in the lobby for two hours, stewing in his own rage, flinging insults and accusations at the frightened receptionist before he was forcibly removed. I also discover from Frances, who makes a second trip to my apartment, that his reaction had only partly to do with my vilification by Wilkerson.

"While you were away Scott sent *Colliers* six thousand words of his manuscript."

I'm puzzled. "That's less than half of what they wanted."

"He was eager to get the deal done. He has an elaborate outline, though between us, he changes it every day. But he felt confident that the editor would fall in love with the book. He saw himself back in business again, getting a dozen big checks, with the completed novel sold to Scribner's." She fishes a crumpled telegram out of her pocket. "Then, this." FIRST 6000 PRETTY CRYPTIC THEREFORE DISAPPOINTING. BUT YOU WARNED US THIS MIGHT BE SO. CAN WE DEFER VERDICT UNTIL FURTHER DEVELOPMENT OF STORY? IF IT HAS TO BE NOW IT HAS TO BE NO.

I may be ill.

"After Scott read it, he looked like he could bite the head off a bat. We immediately sent the manuscript to Max Perkins, but he said Scribner's also requires a bigger hunk of pages, though he offered to send him some money——"

A sympathy vote.

". . . and then the *Saturday Evening Post* passed, too."

A major publishing house and two magazines that once vied for Scott's work.

People will soon forget my attack from Wilkerson, and John Wheeler, who considers the editor a lunatic, has assured me that I won't lose my job. But I'm guessing Scott feels shattered, permanently consigned to the literary dustbin. That evening, he is inconsolable when I attempt to offer sympathy and support. He speaks in barely more than monosyllables, as if he is no longer entitled to complete sentences.

"I can't talk."

"I'm over."

"Nothing as old as last year's new."

Between each response Scott waters his growing self-pity with a heavy pour of gin.

While this frightens me, I understand why he is seeking the comfort of alcohol and make no attempt to stop him. Throughout my life, I've believed that if you show the world your exuberance and desire for a goal and work hard enough, you'll reach it. In that way, I willed myself into existence. All Scott wants is to be recognized as the writer he once was. He must believe the world is conspiring against him.

"You have to write the rest of *Tycoon* no matter what," I plead. "You've read enough to me for me to know it's possibly your best work."

"You're deluded, apparently."

"I know I'm not, Scott, not after all the novels you've made me read. I'm sure Frances would agree. It's essential that you keep going."

For the rest of the meal, he says nothing. After dinner, I walk to his side of the table, circle my arms around his neck, and suggest that we go upstairs. "Darling, let's end this god-awful day and start fresh in the morning."

He gently removes my arms. "Leave me alone, Presh. I know you mean well, but I'm unfit company. I'll call tomorrow." He is beginning to slur his words.

"Shall I sleep in the extra bedroom?"

"No, you go home. Tonight is for sulking."

Scott's hurt is my hurt. I break inside to see him in this much pain. I leave, but before I go, I wrap his gun in newspaper and hide it high up in the pantry, inside a teakettle.

Chapter 42

1939

By November the San Fernando Valley is the yellow-brown of mustard. Scott's been on and off the wagon more times than I can count, dry for weeks, then he takes one drink, twice as many the next day, and eventually, even the ministrations of a changing cast of nurses fail to put a full stop to his binge. When he's on a bender, I pity him, though the intensity of my feelings would be no match for how much, once sober, he loathes himself. Yet he also continues to write and to read from his growing novel, which is showing the glitter of greatness.

And then there was tonight.

It has been a long week, beginning with an interview I'd landed after considerable finagling. For a young woman of vast accomplishment, Judy Garland was sadly insecure, fidgeting and restating her answers two and three times before she was satisfied. "Judy, is something wrong?" I asked when her last nail was bitten.

"It's the damn pills," she said. "I'm on such a crazy schedule the studio feeds me bennies to stay awake. Then I'm so pumped I need a handful of downers to sleep."

"You poor girl, how many are you taking?"

"I've lost count. Ten, twelve, a day."

That's even more than Scott's Nembutal nightcap. "Perhaps it's not my place to say, but I wish you'd stop. You're only seventeen." She looks even younger. In contrast with her giant talent, Judy is less than five feet tall. What will Hollywood do with her when she outgrows child parts?

"I've tried to stop and got so ill I needed to miss a day's work. The producer was ready to hang me out to dry."

I see her eyeing the dishes a waiter is bringing to another table, and sense that I've heard all she wants to unload. "Well, let's see where our food is," I say.

"Great. I'm starving. I'm only allowed lettuce and soup for dinner, you know? To make me lose a few."

We spend the rest of our lunch talking about her Andy Hardy movies while she attacks spaghetti followed by apple pie à la mode and I plan the blind item I will place in my next column.

Which wildly successful young child actress is being starved to death in order to conform to Hollywood standards of slenderness? She is living off pills and being worked like a farm animal. This should be illegal . . .

The next day the phone rings when I'm still in my nightgown. I immediately worry about Scott.

"Good morning, Miss Graham." The mewing belongs to the woman John Barrymore called "the old udder."

"Good day to you, too, Mrs. Parsons."

"I will get right to the point. I see you were taken in by young Miss Garland's lies. We all make these mistakes—in the beginning. I advise you to write an immediate retraction that admits your error . . ."

Is Louella angry because I snagged the story before her, or is she this much in bed with the studio that she's acting as a fixer? And does it matter?

"There was no error," I say.

"You have only the word of a child."

"Since when do any of us have an affidavit? That's why it's called gossip. Now if you'll excuse me, I have work to do."

The work keeps me hopping all week, and on Friday evening, it's a relief to let myself into the Encino house. Frances, already gone for the weekend, has left a note saying she took with her a bundle of bottles. One of Earleen's platters of fried chicken and an angel food cake command center stage on the counter. I call to Scott. "I'm here, darling. I've missed you. Want some chicken? I stopped at the farm stand for huckleberries."

"Up here, Presh," he sings out with glee.

As I walk the stairs, I hear other voices. Doctors? No. When I enter Scott's bedroom, I see two hobos who I suspect he picked up driving to the roadhouse not far from here. One whiskery vagrant is wearing what I recognize as a charcoal Brooks Brothers suit, a recent splurge that I helped Scott select when he decided that his wardrobe looked a decade out of date. Both jacket and pants may now be crawling with lice. The other tramp has draped Scott's blue suit over his arm. On the bed sits a pile of shirts and sweaters. As if he manages a haberdashery, Scott, his bathrobe hanging open, is trying to make a sale. "The red, not the beige, I think, with your coloring, sir."

"What's going on?" I shriek.

"Ah, gentlemen, meet Lily Knish," Scott slurs, "the famous columnist."

"Put those clothes down!"

"Excuse the woman. I believe she's had too much to drink. You go right ahead and take whatever you want, my friends."

"Drop them or I'm calling the police." I avert my eyes as the derelict in the pinstripes strips to soiled undershorts and flings the pants and jacket across the room. The other stranger stands back, leery. Has he never seen an enraged woman?

"Now what did you do that for?" Scott says to the bum who'd worn the suit. "You take whatever you'd like."

"Get out this minute." My voice is a siren. "You're stealing from a sick man."

"First-class bitch," Scott growls.

"You listen to me. Leave or I'm calling the police."

"C'mon, Elmer. We ain't wanted," says the second hobo.

Literally given the bum's rush, they head toward the door. I chase them downstairs and out of the house, Scott's tortoiseshell hairbrush raised like a machete. Where is the latest nurse, the one who spends most of the day flirting?

Scott follows me to the kitchen. "I'm making you some dinner," I say, imitating a normal voice. Given that Scott is clearly drunk—and within shouting distance of becoming a homeless vagrant himself—it is not the moment for an inquisition on how he managed to lure two drifters to Belly Acres. "It will do you good," I add. To accompany Earleen's fried chicken, I heat a can of tomato soup, which I pour into bowls and put on the table.

"Never so embarrassed in my life, the way you chased away my friends," he mumbles, circling the dining room like a rabid dog.

"C'mon, darling. Sit down." Matron Weiss's voice creeps into mine. "Eat something."

Scott comes from behind with surprising agility and hurls a soup bowl. Red liquid, boiling hot, erupts like Old Faithful and leaves wide streaks on the wall and floor.

"God help me, grow up," I scream in frustration. "You could have burned me." I bend down to gather shards of china to dump in the kitchen trash can, trying to avoid skidding. "I'm not the damn sanitation crew at the Thanksgiving parade."

When I return to the dining room with dishrags, my Princeton boxer pulls back his right hand and lands a punch on my jaw. I stumble to the ground. Just as he winds up for another attack, the nurse appears. I am not too startled to notice that she's had her hair set and wears Chanel No. 5 and a snug new uniform.

"Mr. Fitzgerald, what are you doing?" She approaches him, arms outstretched. "Stop it!"

"Oh, you think Sheilah needs protection?" he sneers. "If you knew who she really is. She's a fake, right out of the filthiest privy of London. She's not *Sheilah Graham*," which he says with his nose in the air. "She's a Jew. Lily Shiel. Lily Shiel! Lily Shiel!" He repeats my name as if it were a curse—which to me, it is—betraying my secrets to a woman I despise and who I suspect despises me. Scott shatters our bond as if it were nothing more than one more china bowl.

If the nurse feels triumph, it does not last long, because when she reaches forward to try to restrain the patient he kicks her in the shin as if he were a second-rate goon. "Fuck you, Mr. Fitzgerald, you prick. How dare you?" she screams and runs out of the room.

I take three steps back and try to get to the kitchen, where there is a back door, but Scott, despite his TB and inebriation, is agile. "No, you don't," he says, grabbing my wrist, stating calmly, "You're not leaving this house."

I reach for my bruised jaw, as well as my composure. "You . . . can't . . . stop me."

"Lily Shiel, you will go when I say so."

"I hate you."

Scott's voice continues to be controlled, though sweat beads his forehead. "In that case, Lily Shiel, I will kill you."

He doesn't mean it. Don't panic. He's a caricature of a psychopath. It's all because of booze. This isn't really Scott.

I take a deep breath, hoist myself up to the counter, and sit on its edge, feet dangling, trying to hide my fear. "Well, if I can't leave, would you like to talk? Since you have Jews on your mind, shall we, say, analyze *The Merchant of Venice*?"

"I'm going to kill you. I just need to find my gun." He begins to open drawers and cupboards, tossing the contents to the floor in a clatter. "Where the fuck is it? Tell me, Lily."

"How should I know?"

"I know you know." He continues to rummage and rampage. "Where'd you put it?"

"I have no idea. I swear."

He picks up the telephone, dials, and gentles his tone. "Françoise, my sweet. I've been hearing suspicious noises here tonight, and I wonder if you know where my pistol is, please."

I can hear Frances's voice and she isn't buying it. "No, I'm sorry, I don't know where the gun is."

"You're sure? Because I'm certain there's an intruder."

"Maybe you hid it someplace."

He hangs up, looking befuddled.

"May I leave now, Scott?"

"Like I said, you're not going anywhere." His eyes are red-rimmed, his face locked in an evil squint.

I speak slowly and clearly. "Then I'm going to call the police and say I'm being held against my will. I'll use my real name. Hedda and Louella will serve us for breakfast. The whole world will discover what a savage you are and have a laugh at our expense, to boot. Knowing Hedda, she'll call Scottie and read her the column. Maybe Zelda, too. And if Hedda doesn't do it, Louella will." Especially this week.

While Scott continues to search for the gun at the opposite end of the room, I sprint to the phone and ring the operator. "Get me the police," I choke out. "If I'm cut off this is my number."

Scott seems puzzled by the fact that I am able to make the call and stands by as I recite the Belly Acres address. A squad car will be arriving shortly, a sergeant says.

"You probably heard him. The police are on the way. I think you'd best let me go."

He freezes. Disbelief unravels across Scott's face. I make a run for it, grab my keys left on the table by the front door, bolt to my car, and tear out of the gravel road, the sedan screeching around a corner. I drive thirty miles above the speed limit. As I cry I relive what the French call the *mauvais quart d'heure*, a quarter hour when your whole life changes.

Strike one: the incident in Chicago. Strike two: Malibu. Strike three: our first struggle over his gun. Then his absurd reaction to Billy Wilkerson's editorial, and now tonight. I review these incidents on the way home. Every one leads back to a bottle.

He's unglued. It's over. It's finished.

I am panting by the time I reach my flat, unlock my front door, and race to my kitchen, my jaw smarting. I wrap ice in a towel and collapse onto the living room sofa. I am living the kind of movie I hate to watch.

The phone begins to ring and doesn't stop. "What do you want?" I ask when I finally answer it.

"To make sure you got home safely," Scott says in a mockery of concern, sounding no less plastered than he did an hour ago.

I slam down the receiver. In a fury I run to my new book-shelves and rip out the inscribed page of every one of his novels, all first editions special-ordered from Scribner's. *To Shielah*— Scott never did learn to spell my name—*With love and admiration.* I light the logs in my fireplace and toss the books into the flames, one by one. *Tales of the Jazz Age, Tender Is the Night, This Side of Paradise, The Beautiful and Damned, The Great Gatsby.* With satisfaction, I watch them blaze, every crackle a jeer at Scott's expense.

When the books become ash, I am gripped by a fierce sorrow on behalf of what I've lost—not just precious volumes that represent Scott at his finest, but the man himself. I feel a burning rage for how he tramples his talent along with the love between us. I have made allowances on account of his disappointments and insecurity, but this time, he's gone too far.

The next day, my bruise is a purple that not even a heavy sludge of pancake makeup can cover. When my secretary arrives, I tell her a story she surely doesn't believe about banging into a door, and instruct her to hang up should it be Mr. Fitzgerald. This happens nine times. The tenth time I answer myself. Flustered at hearing my voice, it's Scott's turn to hang up.

Every few hours the doorbell buzzes with the delivery of a

scrawled threat straight out of a Pat Hobby story too overwritten to send to *Esquire*. Anyone but me would laugh.

Leave town or your body will be found in Coldwater Canyon.
Get out of Hollywood or you know what to expect.
You're a corpse.

For days Scott bombards me with angry letters and telegrams. He also wires John Wheeler, who calls me, infuriated to read the telegram. SHEILAH GRAHAM FORBIDDEN TO ENTER EVERY STUDIO STOP WHY DON'T YOU HAVE HER DEPORTED? STOP DO YOU KNOW HER NAME IS REALLY LILY SHIEL?

"Cripes, what kind of godforsaken cesspool have you slipped into now, Graham?" John Wheeler asks. This requires me to convince him that this is Scott's idea of a prank.

The harassment continues, as does my concern for my reputation. What if Louella or Hedda dine out on this or whatever cockamamie thing Scott tries next? A lawyer Jonah knows tells me I have two choices. I can take Scott to court—slow, costly, and public—or for five hundred dollars two policemen could be persuaded to pound on his door at five in the morning and threaten him with arrest.

"We've found this to be a highly effective technique," the attorney explains. As insulted and outraged as I am, I pass on this idea.

Two weeks after the punch, a letter arrives from Scott, typed by Frances, no doubt.

Dear Shielah,
I went haywire and hurt you. I said nasty things that repre-
sent nothing in my consciousness and very little in my sub-
conscious. About as meaningful as the quarrel we used to
have about which was the better holiday, Thanksgiving or
Christmas. I'm glad you no longer think of me with either

esteem or affection. Obviously, I am HORRIBLE for you. I loved you with all I had, but something was terribly wrong. You don't have to look far for the reason. I was it.

I want to die, Shielah. Your image is all over my heart, where Zelda's used to be. Let me remember you up to the end, which is soon. You are the finest, too much for a tubercular neurotic who can be jealous and petty. You can have the first chapter of my novel and its outline. I have no money but it might be worth something. I meant to send this longhand but I don't think it would be intelligible.

Scott

I imagine him writing the letter in a moment of sobriety, but I feel only indignation and hurt. I will not be manipulated. I will not see him. I will not.

To make sure of this, I decide to allow myself to be reabsorbed into the Garden of Allah social life. Bruised or not, Sheilah Graham is not quite ready to take the veil.

Chapter 43

1939

Hollywood is a village. Word gets around, and over the next few weeks, while I nurse my broken heart and bruised jaw ("I'm such an oaf") the single male cavalry fills my dance card. My first date is with Victor Mature, a miniature Johnny Weissmuller built for loincloths who fills me in on what it's like to play a caveman. This includes a vocabulary of grunts. After Scott, it's like spending an evening with a handsome primate. On the other hand, Garson Kanin, the director, has far too much to say, all about himself, and John O'Hara wants to talk only of his friend Scott. On that point, I, too, am speechless.

Robert Taylor invites me to a lunch "so casual you can wear blue jeans." Since I don't own dungarees, I dress in navy-blue trousers, expecting to go to a pier or a park. "I hope you like to ride," he says when he picks me up.

"I haven't been in a saddle since London, but I adore it."

We head for Bob's ranch, where we giddyap for hours along trails in the chaparral, which, as winter approaches, displays a muted beauty, and follow our ride with steaks he grills himself. In his boots and Stetson, with a buckle glinting at his narrow waist, Cowboy Bob is every bit as handsome as Vic—with the added benefit of a human vocabulary. Compared to Scott—no, I can't compare, because Bob is successful, sober, and without a right-hand hook, loaded gun, or secrets he broadcasts about my past. Easy.

"Doesn't Barbara Stanwyck live nearby?" I feign innocence after our ride as we drink strong coffee at a rustic table Bob says he built himself.

"You mean, the Geisha?"

"Careful. I like Barbara."

"As do I."

"Enough to marry?" I grin.

When he smiles I notice a dimple. "The answer depends on whether you're wearing your columnist hat. Remove it and I'll answer."

"Fair enough. Consider this conversation off the record."

The dimple disappears. "Here's the deal. We're already married—since May."

He takes a gold band out of his pocket and slips it on his finger. "At first Mr. Mayer told me not to mess around with Barbara. He thought marriage would jeopardize my image. But when LBM realized we were doing as we damn pleased, he dragged me to the altar by the ear."

The day no longer feels casual, nor does Robert Taylor seem half as clean-cut or uncomplicated. "If you're Barbara Stanwyck's husband, what are we doing together?"

"I like you, Sheilah, I think you feel the same way, and I wouldn't say Barbara and I are exactly bleeding with love. For God's sake, she calls me Junior." He walks around the table and embraces me. I push him away. Do I have "trollop" branded on my behind? If loving a man married to a woman in a sanitarium two thousand miles away is stupid, dating a star who's taken a beloved bride of national renown is nuts.

"Our afternoon is over," I tell Robert.

We have little to say to one another in the car, but when Robert walks me to the door I kiss him on the cheek, adding, "I hope you and Barbara can figure out what the hell you're doing."

It is a relief to be at home, but when I'm inside, I find a note that's been slipped under my door.

Mr. Fitzgerald is himself again and everything he did seems awful to him. He wants to know if he should leave Hollywood, to remove as much of the unhappiness as is possible from what he did.

Sincerely,
Frances Kroll

The handwriting belongs to Frances. The language is pure Scott.

I call Frances at home and tell her I want, please, to be left in peace. Which is how I pass the evening, reading *Pride and Prejudice* with an avocado mask on my face, wearing a flannel nightgown, giving myself a pedicure and listening to Chopin.

Two days later another note arrives, this one in Scott's hand, steeped in self-pity . . . how he thought of the trusting girl whom he "loved more than anything in the world"—to whom he gave sorrow when all he wanted was to give joy. He blames his behavior on fever, liquor, and sedatives. "I hope the last awful impression is fading until someday you can say, 'He can't have been that bad.'"

I don't respond. He was that bad.

The following day, John Wheeler forwards a second telegram from Scott. I SENT YOU THAT EARLIER WIRE WITH A BURNING FEVER AND A GOOD DEAL OF LIQUOR IN MY GUT. DO NOT WORRY ABOUT SHIELAH IN CONNECTION WITH THE STUDIOS. WE HAD SOME PRIVATE TROUBLE WHICH I DEEPLY REGRET.

I read the wire with the same indifference I feel when American Beauty roses arrive from Scott the next day. I consider dropping them in the garbage, then decide the flowers don't deserve to be punished for his asinine behavior and arrange them in a vase that I place in the living room.

The next day Frances stops by. "He's quit drinking for good," she says, bashfully. Frances likes me and I like Frances, but her first allegiance is to Scott.

"I've heard that before."

She glances at the roses. I expect her to report back to Scott that I kept them, which he'll see as a triumph. "He's also finished a second chapter of his book and it's wonderful."

So what? I've enjoyed the last five weeks, though their lightness is the result of pointless conversation, even when Irwin Shaw, the playwright, remarked, "It's amazing how well-read you are." A few months ago this praise would have flattered me. Now that the College of One has helped me grow an armor of confidence, I see that the difference between more articulate people and me has far less to do with IQ than I used to think. My mind is quick. I had only needed to learn to use it. For this I am in Scott's debt—which compounds my anger, because it reminds me of what I have lost.

That night, after dinner at the Coconut Grove and dancing the mambo at Ciro's in the arms of Robert Benchley, I walk through the door and kick off my sandals just as the phone rings. It is exactly midnight. I know that it is Scott even before I answer.

On what may be the first night in five weeks that I managed not to think of him every five minutes, he says, entirely compos mentis, "Thanks for not hanging up. All I want to do is talk, Sheilo. Out of respect for what we had."

I count to ten before I say, "I'm listening. What's on your mind?"

"Would you be willing to see me?"

Silence hangs between us like a wall of glass.

"I torpedoed all that was fine between us by my egotism and lack of self-control," he says. "I miss you like a phantom limb. I wander these rooms saying your name."

Pretty words.

"Be kind. That's all I'm asking. See me once. Let me tell you what's in my heart."

"My jaw is only now healed. How do I know you won't slug me again?"

"I am deeply ashamed of my actions, Sheilo. I've never hit a woman in my entire life. I behaved like an animal that night." I hear his tears. "I'm a broken bird, but I love you and want to apologize in person. Your man is begging you."

I say nothing.

"Do you respect what we had?" he asks.

"I do." I've never experienced such closeness, known such pleasure, or felt as understood.

"In that case . . ."

Chapter 44

1939

Scott calls for me at nine in the morning. On the Fitzgerald clock this is dawn. We greet one another with a chaste peck. I do not invite him in. Rather, we walk to his car, where we are first-date wooden.

"You look well, Sheilah."

"As do you." His cheeks show healthy color and he is smoothly shaven, though for the first time, I notice silver threads in his cornsilk hair. "Are you working?"

"I'm my own drill sergeant. Two chapters solid."

"I'd like to think that's true." I hear the acid in my voice.

"I'm hoping you can withhold skepticism, and in exchange, I promise no more lies, not even to myself."

I almost smile. "Sleeping well?"

"Sleep and I are still fighting the Hundred Years' War, but the wee hours give me time to ruminate on my sins."

"Repenting, are we?"

"In my way. I asked Frances if she'd pray for me last Yom Kippur. She informed me God doesn't allow mercenaries, so I'm one more sucker on his own."

When was I last in a synagogue atoning for my own sins? Twenty-two years ago, and yet, with not a small amount of hubris, I say, "Yom Kippur was last fall, before——"

Scott raises his hand. "Point taken."

We drive wordlessly until we reach Laurel Canyon. Scott parks the car, walks to my side, and offers his arm, which I refuse. I follow him to a grassy slope, stippled by sunlight. Under

the tent of a cloudless January blue sky, he unfolds the plaid
blanket we used for tailgate picnics and spreads it on the ground.
We face one another as we each lean against tree trunks. Our
breath dances in the nippy air. I feel small and awed, as if we
are lone worshipers in a grand cathedral. But I am still angry.

He clears his throat. "If you'll do me the favor of listening, I
want—I need—to explain my drinking. I've been justifying it
for twenty-five years, and it's the source of all my bad conduct."
His voice is low and steady. Rehearsed.

"I'm listening."

"I started in college to try to be something I wasn't, a young
man in the vortex of a brain trust and social whirl. Since childhood I'd been in thrall to the rich, with my nose pressed up
against their window. They're the closest thing we've got to an
aristocracy, and remember, I'm just a middle-class Catholic boy
from nowhere, an unhappy family's show pony, who grew up
with hardly a dollar."

"I'm actually familiar with that experience," though I'd rate
mine ten times sorrier.

"Of course, Sheilo, but you're stronger than I am—most
women are—and don't think I'm not envious or that this isn't
one of fifty reasons I love you." I sense that he wants to reach
for my hand. I lean away. "I pretended I was no different from
any other college man or soldier—boozing was as indigenous to
the army as to Princeton. But I liked the bolder self I was with
alcohol. I liked it very much."

His reader knows the man he is describing. He or she meets
him in any of his books.

"When Zelda and I married, she matched me almost drink
for drink. Carousing on a baroque scale became our life. Both
love and art require a certain defenselessness, and we wanted
the hilarity, the rush—I'm not sure which of us more. I poured
my youth into a highball, too reckless to notice that others had
stopped long before I did. When *This Side of Paradise* hit it big,

I was only twenty-three, undisciplined and puffed with adulation. I made mountains of money, and thought all I needed to make more was paper and pencil."

Scott's hands are shaking. The air is still, but it takes him three tries to light a cigarette.

"I was wrong. I needed gin, too, though I also devoted my attention to Champagne and cognac and triple sec and absinthe and calvados and chartreuse and Frangelico, simply because I liked the name, chased by the odd Pimm's Cup. Every morning was my birthday and every night New Year's Eve. Zelda caught on and hated me for my weakness. Not that I had anyone to blame. My failures were and are entirely mine. One might say I've been consistently imprudent."

"One might."

"I've tried to dry out, only to fall off the wagon. Well, you've seen this."

"And its collateral cruelty."

"Then Zelda broke, and it was all my fault." He lets his tears fall. "My wife lost her mind because I drank . . ."

This stops me. "That can't be true, Scott. Being an alcoholic—"

He backs away as if I've slapped him, but I need to get through. "Call your problem what it is, or not, but I don't think even F. Scott Fitzgerald, with all his magical talent, can make someone else mentally ill. Zelda has her own plight. You have yours."

He dabs his eyes with a handkerchief. "I don't know, but it comes down to this. I drank to find myself, never realizing with each sip my higher reasoning evaporated that much more. First I took a drink, then the drink took a drink, and eventually the drink took me. I drank to keep from being invisible, but the booze has done that job all on its own. It's destroyed my ability to write."

If he thinks this will win my sympathy, he is wrong. "Interesting theories, Scott."

"But now I want to talk about you, Sheilo," he says. "You've stood by when I've been a scoundrel and in return I've hurt you, in the most contemptible ways. I don't deserve you, but that doesn't stop me from wanting you. I'm a glutton for your bright mind, your big heart, your love."

He gets on one knee, as if he might propose. I shiver.

"Sheilah Graham, I adore you with a heart pumped by penitence and passion. I haven't had a drink since December first and I intend never to drink again. I'm so very sorry, for everything." He stops. Could he be praying? "Will you please come back? I need you. You give me the gift of hope."

It's a confession, impassioned, but not an apology. He's left out hitting and humiliating me, and wrangling over a gun. What has changed since the cruelty of his Lily Shiel tirade—everything or nothing?

"I need a true apology."

"Oh. Sheilo, you have it. I am so sorry. Endlessly sorry. Infinitely remorseful."

"I need to know, when you drink, why you change into a beast. Who's the real Scott?"

He shifts to sitting. "The man before you."

Allegedly.

"I don't know the louse I become when I drink. It's as if a ghoul who despises me comes to destroy my life. But I do know I can stop drinking and be a man who can love as you ought to be loved and honored. I've had nurses for weeks and I'm making the cure work, for both of us. We belong together. You are my missing piece, and I hope you agree." Scott is pleading, and seems exhausted from the effort.

I'm dry-eyed. "I hear your remorse, but how can I be sure?"

"Miss Graham, give me a trial run, satisfaction guaranteed. If you're displeased, return me to my solitude, and I won't bother or hurt you again."

We soak up whatever weak sunlight the winter sky offers, until I say, "Please take me home."

We drive stone silent. It's been a good show, but the ability to enchant is, after all, Scott's core. Author and philosopher first, smooth-talker second.

"And now?" he says when we arrive.

And now . . . "I will think."

I try to lose myself in work and intimate in my column that Artie Shaw, the handsome bandleader—the kind of Jewish boy I dreamt about at fifteen—has captured Judy Garland's youthful heart. "What bright-eyed film ingénue has been seduced along with the rest of the country by Artie Shaw's rendering of 'Begin the Beguine'?" I write. "The King of Swing plays a clarinet like he's making love to a woman." That's what I'd *like* to have written. What I actually wrote was "like he's falling in love with a woman."

Meanwhile, Louella lands the far bigger story—and secures her revenge.

After their first date, Artie Shaw eloped with Lana Turner, the girl Billy Wilkerson discovered as she sipped a Coca-Cola on Sunset, causing busloads of fetching young things to empty their piggybanks and invade Hollywood. With her hair turned blond, Louis B. Mayer is grooming Lana "Sweater Girl" Turner to be the next Jean Harlow.

Now that's mean, with a dangling modifier to boot. If poor Judy Garland isn't gobbling pills now, she will be soon.

I labor to come up with a scoop to rival Louella's and settle on letting readers know that dozens of still photographs of Joan Crawford and Clark Gable from *Strange Cargo* were killed by the Hays Office because of the libidinous expression in Clark's eyes.

Despite the drumbeat of work, I can't stop thinking about Scott. It requires no mastery of psychology to discern the symbiosis between his weakness and the self-deception that has allowed my own lies to grow. Nor do I need anyone to point out how attached I am to Scott, and how I miss his laugh and lips. Every time he's gone on a bender, I've gotten closer to figuring out that I need him the way he needs gin.

As the time stretches since the gun incident, I realize, too, how much I want to be on his side. Like me, Scott is alone. In England, I had the kind heart of Johnny—and somewhere on this earth, my brother Morris—but now I only have acquaintances. Who does Scott have? Zelda depends on him, but can give little back. Scottie is still a girl. Frances is an employee. Many long-standing friends adore him, but he opens his heart to none except in his writing. Scott and I need one another. He is my bread and water, the only man who recognizes my flaws, yet loves me nonetheless, and the only man who has come to cherish my mind as well as my body.

I like being seen as Scott alone sees me, with my secrets and broken places. I am his beloved infidel and he is simply my beloved.

Since we met a few weeks ago, there have been no flowers, no notes, no poems. But I sense him waiting. Well into February, when I can no longer stand to be apart for one more hour, I call.

"I need to know you've truly changed," I say, not bothering with hello.

"I have. I promise you." He speaks without hesitation, as if he anticipated the call.

"I want to be able to count on you."

"You can."

"Then I'm ready to see you."

"Sheilo," is all he says as his voice breaks. "Yes, yes, yes."

A few hours later I hear the huff of his car, a sound sweeter to me than a Mozart aria. He walks quickly up my walk, his scruffy trench coat hanging open so I can see my favorite pink shirt. When I open the door, he hands me one red rose. We stand still, taking each other in. At first we embrace tentatively, yet a moment later I crush him in the way I might if he'd escaped a plane crash. I want to be crushed in return, to freeze this moment and never be separated again. One hand ruffles his hair and with the other, I remove his necktie.

"You," is all I say. "Darling."

"Sheilo," he whispers in response.

Upstairs, our lovemaking begins with cautious civility, but as Scott's skin warms mine, passion replaces restraint and kisses become more. I cannot pretend I don't want this gifted soul, with all his complicated humanity. I want us to own one another.

We wake from a doze, arms entangled, our feelings ratified and bodies satisfied. "Day by day, that's the only commitment I'm willing to make," I say.

"I'll take it," he answers.

Our life falls back in place, secluding us in a country cocoon. Were it not for premieres in town, we'd see nothing
of our friends. When spring explodes, Scott pays to have the pool
filled as an enticement for me to stay at Belly Acres during the
weekdays. This is a luxury, but he has money trickling in—he's
been commissioned to write a script from his own short story
"Babylon Revisited," and while the fee is just short of a swin-
dle, Scott is pleased. He swims in his own words, reimagining
them for the screen, though he barely dangles a toe in the water.
"Can't risk it with the old TB," says my favorite hypochondriac,
who now takes his temperature every four hours. At midday we
indulge in a break when Scott paces on the sidelines in a hat and
long-sleeved shirt, bellowing orders on how I should fine-tune
my breaststroke and crawl. "Arm higher! Slice the water! Every
fourth stroke turn to breathe! Kick!"

Our enclosed world is an incubator of creativity. Scott writes
while I finish my column and read for the College of One.
He's starting this faux shiksa on the Gospels of St. Mark and
St. Luke. Perhaps he's called on the same saints for heavenly
forbearance, because when he discovers that I incinerated the
first editions of his novels, he replaces them with rueful grace,
inscribed again, *Encino Edition*. I'm also taking his urging to
heart and trying my hand at my own fiction, which I haven't
attempted since my clumsy detective novel written in London.
I am dotting the *i*'s on "Janey," a short story about a rebellious
daughter with a creamy complexion and widely spaced blue

eyes who wrangles with her professor father, who in the 1920s was the literary mouthpiece for flaming youth.

"I wouldn't exactly call this fiction," Scott said, not unkindly. "You'd better change it up so the characters aren't instantly recognizable."

I take that as a compliment, though I ask, "Since when do you follow this advice?"

The evening hours are when Scott reads me pages from his novel, using his full arsenal of dramatic fireworks. I'm honored when I hear my own descriptions—"at night the Ping-Pong balls on the grass look like stars" or "the cascading California rain sounds like horses weeing"—and hoot when he dismisses a script in the novel as being "flat as an old column of Lolly Parsons."

It's not news that the hero's love interest faintly resembles me, but with additional chapters revealed, I recognize that she transcends a dim replica. Kathleen, who'd been engaged to a king, floats through his pages like my ghost. I once described blueprints a movie director had shown me for a house he wanted to build. There is the construction site where Monroe Stahr and Kathleen consummate their love. "When I'm with you, I don't breathe quite right," she whispers to Stahr, re-creating the honesty I risked in revealing this to Scott the first time we danced. Kathleen, who also has "nice teeth for an English girl," confesses the shame of her past to Stahr, as I did my own history to Scott. Each time I hear new pages I wonder which cadged details will be woven into this fictional tapestry that we hope will reinstate him in the bestseller pantheon. I'm both flattered and horrified.

Tonight when he finishes his reading, I repeat, "Her eyes invited him to a romantic communion of unbelievable intensity," and ask, "Do you realize you're offering the world a glimpse into our own love affair, even to how we give one another pleasure?"

He puts on his most cherubic smile. "Nonsense. These are characters, Presh, though if you feel they're real, I've done my job."

"You're being elusive." I get no answer beyond a short, self-satisfied cackle. "You always write your life, don't you?"

"What else do I have to work with? Even if I were reporting on wrestling alligators, what would interest me isn't the blood and biceps, but why the lady alligator broke the big guy's heart. I shake it all up, the good and the bad, and see where the dice land."

Scott must sense that I'm unconvinced because he says, "If there's anything you want me to change, I will."

"Not change, explain," because I am learning how much Kathleen reminds lonely Stahr of his dead wife. I take the temperature between us, decide that it's smoldering, and ask the question that's been on my mind for three years. "When we're together are you thinking about Zelda?"

I am afraid Scott will brush off my question with a laugh, but he admits, "At the very beginning, I did, a bit. That first night I thought I saw something around your eyes, and the fair hair, which, by the way, Zelda doesn't have anymore. Her hair is dark now, to match the rest of her."

"But when you're looking at me, is she who you see? I need to know."

This is as important a question as who the real Scott is, the drunk or the gentleman.

Now he takes my hands. "I see only you, Sheilo. You are today. Well, today and tomorrow and forever. The Zelda of almost twenty years ago is long gone, and while out of loyalty and human kindness and a tribute to our history, I will always try to take care of the girl I wed, our marriage has expired in every way but legal."

These sentiments are a sonata, though I don't expect to hear what every woman in my position craves: I love you best. You arouse me more. Only you are the true love. Most of all, I want to have a child with you, because I want what you want.

I will never stop hoping that Scott speaks these words, and today I say it straight. "I'd love to have your baby. Could you see us as parents together?"

He looks electrocuted. "Is this humor?"

"With your insomnia the night feeding would be painless."

He isn't chuckling. "You would make a loving mother and we would have a perfect child, but this is something I can never offer you, Presh. Please don't ask. I'm not young enough."

"You're only forty-three. I give you Picasso."

"Or rich enough."

"After *Tycoon* the dollars will pour in and you'll feel thirty-five." As Tatte said, from my mouth to God's ears. "Please think about it."

Scott ends the conversation with a kiss. I read this as a definite maybe.

As spring broils into summer, the heat is like a thick bandage binding the valley to the steaming earth. Belly Acres becomes a furnace where the wind dies in the haze. Leaves stand still, and there aren't enough fans or chilled glasses of Coca-Cola and minty iced tea to make a difference. I dip in the pool first thing in the morning, and again before dinner. It has become too hot to swim at high noon.

"I can't think in this smelter," Scott complains early one evening as we sit in the dining room, fanning ourselves and eating puddles of vanilla ice cream.

"We'll get better cross-ventilation if you push that sticky window higher," I suggest.

He attempts to raise the window, which refuses to budge, tries again, and snaps back, grabbing his right arm, flailing and shrieking, "What the hell?"

"Scott!" I jump from my seat and race across the room.

He stumbles, spins, and reaches to bolster himself against the wall. "Holy Mother of God." He has collapsed, moaning.

"Talk to me!" I say, bending over him.

Scott opens his eyes. "It went black for a minute, as if I'd been torched by a hot poker. The pain shot all the way up here"—he points to his shoulder—"and now my arm's gone stiff." He reaches for it with his left hand and his face contorts.

"You're going straight to bed." I shout for Earleen to help him walk upstairs while I call Dr. Nelson, who promises to get here as fast as possible.

For nearly two hours I hover over Scott, wiping his forehead with towels dipped in ice water. He's been telling me that a novelist becomes his characters and that he's begun to feel and think like Monroe Stahr. Is Stahr's bad heart casting a spell on our newly perfect life?

"Everything's going well—us, the book, Scottie's studies," Scott groans. "Why trouble now?"

"It's probably nothing," I lie. "Just close your eyes and rest."

We wait for Dr. Nelson. And wait. Finally, he arrives, brandishing his stethoscope and forced optimism. After a few "breathe deeplys" and prods he says, "You'll live, my friend, but I want you in my office first thing tomorrow."

The next day, anxiously, we report for the exam. A cardiogram proves that Scott didn't have a heart attack, as we'd both feared. He experienced what the doctor calls a seizure. A warning.

"We're finished with Encino," I say when we leave the physician's office, no less scared. "I'll find you someplace in town, near me"—and the doctor, just in case. "All that heat and the driving, it's too much."

I feel a tremendous yearning to care for Scott now, demonstrating my love in sickness and in health. I wish we could live together, letting me be with him night and day, every day, but Hollywood hypocrisy prevents it. Our relationship may be an open secret, but given showbiz priggishness, should a couple share a household without the holy sacrament of marriage, they're considered shameful, even in 1940. In our case, since the whole world knows about poor Zelda, I would be cast as a hateful hussy and Scott the cruelest sort of philanderer. Louella and Hedda would make us a bigger scoop second to the United States declaring war on Germany.

We opt for a furnished flat I find on Laurel Avenue, only a block away from me and a short stroll from Schwab's, since God forbid that Scott runs low on Raleighs and Hershey bars. It's an entirely unexceptional apartment with a top note of cat-once-lived-here and a saggy couch the green of a rotting pepper, but spacious enough, and given the location, cheap.

We move immediately. The first thing Scott does is hang his map of Europe where he tracks the whereabouts of Hitler's troops, whom he is sure he could defeat if only the English commanders would take his advice. Next to the map are timelines and charts for *The Love of the Last Tycoon*. Together, we make short work of unpacking his suitcases and boxes—his new grey suit and tuxedo and the rest of his small wardrobe, records, a radio with reliable reception for war reports and music, books and more books, and for the bedroom, pictures of Scottie, Zelda, and me, including one of the two of us when we spent a weekend in Tijuana; I'm grinning like the ass I'm sitting on. My caballero wears a serape and sombrero, looking as witless as anyone would in that get-up.

Settling in takes all of an hour. During that time his neighbor down the hall entertains us with ear-piercing shrieks, which the landlord tells us she sells for movie soundtracks. She inflicts her entire repertoire on us, which appears to range from "cockroach ahead" to "girl trips on a cadaver." When the woman finishes a particularly heartfelt screech, we follow it with maniacal laughter of our own. After we calm down, however, I notice that Scott's eyes droop.

"You nap now," I say. "Dinner at eight, at my place." We've hired a maid who'll clean both apartments, go to the market, and cook an evening meal, because even a poor man in Hollywood finds money for a servant. I walk to my flat and unpack the few items I kept in Encino—nightgowns, slippers, lingerie, a blue silk kimono, books, the remaining half inch of my Elsa Schiaparelli perfume, cosmetics, and toiletries. I think about what Dr. Nelson promises: Scott's heart will heal. It's a muscle like any other. But for six more weeks, he forbids sexual activity.

Tonight we sleep together at his place. We spoon and the closeness of his warm flesh next to me fills my heart. I am counting the days . . .

Chapter 46

1940

After Dr. Nelson's pronouncement of a heart seizure, I half expect Scott to limp about with a cane, chewing on a thermometer. I am wrong. Whether the cause is the change of scenery or fear of being classified as a legitimate invalid, I cannot say, but he displays a defiant energy that is resulting in a personal Industrial Revolution. Pages for *Tycoon* pour from Frances's typewriter, typed three times: triple-spaced, so her boss can eviscerate the draft with pencil edits; a double-spaced version that suffers through a second polishing, and finally, another double-spaced manuscript Scott may or may not consider to be "finished."

As someone who zips through one draft of her column, meets her deadline, and moves on, I never fail to be awed by Scott's perfectionism. Nor is his novel all he is producing. He has another quickie script job, adapting an English play whose plot revolves around a matinee idol undone by drink; Darryl Zanuck seems to think Scott Fitzgerald has the insight to turn this into a wry comedy. Every morning my cinematic soldier marches off with a briefcase of Coca-Cola to meet Frances at the Fox studio. When he returns there are Pat Hobby tales and other stories to churn out, and his continuing correspondence with Scottie, Zelda, Max Perkins, and other regulars. Scott and the United States Postal Service maintain an intimate relationship. With a flourish of epic grandeur, he keeps duplicates of his letters, in case posterity gives a damn. Destiny, take note.

Scott thrums with energy, and appears too occupied to take

more than the occasional drink. Does he suppose I don't notice the odd bottle poking out of the trash? What's different
is that for the first time since I've known him, he is drinking
to the point of joie de vivre, not oblivion, able to have one or
two gins—though never in front of me—sleep them off, and
get cracking in the morning. My deepest regret now isn't for
the hurt he's caused me, almost a year gone, but for the books
he might have written during the past decade's vast swaths of
squandered time. At nearly forty-four—his birthday is in September, two months away—I believe Scott is belatedly saying
ta-ta to his endless adolescence, as Dr. Hoffman urged last year.
He's trading clownery that brought bums to the house for a
muffled quiet that brings chapters to completion. If he seems
older, he is also happier.

I say the same for myself. This busy yet tranquil life is one I
choose with a full heart. I enjoy reporting, reading, and tinker-
ing with my short story, though I'm not going to turn down a
junket to Dallas for Gary Cooper's premiere of *The Westerner*,
nor would I mind occasionally dancing to Benny Goodman or
Artie Shaw. I can't say I miss the charades. At thirty-six what I
do miss is marriage—going to bed every night with a husband
and waking up with him by my side in the morning. I also miss
a child, but when I float that subject, as I have now more than
once, Scott shuts me down.

This evening—Scott's birthday—marks two months since we've
been back together.

We splurge on dinner at the Brown Derby rather than eat the
maid's unrelenting steak, peas, and baked potato. Feasting on
shrimp cocktails followed by lobsters big as footballs, we bask in
the attention of fawning waiters and random acquaintances. At
home later on Hayworth, I dim the living room lights.

"Are you preparing a naughty seduction?" Scott asks.

"That depends on what you wish for. Close your eyes." My maiden baking effort is a fudge cake that lists at a rakish angle, with shaved coconut rained over the top to hide its patchy, crumb-flecked icing. I ignite an infantry of candles.

Despite Scott's orations on the theme of tuberculosis, he blows out every flame.

"Well done, Mr. Fitzgerald." I throw my arms around him. "Happy Birthday, darling."

"May I assume this lovely confection is your handiwork?"

"This cake may be the inspiration for the word 'slapdash.'"

"*You* are a confection, and do you know this is the first cake anyone's baked for me since I left St. Paul? Sheilo, you do make me more content than I have a right to be."

"Should I cross-stitch those words on a sampler?"

"I fell in love with a pugnacious reporter who has become as domestic as a tabby cat. Tomorrow, darning socks?"

"I have other ideas."

Tonight ends our forced celibacy. We are nervous as virgins. Scott unwraps me like a present down to my newly bought garland of lacy underthings, and we proceed in a courtly minuet that turns into voluptuous, elongated movement. He smiles above me, purring verbal caresses I return.

"Good to be back where we belong," he says when it ends, blowing smoke rings, looking rather pugnacious himself.

"To the future."

The following week, I come home from a shopping trip, eager to show Scott three new dresses, each more heavenly than the next.

"Don't you think three is a bit extravagant?" he chides in the hectoring tone I've heard in letters to Scottie that he's read aloud.

"You know I have to look the part." Conscientious coquette.

"Nevertheless, I think I've made myself clear." He galumphs out of the room, his verbal spanking leaving me peeved. I pay for my clothing, along with my rent, and I've recently gotten a raise.

The next chance I have to corner Frances, who does Scott's banking, I ask how much money he has in his account. She hesitates.

"Franny," I say, "this may seem intrusive, but I assure you my inquiry is in Scott's best interest."

"He has enough left to get him through the next four months," she says, "if he's frugal." No more Brown Derby blowouts, no trips to Santa Barbara as we made a few weeks ago, no more hand-built bookshelves or expensive records. I thank her and hatch a plan.

What I know of Max Perkins, Scott's editor at Scribner's, is that he is not merely skilled, but fatherly, generous, and fond of Scott. We have never met, though Scott has made him aware of our relationship. Understanding how Scott appropriates his life in his fiction, I'm certain Max recognizes me as Kathleen in the early chapters he read of *Tycoon*.

Dear Max, the muse decides to write.

I want you to know that The Love of the Last Tycoon *is coming along beautifully and furthermore, that Scott has not had a drink for a year. He has become devoted to finishing his novel, which, I am convinced, may be his best work yet. I hope you will agree. Beyond reporting this, I have another reason for writing, though I ask you to never mention this correspondence to Scott. What I propose would injure his pride.*

I am enclosing a check for two thousand dollars. I would like you to give it to Scott as an advance against future royalties of Tycoon. *A vote of confidence, as it were. If you would add a few thousand to this amount I—and, I'm sure, Scott—*

would be very grateful. Were he to get this money now, he
would be able to fully commit to his novel rather than in-
terrupt his work to take studio jobs in order to pay his bills,
which as you know, include Scottie's tuition at Vassar and
Zelda's fees for Highland Hospital.

My initiative may be unorthodox, but I believe it would
make all the difference to Scott if he knew that you and Scrib-
ner's were behind him. Also, please understand that even if
the novel makes millions, I do not expect to be reimbursed.

The money is Scott's that he gave me last year, deposited in
the bank, earning interest. I mail my letter with no regret and
wait to see if my conniving will pay dividends.

It is a shock when I notice that Scott's weekly letter to Zelda,
which he leaves next to the front door for Frances to mail, is addressed not to North Carolina, but Alabama. I sit on this discov-
ery for a few days, but over dinner one night try to ask casually,
"Has Zelda been discharged?"

Scott reacts as if I've hosed him with cold water. "Why do
you ask?"

"Just curious. It's wonderful news if she's healthy enough to
no longer live in the sanitarium." Wonderful for her.

"She hasn't been in Highland for six months. Her doctor decided she can live with her mother in Montgomery, just as the
Sayres always wanted."

I have many questions, but the one I ask is, "How's it going?"

"It depends on whom you ask. Mama Sayre says it's perfectly
splendid and long overdue, but she's always blamed the cuckoo
husband for her daughter's situation. If you ask Scottie, poor
girl, her mother is babbling nonsense half the time. I tell Scottie if you live in the South, no one will notice."

But it isn't funny. What if Zelda improves enough to reunite with Scott? What if she joins him in Hollywood? Worse, what if he moves to Alabama?

"Well, good for Zelda," I say. "She must have excellent doctors."

"Charlatans I no longer have to pay, so at least there's that."

For days I can barely breathe. Scott has told me his marriage binds him only legally, but I know the depth of his Catholic-boy guilt and sense of obligation. Now that Scott has his drinking under control, I cannot risk having Zelda decimate our relationship.

I choose to respond in the best way I can imagine. Following the ancient wisdom of *act first, apologize later,* I toss my diaphragm.

Chapter 47

1940

I've finished my story about the character not-to-be-mistaken-for-Scottie. Scott tells me it's possibly publishable and is determined to turn me into a writer capable of crafting more than another story or gee-whiz conjecture about whether Charles Boyer wears a toupee. He believes the world is waiting for a memoir by the gorgeous Miss Graham and to that end, has bought me a costly ledger of tobacco-colored leather embossed with my initials. In it, he expects me to plan my future book.

"Have you noticed how I work?" he asks.

Would it be possible to spend any time with the man and not notice?

"If I think of something, I write it down, right away. I dig it all out like diamonds—one sparkler to the cubic ton of dull, grey coal. You can always rewrite, but you may never recapture what you notice or think as vividly as the first time. Take notes, not just your own observations and things people say, but what you remember from your childhood."

"What little I remember, I'm trying to forget."

"Nonsense, Sheilo. Be proud of how far you've come. You're my Gatsby."

Poor imposter got involved with careless people, but Gatsby had his good points. "Nothing is more insufferable than a flawless character and you, sweetheart, have somewhat contradictory qualities that make for an interesting heroine—optimistic but cautious, brave but secretive, dreamy but sensible."

"Cautious? Secretive? Sensible?" though it's true and said

with affection. When Scott's writing goes well, he's as light as a dancing sunbeam, which is the sort of hackneyed phrase that comes to my mind, proof that the author Scott thinks I can be will never exist. I remember the metaphors I tossed about like rice at a wedding in *Gentleman Crook,* and have no confidence that I can do better all these years later.

"Thank you for the handsome notebook. I promise I'll try to be worthy of it."

"You'll use it?"

"Yes, Scott." Eventually. Maybe. Unlikely.

We are sitting in my living room and start to play a recording of Mozart's *Così fan tutte.* I try to listen while I read the libretto and Scott works out military tactics. He is winning the war with his book, but General Fitzgerald has lost every battle in Europe. When the opera ends, he announces that he needs some air and is off for cigarettes.

"Start the Bach. I'll be back soon," he says. "Twenty minutes." Although the temperature is sixty-one degrees, he bundles himself into a grey topcoat, black scarf, and a homburg, as if he just parachuted in from Wall Street.

Twenty minutes pass. No Scott. I picture him at Schwab's paging through magazines. I've never seen him walk by a *Colliers* or *Saturday Evening Post* that he wasn't tempted to open so he could rant about the inferiors being published rather than F. Scott Fitzgerald.

Forty minutes pass. I begin to worry in earnest and am grateful when he staggers through the door, though I see at once that he is pale. I rush to his side as he flops into my green armchair. "What happened?"

He plucks a Raleigh from his pocket, lights it with disquieting slowness, takes a long drag, and speaks in a voice worthy of Edgar Allan Poe. "I had the spookiest sensation at Schwab's, as if the world around me was going dim, little by little."

The chorus swelling to Bach's *Singet dem Herrn* adds melodrama to Scott's narration that I do not need. I switch off the music. "Do you think you had another seizure?"

"No, there wasn't pain. This time I was dizzy and clammy and faint. I had to ask the man at the counter if I could sit somewhere." He puts his hat in his lap, loosens his scarf, and shakes his head. "I felt like my own grandpa. Thoroughly embarrassing."

"I'll get you some water and help you out of this coat. You're overheated." I'm also thinking it wasn't prudent to have enjoyed one another in bed both this morning and last night, even if the second time my middle-aged lover boy initiated it. Scott most likely needs just ordinary rest.

The next day he insists on seeing the doctor—alone. "It was a cardiac spasm," he announces on his return.

"Not a heart attack?"

"The doc didn't use those words."

Thank God. When John Wheeler had a heart attack he was out flat on his back for six weeks, though now he has returned to work and is, he claims, in the pink.

"Do you have any restrictions?"

"No stairs."

The next step comes to me as if foreordained. "You'll move into my second bedroom till we find you your own place."

Scott's eyebrows arch to his high forehead. "But Sheilo, that's where you and your secretary work."

"Don't be silly. We'll switch to the dining room, and Frances and I will look for a different apartment for you, on the ground floor, somewhere nearby. You'll be able to move soon enough. Staying with me is simply temporary."

I try to feign nonchalance, but inside I am cheering. Scott will now be as physically close as I feel him to be emotionally. I'll watch over my love with vigilance and affection, offering him the attention he requires and that I am as eager as a bride to bestow. I'll be the next best thing to Mrs. Fitzgerald. The

real version may elude me, but having spent half my life playing let's-pretend, I believe I can be at peace with an almost-
marriage.

Taking care of Scott will be different from the vile servitude
of nursing my mother, because I'm convinced she never loved
me. I certainly stopped loving her the moment I was left at the
Asylum. For all his failings, Scott does love me, deeply, and I
love him. What's more, looking after him will be my choice, as
it wasn't when Mama fell ill. No one is destroying my future.
Scott *is* my future.

"One more thing. Intimacy is out again," he says primly,
"until the cardiograms improve. But they will. You know what
Dr. Nelson says, 'the heart heals.'" He imitates the doctor's bari-
tone. "Your old man isn't finished yet."

"I never thought you were. We'll be back in business soon
enough," I say, and I kiss him long and sweetly.

Scott moves to Hayworth Avenue. For the first time in our
almost four years together, we thumb our nose at the movie
industry's smug moralism by openly living together.

Scott has had a lifetime of dress rehearsals for being an invalid.
They serve him well. Ensconced at his lap desk during the day,
he becomes king of his bed, fluffing pillows, twirling the dial
on the radio, and churning out pages by the dozen. Frances fer-
ries them to his flat on Laurel, returns the typed copy to the
author to correct, and the loop begins anew, as if Scott is manu-
facturing shoes or gloves. He's chipper, partly because he's heard
from Max, who said he'd reconsidered and would be pleased to
give him a small advance after all. Two thousand. It's a partial
victory for me, but a bigger victory for Scott.

"Aha! Told you so!" is all he says the day the letter and check
arrive, but Scott's confidence orbits throughout my flat. I love
when he calls out remarks like "What film-land feast are you

serving readers in Milwaukee today?" when he sees my secretary or me pass in the hall. Our life is harried in the same buoyant way it might be if we were preparing for a party.

Every weekday at five o'clock, my assistant leaves and at six we eat the maid's T-bone, peas, and baked potatoes. After dinner we stroll to Schwab's and treat ourselves to chocolate malts while we discuss *Bleak House*, the current assignment for College of One.

"Dickens's best novel," Scott proclaims.

"I have to disagree." Which I dare to do now. "I love the description of London's jumbled shops, but Esther is too good to be believable."

"You're reading only for story," Scott says. "You need to look at craft. It's astonishing. Before I start writing a novel I always reread Dickens along with Dostoevsky."

At night we snuggle in my room, breathing in unison until Scott returns to the bed next door or, when insomnia wins, walks the flat. Hearing him quietly tuning in to the radio in the middle of the night, when he thinks I'm asleep, makes me smile, as it does to see his toothbrush parked next to mine. I love having Scott nearby, although it will be for merely weeks. In January, he'll move into an apartment only blocks away on Fountain Avenue that Frances found.

Since cardiograms show slight improvement, we decide to attend a screening of *Little Nellie Kelly*, adapted from George M. Cohan's Broadway hit. We can use a shot of musical comedy, especially with my young friend Judy Garland in the lead. Only when we pull into the parking lot do I remember that tonight's projection room is a Sisyphean vault to the second floor. If I point this out, I worry that in a fit of irrational rebellion, Scott will attempt to sprint up the stairs like a Princeton freshman.

To preempt that disaster, I take one step out of the car, flinch, and cry out, "Oh bugger! These shoes. I never should have worn such high heels." I turn to Scott and groan, "I've twisted my ankle. Could you please help me?" Trying not to lean on him, I take his arm and at a stately pace we proceed upstairs. It takes a solid five minutes.

During movies, I look forward to Scott's whispering punditry as he points out abysmal acting, stilted dialogue, and specious plot twists. His critique is better than most films. But tonight, despite a heavy pour of Irish accents he usually mimics, he's mute. Even Judy's first, decidedly awkward, on-film kiss to the fatherly George Murphy fails to spark a reaction. I attribute this to the story line—newlyweds move to New York City, as did he and Zelda—and I worry about a siege of melancholia. But when the film ends, Scott admits that for the last two hours he's been light-headed and queasy.

"Take my arm when we walk out," I say under my breath. "It might be the grippe. You've been working too hard."

"People will assume I'm drunk." After a year of fortitude to stay on his custom model of the wagon, Scott's dignity is at stake, but his distress wins. I smile at people we know, point to my ankle, and shrug as we slowly walk to the car, which I proceed to drive. At home, he falls immediately to sleep and stays that way for ten hours—a personal best.

"If I could sleep like that every night," he says in the morning, stretching, "I'd already be starting my next novel while we sailed around the world on *Tycoon's* royalties."

"Do you think you should call Dr. Nelson and tell him about last night?"

"I was just worn out," he insists. "I'm all better now."

I don't argue. Scott's expansive mood continues to the afternoon, when he asks me what I'd like for Christmas.

"Your good health." It's the truth, although I do have a second, bigger wish.

"Then we'll leave it up to God and Santa, but I want to think of something special for Frances," he says. "Perfume?"

"Too personal. She might misinterpret. How about a cashmere cardigan? I saw one at Saks and that apartment of yours is chilly."

"I knew you'd know. And Scottie? She's a tough one."

Not really. Scottie wants the same luxuries most girls find indispensable at nineteen. Last year she asked Papa for twenty dollars to buy a gown for her debut. He not only refused, but he belittled the notion of a coming-out party—because, I suspect, he had no money to stage or attend it. Where Scottie is concerned, Scott is maddeningly inconsistent. He insists on Vassar—not, say, UCLA, whose tuition is more within his budget—yet he denigrates Scottie when she wants to participate in one of the grand traditions of the set to which she belongs. I try to intervene, but tread lightly. Scottie Fitzgerald is Zelda's daughter, not mine.

This didn't stop me from secretly sending her money to buy the dress. The loneliness of being a girl on her own is something I know all too well, and while no child in America gets more letters from Daddy, Scott hasn't seen his daughter for fourteen months. I adore that girl, and have been waiting to present another idea.

"Why don't you give my silver-fox jacket to Scottie?" With our decorous social life, I rarely wear it. I expect Scott to suggest that I'm ungrateful for wanting to give away his gift to me. I am wrong.

"Isn't the style too mature? She's a little bug of a thing."

"Isn't Frances's father a furrier?"

Mr. Kroll remodels the coat—at no cost—and my fox migrates East for its own coming-out party, accompanied by a letter Scott dictates, signed by me.

Please send your father a picture of you in the fur or he won't be able to recognize you next you meet, which he hopes is soon. Warm wishes for everything you want in the New Year, and know that while your father has not been well, he is better and—this is the best part—hasn't had a drink in a year.

The next day Scott sends a letter signed by Ecclesiastes Fitz-gerald, reminding Scottie to write three notes: to me, to Frances, and to him to show to me. "A giver gets no pleasure in a letter acknowledging a gift late even though it crawls with apologies," says sermonizing dad. I, however, am not paying note to when an acknowledgment arrives from Scottie. I am counting the days in another matter.

Chapter 48

1940

Three weeks is how late I am. Every day I make a note in my new leather ledger. Scott notices me writing. May I see, he asks? Later, darling. At least a month from now when I'm absolutely sure.

Dec. 3, Is it just nerves or could I be pregnant?

Dec. 4, IF I'm pregnant I will be the happiest woman on earth. I will never 1) give my child to an orphanage, 2) shave her head, 3) berate her in front of others . . .

Dec. 5, How will I tell Scott? He will feel tricked and furious, but after his anger ebbs, happy and proud, I am sure of it. New book, new baby . . . I love him. He loves me. We belong together. If there is a baby, how can it be wrong?

Dec. 6, There might truly be a child growing within me, a living soul made by Scott and me. I am overwhelmed. Overjoyed. Scared. Shocked. Expecting???

Dec. 7, I can win over Scott, but what about Zelda?

This is where I stalemate. Scott has said, time and time again: he will always take care of Zelda. I respect him for his Ashley Wilkes honor, proper and right. He is a man of ethics. But since Zelda has left the sanitarium and Scott has recently assured me that he and his wife haven't been sexual for years—and never will be again—must they continue to be *married*?

He hasn't practiced his religion since childhood. Is it inconceivable for them to divorce, as Johnny and I did when the intimacy of marriage ceased? If a child is on the way, Scott would want his baby, whom I'm sure is a boy, to carry the Fitzgerald name . . .

Dec. 8, Francis Scott Fitzgerald, II. We will call him Frank, like Frank Sinatra. Blue eyes, like Scott, Mr. Sinatra, and me. Is Frankie better? Frankie Fitzgerald. Yes.

Dec. 9, Francesca? Francine?

Dec. 11, Do I dare write to Zelda?

Dec. 12, I could never write to Zelda. It's cruel and Scott will feel duped. I am out of my mind, shanghaied by hormones and doubt.

Dec. 13, Aren't I allotted a full measure of happiness? I must write to Zelda . . .

Dec. 14, If I were Zelda, I would release him, so he could start anew and admit that our best times are long gone. I wouldn't want my husband shackled forever.

Dear Zelda . . . This is the hardest letter I have ever tried to write. You do not know me, but I say at the outset, I intend no harm. Scott and I didn't mean to, but fate brought us together. For the last three and a half years . . .

Do I dare send this letter?

I do.

Chapter 49

1940

always wanted to be a dandy." Scott winks in the mirror while I watch him straighten his bow tie. In honor of Christmas, less than a week away, he's chosen a bright red, as if he is a cross between Baudelaire and Lucius Beebe, the New York society columnist. I am wearing one of my new dresses, a rustling violet silk. God willing, soon enough it will not fit.

Tonight is the premiere for a movie banned by the Catholic Legion of Decency. "You couldn't keep me away if I were on my deathbed," Scott says. It's the first gala we've attended in months. I'm ready for some sparkle, or at the very least, a waltz and a kiss under the mistletoe.

We walk the red carpet. Scott looks smart—and more important, healthy. It's been longer than a year since his heavy drinking and for the last day I haven't heard his cough, which had become a public menace. He circles my waist in a gesture of pride and protection. *If you only knew,* I think, though I rather like concealing such a tasty secret and intend to until I'm entirely sure. No lightbulbs flash when we pass, but inside, we mingle in the palatial lobby of the Pantages Theatre and greet friendly faces. Among them are Barbara Stanwyck escorted by Robert Taylor, to whom Scott is remarkably civil. We admire the gilded sculptures in this shrine to Hollywood, and pay homage to the headliners, Rosalind Russell and Melvyn Douglas. They're poised, though most likely feeling the heebie-jeebies all stars must experience before a reckoning by their peers.

We find our seats next to Alan and Dorothy. I admire the

new pearls dripping down her black velvet bodice. Screenwriting is treating my friend well.

"How's the ticker?" she leans over to ask.

"Ba-bum, ba-bum, ba-bum," Scott says, tapping his chest. "He who fights and runs away, lives to fight another day."

The curtain parts and reveals an inane plot in which newlyweds elect to endure three months of abstinence. "Heaven forbid ours lasts that long," Scott whispers. I am glad to hear him once again gab during a movie, and there is plenty to critique. *This Thing Called Love* adheres to the Hays Code—with ample sexual innuendo.

At the after-party we remain wallflowers until the band strikes up "I Could Write a Book." "My cue," Scott says as he stands, bows, and reaches for my hand. It's been more than a year since we've circled a dance floor. I close my eyes as the soloist sings, "*I could write a preface on how we met, so the world would never forget.*" Precisely what Scott is doing.

When the music ends, we hold each other on the dance floor, my eyes closed. I'd like to make this feeling last forever.

Thanks to a handful of phenobarb, Scott sleeps late but wakes cheerful and drinks the coffee I bring him in bed while he makes notes for his sixth chapter. I arrange pine boughs on the mantel and string lights on a thigh-high tree I bought at a lot on Pico—no giant spruce this year for Scott to strap to the top of his car. I stand back and breathe in the evergreen scent. Under the tree two gifts wait, one for me from Scott in tartan paper and for him, a box with a big red bow. Nothing extravagant, a cashmere cardigan in cadet blue. As a favor to his most dogged patient, Dr. Nelson, who will be traveling over the holidays, is paying Scott a visit this afternoon with his portable cardiograph. Assuming good news—knock wood—I look forward to a holiday with music on the phonograph, simple meals I'll cook myself, and Scott reciting poetry, and writing and reading more of *Tycoon*.

The doorbell rings. It is Frances, who drops off Scott's mail, which she piles on a table by the door. She wishes both of us a happy holiday and adds, "Scott, your *Princeton Alumni Weekly* arrived, by the way."

That's not all. While the two of them chat, I check. Amid the bills I see an envelope addressed to Scott in Zelda's loopy handwriting. My stomach lurches, and I doubt it's morning sickness. In this letter there could be a piece of news that will transform my life. I feel quashed by joyous excitement along with what-have-I-done? shame spiked with be-careful-what-you-wish-for curiosity.

I am restless, and need to get out of the house. "How about sandwiches for lunch?" I call out to Scott.

"I could go for a turkey on rye, Presh, if you don't mind walking to Greenblatt's."

I welcome the outing, though it's the shortest day of the year and we're only a few more hours away from darkness. When I return, Scott has settled into my green armchair with his magazine. The letter from Zelda, I notice, remains unopened. I choose a record and place it on the phonograph, Beethoven's Third Symphony, *Eroica*—as grand a piece of music as anyone has ever written—kick off my shoes, relax on the sofa, and try, unsuccessfully, to put the letter out of my mind. Fortunately, Scott interrupts my train of thought.

"1941 might be Princeton's best football team in seasons," he says.

This is a topic on which I have nothing to contribute beyond "I certainly hope you're right." I smile and return to my biography of our friend Ludwig, who is beginning to lose his hearing, poor savant. I reread the same page three times.

A few minutes later Scott looks up. "You know, Sheilo, I think *Tycoon*'s going to be big."

"I think so, too. I truly do," and not simply because it's both love story and blistering exposé. With this novel, Scott has been restored to top form, his writing steeped with cinematic imagery, and I can't imagine a better book about the movies. Monroe Stahr is a true businessman hero, Jay Gatsby plus genius. I also admire the way Scott described his heroine when he wrote to Max, "dowering her with a little misfortune because people don't sympathize deeply with those who've had *all* the breaks." There, there.

"When the royalties start rolling in I want us to leave Hollywood," Scott says. "I've had it. I'd like to volunteer as a war correspondent, should the United States join the fight."

"I pray it doesn't come to that, but if you really would go abroad, I'd do the same. We could work side by side." If only Scott's health would be restored to allow this kind of patriotic adventure.

"I was hoping you'd say that, intrepid Sheilo, and when the war is won and Hitler's moldering in his grave, how about Paris?"

Paris, for me, recalls Monte and deception and I'd worry that for Scott, Zelda will lurk in every café. "I'm all for leaving Hollywood, but not Paris."

"London, then? We could lend moral support to your countrymen—help dig them out."

"I'm finished with London." Too much history. "How about going East, so I can still work and we'll be on the same coast as Scottie?"

I may not be part of Scott's treasured youthful memories, but we can build decades of new ones. He is, after all, just forty-four. We'll live in harmony, without the intramural competition that dogged his marriage. I can imagine the home we would make for the two—or three—of us. Laughter. Books. Music. Work. Warmth. Sex.

Instinctively, my hand goes to my stomach. Perhaps also a child.

"I didn't think you'd want Manhattan or Long Island," he says, reeling me back.

"How about Connecticut?"

"There you go. Westport, perhaps, where I lived after *This Side of Paradise*. That book was a bestseller, so it would be a lucky charm to return. I'll ride the train with Max, and torment him all the way to Grand Central."

Wherever our future takes us, for the first time I can see it shimmering ahead.

Scott returns to his football for a few minutes, looks up, and says, "I need something sweet, Presh. I think I'll walk down to Schwab's for ice cream."

"You might miss Dr. Nelson. How about a Hershey bar?" I've squirrelled one away next to my bed.

"Fair enough," he answers. I walk upstairs, get the chocolate, and hand it to Scott.

"Want a Coca-Cola with it?"

"Perfect."

I'm in the kitchen when I hear Scott shout. I smile as I imagine him cheering for Princeton at the victory he is reliving against Yale. But when there is a second sound, more of an animal howl, almost muffled by the rising crescendo of *Eroica*, I run to the living room. Scott is standing. He lurches toward the hearth and grabs the mantel. I'm afraid he will fall into the fire I kindled when I returned from Greenblatt's, but he totters backward, tumbles with a thud, and lands splayed on his back. From someplace deep in his throat I hear a short, low gurgle.

A piece of paper has fallen from his hand.

"Scott! Scott!" Now it's my turn to scream. I run to him, afraid he might have suffered a concussion. He doesn't answer, and when I reach him, I see he has fainted. *Oh my God.* I need to revive him. I slap his face, but he stares strangely and fails to respond. I slap him again. Nothing.

I've watched enough movies to know what Scott needs. I rush to the kitchen for the brandy I've stashed in the back cupboard, decanted into an empty vinegar bottle. I don't give a damn if it pushes him off the wagon. I race back, and try to pour the liquid straight down Scott's throat, but his mouth is clenched. He's out cold. The alcohol trickles onto his sweater.

"Wake up! No! Scott, wake up!"

I reach for his wrist and fail to find a pulse. I'm frantic, not sure if I'm looking in the right place. I can almost hear him say, *Don't get hysterical, Sheilo. You have your talents, but nursing isn't among them.* I drop his hand, smeared by chocolate, and dial Dr. Nelson's number, which I know by heart. Of course there's no answer—he's most likely in his car, on his way over now. I hate leaving Scott alone, but I will need to find a neighbor. I dash out into the hall and bang on the door of the building manager's door.

"Mr. Culver! Mr. Fitzgerald's fainted! Come quick!" My voice is as loud as I can make it. Fortunately, our neighbor is home.

Henry Culver runs faster than I think a fat man can move. He kneels next to Scott, who is eerily still, disguised as a wax-work figure, and puts two fingers on the inside of his wrist and waits. Holding his wrist, Mr. Culver looks at me as I crouch by his side.

"I'm so sorry, Miss Graham," he says gently, "but I'm quite sure Mr. Fitzgerald is gone."

I swirl in an eddy of confusion. "Whatever do you mean, gone?"

"I'll call the police and the fire department. Where is your telephone, dear?"

"Please use the one in the kitchen," I manage to say.

"Scott, oh Scott," I wail as I bend next to him and lift his beautiful head in my hands. My tears wet his face. "Darling, what happened? What have I done? Don't leave me! Scott, Scott,

Scott. I love you, sweetheart." I tenderly rock him and stroke the high forehead I know so well.

A letter is lying next to him, only one paragraph long. I read it quickly and toss it into the flames.

What was Scott's last word? I'm quite sure it was *perfect*.

gently remove photographs from my office wall. It's time to pack.

Here I am beaming as a young mother, holding an infant Wendy . . . with Marilyn Monroe, two bosomy blondes disproving the myth that no one in Hollywood makes a close friend . . . Robert Taylor cooing over my own sweet baby boy Robby— grist for the rumor mill . . . Scott in Tijuana wearing a sombrero, looking ridiculous and dear. And there I am in England during my year as a correspondent, pounding on a typewriter, all sensible shoes and tweed.

Following Scott's death, everything we'd shared seemed to have been swept away like a pile of dust. I needed to escape. He believed I could report on the war, and once again, he was right. With Scott as my emotional compass, I took myself to London. The city was as battered as I, but I found solace where resilience ruled. I didn't return to Hollywood until the war ended.

Now, after all these years of bustle and bluster, I'm decamping again, from my home in Beverly Hills to a sleepy Connecticut village not far from Manhattan. Hollywood is less amusing at fifty-five than at thirty-five, though I continue to inflict my signature ripostes upon the reading public. My columns, with twenty million readers—published in more papers than Hedda and Louella combined—earn me movie star money. Five thousand dollars a week, with my fame enriched by my own television show.

Gossip has been good to me. People would rather scoff at the foibles of others than examine their own lives. They always did. No wonder Scott wrote fiction. I can picture him in the frayed green armchair that will also be moving East. He is a revenant, back from the dead, blowing smoke rings. This is how I'll always remember him, his handsome face younger than my own, ready to break into a laugh. As for me, I need a bit of blonding and weeks of dieting; menopause and Danish pastry have stolen my waist.

An antiques agent came by last week to bid on my Faulkners and Wolfes and O'Haras and Hemingways. When he saw that I owned a complete set of F. Scott Fitzgerald's first editions, the man's eyes bugged out: he offered me as much for my collection as all the other novels together. Not for sale, I informed him.

After Scott died, it didn't take long for the skeptics to come around. Resurrected, he became the patron saint of English majors, with no liberal arts education complete without F. Scott Fitzgerald. Biographies, doctoral theses, lectures, Gatsbyesque anointed as an adjective, albeit one Scott would never use. Not bad for a man who died believing he was a failure, with a final royalty check of $13.13—for books he bought himself.

Scott would call this "peripeteia," a sudden reversal of fortune. This takes me back to our College of One, from which I never got to graduate but has made all the difference in my life. I will always continue the education that Scott started, because it grows, giving me strength and ballast. I have dreamed, wandered, gotten lost, and invented myself again and again, ultimately as a woman able to raise two children alone. Where I used to be tough outside and soft inside, I am now soft outside and tough inside.

With the walls stripped bare, I turn to my desk. Tenderly, I lift my scuffed leather ledger, its pages filled by outlines and lists, and tuck it in next to *Beloved Infidel*, the memoir Scott urged me to write.

When I told my story, did I reveal the truth? Occasionally.

Honesty and I have been known to intersect on numerous occasions.

I think of the Seder I attended last year. When my hosts recited the prayers—in the wrong order, with faulty pronunciation—the Lily Shiel within me couldn't help herself, and corrected them. Little did my friends know they'd invited not a secret biblical scholar, but the winner of the Jews' Orphan Asylum's Hebrew prize. But my background isn't for public consumption. Let my tombstone read *Sheilah Graham, Unreliable Narrator.* I can live with that.

Half-truths notwithstanding, my book became a bestseller. Framed and sitting on my desk is its *New Yorker* review by Scott's friend Bunny Wilson, with my favorite part underscored: *The very best portrait of Fitzgerald that has yet been put into print.* Not every critic, of course, agreed. Dorothy trashed the book in *Esquire.* Jealous shrew. She also bashed the movie, although in that case, I agree. Gregory Peck was no Scott—too tall, too dark-haired, too stiff, not even a convincing drunk. And Deborah Kerr, twice as elegant but half as earthy, playing *me*? "Why'd you ever cast her when you could have hired Marilyn?" I ask aloud.

"Whomever are you talking to?" says a voice false with concern.

I laugh and turn. "Don't mind your old mother, Wendy."

"Sorry, Mom." I am not Mum or Mummy. My son and daughter want a thoroughly American parent. "But I worry about you." She rolls her eyes as young women have forever. "I wanted to tell you Princeton called. Their boxes need to ship tomorrow."

I have decided that Scott's letters, notes, and poems aren't mine to keep. They should belong to the world, for scholars to study, and I'm donating them to his college for the library that's being established in his honor.

"Do you need any help here?" my daughter asks.

"Thanks but no, darling." I like being surrounded by memories, a chorus of bells only I can hear.

"Call if you need me," says my fair-haired Wendy Frances with her blue eyes and love of books. Who is her father? No one need know. I will always be the sum of my secrets, as tangled as a handful of shiny gold chains tossed into a box and hidden away.

My shelves are almost empty. The F. Scott Fitzgerald *Encino Editions* I will pack last. They hold pride of place next to the sterling silver pitcher that was my last Christmas gift from Scott, which I had to open alone. I will wrap it in his frayed pink shirt, and nestle it next to his red bow tie and the blue cashmere sweater he never got to wear. I feel its warmth—and Scott's—as I work this afternoon.

How do you get over F. Scott Fitzgerald? You don't. The moment we met my life began to snap into focus, revealing a gate to which only he had a key. Like a 1930s torch song, his spirit will always glide next to me, seducing, teasing, praising, and sometimes asking for a dance. I remember us as a couple in the grand tradition, when men were men and music made women swoon. That we never married is a minor footnote.

Long ago I tallied the days of our romance when Scott was drunk: nine whole months of our three and a half years together. There are those who believed I should have broken off with him when he misbehaved. They were wrong. We were always worth keeping, and his faults, despite their epic scale, never diminished our bond, which ran deep. Only the two of us knew what we meant to each other.

At times Scott broke my heart, but he also taught me to be strong, brave, and perhaps even wise. He accomplished this with his own magic—by believing in me—and in doing so, he has kept me as safe as he once promised. My inheritance.

I live without regret because Scott Fitzgerald was no fever dream. He made me who I am today, following me through countless flirtations, numerous flings, and two incidental marriages. None succeeded because I have always loved him most.

Destiny truly *is* what you make of fate. Thank you, Matron Weiss, and thank you, Scott.

Every night, before I go to bed, I kiss his portrait, which will go into the final box alongside my dog-eared copy of *The Last Tycoon*, where our love enriches every word. Scott's novel was never truly finished. Neither, I know, are we.

Acknowledgments

It's fair to say I wrote the novel I wanted to read. In doing so, I fell in love with F. Scott Fitzgerald, who was, when he wasn't knockdown drunk, the world's best boyfriend—at least to an English major. I wish I could have known him. And Sheilah Graham, too, with her exceptional blitz of qualities I admire: grit, wit, cunning, generosity, and a powerful work ethic. I hope that both of them—along with Sheilah's children, Wendy Fairey and Robert Westbrook—would approve of this novel and understand why, in reaching for emotional truth, I blurred timelines and a handful of details.

Sara Nelson, my editor, said she feels that for us to work together is *beshert*, a Yiddish word for "destined" that Sheilah might have taught Scott. I feel the same way. With Sara's deep publishing background and our shared affection for this book's leading male, I could not imagine a finer editor. Deep gratitude as well to the entire Harper team—notably Robin Bilardello for designing this beautiful cover; Leah Carlson-Stanisic for its vintage-inspired interior design; Leah Wasielewski and Katie O'Callaghan for overseeing an extensive marketing campaign; Tracy Locke for masterminding publicity; and Daniel Vazquez and Christina Polizoto for patiently juggling countless other details.

I am long indebted to Christy Fletcher, who warmed instantly to the idea of this novel. She deserves special gratitude, which I also extend to her gifted colleagues Sarah Fuentes, Melissa Chinchilla, Erin McFadden, and Grainne Fox.

Writing is a lonely business, which makes me grateful to

be in the trench with a tribe of readers/writers/friends with equally big brains and hearts. Vivian Conan, Chaya Deitsch, Barbara Fisher, and Sally Hoskins showed unwavering enthusiasm for this unfolding story while helping to blow the whistle on anachronisms, ill-conceived metaphors, and missing commas. Thanks, too, to Janet Chan, Patty Dann, Evelyn Renold, and Charles Salzberg, who read the manuscript in its early days. A big hug goes to members of my two smarty-pants book clubs—Meakin Armstrong, Betsy Carter, Cathy Cavender, Alexandra Horowitz, Aryn Kyle, Judith Roth, Patrice Samuels, Carol Tannenhauser, and Jennifer Vanderbes—for their analysis of distinguished authors who inspire my humbler efforts. Michele Willens, what would I do without our breakfasts, and Jane Greenberg, our calls?

Befriending writers and booklovers on social media has widened my community in ways I could never have imagined when I published my first novel ten years ago. Thank you, cyberfriends—in particular, Andrea Peskind Katz, Robin Kall Homonoff, and the remarkable Tall Poppies and NextTribe writers. Age boldly! Thanks, too, to Dale Berger, Rochelle Caplan, Vicki Kriser, and Betsey Teutsch—sisters all—and my amazing mother-in-law, Helen Sweig, for never failing to ask, "What's up with the book?"

Last, but first in my heart, thank you to Robby, who puts up with a wife too often glued to her laptop; to Jed, Anne, Rory, and Kim; and to our next generation of readers, Emil, Madeline, Fin, and William. You make me proud in countless ways.

About the Author

SALLY KOSLOW is the author of *The Widow Waltz*; *The Late, Lamented Molly Marx*; and *With Friends Like These*, and the nonfiction work *Slouching Toward Adulthood*. Her debut novel, *Little Pink Slips*, was inspired by her long career as the editor in chief of the iconic *McCall's* magazine. Her books have been published in a dozen countries.